Praise for the DS M...

'In terms of food analogies ... d or subtly flavoured, while others are ... vid Mark's DS McAvoy books are unarguably ... gory.' *Independent*

'David Mark takes you to the darkest ...s of Hull and Back, but be prepared for a late night, as *Dead Pretty* will make you see dawn.' Martina Cole

'Dark, compelling crime writing of the highest order.' *Daily Mail*

'More twists and turns than a corkscrew through the eyeball.' Val McDermid

'Not for the faint-hearted ... Richly satisfying and told with remarkable flair, it confirms Mark as one of the darkest of the new faces in British crime writing, and one not to miss.' *Mail on Sunday*

'Truly exhilarating and inventive. Mark is a wonderfully descriptive writer and an exciting young talent.' Peter James

'Compelling and harrowing.' *Daily Express*

'In McAvoy, David Mark has created a big hero with a huge heart. His skill at weaving threads of light through the darkest fabric has rightly won him a legion of fans who like their crime fiction to be real and compassionate.' Sarah Hilary

'Gripping story lines steeped in emotion and menace, with a larger than life character whom I love to reacquaint myself with. Always right on the Mark for me.' Mel Sherratt

About the author

David spent more than fifteen years as a journalist, including seven years as a crime reporter with the *Yorkshire Post* – walking the Hull streets that would later become the setting for the Detective Sergeant Aector McAvoy novels.

He has written six novels in the McAvoy series: *Dark Winter*, *Original Skin*, *Sorrow Bound*, *Taking Pity*, *Dead Pretty* and *Cruel Mercy*, as well as two McAvoy novellas, *A Bad Death* and *Fire of Lies*, which are available as ebooks. *Dark Winter* was selected for the Harrogate New Blood panel and was a Richard & Judy pick and a *Sunday Times* bestseller.

Also by David Mark

The DS McAvoy Series

Dark Winter
Original Skin
Taking Pity
Dead Pretty
Cruel Mercy
A Bad Death: an ebook short story
Fire of Lies: an ebook short story

DAVID
MARK

SORROW
BOUND

MULHOLLAND
BOOKS
HODDER

First published in Great Britain in 2014 by Quercus

This paperback edition first published in 2017 by Mulholland Books
An imprint of Hodder & Stoughton
An Hachette UK company

1

A CIP catalogue record for this title is
available from the British Library

Paperback ISBN 978 1 473 66884 3
eBook ISBN 978 1 473 66885 0

Printed and bound by Clays Ltd, St Ives plc

Hodder & Stoughton policy is to use papers that are
natural, renewable and recyclable products and made
from wood grown in sustainable forests. The logging and
manufacturing processes are expected to conform to the
environmental regulations of the country of origin.

Hodder & Stoughton Ltd
Carmelite House
50 Victoria Embankment
London EC4Y 0DZ

www.hodder.co.uk

For my children, George and Elora.
I hope you never stop being seriously frigging odd.

Oft have I heard that grief softens the mind,
And makes it fearful and degenerate;
Think therefore on revenge and cease to weep.

Henry VI, Part 2, 4.4.1–3

PROLOGUE

Keep going, keep going, it's only pain, just breathe and run, breathe, and fucking run!

He skids. Slips on blood and ice. Tumbles into the snow and hears the sound of paper tearing. Feels the flap of burned skin that was hanging, sail-like, across his chest, being torn away on unforgiving stone.

His scream is an inhuman thing; primal, untamed.

Get up, run, run . . .

Sobbing, he bites into the fat of his hand. Tastes his own roasted flesh. Spits blood and skin and bile. Petrol. Somebody else's hair.

Not like this. Not now . . .

He tries to pull himself upright, but his naked, frozen toes fail to respond to his commands. He thrusts his ruined hands into the snow and pushes his body up, but slips again and feels his head hit the pavement.

Stay awake. Stay alive.

His vision is blurring. From nowhere, he finds himself remembering the television in his old student flat – the way the picture disappeared down a dwindling circle of colour in the centre of the screen, creating a miniature whirlpool of swirling patterns and pictures. That is what he sees now, his whole world diminishing. His senses, his understanding, are turning in a shrinking kaleidoscope of crimsons and darks.

Half-undone, almost broken, he raises his head and looks back at the grisly path his feet have punched in the snow. Miniature ink-bombs of blue-black blood, scattered haphazardly among ragged craters.

'There! There he is! Stop him. Stop!'

The voices force him upright, boost his vision, his perception, and for a blessed moment he gathers himself and takes in his surroundings. Looks up at the Victorian terraces with their big front windows and bare hanging baskets: their 'vacancies' signs and joyless rainbows of unlit coloured bulbs.

His own voice: 'Bitch, bitch.'

He realises he can hear the sea; a crackle of static and sliding stones, slapping onto the mud and sand beyond the harbour wall.

And suddenly he is adrift in a symphony of senses.

Sounds.

Scents.

Flavours.

He smells the salt and vinegar of the chip shop; the stale ale of a pub cellar. Hears the scream of gulls and the wet kisses of rotting timbers knocking against one another as bobbing fishing boats softly collide. Doors opening. Sash windows sliding up. Glasses on varnished wood. Faintly, the triumphant song of a slot machine as it pays out. A cheer. The rattle of coins . . .

Up. Run!

He has taken no more than a dozen steps when his strength

leaves him. He slides onto his belly. Feels the snow become a blanket. Deliriously, tries to pull it around himself. To make a pillow of the kerb.

Running feet. Voices.

Up. Up!

A hand around his throat, hauling him to his feet. An impact to the side of his head. Perhaps a fist, perhaps a knee.

'Bastard. Bastard!'

His teeth slam together: the impact a blade biting into wood.

Stars and mud, snow and cloud, boots and fists and the kerb against his skull, again, again, again . . .

He is drifting into the tunnel of shapes, now. Disappearing. Everything is getting smaller. Darker.

All over. All gone . . .

The snow so soft. The dark so welcoming.

Fresh hands upon him. Hands, not fists. Soft. Firm, but tender. Flesh on flesh.

A face, looming over him.

'Look what you've done to him.'

A moment's clarity, before the black ocean pulls him under . . .

'Let him die. Please, let him fucking die.'

Part One

Part One

1

Monday morning. 9.16 a.m.

A small and airless room above the health centre on Cottingham Road.

Detective Sergeant Aector McAvoy, uncomfortable and ridiculous on a plastic school chair, knees halfway up to his ears.

'Aector?'

He notices that his left leg is jiggling up and down. *Damn!* The shrink must have seen it too. He decides to keep jiggling it, so she doesn't read anything into his decision to stop.

He catches her eye.

Looks away.

Stops jiggling his leg.

'Aector, I'm not trying to trick you. You don't need to second-guess yourself all the time.'

McAvoy nods, and feels a fresh bead of sweat run down the back of his shirt collar. It's too hot in here. The walls, with their Elastoplast-coloured wallpaper, seem to be perspiring, and the painted-shut windows are misting up.

She's talking again. *Words, words, words . . .*

'I have apologised, haven't I? About the room? I tried to get another one but there's nothing available. I think if we gave that window a good shove we could get it open, but then you have the sound of the road to contend with.'

McAvoy raises his hands to tell her not to worry, though in truth, he is so hot and uncomfortable, he's considering diving head-first through the glass. McAvoy was dripping before he even walked through the door. For two weeks it has felt as though a great wet dog has been lying on the city, but it is a heatwave that has brought no blue skies. Instead, Hull has sweated beneath heavens the colour of damp concrete. It is weather that frays tempers, induces lethargy, and makes life an ongoing torture for big, flame-haired men like Detective Sergeant Aector McAvoy, who has felt damp, cross and self-conscious for days. It's a feverish heat; a pestilent, buzzing cloak. To McAvoy, even walking a few steps feels like fighting through laundry lines of damp linen. Everybody agrees that the city needs a good storm to clear the air, but lightning has yet to split the sky.

'I thought you had enjoyed the last session. You seemed to warm up as we went along.' She looks at her notes. 'We were talking about your father . . .'

McAvoy closes his eyes. He doesn't want to appear rude, so bites his tongue. As far as he can recall, he hadn't been talking about his father at all. She had.

'Okay, how about we try something a bit less personal? Your career, perhaps? Your ambitions?'

McAvoy looks longingly at the window. The scene it frames could be a photograph. The leaves and branches of the rowan tree are lifeless, unmoving, blocking out the view of the university across the busy road, but he can picture it in his imagination clearly enough. Can see the female students with their bare midriffs and tiny denim shorts; their knee socks and back-combed hair. He closes his eyes, and sees nothing but victims. They will hit the beer gardens this afternoon. They will drink more than they should. They will catch the eye and, emboldened by alcohol, some will smile and flirt and revel in the sensation of exposed skin. They will make mistakes. There will be confusion and heat and desire and fear. By morning, detectives will be investigating assaults. Maybe a stabbing. Parents will be grieving and innocence will be lost.

He shakes it away. Curses himself. Hears Roisin's voice, as always, telling him to stop being silly and just enjoy the sunshine. Pictures her, bikini-clad and feet bare, soaking up the heat as she basks, uncaring, on their small patch of brown front lawn.

Had he been asked a question? Oh, yeah . . .

'I'm not being evasive,' he says, at last. 'I know for some people there are real benefits to what you do. I studied some psychology at university. I admire your profession immensely. I'm just not sure what I can tell you that will be of any benefit to either of us. I don't bottle things up. I talk to my wife. I have outlets for my dark feelings, as you call them. I'm okay. I wish my brain didn't do some things and I'm grateful it does others. I'm pretty normal, really.'

The psychologist puts her head on one side, like a Labrador delicately broaching the subject of a walk.

'Aector, these sessions are for whatever you want them to be. I've told you this. If you want to discuss police work, you can. If you want to talk about things in your personal life, that's fine too. I want to help. If you sit here in silence, that's what I have to put in my report.'

McAvoy drops his head and stares at the carpet for a moment. He's bone-tired. The hot weather has made his baby daughter irritable and she is refusing to sleep anywhere other than on Daddy. He spent last night in a deckchair in the back yard, wrapped in a blanket and holding her little body against his chest, her fingers gripping the collar of his rugby shirt as she grizzled and sniffled in her sleep.

'The rowan tree,' says McAvoy, suddenly, and points at the window. 'They used to plant them in churchyards to keep away witches. Did you know that? I did a project on trees when I was eight. *Sorbus aucuparia*, it's called, in Latin. I know the names of about twenty different trees in Latin. Don't know why they stayed in my mind but they did. Don't really know why I'm telling you this, to be honest. It just came to me. I suppose it's nice to be able to say something without worrying that people will think I'm being a smart-arse.'

The psychologist steeples her fingers. 'But you're not worried about that at this moment? That's interesting in itself . . .'

McAvoy sighs, exasperated at being analysed by anybody other than himself. He knows what makes him tick. He doesn't want to be deconstructed in case the pieces don't fit back together.

'Aector? Look, is there somewhere else you would rather be?'

He looks up at the psychologist. Sabine Keane, she's called. McAvoy reckons she's divorced. She wears no ring but would be unlikely to have been saddled with a rhyming name from birth. She's in her early forties and very slim, with longish hair tied back in a mess of straw and grey strands. She's dressed for the hot weather, in sandals, linen skirt and a plain black T-shirt that exposes arms that sag a little underneath. She wears no make-up and there is a blob of something that may be jam halfway up her right arm. She has one of those sing-song, storytelling voices that are intended to comfort, but often grate. McAvoy has nothing against her and would love to be able to tell her something worthwhile, but is struggling to see the point of these sessions. He's grateful that she learned to pronounce his name the Celtic way, and she has a friendly enough smile, but there are doors in his head he doesn't want to unlock. It doesn't help that they got off to such an inauspicious start. On his way to the first session, he had witnessed her involvement in a minor incident of cycle rage. It's hard to believe in somebody's power to heal your soul when you have seen them pedalling furiously down a bus lane and screaming obscenities at a Volvo.

McAvoy tries again.

'Look, the people at occupational health have insisted I come for six sessions with a police-approved counsellor. I'm doing that. I'm here. I'll answer your questions and I'm at great pains not to be rude to you but it's hot and I'm tired and I have work to do, and yes, there are lots of places I would rather be. I'm sure you would too.'

There is silence for a second. McAvoy hears the beep of an appointment being announced in the waiting room for the main doctor's surgery downstairs. He pictures the scene. The waiting room of sick students and chattering foreigners, of middle-class bohemians waiting for their malaria pills and yellow fever jabs before they jet off to Goa with their little Jeremiahs and Hermiones.

Eventually, Sabine tries again. 'You have three children, is that right?'

'Two,' says McAvoy.

'Youngest keeping you up?'

'Comes with the job.'

'It's your duty, yes?'

'Of course.'

'Tell me about duty, Aector. Tell me what it means to you.'

McAvoy makes fists. Thinks about it. 'It's what's expected.'

'By whom?'

'By everyone. By yourself. It's the right thing.'

Sabine says nothing for a moment, then reaches down and pulls a notepad from her satchel. She writes something on the open page, but whether it is some clinical insight or a reminder to pick up toilet rolls on the way home, McAvoy cannot tell.

'You've picked a job that is all about duty, haven't you? Did you always want to be a policeman?'

McAvoy rubs a hand across his forehead. Straightens his green and gold tie. Rolls back the cuffs on his black shirt, then rolls them down again.

'It wasn't like that,' he says, eventually. 'Where I grew up. The set-up at home. The script was kind of written.'

Sabine looks at her notepad again, and shuffles through the pages to find something. She looks up. 'You grew up in the Highlands, yes? On a croft? A little farm, I believe . . .'

'Until I was ten.'

'And that's when you went to boarding school?'

McAvoy looks away. He straightens the crease in his grey suit trousers and fiddles with the pocket of the matching waistcoat. 'After a while.'

'Expensive, for a crofter, I presume.' Her voice is soft but probing.

'Mam's new partner was quite well off.'

The psychologist makes another note. 'And you and your mother are close?'

McAvoy looks away.

'How about you and your father?'

'Off and on.'

'How does he feel about your success?'

McAvoy gives in to a smile. 'What success?'

Sabine gestures at her notes, and the cardboard file on the floor at her feet. 'The cases you have solved.'

He shakes his head. 'It doesn't work like that. I didn't solve anything.' He stops. Considers it properly, shrugs. 'Maybe I did. Maybe I was just, well, there. And when it was just me, on my own, when nobody else gave a damn, I ended up thinking I shouldn't have bothered. Or maybe I should have bothered more.'

There is silence in the room. McAvoy rocks the small plastic chair back on two legs, then puts it down again when he feels it lurch.

After a moment, Sabine nods, as if making up her mind.

'Tell me about Doug Roper,' she says, without looking at her pad.

Involuntarily, McAvoy clenches his jaw. He feels the insides of his cheeks go dry. He says nothing, for fear his tongue will be too fat and useless to make any sense.

'We only get the most basic details in the reports, Aector. But I can read between the lines.'

'He was my first detective chief superintendent in CID,' says McAvoy, softly.

'And?'

'And what? You've probably heard of him.'

Sabine gives a little shrug. 'I Googled him. Bit of a celebrity policeman, I see.'

'He's retired now.'

'And you had something to do with that?'

McAvoy runs his tongue around his mouth. 'Some people think so.'

'And that made you unpopular?'

'It's getting better now. Trish Pharaoh has been very helpful.'

'That's your new boss, yes? Serious and Organised Crime Unit, is that right? Yes, you mentioned her last time. You mention her quite a lot.'

McAvoy manages a faint smile. 'You sound like my wife.'

Sabine cocks her head. 'She means a lot to you?'

'My wife? She's everything . . .'

'No. Your boss.'

McAvoy's leg starts jiggling again. 'She's a very good police officer. I think so, anyway. Maybe she isn't. Maybe Doug Roper had it right. I don't know. I don't know anything very much. Somebody once told me that I would drive myself insane trying to understand what it's all about. Justice, I mean. Goodness. Badness. Sometimes I think I'm halfway there. Other times I just feel like I'm only clever enough to realise how little I know.'

'There's a line in the report we have that says you take the rules very seriously. Can you tell me what you think that might mean?'

McAvoy holds her gaze. Is she making fun of him? He doesn't know what to say. Is there something in the file about his adherence to the rule book? He's a man who completes his paperwork in triplicate in case the original is mislaid and who won't requisition a new Biro from the stationery cupboard until his last one is out of ink.

He says nothing. Just listens to the tyres on the bone-dry road and the sound of blood in his ears.

'The report says you have lots of physical scars, Aector.'

'I'm okay.'

McAvoy tries to be an honest man, and so does not reproach himself for the answer. He is okay. He's as well as can be expected. He's getting by. Doing his bit. Making do. He has plenty of glib, meaningless ways to describe how he is, and knows that were he to sit here trying to explain it all properly, he would turn to ash. At home, he's more than okay. He's perfect. With his arms around his wife and children, he feels like he is glowing. It is only at work that he has no bloody clue how he feels. Whether he regrets his actions. What he really feels about the corrupt and pitiless detective superintendent whose tenure at the head of Humberside CID only ended when McAvoy tried to bring his crimes into the light. Whether noble or naïve, McAvoy's actions cost him his reputation as rising star. This gentle, humble, shy giant of a man was made a distrusted, despised pariah by many of his fellow officers. He was dumped on the Serious and Organised Crime Unit as little more than accountant and mouthpiece, expected by all to be chewed up and spat out by the squad boss, Detective Superintendent Trish Pharaoh, with her biker boots, mascara and truckloads of attitude. Instead she had found a protégé. Almost a friend. And at her side, he has caught bad people.

The burns on McAvoy's back and the slash wound to the bone on his left breast are not the only scars he carries, but they have become almost medals of redemption. He has suffered for what he believes.

Sabine puts down her pen and pulls her phone from her bag. She looks at the display and then up at McAvoy. 'We have half an hour left. You must want to get some of this off your chest.'

McAvoy pulls out his own phone to check that she is right, and sees that he has had eight missed calls, all from the same number. He pulls an apologetic face and before Sabine can object, rings back.

Trish Pharaoh answers on the second ring. Spits his name the only way she can pronounce it, with a mixture of sugar and steel.

'Hector, thank fuck for that. We've got a body. Tell the shrink to tick your chart and let you go. You're in fine shape. Let's just hope your gag reflex isn't. This one's going to make you sick.'

Tick-tock, tick-tock, indicator flashing right. A bluebottle buzzing fatly against the back window. Horns honking and the drone of a pneumatic drill. Shirtless workmen lying back against the wall of the convenience store on the corner, egg-and-bacon sandwiches dripping from greasy paper bags onto dirty hands.

The lights turn green, but nobody moves. The traffic stays still. Two different radio stations blare from open windows. Lady Gaga fights for supremacy with The Mamas and the Papas . . .

A city in the grip of a fever: irritable, agitated, raw.

McAvoy checks his phone. Nothing new. Tries to read the sticker on the back windscreen of the Peugeot two cars in front, but gives up when the squinting makes his temples sweat.

Looks right, at the Polish convenience store: its sign a jumble of angry consonants. Left, at the gym with its massive advert for pole-dancing fitness classes. Wonders if any of the immigrants in this part of town have become champion Pole dancers . . .

He's at the bottom of Anlaby Road, already regretting his decision to turn right out of the doctor's surgery. He's driving the five-year-old people-carrier that he and Roisin had settled on a month ago. There are two child seats in the back, leaving

McAvoy constantly worried about being asked to chauffeur any more than one colleague at a time.

The lights turn green again, and he noses the car forward, into the shadow of a boarded-up theme pub. He remembers when it opened. A local businessman spent more than a million on revamping the building, convinced there was a need for a sophisticated and luxurious nightspot in this part of town. It lasted a year. Its demise could serve as a mirror for so much of this area. The bottom end of Anlaby Road is all charity shops and pizza parlours, cash-for-gold centres and pubs where the barman and the only customer take it in turns to go outside for a cigarette. The streets are a maze of small terraced houses with front rooms where a man of McAvoy's size would struggle to lie down. Once upon a time, the people would have been called 'poor but honest'. Perhaps even 'working class'. There is no term in the official police guidance to describe the locals now. Just people. Ordinary people, with their faults and flaws and wishes and dreams. Hull folk, all tempers and pride.

The lights change again, and McAvoy finally edges into Walliker Street.

Second gear. Third.

He is at the crime scene before he can get into fourth gear. There are three police cars blocking the road, and a white tent is being erected by two constables and a figure in a white suit. Pharaoh's little red convertible is parked next to a forensics van, outside a house with brown-painted bay windows and dirty net curtains pulled tight shut. Next door, a woman in combat trousers and a Hull City shirt is talking to a man in a dressing gown in the front yard. McAvoy fancies they will have already solved the case.

He abandons the car in the middle of the road and reaches into the back seat for his leather satchel. It was a gift a couple of years ago from his wife, and is the source of endless amusement to his colleagues.

'Hector. At last.'

McAvoy bangs his head on the doorframe as he hears his boss's voice. He looks up and sees Pharaoh making her way towards him. Despite the heat, she has refused to shed her biker boots, though she has made a few concessions to the weather. She's wearing a red dress with white spots, and has a cream linen scarf around her neck, which McAvoy presumes she has placed there to disguise her impressive cleavage. She is wearing large, expensive sunglasses, and her dark hair has a kink to it that suggests it dried naturally on the hot air, without the attentions of a brush.

'Guv?'

She looks at her sergeant for a moment too long, then nods. 'No suit jacket, Hector?'

McAvoy looks at himself, neat and pressed in designer suit trousers, waistcoat, shirt with top button done up and his tie perfectly tied in a double Windsor. 'I can pop home if . . .'

Pharaoh laughs. 'Christ, you must be boiling. Undo a button, for God's sake.'

McAvoy begins to colour. Pharaoh can make any man blush but has an ability to transform her sergeant into a lava lamp with nothing more than a sentence or a smile. He has refused to wear a white shirt since she told him she could see the outline of his nipples, and has yet to find a way of looking at her that doesn't take in at least one of her many curves. He raises his hands to his throat but can't bring himself to give in to slovenliness. 'I'll be fine.'

Pharaoh sighs and shakes her head. 'All okay at the shrink?'

He spreads his hands. 'She wants me to have more problems than I have.'

'That's what she's paid for.'

'Came as a relief to get your call.'

'You haven't seen the poor lass yet.'

Together they cross the little street, passing a closed fish and chip shop that appears to have been built in the front room of one of the terraced houses. The row of houses stops abruptly and behind the wall of the last house is a large parking area, its concrete surface broken up and pitted, and the beads of broken glass on its surface testament to the fact that this is no safe place to leave your car.

The forensics tent has been pitched on a patch of grass beyond the car park, behind a small copse of trees that stand in a dry, litter-strewn patch of dirt. Behind it is the railway bridge that leads over the tracks to another estate.

'Brace yourself,' says Pharaoh, as she lifts the flap of the tent and steps inside.

'Guv?'

'Take a look.'

A forensics officer in a white suit is crouching down over the body, but he stops taking photographs and backs away, crablike, as McAvoy enters the tent. Breathing slowly, he crosses to where the corpse lies.

The victim is on her back. The first thing that strikes him is the angle of her head. She seems to be looking up, craning her neck so as not to see the ruination of what has happened to her body. Even so, her expression is one of anguish. The tendons in her neck seem to have stretched to breaking point and her face is locked mid-scream. Her mouth is open, and her blue eyes have rolled back in her head, as if trying to get away.

McAvoy swallows. Forces himself to look at more than just the wounds.

She is in her late fifties, with short brown hair, greying at the roots. She is wearing black leggings and old, strappy sandals that display bare toes with nails painted dark blue. Her fingers are short but not unsightly, with neatly clipped nails and a gold engagement ring and wedding band, third finger, left hand.

Only now does he allow himself to consider her midsection.

His bile rises. He swallows it down.

The woman's chest has been caved in. The bones of her ribs have been snapped, splintered and pushed up and into her breasts and lungs. Her upper torso is a mass of flattened skin and tissue, black blood and mangled organs. Her white bra, together with what looks like the remains of her breasts, sit in the miasma of churned meat. For a hideous moment, McAvoy imagines the noise that will be made when the pathologist disentangles them for examination.

He turns away. Takes a breath that is not as deeply scented with gore.

He turns back to the horror, and flinches.

Though it shames him to have considered it, McAvoy finds himself in mind of a spatchcocked chicken; split at the breast and flattened out to be roasted.

He feels Pharaoh's hand on his shoulder, and looks into her face. She nods, and they step outside the tent.

'Bloody hell, Guv,' says McAvoy, breathlessly.

'I know.'

He breathes out, slowly. Realises that the world has been

spinning a little, and waits for the dizziness to pass. Forces himself to be a policeman.

'What sort of weapon does that?'

Pharaoh shrugs. 'I reckon we're after a bloke on a horse, swinging a fucking mace.'

'That can't have been the cause of death, though, can it? There must be a head wound, or a stab somewhere under all that . . .'

'Pathologist will get to all that. All I can say for certain is it wasn't suicide.'

McAvoy looks up at the sky. It remains the colour of dirty bathwater. He feels the perspiration at his lower back and when he rubs a hand over his face it comes away soaking. Although he knows nothing about the life of the woman in the tent, the little he knows of her death makes him angry. Nobody should die like that.

'Handbag? Purse?'

Pharaoh nods. 'The lot. Was only a few feet from the body.'

'What time?'

'She was found a couple of hours ago. Bloke on his way to get the morning papers. Saw her foot sticking out and phoned 999.'

'Regular CID can't have had a look, then . . .'

'Came straight to us.'

'Guv?'

Pharaoh makes a blade of her fingers and waves them in front of her throat, suggesting he cut short his questions. As head of the Serious and Organised Crime Unit, Pharaoh is used to the infighting and internecine warfare that pollutes the upper strata of Humberside Police. Her unit was established as a murder squad, set apart from the main body of detectives, but budget cuts and personnel changes have left the team with no clearly defined role. At present, Pharaoh and her officers are loosely tasked with investigating a highly organised criminal outfit that appears to have taken over most of the drugs trafficking on the east coast. Its emergence has coincided with a marked spike in the incidents of violent crime, and both McAvoy and Pharaoh know for certain that the gang's foot soldiers are responsible for several deaths. Their methods are efficient and brutal, their favoured weapons the nailgun and blowtorch. Pharaoh's unit have locked up three of the outfit's significant players but so far the information they have managed to glean about the chain of command has been pitiful. Ruthless, efficient, single-minded and worryingly well informed, each tier of the gang seems to be insulated from the next. The soldiers have little or no knowledge of who gives them their orders. It is an operation based on mobile phones and complex codes, which has recruited a better class of muscle through a combination of high reward and justified fear.

'This is down as gang-related?' asks McAvoy, incredulously. It is the only way the crime would have come straight to Pharaoh.

Pharaoh gives a rueful smile. 'She runs a residents' group. Spoke out at a recent public meeting about street dealers ruining the neighbourhood.'

McAvoy closes his eyes. 'So what do we know?'

Pharaoh doesn't need to consult her notes. She has already committed the details to memory.

'Philippa Longman. Fifty-three. Lived up Conway Close. Past Boulevard, near the playing fields. There's a uniform inspector from Gordon Street with the family now. Philippa worked at the late shop that you passed driving in. Was working last night, before you ask. And this would have been on her way home. Somebody grabbed her. Pulled her behind the trees. Did this.'

'Family?'

'Our next stop, my boy.'

'Bloke who found her?'

'Still shaking. Hasn't got the taste of sick out of his mouth yet.'

'And we're taking it, yes? There won't be a stink from CID?'

Pharaoh looks at him over the top of her sunglasses. 'Of course there will. There'll be a stink whatever happens.'

McAvoy takes a deep breath. 'I'm supposed to be prepping for court. Ronan Gill's trial is only a month away and the witnesses are getting jumpy . . .'

Without changing her facial expression, Pharaoh reaches up and puts a warm palm across McAvoy's mouth. He smiles, his stubble making a soft rasp against her skin.

'I have a hand free for a kidney punch if you need it,' she says sweetly.

McAvoy looks back at the tent. Sees, in his mind's eye the devastation within. He wants to know who did it. Why. Wants to stop it happening again. Wants to ensure that whoever loved this woman is at least given a face to hate.

He wishes the bloody psychologist were here, now. It would be the only way she could ever understand what makes him do a job he hates. Wants to tell her that this is what he is. What he forces himself to be. Here, at the place between sorrow and goodbye.

'Okay.'

2

'Poor lass.'

'Aye.'

'You can hear it, can't you? When it goes from panic, to something else . . .'

'Bloody terrifying is what it is. They should play that to anybody who thinks about leaving the house without a pitbull terrier and a spear.'

McAvoy is holding Philippa Longman's mobile phone to his ear, still inside the polythene evidence bag. He is listening to her voicemails. There are ten of them, starting with a gentle enquiry from a man with a West Yorkshire accent, wondering if she is on her way home, and progressing through an assortment of sons and daughters, increasingly desperate, asking where she is, if she's okay, to please call, just please call . . .

'Out of character, least we know that,' says McAvoy, switching off the phone and putting it back in Pharaoh's red leather handbag, which he is holding between his knees in the passenger seat of the convertible.

'Getting murdered? Yeah, it definitely hasn't happened to her before.'

'No, I mean—'

'I know what you mean.'

McAvoy looks out of the window. He doesn't really know this part of Hull. They are on an estate towards the back end of Hessle Road, where those who made their living from the fishing industry used to make their homes. It's pretty run down, but in this grey light, nothing would look pretty.

'Tenner for the first person to spot an up-to-date tax disc,' mutters Pharaoh.

None of the cars that are parked on the kerbs and grass verges looks younger than ten years old, and Pharaoh's convertible draws stares as they pass a group of people lounging by a low wall that leads to a fenced-off storage yard. They are of mixed ages. Two youngsters, shirtless, with buzzcuts, lounging over the frames of BMX bikes. Three men, tattoos on their necks and roll-ups in their fingers. A woman in her late sixties, with grey hair and tracksuit bottoms, sipping from a can of lager and telling a story. One of them says something, but the convertible's roof is up, and the words are lost in the sound of tyres on bone-dry road.

They pass a sign declaring that they are on Woodcock Street, and he vaguely remembers reading that the army had used this neighbourhood to practise their tank manoeuvres before being deployed to Afghanistan. He wonders if that was true.

'Up here. Playing fields.'

Ahead, several acres of untended grass stretch away: a play park in one direction, and some form of stone memorial in the other. A police car sits abandoned in the road, among half a dozen vehicles parked haphazardly around a corner terraced house. The cars look as though they have arrived at speed and been abandoned.

Pharaoh and McAvoy step from the car. As McAvoy arranges his clothes and makes himself a little more presentable, he peers over the wall that marks the boundary of the park. Old gravestones have been laid against the far side of it, their inscriptions mossed over and names lost to wind and time.

'Shall we?'

McAvoy takes a deep breath. He has done this too many times. Sat in too many rooms with too much grief; felt too many eyes upon him as he made his promises to the dead.

They head towards the house. It sits on the far side of a low flower bed which carries nothing but dry earth and hacked-back stumps. Beyond that is a footpath, its surface a camouflage pattern of different tarmac patches.

'Poor lass,' says McAvoy, again, pushing open the gate.

The house where Philippa Longman lived is the nicest in the row. Freshly painted black railings edge a driveway of neat bricks, upon which sits a tastefully varnished shed, with double locks, and a child's plastic playhouse. There are two hanging baskets by the double-glazed front door, and the front window carries posters for a charity coffee morning and a reading initiative at a local nursery.

Pharaoh reaches up to knock on the door, but it opens before she can do so. In the hall is a Family Liaison Officer that McAvoy remembers having met before. He is pushing forty, with receding hair and slightly crooked teeth, set in a face that always looks to be squinting against harsh light. He's a nice enough guy, who understands what he is there for. His job is not to heal these people or make sense of things. He's just there to show that the police are doing something. That these people matter. That this death is important . . .

'They're in the lounge,' he says, his accent broad Hull. 'Husband. Jim. Nice old boy. Two sons, one furious, one falling apart. Couple of daughters-in-law. A neighbour. A sister, too, if I got the family tree straight. Eldest daughter bolted about twenty minutes ago. Took the nippers to the park, I think. Boy and a girl. A cousin, too. Was all too much. Inspector Moreton and PC Audrey Stretton are holding the fort. Family know Mum isn't coming back. They know that we found a body that matches her description. They had called her in as missing about five this morning.'

Pharaoh nods, turns to McAvoy, and without a word passing between them, he turns away from the house. The FLO opens the door to the living room and as Pharaoh continues inside, McAvoy hears the soft patter of emotionless conversation, pierced by a wet, choking wail . . .

He makes his way over to the entrance to the playing fields and follows the footpath through the long, straggly grass to the play area beyond a line of oak trees. *Quercus robur*, he remembers, unprompted, and has a sudden image of sitting at the kitchen table, breathing in peat smoke and wood shavings, mopping up potato soup with a hunk of soda bread: his dad washing pots at a deep stone sink and softly imparting facts over his broad shoulder at his eight-year-old son. *They call it "petraea" in some places. Flowers in May and leaves soon after. Sometimes they have a second flush of leaves if it's been a bad year for caterpillars. They call it Lammas growth. Can you spell that? You write it down and I'll check it. Best charcoal for making swords, the oak. Burns slow. They use the bark for tanning, Aector. High-quality leathers, especially . . .'

He shakes himself back to the present. Looks ahead. It's a modern swing park, with a protective rubber surface and plenty of padding. He remembers mentioning to Roisin that parks seem a little too safe these days. Said he couldn't see the point of bubble-wrapping all of the equipment when children have such a habit of banging their heads into one another. He had predicted crash helmets becoming compulsory on roundabouts within five years.

There are several adults in the play park but McAvoy spots Philippa Longman's daughter straight away. She is pushing a child on a swing, and between each shove she is raising her hands to her face to cuff away tears that have turned her fleshy cheeks red and sore. She is wearing a denim skirt and a green vest top, her hair pulled back in a ponytail to leave a severe fringe at the front. It doesn't suit her. Hers is a warm, open face that looks as though it hides a pleasant smile.

She sees McAvoy approaching. Immediately identifying him as a policeman, she gives a slight nod and then grabs the swing to halt its momentum. She lifts the toddler out and gives him a gentle pat on the bottom, before pointing at a climbing frame where an older child is dangling upside down. She tells him to go play with his cousin. He wobbles off, and the woman extends her hand.

'Elaine,' she says, and her voice catches. 'Elaine,' she says, again.

'I'm Aector,' says McAvoy, taking her hand in his. It's cold, tiny and birdlike in his large, fleshy palm. 'I'm a detective.'

'The house is over there,' says Elaine, waving, vaguely. 'They're all in there. Crying and bloody carrying on. I couldn't take it.'

McAvoy recognises her voice from Philippa's answering machine. She had left the most messages. By the last, her voice was just a staggered breath, broken up around the word 'please'.

'People are different,' says McAvoy, leading Elaine to a bench that overlooks the park. 'Some need company, others needs space. It's agony whatever you do.'

Elaine meets McAvoy's eyes. Holds his gaze. He watches as tears spill afresh.

'I don't know what to do,' says Elaine, looking away. 'Last night I had a mum. The kids had a grandma. It was all normal, you know? I watched a DVD and had a bottle of white wine and I tucked in my son and I went to bed. Dad woke me up, ringing. Mum hadn't come home. Was she with me, had I heard from her, did I know where she might be. I rang her, as if he hadn't already tried that. Nothing. Phoned her work and there was nobody there. I got Lucas up and we went to her shop. Walked her route. Christ, I must have walked right past where she was bloody lying . . .'

A shudder racks her body.

'What if he was doing it as I walked past? What if I could have saved her . . .'

Elaine dissolves. She shrinks inwards, a creased fist of pain and despair. Her head falls forward, tears and snot pouring unimpeded down her face, and it only takes the slightest of touches on the back of her head before she is steered into McAvoy's arms, where he feels her shudders like those of a dying animal.

McAvoy had not meant to hold her. He knows officers who have no difficulty with the professional detachment encouraged in the national guidelines, but he cannot witness pain without providing comfort.

'Oh my God, oh my God . . .'

He senses her words as much as hears them, whispered against his skin. Gently, as if she is made of shattered porcelain, he lifts her back into a seated position and tries to raise her head to look in her eyes. She ducks from his gaze and then, unexpectedly, gives a little pop of laughter.

'Your shirt, I'm so sorry . . .'

McAvoy looks down at his waistcoat, and the mess of mucus and tears.

'It doesn't matter.'

'Here, I have a tissue . . .'

'Your need is greater than mine.'

She stops talking then. Just looks at him. Then she uses her wrists to dry her eyes, and pulls a paper tissue from the pocket of her skirt. She dabs her nose.

'Don't. Give it a proper blow,' says McAvoy.

Elaine blows her nose. Folds the hankie. Blows it again.

'You're a dad, then?' she asks, tucking the tissue away. She manages a smile, at a memory. 'My dad always speaks to me like that. Still takes my arm when we cross the road. What you got?'

'Boy and a baby girl.'

She looks him up and down. 'Bet the lads won't give her any trouble when she's older, eh? You could snap them in two.'

McAvoy smiles. 'She'll be able to look out for herself. That's what you want for your kids, isn't it? That they're good people. Responsible. Able to take care of themselves.'

Elaine nods and presses her lips together. 'I think Mum did okay with us. Did her best, anyway. There's me and my two brothers. Two grandkids now. Mine and Don's. Don's the middle kid, if you need to know that.' She stops herself. 'What is it you need to know? Really? I'm no good back at the house. Don's wife's such a bloody drama queen. If I go in there I'll say something. Dad doesn't need all that around him. He doesn't know what to bloody do either, but once he's stopped making everybody cups of tea this is going to kill him too. They were together thirty-three years, you know. Got married as soon as she found out she was pregnant with me. Dad could have done a runner, couldn't he? But he didn't. Married her in a flash. Last time they agreed on anything was when they both said "I do" but they loved each other.'

Elaine falls silent. She doesn't seem to know what to do with her hands so just holds them in her lap. McAvoy looks past her. The other parents in the park have drifted together and the pair of them are receiving repeated glances. McAvoy wonders if they already know what has happened to Philippa, or whether they think he is some hulking great brute of a boyfriend who has just made his girl cry.

'Mum helped get the funding for this park,' says Elaine, gesturing at the assemblage of brightly painted swings and slides. 'Badgered the council until they couldn't say no . . .'

McAvoy looks around him. Wonders whether it is too soon to suggest they name it after the dead woman. He tries to find something to say but finds his gaze falling on Elaine's son, sitting on a roundabout and hoping somebody will come and give him a push. His cousin seems to have wandered off. McAvoy stands up and walks over to the roundabout. He smiles at the toddler, and then gently gives it a push, walking around at the same speed in case the child topples over and falls. He feels a presence beside him and turns to see Elaine, smiling weakly.

'What am I going to do without her? What will he?'

McAvoy reaches down and picks up the boy. He tickles his tummy, then under his chin, and is rewarded with a delicious peal of laughter.

Still holding the boy, he chooses his words carefully. 'Elaine, the unit I work for deals with organised crime. There is some suggestion that your mother was a little outspoken about some of the more unsavoury elements in the neighbourhood.'

Elaine's expression doesn't change. 'Is that something to do with this?'

'We don't know.'

She turns away and stares across the grass in the direction of her mother's home.

'I don't live around here,' she says, after a time. 'I live up Kirk Ella. Nice little place, just the two of us. I didn't grow up here either. We're from Batley. West Yorkshire. Dad came over here for a job about fifteen years ago and they bought this place. I can't say I thought much of the area but Mum said the people seemed nice. She made it a lovely home. Well, you can see that, can't you? And she was never one to keep herself to herself. Couldn't help but get involved. She'd lived here a year and she'd started a neighbourhood association. Even ran for the city council as an independent. The papers used to come to her for a quote and she was always good value. Told them this was a nice neighbourhood but that a few rotten apples were spoiling it for everyone. She meant that too.'

'Did she ever name names?'

'I don't think she knew any,' says Elaine. 'Everybody on this estate knows how to buy a bit of this or that, but Mum was no threat to anybody's business. Not really. She was probably a nuisance, if anything. She used to give your lot hell about the lack of police patrols and not seeing any policemen on the streets any more but it was busybody stuff, really. She wasn't some supergrass. She worked in a bloody late shop, for goodness' sake . . .'

'And she always walked home? It's quite a hike.'

'That's my fault,' says Elaine, kicking at a clump of grass that is pushing through a crack in the spongy surface of the park. 'We started this health challenge a couple of years ago. You have to do a certain amount of steps each day and enter the number on this website and it tells you how far around the world your team has got. She was well into it. They gave us pedometers and we both lost a bit of weight chalking up the miles. I packed it in when I got pregnant but Mum stuck with it. Said she wanted to be able to say she had walked to Mexico. Worked out that if she walked to and from work for her shifts and did a big walk on a weekend, she could be there before she was sixty.'

'So anybody who knew her would know she always walked, yes? Anybody waiting for her would know.'

Elaine reaches out and takes Lucas, holding him like a teddy bear.

'This isn't anything to do with drugs or gangs,' she says, softly. 'It can't be.'

'Do you know anybody who would want to harm her?'

'She was a good person. My best friend . . .'

'Elaine, this is a very early stage in the investigation but we need to build up as clear a picture of your mum as possible. Did she have any enemies? Had she ever been threatened?'

The dead woman's daughter shakes her head. 'She was everybody's friend. She was a lifesaver. There was . . .'

Elaine stops herself, her hand raised to her mouth.

'Darren,' she says, softly.

'I'm sorry?'

Elaine puts down her son. Tells him to go play.

'My ex.'

'Elaine?'

She grabs a handful of her fringe, eyes suddenly alive with more than tears.

'Shit, I didn't think . . .'

McAvoy takes her shoulders and turns her eyes to his. Tries to make it okay.

'Elaine, you can tell me.'

She sobs, and covers her mouth with her hand.

'He said if he ever saw her again he would kill her. That he would tear her heart out the way I tore out his . . .'

3

'Lemon-scented.'

Helen Tremberg walks back to the car and pokes her head through the open window.

'Sorry, Ma'am?'

Sharon Archer punches the steering wheel with the flat of her hand. When she speaks, it is through bared teeth and unmoving lips, and for a moment, she takes on the look of a psychotic ventriloquist.

'I said lemon fucking scented.'

Tremberg nods, pressing her lips down hard on the smile that is threatening to become a snigger. It is an act as hard as calling a woman two years older than herself 'Ma'am'.

'Sandwich, or anything?'

Archer's eyes flash fury as she turns.

'Do I look like I'm in the mood for a fucking snack?'

Tremberg turns away and heads for the pharmacy that represents the only high-street name on this little parade of independent shops and salons. She pauses for a moment to look at the display of cupcakes in the window of a bakery, but an angry blaring of the car horn indicates that Archer is watching her in the rear-view mirror and is not in the mood for waiting.

'Okay, okay,' she mutters, accepting that for now, there is no time for cake.

It's cool inside the brightly lit store and for the first time in days, Tremberg's skin goose-pimples as the sweat turns cold upon her bare arms. It's rare that she exposes any flesh while on duty but today she has acquiesced to a short-sleeved blouse, which she has not tucked into her pinstripe trousers.

'Wipes, wipes . . .'

She finds the right shelf, and pretends she can't see the lemon-scented ones. She picks the packet with the most overtly chemical smell, then heads to the counter, where a short Asian lady gives her a bright smile.

'It's two for one,' she says, conspiratorially. 'Special offer.'

Tremberg shrugs. 'They're for my boss. She can make do.'

The lady grins, and Tremberg hands over the five-pound note Archer has given her. 'Put the change in the charity box,' she says, crumpling the receipt.

'We don't have one.'

'Then get yourself an ice cream.'

Tremberg heads for the exit, catching a glimpse of her reflection in the mirror behind the make-up display as she leaves. She's at ease with what she sees. At thirty-one, she's happily single and rarely lonely, and though she may be a little more broad shouldered than she would like, there is nothing offensive about her round face with its narrow features, or her simply styled brown hair.

He'll like it, she tells herself. *Get up the courage to suggest a drink. And stop checking your phone!*

For the past few weeks Helen has been receiving increasingly colourful messages from a solicitor she met while waiting for a court case. His emails are the favourite part of her day and she has taken to checking her phone almost obsessively. Although she is no stranger to relationships, she is nervous about being the first to get in touch each day. It seems important to her that she is the respondent to his overtures, rather than making the running herself.

Helen emerges back into the muggy air and takes in the view. She's never got out of the car on this stretch of road before and wonders if she ever will again. It's no shabbier than anywhere else, and there are only a few untenanted shops. Each of the parking spaces by the side of the road is taken, and there is a steady procession of shoppers wandering from store to store, filling shopping bags with fruit and veg, bread rolls, sliced meat, saying hello over the noise of the traffic and thinking about how best to jazz up the salad they are considering for tonight's tea. It reminds Tremberg of the Grimsby neighbourhood where she grew up. Normal folk. Normal people. Bit skint by the third week of the month, and a week in Benidorm each June. Fish and chip tea on a Friday, and six-packs of supermarket lager in front of the Grand Prix on a Sunday. The people she became a copper for. The people worth protecting.

Tremberg tries to get her bearings. Works out where she is. She's half a mile from the prison on the road that leads to the Preston Road Estate. She has only been working in Hull for a year and has not had time to familiarise herself with every neighbourhood, but knows the PRE by reputation and is grateful that it was never her beat when she was still in uniform. More Anti-social Behaviour Orders have been handed out here than on any other estate in the city boundary, and barely an edition of the *Hull Daily Mail* is published without it containing some report or another about teenage gangs making life miserable for 'decent' people.

Tremberg rarely troubles herself with the politics of her job or the social background to the crimes she investigates. She does what she's asked, and enjoys catching villains. She's good at it too, even if she is currently feeling less than happy in her work. As one of four detective constables on the Serious and Organised Crime Unit, she has little say in which of her senior colleagues she is paired with, but she enjoys her working days considerably more when helping McAvoy or Pharaoh. At the moment, she is working for Detective Inspector Shaz Archer, and loathing every moment of it. Archer and DCI Colin Ray are effectively leading the unit's investigation into the spike in organised crime. Pharaoh is overseeing, but her day is so filled with paperwork and budget meetings that Ray and Archer are running the show, revelling in being top dogs.

This morning, Ray had told Tremberg to accompany Archer to HMP Hull because there was a good chance that the man they were seeing would warm to two women more than he would to Ray himself. Tremberg had seen the logic in that. It is impossible to warm to Colin Ray. He's a walking sneer, all yellow teeth and nicotine-stained fingers; all curses and spittle and ratty little eyes.

Tremberg had accepted Ray's orders with good grace, even though she had despaired at the thought of spending the morning with the snotty detective inspector who seems to be the only female that Colin Ray has any time for. The two are pretty much inseparable, though they make for unlikely friends. Archer is part of the horsey crowd and spends her free time playing polo and knocking back Pimm's with people called Savannah and

Sheridan. Ray coaches football in his spare time and spends his money on greyhounds, lager and ex-wives.

Tremberg is not the sort to be jealous of her female colleagues and does not object to the fact that Shaz Archer is extraordinarily attractive. It's her personality she bridles at. She puts Tremberg in a mind of a California high school bully in a film for teens. She holds everybody and everything in open contempt, and uses her looks to manipulate colleagues and crooks alike. Her arrest record is impressive, but Tremberg finds the way she flaunts herself distasteful. While she admires Trish Pharaoh for just being herself – for being sexy and mumsy and hard as fucking nails – with Archer it's all strategic. Every time she purses her lips or blows on her perfect fingernails, she's doing it to get a reaction out of somebody. She keeps miniskirts and crop-tops in her desk so she can get changed into something exotic if she's interviewing some easily led pervert, and there are rumours she has traded her affections for confessions in the past. Tremberg knows police stations to be termite mounds of malicious gossip and had originally decided to ignore such slander about a female colleague. Then she got to know Archer herself, and decided the woman was, if nothing else, a bitch of the first order.

Still, she didn't look quite so well groomed this morning . . .

As Tremberg passes the cake shop, she has to bite down on her smile again. The morning's interview at Hull Prison had been fruitless in terms of information, but Tremberg wouldn't call the day a waste of time. It's hard to think of any morning as a write-off when it involves watching a drug dealer chuck a polystyrene cup full of piss over your boss.

'How did he even do it?' Archer had spat, furious, as the guards led the laughing Jackson away, and her waterproof mascara began to prove it wasn't piss-proof by running down her cheeks.

Tremberg had had no answer. She had thought Jackson was just ignoring them. Instead he was busily urinating beneath the desk, waiting for the right moment in proceedings to demonstrate his strength of feeling about their questions. It had worked, too. The interview was terminated without him even confirming his name, let alone who had paid him to be at the wheel of the marijuana-filled Transit van that had been pulled over by traffic officers eight weeks before. Tremberg had been planning to tell the middle-aged convict that it was in his interests to talk to them; to point out that his employers had lost money, and face, because of his decision to drive at 53 mph on the bend of the A63. She wonders if Jackson will learn the hard way.

Tremberg turns her head away from the cake shop as she passes, avoiding the temptation to stop and drool. Across the busy street, an attractive, pink-haired woman is hanging a special offers poster up in the window of a nice-looking hair salon. Inside, a pretty young blonde looks as though she may eventually stop talking for long enough to cut some hair. Next to it is a smaller shop that looks as though it has not been open long. 'Snips and Rips' says the sign, and the lettering on the large front window declares it to be a specialist in clothing repair, dressmaking and curtain alterations. Tremberg, who has a nasty habit of pulling buttons off shirts and snagging the turn-ups of her trousers on chair legs, makes a mental note to remember that it is there.

'It's Helen, isn'it?'

Tremberg turns, startled. Police officers are rarely pleased to be taken by surprise.

'It is! Jaysus, how are you?'

The girl is stunning, in a mucky kind of way. Petite, tanned and toned, she is wearing a purple bikini top, jogging trousers and Ugg boots, and is pushing a stroller in which a dark-haired baby is chewing on a sunhat. She has a tangle of golden necklaces at her throat, and several earrings in each ear.

Tremberg tries not to frown as she struggles to remember where she knows the girl from. Is she one of the travellers from the Cottingham site? Has she tipped them the wink on some stolen goods, maybe. But *Helen*? Not 'Detective Constable'? Who the bloody hell . . .

'Roisin,' says the girl, helpfully, in an accent tinged with Irish. 'Roisin McAvoy.'

Tremberg finds herself flustered, suddenly embarrassed at not having remembered her sergeant's wife. They have only met once, and then only briefly, but McAvoy had once opened up to her about the circumstances of his meeting Roisin, and Tremberg hopes her face does not betray her as the memories flood in. This is the traveller girl that McAvoy saved. The girl who suffered agonies at the hands of attackers when not yet a teen. Whom McAvoy revenged, and to whom he later gave himself completely.

'Roisin, of course, I'm sorry, it must be the heat. How are things? Warm isn't it? And goodness, who's this little thing? Lovely, lovely.'

If Roisin finds Tremberg's gabbling amusing, she hides it well. She smiles at the constable and then crouches down by the stroller. 'This is Lilah,' she says, proudly. 'Our youngest. Seven months now. Hasn't she got her daddy's eyes?'

Tremberg is never comfortable around children, but as she bends down she does at least appreciate the sloppy, gummy grin the child turns her way. Lilah's eyes, as promised, are brown and innocent, looking out at the world in confused fascination.

'She's a stunner,' says Tremberg, and then winces as she hears Archer honk the car horn.

'That for you?' asks Roisin. 'Tell them to hold their horses.'

'It's my boss. Well, one of them. Bit of an incident at the prison this morning.' Tremberg holds up the packet of wipes by way of explanation. 'She needs these, fast.'

'Have an accident, did she? Scary places, prisons. There's some Sudocrem in my bag if she thinks she might get a rash . . .'

Roisin says it with a smile, but her accent is pure traveller, and Tremberg finds herself wondering how difficult it must be for this young girl to be married to a policeman when she grew up thinking of them as the enemy. There must be times when the worlds collide, she thinks, and remembers the night Ray and Archer put the cuffs on the drugs outfit's enforcers up at the traveller site. There had been rumours that McAvoy was there too: bloodied and dirty, his great fists grazed to the bone.

There is another angry blast on the horn.

'Patient woman,' smiles Roisin.

'Oh she's a love,' says Tremberg. 'What brings you up this way, anyhow? Kingswood you live, isn't it? Or did your husband tell me you were moving?'

Roisin nods, like a teenager about to tell a friend what she is getting for Christmas. 'We're living out of boxes at the moment but we should exchange contracts next week. Aector's taking care of all that. Lovely house though, down by the foreshore, under the bridge. Old cottages, done up a treat, so they are. I've got a load of ideas. I've spoken to Aector about having a few people over when we get moved in, so it would be lovely to see you. Bring a friend or two. Maybe not whoever's honking that horn, though . . .'

Tremberg smiles. She can see how McAvoy fell for this girl. She's not just beautiful; she has some inner light, some warmth. She is a soothing presence. *This is what McAvoy comes home to*, she thinks. This is what keeps him upright. Keeps him good. Keeps him alive . . .

'Oh, before you rush off, can I give you one of these?' Roisin reaches behind the stroller and hands Tremberg a flier for the alterations service across the street. 'My friend's place. Mel. Met her at salsa not so long ago. Such a nice person. This is her dream, running her own place. She's dead good, too. I'm just here for a bit of moral support because she feels a bit daft sitting there when there's no customers. No air conditioning in there either, so she'll probably have me wafting the door! Anyway, I'll let you go but it's lovely to see you again.'

To Tremberg's surprise, Roisin reaches up and gives her a clumsy kiss on the cheek. Tremberg gets a whiff of sugary pop, of expensive perfume and hand-rolled cigarettes, then gives a vague wave as she heads back to the car. She stops after a few paces, when she remembers that she owes Roisin a thank you. A few months back, Tremberg had been badly cut during the hunt for a killer, and through McAvoy, Roisin had sent her a pot of some herbal remedy that had helped take the sting out of the wound. At the time, Tremberg had tried to make a joke of it, and asked her sergeant if his perfect wife was a white witch as well as everything else. McAvoy had looked hurt, and Tremberg had ended up scolding herself for being mean and feeling like she had just punched a rabbit in the face.

'Next time,' she says, under her breath, opens the car door.

'Could you have taken any fucking longer?' demands Archer, as she snatches the packet and begins pulling out fistfuls of wet-wipes. She scrubs at her tanned brown arms, her made-up face, down into the cleavage of her pink tennis shirt. 'No lemon?'

'They were out of lemon,' says Tremberg, wincing as her sweat-soaked shirt presses against the skin of her back as she sits down. She looks into the rear-view mirror and watches Roisin waiting for a gap in the traffic, singing gently to baby Lilah.

Archer scoffs, and then reaches into her designer handbag and starts pulling out lipsticks and assorted blushers.

'Who was that, anyway?'

'Ma'am?'

'The tart? Tits out. Fat arse. Asking the world to fucking look at her.'

Tremberg opens her mouth to explain, then changes her mind. 'Just somebody I know from a case.'

Archer loses interest as she begins applying eyeliner. 'On the game, is she?'

Tremberg looks at her boss and lets a little temper bubble to the surface. 'I think you've missed a bit.'

11.44 a.m.

A taxi office off Hull's Hedon Road, halfway between the prison and the docks.

In the back office, Adam Downey is sipping whisky. It's an expensive bottle. Japanese. It came in a metal casket with a samurai on the front. It's supposed to be one of the finest spirits in the world and he's drinking it from a crystal tumbler that weighs as much as his head. To Downey, the tipple tastes like petrol and heartburn, but he reckons he looks good while sipping at it, so tolerates the bad taste.

Downey is in his early twenties. He's a handsome lad who takes his appearance seriously. He's in good shape, with muscles built for showing off rather than for lifting anything heavy. He looks like he should be auditioning for a TV talent show. He has a pop-star appearance. He's a vision in designer white trainers, slashed-neck T-shirt and £100 haircut. The diamond in his earlobe cost him a mint and the little stars he has tattooed behind his ear show he can take a bit of pain if the reward is worth it.

He's flicking through a porn mag. He likes black women best of all. Usually he looks for something stimulating on his top-of-the-range mobile phone but the reception here is terrible so he has resorted to old-school thrills.

Out front, half a dozen drivers sit snacking and sweating, waiting for the phone to ring. Three of them are Turks. Dominating the scene is Bruno, a mountain of muscle and dreadlocks. They're his team. His boys. They do what he fucking says.

For the past few months, Adam Downey has been somebody to fear. He has been a drug dealer since his teens. He was always going to be trouble. He grew up in a nice house with a stable family unit, but he was never any good at living the quiet life. Downey wanted to be respected. Admired. Feared. He had put himself in harm's way from an early age and by his mid-teens he was running drugs for the punk rocker who used to run the trade in the east of the city. Orton, his name was. He didn't look like much of a drug dealer. He had little in the way of style. He was all tattoos and combat pants, lace-up boots and piercings. But for the best part of fifteen years he was responsible for most of the gear that came through the docks. Downey was never his muscle or the brains, but he was reliable and ambitious and soon became one of Orton's confidants.

It was when Downey got sent to prison that things changed. He showed up on somebody's radar. He got headhunted. A phone was pressed to his ear as he lay in his bunk and a man with a refined accent and perfect diction told him he had been talent-spotted. A new outfit was safeguarding the interests of a number of established crime organisations on the east coast. Orton was refusing to see the benefits of following suit. They were seeking somebody young, ambitious and capable who could step into the gap that would be left by his imminent departure. Would he be interested in the position? It hadn't taken Downey long to make up his mind. For as long as he could remember he'd secretly thought of himself as the prince of the city. He daydreamed about people doing his bidding. He fantasised about dispensing mercy and justice in equal measure. He wanted to point, nod, and know that whoever had wronged him was going to learn just how very special he was.

Downey had said yes.

Soon after, his sentence was inexplicably cut. He found himself back on his own streets. A grateful, oblivious Orton came to pick him up from the prison gates. He had Big Bruno by his side. Orton handed over an envelope full of cash, which Downey pocketed. Then Bruno drove them to the woods. They were barely free of the city when Orton began to realise things were not going as he had planned. He began asking Bruno where he was going. Asking him who had been in his ear. Offering him cash and blubbing about his family.

Ten miles from Hull, Bruno pulled Orton from the car. He

smashed the old punk's head open with a hammer. Then Downey joined in too.

Downey likes being a drug dealer. He likes the fact that the police don't seem to know anything about him but know that somebody like him must exist. He likes that the men he has recruited to his cause are so international. It makes him feel sophisticated and cosmopolitan. He likes the occasional phone calls he gets from his employers, praising him for his initiative and tenacity. He likes feeling like a somebody.

The taxi firm is the perfect front for his operation. His drivers rarely pick up real fares. They just attend the addresses they are given and hand over the packages that Downey has carefully weighed out for them. Their customers are all approved and trusted. It's a slick operation with a huge turnover. Downey doesn't have to worry about how to get the gear into the country. His job is to get it from Point B to Point C, where it will be cut, packaged, and passed on to other people in the chain. Downey's drivers know what they are involved in. They get paid handsomely for it. It's a system that works, and that makes Adam Downey feel blissfully fucking untouchable.

He sips his whisky again. Grimaces.

It's hot here, in this small, bare office, and Downey wants to go and sit out the front with the lads. They're a good crowd and seem to respect him. But he believes that being aloof adds to his image, and Downey loves image. He watches himself in the mirror, and plays with the grenade.

Downey had nicked the grenade when he was picking up a wholesale delivery. Among the crates of white powder were half a dozen handguns and a leather holdall full of grenades and plastic explosives. Impulsively, Downey had wanted one.

He knew the guns would be missed were he to help himself, but the grenades seemed deliciously inviting. They didn't look the way he had seen them in war films. The one he holds in his palm is black and square: no bigger than his mobile phone. It has a pin through the top and Russian lettering down its side. He likes to hold it. Likes to play with the pin. Dares himself to throw the grenade in the air and catch it again before it can detonate.

Downey hears the front door of the taxi office bang. There is a muttering from beyond the door to his office, then it is pushed open by a tall dark man in a football shirt and camouflage trousers.

'We knock in this country, Hakan,' says Downey, over the lip of his glass. 'Remember? We flush toilets too? None of that folding up the bog-roll and putting it in the bin. We're not keen on shit samosas.'

Hakan doesn't seem to understand. His English is good but he seems too flustered to pay attention.

'What's the matter?' asks Downey.

Hakan closes the door behind him then leans against it. He's quite a good-looking guy, though he is hairy enough to blunt a lawnmower.

'I fuck up.'

Downey spreads his hands. He's not worried. There's nothing he can't handle.

'Police,' says Hakan. 'I think they follow me. I not know what do. I park. Put parcel in coat. Take coat seamstress. Seamstress has coat.'

Downey sits forward in his chair. He spits his whisky back in the glass.

'Again, Hakan. In fucking English.'

Downey sinks lower in his seat as the driver tells him what happened. He'd been delivering a wallet-sized package of white powder to the address that had been phoned through just an hour ago. He'd been driving normally, doing as he was told. Then he saw the flashing lights in his mirror. Panicked. Started seeing a conspiracy. Every parked car was suddenly a plain-clothes officer. Every van was a surveillance unit.

'I have coat with me. I see shop, yes? Southcoates Lane. I have idea. Put package in coat. Take coat in shop. Ask for them to fix zip. She nice lady. We talk. I go back when all quiet, yes. I do right, yes?'

Downey chews on his lip.

'You gave the parcel away, Hakan. You gave it to a stranger. What if she looks in the fucking pocket?'

Hakan waves his hands.

'She say she busy. I say "No rush." I go back for it in a week, perhaps. Tell her I not need work done at all . . .'

Downey throws his glass at the wall. It shatters in a rain of jagged crystal.

'Ticket,' he says, furious.

'Ticket?'

'The fucking ticket, you Turkish prick,' says Downey. 'The ticket for the alterations shop. I'll go for it. Christ, if she finds it. If we lose that parcel . . .'

Downey doesn't finish the sentence. Everything he has could be yanked away from him with one swift tug. Being prince of the city depends on staying in the good graces of the powers behind the throne.

He drains his whisky. It burns, and tastes like shite.

He snatches the ticket from Hakan's hand. Looks at the words.
'Snips and Rips – alterations a speciality'.

Downey grunts.

'Story of my fucking life.'

4

'If you weren't such a pansy you would be a hell of a Romeo.'

'Guv?'

'Women. They bloody love you, don't they? One look at those big sad eyes and they're pussy in your hand.'

'Putty, you mean.'

'I know what I mean. It's just funny. They don't know what they want to do with you, do they? Don't know whether they want you to throw them around like a ragdoll or put them in the bath and wash their hair.'

McAvoy keeps his eyes on the road. He swallows, and is aware of his Adam's apple rubbing against his shirt collar.

'Do you do that? Do you wash Roisin's hair?'

He can feel his boss staring at the side of his face. Senses that she is shaking her head slightly, and smiling with only one half of her mouth.

'Paint her nails? Read her bedtime stories? Cut her fish fingers up for her . . .'

McAvoy turns in the driver's seat and looks into Pharaoh's blue eyes. She's gone too far, and she raises her hands, acknowledging it. She does this, sometimes. Teases until she feels bad. He has come to understand her pretty well these past months. He knows all about so-called 'gallows humour' – cops cracking off-colour gags so the misery of their jobs has to work harder to reach their souls. With Trish it's different. Her job does affect her. The sights she sees make her cry. She never makes jokes about the dead. She just performs with the living the way she has learned to in two decades of policing. She's Trish Fucking Pharaoh: brash and seductive, loud and maternal, hard as fucking nails. She gets the job done, and then she goes home to her four kids and crippled husband and drinks until the screaming in her head goes away.

'Sorry. It's the heat.'

He nods. Turns back to the road. Tries to be jolly British about the whole thing and move the conversation on to the weather. 'It's just so sticky, isn't it? Back home, there would be clouds of midges in this heat. You rub your hand over your face and it comes away black with the little sods.'

'I've heard. Coming back with bites is not my idea of a holiday. Not unless they're on your thigh, anyway.'

McAvoy gives the tiniest of laughs, and that seems to satisfy her. She goes back to reading her phone.

Home, he thinks. Why did I call the Highlands 'home'? Roisin is *home*. The kids are *home*. What did I mean by that? What would Sabine make of it . . .

McAvoy gets annoyed with himself and curtails the train of introspection. Concentrates on driving, his hands where they should be at a precise ten-to-two on the steering wheel. Looks out through dead flies and dust. It's a boring road, all bland fields, four-house hamlets and dead farms. It seems popular with boy racers intent on risking their lives on hairpin bends, and McAvoy has winced several times in anticipation of a horrific smash as souped-up Vauxhall Corsas and Subarus tore past him at 90 mph.

The journey is giving him the beginnings of a migraine. He's been squinting for half an hour. The windscreen wash is empty. He is staring through grease and dirt, smeared into a khaki, blood-speckled rainbow by the wipers that squeak across the glass.

'I'm getting a stuffy nose,' says Pharaoh, giving a sniff.

'It's the rape fields,' says McAvoy, waving a hand in the direction of the luminous yellow crops either side of the winding B-road.

'*Rape Fields*? Think I rented that from Lovefilm . . .'

'Rapeseed, Guv. A lot of people are allergic to it. Really, you should plant a blue crop called borage nearby to counteract it, but the European Union didn't insist, so nobody does. A lot of people think they have hay fever when they don't. Gives you runny eyes, a stuffy nose . . .'

'You seem fine.'

'I'm not allergic to it. Penicillin and coconut, that's me.'

'Yeah?' Pharaoh takes a handkerchief from her bag and tries to blow her nose. 'Fuck, one nostril's blocked.'

'Sea air will help.'

'So will a vodka.'

A minute later they are drifting through the centre of Hornsea, a seaside town half an hour from the outskirts of Hull. It's not really a resort. Holidaymakers head for Bridlington and Scarborough, and though the place does have a few guest houses and some amusement arcades jangle and bleep on the seafront, they're more for listless local teens than to satisfy any deluge of tourists. It's a presentable, quiet place that's doing okay for itself and doesn't make much noise. It's a jumble of coffee shops, curiosity shops and estate agents, with ornate awnings and

Victorian roofs, huddling together between the new all-night mini-supermarkets and chain pubs.

McAvoy parks outside a strip of attractive townhouses, opposite a large white Art Deco building with huge bay windows. He can tell they'll offer awesome views of the bay. Having spent the past few weeks mired in real-estate dealings, he instinctively wonders how much the view adds to the asking price.

'He'd better be bloody in,' says Pharaoh, getting out of the car.

McAvoy purses his lips, blows out a stream of silent concerns, closes his eyes, and becomes a detective again as they walk up to the red-painted front door. Darren Robb lives in Flat 3, and works from home as a website designer. Elaine has given them a brief sketch of his background; told them he's a bit of a useless lump who likes computer games and crisps. A quick search of the police database has come up with nothing exciting in his file. He once got a caution for urinating in a side street off Holderness Road, but having been to Holderness Road, McAvoy finds it hard to think of that as much of a crime.

It is Pharaoh, as the senior officer, who is allowed the honour of leaning on the doorbell. She does so for a full ten seconds. McAvoy turns back to the street. There are houses both to his left and right, but directly in front of this building is a swathe of stubby grass. The view to the sea is unimpeded. Some kids are kicking a football around. A mum with a pushchair is lying on the grass reading a magazine. The kids who were leaning by the sea wall are now squatting in a rough semicircle, eating chips from polystyrene cones. Normal people, normal day . . .

'Hello.'

The voice is made tinny by the intercom.

'Mr Robb?'

'Aye.'

'This is the police. Can we come up?'

There is a pause.

'I didn't do it.'

Pharaoh gives a little laugh. Rolls her eyes.

'Okay then, we'll be off.'

After a moment, the door clicks open, and both officers step into the wide hallway. The corridor is bare brick and linoleum, leading down to a ground-floor flat with a black front door. To their left is a set of stairs with a black handrail.

'Up,' says McAvoy, needlessly, and begins to climb.

Darren Robb is standing in the doorway of Flat 3. He's shaking with so much nervous energy that he puts McAvoy in mind of a stationary car with its motor running. The information they have on him suggests that Robb is forty-one years old, but there was nothing in the files about him having put on a stone each birthday. The man is enormous. Grotesquely fat. He's wearing grey jogging bottoms and a black T-shirt which is stretched almost to breaking point over fleshy arms, tits and belly. His skin has the mottled, waxy hue that makes McAvoy think of bodies pulled from water. His round head is bald on top and close-cropped at the back and sides, while his face, locked as it is in a mask of worry and annoyance, is all fleshy lips and blackheads. McAvoy briefly pictures Elaine, and wonders how the hell she fell for this monstrosity. Pharaoh is clearly thinking the same thing. As she reaches the top of the stairs, he hears her laugh.

'I wouldn't have picked you out for living on the second floor, Mr Robb. Can you imagine if you were a ground-floor guy? You might lose your figure.'

If Darren Robb is offended, he gives no sign of it. He just stands in the doorway, all but blocking out the light, jiggling up and down like he's driving over cobbles. He turns his gaze on McAvoy, realises he has no chance of getting past the big man, and seems to sag. He steps back into the flat, vaguely waving them in.

The door opens into a tasteful apartment. The floor is natural wood and the sofa is cream leather. A black-and-white cowhide serves as an island between the pine coffee table and the large flat-screen TV, and the walls are decorated with colourful landscapes, all purple mountains and shimmering lakes. The big bay window gives the kind of view that would cost a million in Brighton, and McAvoy crosses to it, looking out over the grassed area and down past the sea wall to the grey ocean. It moves as if being sifted for gold in a prospector's pan. As he hears the sound of Pharaoh plonking herself into the sofa, he gently moves aside one of the velvet curtains that hang to the floor, and spots the binoculars that sit on the windowsill. McAvoy looks again at the sea, wondering whether Robb enjoys watching the waves and the gulls, following the spirals of the kittiwakes and the razorbills. Then his gaze falls upon the woman with the pushchair on the grass. McAvoy decides not to make up his mind about the man until later.

'I didn't do it.'

Robb is standing by the far wall, between the door to the kitchen and a closed serving hatch set into the brickwork.

'Didn't do what, Mr Robb?' asks Pharaoh, sweetly.

'Philippa. I didn't do it. I couldn't.'

Pharaoh looks up at McAvoy. Pulls a theatrically confused face. 'Has the body been formally identified, Sergeant?'

57

McAvoy shakes his head.

'Identity released to the media?'

'No, Guv.'

'So, Mr Robb, what the fuck are you talking about?'

Robb raises his hands to his head. If his hair were long enough, he would be pulling at its roots. His breath is shallow and ragged. Suddenly, he starts forward and drops onto the arm of the chair, his T-shirt rolling up to reveal a stomach that appears to have been boiled in onion skins and leaves.

'Elaine's Facebook. Somebody posted how sorry they were. It's had five "likes" . . .'

Pharaoh runs a hand through her hair and scowls.

'And you put two and two together? Big leap.'

He shakes his head, frantic now. 'Radio said there'd been a murder, near where Philippa worked. I used to do that walk with her, now and again, when we were together like. Me and Elaine. I started that whole weight-loss thing with her. Couldn't keep it up—'

'Get to the point, Mr Robb.'

'Elaine's brother, Don. He has a Twitter account. Said this morning his mum was missing. Was asking for help on there. He only has a few followers so I don't know what he was expecting –'

'Oh for fuck's sake.'

'And I tried to phone Elaine and some copper answered. Family Liaison, or something . . .'

Pharaoh kicks out, a biker boot catching the corner of the coffee table. There is a bowl of glass beads at its centre, and they give a little tambourine sound before settling back.

'Don doesn't know I follow him. On Twitter, I mean. I use a different name. Same with Elaine's Facebook. And her friends.

Shit, I know all this sounds shite for me, but, look, I haven't done anything wrong . . .'

Pharaoh waves a hand to silence him. She looks at McAvoy then rubs her hand across the back of her neck. It comes away damp.

'Mr Robb, if you sit quietly for a moment, we can get this over with quickly. Now, as I should have said at the door, we are investigating the murder of Philippa Longman. Her body was found this morning, not far from where she works. Somebody had caved her chest in and left her for the birds. It was one of the most unpleasant things I've ever seen, and though I never met Mrs Longman when she was alive, my sergeant and I have just been sitting with a family that is so broken, they'll never be whole again. And your ex-partner, Elaine, has given us reason to believe you had made threats against Mrs Longman. She told my sergeant here that you threatened to rip out her heart. Now, we couldn't tell whether anybody had ripped out her heart because it was too much of a fucking mess. We'll have the post-mortem results back this evening. But I think that means you have some questions to answer, okay? I don't want to hear about Facebook, or who's following who, or who's been Tweeting or Twatting or whatever it is people do for fun when they should be drinking and watching *X-Factor*. Just tell me where you were last night, where you were in the middle of the night, and why I shouldn't get this big bugger here to slap the cuffs on you while I kick you in the knackers. Got it? On board? Fire away.'

Robb looks from one detective to the other. McAvoy has crossed his arms. Framed by the window, the light defines his muscles and casts a shadow across his eyes, leaving only the set of his jaw illuminated. Robb has no friends in this room. He looks down at his feet, stuffed into dirty white trainers, then addresses himself to Pharaoh.

'We were together, yeah? Elaine and me. Three years, all in all, off and on.'

'How exactly did you meet?' asks McAvoy, unable to hide his surprise that the two were ever a couple.

'Her brother. We were mates. Still would be if things turned out differently. He introduced us.'

'So you were a friend of the family?'

He shakes his head. 'No, just Don. He's a delivery driver. Dropped some stuff off at the office where I used to work. He's a rugby man. Bradford Bulls. We hit it off.'

'And?'

'His sister came to a match with us. Her and a friend. We hit it off too.'

Pharaoh looks Robb up and down. He sees her looking and can't help but let his annoyance show on his face. 'I've put weight on since we split.'

'Comfort eating?'

'Yeah, if you like. I was slimmer. Better-looking. Less bald.'

'Sorry I missed out on you. You sound a catch.'

Robb looks down at the wooden floor. Sees himself, blurred and colossal, in the polished surface of the wood. 'You see any mirrors in this room? There are none in the flat. I know what I am. You don't have to remind me.'

Pharaoh looks at the side of his head until he looks up and meets her gaze. She nods, and while it is short of an apology, it is at least an acknowledgement.

'You fell for her hard?' asks McAvoy.

'She was everything I wanted. I've had a few girlfriends over the years but I never thought it would feel the way it did with Elaine. She just made the world better, you know?'

'You lived together?'

'Yeah. Lovely place. Bought it cheap and did it up. I like all that stuff. Made it nice for her and the kids.'

'And you met her family.'

Robb doesn't seem to be able to cough up the ball of gristle in his throat. He swallows painfully. 'Philippa, you mean?'

'I mean her family.'

'Yeah. Nice family. Close. Proper family, you know? Don was well happy with the way things worked out.'

'And your relationship with Philippa?'

Robb looks away, past McAvoy, to the slate sea and stone sky. 'We were close. All those jokes about mothers-in-law? It wasn't like that. We were mates. She was a laugh. I helped her with her work on the council. Computer stuff. Research. I typed up her speeches. Set up a spreadsheet for her expenses. She used to make ginger biscuits for me as a thanks. Proper ones, with stem ginger.' He gives a tiny smile at the memory. 'It was all nice.'

'So what happened with you and Elaine?'

Robb blows air through his nostrils. Scratches at his throat. He seems to be about to stand up, to offer to make tea, to straighten a picture or move the rug, but he appears to see the actions for the distractions they are, and stays where he is. When he speaks, his voice is soft as tears falling on wood.

'Philippa was at our place. I was showing her how to use a website. Might even have been that walking challenge website. I can't remember. Anyway, I left her in my office for a bit. Went for a pee or a cup of tea or whatever. Next thing she's pulling on her coat and slamming the door behind her. I didn't know what was going on until I went back into my office.' He looks at the wall, shame creeping up into his cheeks. 'She'd clicked the wrong thing. Gone into my private files. Seen some of the things in there.'

Pharaoh gives a whistle. 'Worst nightmare, eh?'

'It was nowt weird,' he says, despairingly.

'Just good wholesome stuff, was it?' asks Pharaoh.

Robb doesn't reply.

'Mr Robb, I don't want to be crass, but everybody in the world has the occasional glimpse at stuff like that. She'd be embarrassed, sure, but she'd hardly cut you off for that, would she? These days? Really?'

Robb looks at her, quizzically, then his mouth opens wide as realisation dawns.

'It was drawings!' he splutters. 'Drawings I'd done. I like to draw.'

Pharaoh is getting frustrated. 'What?'

'I'd done some drawings. Portraits, if you like. Sketches. Some still-life. Some from memory. Other times, they'd sit for me . . .'

'Who?'

'The kids. Elaine's kids.'

Pharaoh's mouth drops open and she turns to McAvoy. 'Are you hearing this? Can you get a straight answer out of this bloke for me please, Hector, because I'm starting to get angry.'

McAvoy takes three steps to the middle of the room and looms over Darren Robb. Were he here alone, he would never consider using his size, would never threaten or intimidate, but in Pharaoh's presence, he knows his role. He is both her enforcer and gentle poet. His job is to keep the suspect off-balance. To become his friend, and then step into his personal space with the softest of snarls. 'Were they naked pictures, sir? The drawings you did of your girlfriend's children?'

Robb stares up at the big man. 'It's art. Like Rubens. Cherubs and stuff. I like all that. I scanned them into the computer so I could use some art software. I wasn't sending them to anyone. I wasn't doing anything wrong! It's just pictures.'

'Nothing that could be considered inappropriate?'

'Not unless there's something wrong with you.'

'But Philippa didn't like what she saw?'

'She wouldn't answer her phone. Wouldn't come to the door when I called for her. She just cut me off.'

'And Elaine?'

'She didn't understand. Her mum sent her this message, telling her that her boyfriend was sick. Twisted. Disgusting.'

'Did you explain?'

'I deleted the pictures as soon as Philippa left.'

'Why?'

'I panicked.'

McAvoy runs his tongue around the inside of his mouth. 'So when Philippa told her daughter that you had naked pictures of her children on your computer, you had no evidence to the contrary.'

Robb looks back at his feet.

'Elaine left you?'

He nods. 'She wouldn't listen.'

'Did you try and make her?'

Robb bites at his lip. 'Over and over. I tried to get Don to talk to her but he wouldn't take my calls either. I went to Elaine's work, to the kids' schools, I just wanted her to listen.'

McAvoy pushes a fist into his palm. 'You must have been frustrated. Angry.'

'Everything was ruined, over a mistake. A misunderstanding. I'd never hurt those kids. I loved those kids.'

'But Elaine didn't know you were drawing them naked, did she? If it was innocent, why not tell her?'

Robb is silent. He tries to find somewhere to direct his gaze, but finds nothing to his satisfaction. He gets up, and adjusts one of the pictures on the wall. 'It was just art,' he mutters to himself.

'And if we took away your computer, Mr Robb, would we find more art?'

A look of horror passes over Darren Robb's face, and McAvoy takes a step towards him, using his size to put the fat man almost into shadow.

'You've been stalking your ex, Mr Robb. You've been following her on Facebook with a fake alias. You've been making a nuisance of yourself. You've made threats about a woman who is now dead.'

Robb's lower lip trembles. He seems to be about to cry.

'Where were you last night?' asks Pharaoh from the sofa.

'I was here,' he says.

'Doing what?'

'I was on the computer. I'm often on the computer.'

'Doing what?'

Slowly, like a bouncy castle deflating, Darren Robb sinks to his knees. 'Same as fucking always,' he says, between sobs. 'Reading her emails. Reading her messages.'

'You hack her emails?'

'Elaine's. Don's. Philippa's. I just want to stay close to them. They were my family too. It was just a misunderstanding.'

'You can show us your search history, then. You can show us that you were here all night, I presume.'

'I stopped about 2 a.m. Then I went to bed.'

'Alone?'

'Of course alone.'

Pharaoh turns to her sergeant. 'We don't know what time she was killed yet. Not for certain.'

'If he's good enough with computers he could do his Internet browsing remotely and make it look like he was on his home terminal. But if he did that on his mobile, we can pinpoint the location from the signal. Will be easier once the forensics people have had their fun.'

'Aye, if he was there we'll probably have found a crisp packet in the vicinity.'

Robb looks at each of them in turn, as if they are passing his fate between them like a tennis ball.

'I can't drive,' he blurts out, as if the admission is the most important thought he has ever had. 'I haven't got a car. I don't have a licence. I work from home. How the hell would I even get there?'

Pharaoh lets the annoyance show in her face. 'You can't drive? How did you bother Elaine then? See her at work? At the kids' school?'

'I took cabs. Buses. I've only moved back to Hornsea the past few weeks. I kept this place on when Elaine and me moved in together. I don't go anywhere. I couldn't.'

Pharaoh looks at the fat man on the floor. 'Pathetic,' she says, and her sneer is an ugly, powerful thing.

McAvoy has been running his tongue around his mouth for the past few moments, his thoughts sliding into one another like coins inside a slot machine. 'The emails,' he says, at length. 'You've been reading them for a while?'

Robb nods, seemingly unsure whether to stay on his knees or get up.

'Did Philippa ever receive any threats of any kind? And I advise you to think carefully about this, because at the moment, we're staring very hard at you for the murder of Philippa Longman.'

Robb screws up his eyes, like a child pretending to concentrate. 'Philippa's emails were just council stuff. Vouchers. Special offers. Sometimes she'd get pictures from friends. I used to search under my name in her correspondence and there wasn't a thing. They'd just moved on. Cut me out like I was something disgusting.'

'And Elaine?'

'She mentioned me sometimes. After I'd been to see her, or sent her a letter or texted her or whatever, she'd message a friend about me. She never sounded cross with me, just sorry for me.'

'But you were cross with her. With Philippa too.'

'I said things I shouldn't have. I was just trying to shock her into listening.'

'You said you would cut out her mum's heart.'

Robb shifts his position, moving the fat around. 'I've never hurt anybody in my life.'

Pharaoh clicks her tongue against the roof of her mouth. She seems to be weighing things up.

'Hector?'

McAvoy looks at the morbidly obese specimen before him. He sees something pitiful, but he does not yet see a killer.

'Don't go anywhere,' he says, to Robb.

Pharaoh scoffs. 'He can't drive, remember?'

'Let's check that, eh?'

'And we'd better tell the boys in the tech unit to remotely access his hard drive. Make sure nothing gets deleted in the next few days.'

McAvoy manages to keep the look of confusion off his face. Pharaoh knows nothing about computers, but has a quality poker face and knows how to scare a suspect.

They turn away from the snivelling man on the floor and head for the door. Halfway across the living room, McAvoy turns back.

'Are you sorry she's dead?'

Robb raises his head. There is nothing but sorrow in his face, though most of that seems to be for himself.

'Did she suffer?' he asks, at length.

McAvoy nods. 'More than anybody should.'

Robb drops his head. The only sound in the room is the soft snuffling of a fat man crying into his T-shirt, and the distant peal of children laughing beneath the crashing of the waves.

5

3.28 p.m. Courtland Road Police Station. Hull.

A three-storey building, all bare brick and dirty windows, painted the colour of storm clouds, shielded from the estate it watches over by bent silver railings and untended grass.

First floor. Home of the Serious and Organised Crime Unit.

Flickering monitors, overstuffed folders and cardboard boxes cluttering the pathways between desks. Home Office posters on the walls and every window pushed open as far as it will go. Phones, answered with coughs and grunts; fingers bashing inexpertly on keyboards that are missing letters and patterned with crumbs. Bluebottles buzzing helplessly on dirty windowsills varnished in coffee stains and smudges of printer ink.

Helen Tremberg, wrist-deep in a packet of crisps, salt sticking to her damp fingers and chipped nails, sweat on her upper lip, fringe twisting itself in knots every time the fan turns in her direction and the edges of her paperwork lift their skirts.

She types, one-handed, on a keyboard that sits in front of a monitor garlanded with Post-it notes. They contain reminders. Phone numbers. Her passwords.

She's hunched. Furtive. Trying to stay below the plastic barrier that divides her desk from DC Ben Nielsen's. There is a tiny smile on her face.

Helen has been officially single for three years. She had two serious relationships before that, with men she was pretty sure she loved. Each ended within a year of them moving in together. In both cases, it was the men who made the decision to go, and Helen who had done nothing to change their minds. She enjoyed cohabiting, liked the intimacy of it all: the foot-rubs during the movie; the unexpected cups of tea; the feeling of slipping on a man's big cosy jumper to pad downstairs in the middle of the night and having somebody warm to spoon up beside when she worked a late shift. It was the other side of it that caused the rifts. Bills. Sensible stuff. Which electricity supplier to use. Getting the broadband to work properly. Whether to do a big shop once a month for freezable stuff, or pop out every night for perishables. Them, forgetting to keep the shower curtain inside the bathtub and soaking the floor. Her with her stubbornness. Her refusal to compromise. Even to be guided. Steered. Told. Sitting there with her fingers digging into the leather of the sofa as some great interloper held the remote control for her TV and decided what they should watch. Both of her failed relationships were so similar in their pattern and make-up that sometimes she forgets which was which, and has to consider the length of her hair in each snapshot of memory to know which lover she went where with, and when.

While she has enjoyed the company of a few blokes over the last few months, she has lacked any real enthusiasm for taking things further. She likes her own space, her own company. Has a few mates, both inside and outside the police service, and has years left before her biological clock starts trying to get her attention. She even has the odd Friday night out on Cleethorpes seafront. Has some fancy sequinned dresses and painful strappy shoes. Knows how to do her make-up and ruffle her short hair in a way that takes the attention away from her broad shoulders and weightlifter thighs. She's okay with herself.

So why are you so giddy, you silly girl?

Helen tries to focus on the half of the computer screen she gets paid to give a damn about. She's cross-referencing between two databases, trying to spot any familiar names among the owners of white, 2003-registered Land Rovers. Such a vehicle was captured on blurry CCTV, heading away at speed from a petrol bombing on the Preston Road estate. The target was an empty bottle shop, and the motive most likely insurance or boredom. It comes under Helen's purview because she is attached to Colin Ray's investigation into the spike in organised crime, and because there had once been a Drugs Squad raid on the shop amid accusations it was being used as a halfway house for cocaine coming off the nearby docks. That raid had proven fruitless, but with the top brass happy to throw resources at making the drugs problem go away before the end-of-year figures are collated, anything with even a sniff of organised criminality about it comes to Colin Ray, and anything he doesn't think is worth his time goes to Shaz Archer, who dutifully passes it on to the people she likes least.

Having already wasted a morning on the entertaining but fruitless trip to Hull Prison, Helen is resigned to a day of futility and irritation, made worse by the buzzing flies and oppressive heat. She had been gutted to hear that Pharaoh was looking into the murder off Anlaby Road. Tremberg is an ambitious woman, hoping to be put forward for the sergeant examination, and had cautiously celebrated when placed on Colin Ray's side of the squad not so long ago. That joy has faded now. She is on a unit that is making no progress, led by a man who is at best tenacious, and at worst, dangerous. Her immediate superior is a tart who doesn't rate her and the last bit of work Helen did that in any way helped make the east coast a safer place was when she put Colin Ray in the back of a taxi before he made good on his promise to cut DC Andy Daniells's head off with a glass bottle at the last CID quiz night.

Her computer suddenly beeps and Helen takes a deep breath. Her left leg bounces up and down.

Stop it, you silly girl . . .

She opens the email. It's him. Mark. The one she can't get out of her bloody head.

Couldn't wait another minute to hear from you. I have no excuse. Are we not past that? Do I need to pretend I have something work-related to discuss? I just wanted to send you a message. Honestly Helen, even seeing your name written down makes me excited. What are you doing to me? Tell me something personal. Can't wait. Xx

Helen smiles and exhales at the same time. She rubs the back of her hand across her face, and prepares to compose a reply. She's no poet. She wishes she'd read the Philip Larkin collection McAvoy had sent her when she was in hospital a few months back. Wishes, even more, that McAvoy himself were here. There are few moments when she is not second-guessing herself in his voice, wondering whether he would approve of her decisions, her police work, her heart. He has somehow become her conscience.

Her thoughts drift to his wife. Helen knows what McAvoy did for her. Remembers that day in the greasy spoon café when her senior officer opened up. Told her about the men who hurt Roisin when she was not yet a teen. McAvoy was just a constable then. A young man in uniform, called to a traveller camp. A man who heard screams and went to investigate. Who carried the crying girl from a burning building and did things to her attackers that scarred his soul. Helen has never asked him what he did to those men. Never asked how he and the child he saved came to be lovers as adults. She has not made up her mind whether she truly wants to know. Whether she wants to unpick the perfection of the image she carries of the McAvoys. She just knows his love for his family is a palpable, magical thing. When he talks of Roisin and his children, the air around him is thick enough to be scooped up with a ladle. She wants some of that. Some of that honesty. That perfect, powerful thing he carries inside him.

You don't need excuses. Message me whenever you want. I won't ever be disappointed to hear from you. xx

It's the best she can do. She makes sure the number of kisses she types is no more or less than the number he placed on his. She runs a quick spell-check, just to make sure she hasn't embarrassed herself, then sends it back, hoping she will not have to wait too long for a reply. She is using her personal email account on the work computer, which is strictly against the rules. She has heard of other forces where viruses have been uploaded simply by opening an unvetted file, but she is so eager to hear from the man that she is willing to take the risk.

Sort yourself out, Helen.

He's not her usual sort. She likes sporty, athletic types. She likes men bigger than her, who know their Grand Prix history and don't shave on a weekend. Mark seems the complete opposite. He's a lawyer with a local firm, dealing mainly in divorce cases and the occasional bit of blame-and-claim litigation. They got talking last month in the canteen at Hull Magistrates' Court, where Helen was giving evidence in a youth offending case she had dealt with in her first plain-clothes job. It had taken an age to come to court and Helen had been sitting there struggling to remember which little bastard had punched which other little bastard. Her mood had been foul, as a man in tracksuit bottoms, shirt, tie and baseball cap had discovered when he told his toddler son to shut the fuck up and cuffed him around the head. Helen, pretending to fall as she passed him, had found a way to tread on the man's instep and knee him in the groin at the same time, all the while apologising out loud – even as she nipped the skin beneath his armpit and whispered cold threats in his ear.

If anyone saw what she'd done then they had the sense to keep quiet about it, but she was soon the only person sitting in the waiting area with an empty chair beside her. Despite the chaos of the court, nobody had wanted to sit next to her. Nobody except Mark. He sat down with a smile, whispered 'Nice work' and waited for her to meet his gaze. He smelled nice. Clean, but not soapy. No aftershave, but somehow fresh, like line-dried laundry. He was small and wiry, his physique putting her in mind of a cyclist's. His sideburns were slightly too long for a man in his mid-thirties, but his designer, frameless glasses and blue pinstriped suit went well together, while the Maori-patterned leather strap around his wrist made him seem just intriguing enough to warrant further investigation.

She'd noticed, even then, that he wore no wedding band. Had it been mercenary? Predatory? Had she been eyeing him up as a potential mate? She didn't know. But he did not run a mile when she told him she was a police officer, which was a hell of a good start, and when he gave her his business card, she had waited less than an hour before sending him an email saying how much she had enjoyed their chat, even though not a word of it had stuck in her head. Since then their correspondence has grown more regular and passionate. She looks forward to his words and spends time thinking up her own. She wants to tell him about her day. Her life. She wants to look at him over the lip of a wine glass and smile as she offloads the dirt and sweat of the day. She wants to know whether his chest is hairy or smooth. Wants to look down on him as she moves . . .

Ask him. Make a date, girl . . .

Helen wishes she were brave enough to suggest a drink tonight. Hopes that in his next email he takes the initiative and does so himself. Oh Christ, how she hopes . . .

'Now then, children!'

The door to the office is already open but Trish Pharaoh still manages to make enough noise as she barges into the room to get everybody's attention. Like worried meerkats, heads pop up above monitors and phones are silenced. Ben Nielsen leans over and switches off the fan and a hush falls on the room. Helen sees them as canaries, their cage suddenly shrouded and silent. Pharaoh is rarely here. She has an office of her own, up another flight of stairs, where she does complicated and exasperating things with spreadsheets and budgets. She is one of CID's most senior figures, having got to a position where she can do little actual police work by being very good at police work.

Tremberg waits for McAvoy to come in as well, and is surprised by his absence. Pharaoh catches her looking at the door, and gives an indulgent smile. 'He's busy,' she mouths. 'We'll be okay without him.'

Helen nods. Joins the rest of the officers in watching Pharaoh stride to the far end of the room, where she starts rubbing Colin Ray's scribblings off the whiteboard. She doesn't even stop to read them.

'Right, you lot. I'm talking to the whole room here because I can't remember which of you lot are still mine and which are Colin's. So, if this is nowt to do with you, just be quiet. In a minute, some very efficient people are going to turn this part of the room into a murder suite. I've spoken to the brass and we've agreed that Philippa Longman's death should be looked at by this unit. Regular CID are about as happy about that as you'd expect, but it will be me that gets the earache and none of you, so don't worry about it. More importantly, don't go approaching any of this thinking that it's got anything to do with bloody organised crime. It hasn't. The gang we're all looking for wouldn't give a shit about some local community activist kicking up a stink about drugs. But by the time that information reaches the Assistant Chief Constable, we'll have found who did it and there will be champagne and cigars all round. Savvy?'

There are smiles and snorts of laughter at that. Tremberg finds herself turning around, half-hoping that Colin Ray and Shaz Archer return from whatever errand they're running and walk into the middle of the briefing.

'Colin and I will be having a chat about which officers stay on current cases and which assist me in the murder enquiry. For now, I've got uniforms doing door-to-door in the immediate vicinity.

It's bloody hot at the moment so people will be sleeping with the windows open and may well have heard something. You can't do that much damage to a person without it waking somebody. I've insisted the forensics be fast-tracked and the PME will be done this evening. McAvoy and me have already interviewed a suspect – the former partner of Longman's daughter. Document wallets will be going around when my secretary or whatever they're supposed to be called these days finishes trying to turn my handwriting into English.'

There are a few mutters at McAvoy's name. Some people are holding a grudge longer than others.

'We've got one lead that needs your immediate attention. Sophie, Andy, I'm thinking of you two.'

Helen lets the disappointment show on her face, but Pharaoh does not acknowledge it.

'We've got a footprint. Almost a perfect one. Size eight, big grips, heavy indent at the toe.'

'Work boots?' asks Helen, hoping to make herself noticed.

'Give that lass a gold star,' says Pharaoh. 'Yes, work boots. We've got plaster casts on their way over, so you need to be hitting the warehouses, the builders' merchants, trying to find a match, and see how widespread those kind of shoes are.'

'It could be anybody's boots, Guv,' comes a dissenting voice. Helen traces it to Stan Lyons. He was a detective sergeant before his retirement, and now works part-time for the unit as one of its complement of civilian officers. He's a nice old boy in his early sixties who takes tablets for his blood pressure and as such is always cold. Even today, in this heat, he's wearing vest, shirt and golfing jumper.

'It could indeed, Stan,' says Pharaoh, 'but given that he's trodden some of Philippa Longman's blood into the grass, I reckon it's worth thinking about, yes?'

'We got anything else?' asks Ben Nielsen, optimistically.

'Early days, my boy, and given you haven't read the paperwork yet, you'll forgive me if I don't hold your hand and baby-step you through every last detail.'

Ben smiles. 'Sorry, boss.'

She nods, looks at the expectant faces, then raises her hands to tell her team to get on with it. This is how she works. She doesn't micro-manage. Sometimes they go days without hearing from her. She hand-picked most of the officers on the unit, and trusts them to do their jobs. The only people she didn't want, and still doesn't, are Colin Ray and Sharon Archer, but she respects them enough to know they won't make waves when it comes to a murder investigation.

Pharaoh heads for the door, stopping only briefly at Helen Tremberg's desk.

'Sorry, Helen. I wanted you. It seems Colin can't spare you. The ACC mentioned you by name.'

Helen looks confused. 'Guv?'

'Seems you're doing a good job. Keep it up.'

With a warm, motherly squeeze of her shoulder, Pharaoh bustles away. For a brief moment, there is silence in the room. Then the fan is switched back on, and officers start to pick up phones. A middle-aged woman in pleated skirt and round-neck T-shirt enters carrying a pile of folders, which she begins to distribute to the team members like a teacher handing back homework.

Helen scowls for a while, then decides to accentuate the positive. Whatever it is she's doing, she's doing it well. She's essential to the ongoing investigation into a criminal gang responsible for countless deaths. That must be something to celebrate.

Quickly, before she can change her mind, she types Mark a new message.

> Let's stop messing around. Drink. Tonight. I have so much I want to tell you. xxx

*

McAvoy pushes his hair back from his face and looks in disgust at the sweat on his palm. He feels like he's melting. His insides feel wrong. He's hungry but the heat of the day is making him feel sick. He wants something sweet and cooling but thinks it would probably be unseemly if he conducted his section of the murder enquiry while licking an ice lolly. He resigns himself to stopping in at a newsagent's for a bar of chocolate on his way back to Arthur Street, where he has another twenty-five houses to doorstep before his section of the house-to-house is completed. People are cooperating, as much as they can. Police are tolerated around here. It's not a bad neighbourhood, all told, and nobody wants to live in an area where the nice lady from the late shop can have her chest caved in on her walk home. The trouble is, nobody saw anything. Nobody heard anything. And while everybody that he and the uniformed officers have spoken to has been only too willing to take his business cards and to promise to call if anything comes back to them, they have yet to find a witness.

McAvoy puffs out his cheeks and lets out a sigh. In front of him, the traffic is still moving at a crawl. Horns are honking. Drivers are revving their engines and the music from competing stereos

blends with the sound of a distant pneumatic drill. The whole
scene throbs with grinding noise. He stares straight ahead, not
really seeing, jolting slightly as he realises his gaze is fixed on a
group of pre-teens who are making a nuisance of themselves on
the single-decker bus in front of him. They see him looking and
mouth a variety of insults, punctuated by fulsome use of mid-
finger salutes. Banging on the window, they laugh as if they have
just committed the century's greatest act of social disobedience,
then sit down as the driver turns around and threatens to let his
fraying temper snap.

McAvoy gives a little nod. Fair enough, he supposes. Makes a
V-sign of his own in the pocket of his trousers and wishes that
the rule book allowed him to show it. He pushes off from the
wall, feeling his shirt sticking to his back. He's sick of this heat.
Sick of the oppressive grey skies, and the fact that his palms
are sweaty every time he proffers one to a potential witness.
He knows his hair looks nearly black at the temples, slick with
perspiration, and while he is wearing enough anti-perspirant to
ensure he doesn't embarrass himself, he wishes he had listened
when Roisin suggested this morning he use some of the powder
she had knocked up from cornstarch and oatmeal, and which
she swears by when it comes to avoiding heat rashes anywhere
too painful. 'Too late for that now,' he mutters, as he crosses
between two barely moving vehicles and jogs painfully back to
the other side of Anlaby Road.

As he reaches into his pocket for the change to buy a bar of
chocolate, he grips nothing but empty cloth. He's out of money.
Shit. It's nothing new. Buying the new car cleaned out his
savings, while every spare penny he can muster is going on the
new house. He qualified for the mortgage without any problems.

On paper, he owns a small croft near Gairloch in the Western Highlands, five or six miles from his father's, though he has only visited it a couple of times and sublets to an arty English couple who make their living doing complicated things with seashells. As a crofter's son, he qualified for government subsidy and had bought the place for a steal while still a young man. The bank had considered the property sufficient guarantee to give him a larger than usual mortgage and he will be moving the family into the new house on Hessle Foreshore next weekend. He's paying for a removals company to do some of the hard work. Paying for a proper wooden summerhouse for the back garden. Paying out too much, truth be told, but each purchase is making Roisin squeal, and if there is a better sound in the universe, he has yet to hear it.

Over the noise of the road, McAvoy hears his radio crackle. The uniformed officers still prefer to use radios, while he and his CID colleagues have made the transition to mobile phones, but McAvoy has no issue with doing things the way the uniformed sergeant coordinating the majority of the house-to-house preferred, and had taken the radio without argument. The team know who to contact if they came up with anything useful.

'McAvoy,' he says, into the radio.

'Sarge, this might be nothing, but I think we have somebody for you to come talk to . . .'

Five minutes later, McAvoy arrives back on Granville Street. He had run the first 500 yards, then slowed when he came in sight of one of the patrol cars so he could catch his breath.

PC Joseph Pearl is waiting by the door. He's a tall, strikingly handsome black man whom McAvoy has only met briefly, but whom he seems to remember as coming from somewhere over

Lancashire way. When he had briefed the officers, McAvoy had felt like warning PC Pearl that his colour would barely provoke a comment in this relatively multicultural area, but that he should keep his Lancashire accent under wraps for fear of abuse. Yorkshire folk have complicated prejudices.

'Nice lady,' says PC Pearl, nodding into the open doorway. 'Hard to shut her up.'

McAvoy steps inside the nondescript terrace, two minutes from where Philippa Longman lost her life. He had intended to make this row of properties part of his own house-to-house, but for fear of being accused of cherry-picking, he had left it to uniform.

The nice lady in question is Lavinia Mantell. She's sitting with her feet drawn up in the corner of a large, squashy, three-seater sofa, which dominates the small living room. On the walls are framed posters of various local theatre nights, and the carpet is a maddening swirl of purples and golds. McAvoy takes a quick look around and decides it must be rented. Lavinia has put her stamp on the place but has not gone to the trouble of replacing the vile soft furnishings or the woodchipped wallpaper. On the table in front of her is a laptop and a pile of papers, held in place by a biscuit tin, which stops the half-hearted breeze from the open window from making a mess. McAvoy recognises the salmon-pink colour of Hull Council Scrutiny Committee reports.

'Miss Mantell,' he says, edging his way around the huge sofa and coming to stand in front of the TV. He introduces himself. 'My colleague tells me you may have some information that would help us.'

She nods, then holds up her hands, as if urging him to wait.

She is chewing on a biscuit. She reaches down beside her and takes a swig from the mug of coffee on the floor.

'Sorry, you caught me.'

He smiles. 'The day biscuits are a crime, I'll be doing life.'

She's in her late thirties, and attractive in a bookish and careworn kind of way. She has brown hair that was probably cut into a sleek and sophisticated bob a couple of months ago but looks a little wilder now. She's wearing Red or Dead glasses and has the sort of figure that men are perfectly at ease with, but women would like to tighten up.

'I presume you work for the local authority,' says McAvoy, indicating the paperwork.

Lavinia pulls a face. 'I'm freelance. I work for whoever.'

'Journalist?'

She shakes her head and laughs. 'Chance would be a fine thing! No, my spelling's terrible. Good enough for marketing though.'

'Ah, right. Press officer?'

'That's what they used to be called. I'm a communications consultant, I'll have you know.' She adopts a haughty tone as she says it, and makes herself giggle. She raises a hand to her mouth suddenly, as if deciding that she is being overly jolly, given the circumstances, and takes on a solemn expression to make up for it.

'I presume you've been told about the events of last night,' says McAvoy, sitting down on the centre cushion of the sofa. 'Did you know Philippa Longman?'

'Not personally. Not really. I knew her face when your mate showed me the photo, and I'd seen her in the late shop.'

'Did you ever speak?'

Lavinia rubs at the tip of her nose with an index finger, trying to be helpful. 'Well, only in the shop. I think she once said the wine I was buying was nice. Something like that.'

'Anything else?'

'I think this was her walk home. I sometimes have a cigarette if I've had a really shit day, and the landlord doesn't like me smoking indoors. I'll sit on the front step with a coffee and a fag and I've said hello to her once or twice like that.'

'And last night?'

Lavinia opens her mouth and sits forward, nodding even before she speaks. 'Sort of. I wasn't on the doorstep last night, I was having a fag out of the window upstairs. I hardly ever do that, but it was so bloody hot last night I couldn't sleep and sometimes a cigarette calms me down. I was sitting on the windowsill.'

'And what time was this?'

'Oh, some time around midnight. Maybe a little earlier. I was reading a book on my phone. There's just enough light from the street lamp for me not to have to put the bedroom light on, you see. I'm on an electricity meter—'

'And you saw Mrs Longman?' asks McAvoy, moving forward in his chair so he can maintain eye contact with her as she wriggles around on the edge of the seat.

'Definitely. She was walking that way.'

She points in the direction the murdered woman would have had to walk to get home, and where, a few yards further on, she was torn to pieces.

'Was she alone?'

'At first,' says Lavinia, reaching forward for a piece of paper from the coffee table then discarding it, distractedly. 'As she came past the window she was. I'd looked up to drop some ash out the window and saw her walking by. Then the next time I was dropping the ash she was with somebody else.'

McAvoy takes out his notebook from his waistcoat pocket. He will remember every single detail, but Lavinia seems the sort of person who will respond well to him taking her words as hugely important, and he holds his pen invitingly over a blank page.

'Were they walking together, or standing still?'

Lavinia appears to think. 'They were talking. It looked like he'd come from the other direction.'

'What makes you say that?'

'The way they were standing. She had her back to me. He was sort of facing me. It's the way you'd stand if you'd just bumped into somebody.'

McAvoy nods, a picture forming in his mind. 'This was at the far end of the street, you say. Near the car park where she was found?'

'Not more than a few feet away from the entrance.'

McAvoy makes a note, moving the notebook just enough for her to see that he is taking down her words in shorthand – the result of an intensive night class he paid for himself.

'How long did you watch them for?'

'It was literally a moment,' says Lavinia, sadly. She seems to be wishing she had seen the whole attack and then taken pictures of the killer.

'And the person she was talking to – it was definitely a man?'

'Definitely,' says Lavinia.

'Big? Small? White? Black?' He checks the door and sees PC Pearl lounging in the doorframe. Begins to explain himself to both of them. 'These questions are crucial, you understand . . .'

'I'd say average. White, I'm pretty certain.' Lavinia looks sorry to be able to offer so little.

'Age?'

'Not old. Not young, either.'

'And they were talking. Not arguing?'

She shakes her head. 'They didn't seem to be. They looked like they had just stopped for a natter.'

McAvoy closes the notepad around his pen. 'Could you show me your room, please, Miss Mantell? PC Pearl, could you please ask a uniformed colleague to stand at the point Miss Mantell has described? Thanks.'

Lavinia looks surprised, but also quite pleased that there is more of this rather exciting aspect of her day still to come. She stands up, straightening her flared pinstripe trousers and white strappy vest. She leads him through the living-room door and into an L-shaped kitchen, then up a flight of stairs, covered with posters from foreign films.

'You like the arts?' he asks, as he follows her up.

She turns back. 'I do a lot of work with theatre companies, and in a perfect world that's all I'd do. That, watch films and smoke cigarettes. Not a perfect world, is it?'

Lavinia pushes open the door to her bedroom and scurries inside, throwing the duvet over the unmade bed and picking up a few items of laundry from the floor to stuff in a wicker hamper next to an open wardrobe. It's a bit of a mess, but comfortably so.

'There,' she says, pointing, rather unnecessarily, at the window. 'You have to reach up to blow the smoke out or dock your ash.'

McAvoy crosses to the window. A young WPC is talking into her radio and crossing to the spot McAvoy has requested. Behind her, he can see the edge of the white forensics tent and behind that, the bridge across the railway lines that would have led Philippa Longman home. He sits on the windowsill and looks out through a single-glazed pane, smears on its surface and dead flies at its edges.

The WPC has come to a halt as instructed. McAvoy squints. He does not know the officer. Could not, now, pick her out of a line-up. He turns to Lavinia. 'Can I borrow you for a moment, Miss Mantell?' He pushes himself back against the wall and invites her to lean past him. He gets a smell of medicated shampoo and Impulse body spray. Could count the freckles on her bare right shoulder, should he so choose. 'Describe the officer for me, please.'

She squints, theatrically. 'It's a woman,' she says. 'Brownish hair. Young.'

'Anything else?'

'I can't tell you the colour of her eyes, no.'

They both stand, unsure whether to be pleased or not with how the past few minutes have gone. Eventually, McAvoy smiles and gives her a card. 'An officer will take a formal statement. In the meantime, if you remember anything else, please give me a call.'

She looks at the card with its variety of numbers. Work. Personal. Email. Home.

'Do you think you'll catch him?' asks Lavinia, looking up. 'It's not very nice, is it? That sort of thing happening where you live. I mean, you get yobs and boy racers and the odd fight after Hull Fair or the football, but somebody being killed like that? I mean, it could have been me. It could have been anyone.'

McAvoy holds her gaze, then breaks away and crosses back to the window. 'It couldn't,' he says, softly. 'He wanted her. She knew him.'

6

8.48 p.m. Hessle foreshore.

A wide strip of grey-brown water, separating East Yorkshire from Northern Lincolnshire; the bridge overhead a loose stitch of concrete and steel, holding two counties together.

Aector and Roisin McAvoy: standing on the strip of muddy shingle, smiling indulgently as their son throws dirty pebbles at the rotten timbers sunk deep into the sucking sands.

He breathes deep. Catches the scent of sun cream and citrus. Her skin lotion and cigarettes. He wants her, as he always wants her. Wants to wash himself, lose himself, in her movements, her affection . . .

He breathes in again. And there it is. That faint chemical tang. The merest whiff of disinfectant and grey steel, still suffusing his skin. The post-mortem. The mortuary. That ghastly tapestry of guts and innards made art by the precision of the incisions and stitches.

If Philippa Longman suffered in her final moments, the wounds are as naught compared with the indignities wreaked upon her corpse by Dr Gene Woodmansey. He was a lot more tender, more dispassionate about it, than whoever tore her ribcage open, but there is no tender way of slicing up human flesh, and McAvoy's hour at the mortuary had been vile. McAvoy has witnessed post-mortem exams before. He saw enough animal corpses and butchered enough cattle in his youth not to be rendered nauseous by the pathologist's work. He is not the sort of officer who would rather do anything than visit the mortuary. He has seen fellow officers volunteer to break the news of violent death to the victim's family rather than visit that anodyne, sterile cathedral of human deconstruction, with its grey walls and floors.

McAvoy is okay with blood. He had not raised objections when asked by Pharaoh to attend the autopsy on her behalf. But he had never seen a corpse like Philippa's before. Nor had he seen Dr Woodmansey give that tiny little shake of the head, that muted exhalation of breath, that suggested, he, too, was at once disgusted and appalled by what had been done to the woman who lay naked and mangled, scrubbed and exposed, upon the metal table before him.

As he holds his wife and watches his son throw stones into the water, McAvoy pictures the scene that played out before him just a couple of hours ago. Sees himself, wraith-like in his disposable white coat and with blue bags on his shoes, standing back against a wall so joyless in hue that it seemed to have been coloured in with a pencil. In front of him are two steel tables. Philippa Longman lies upon one – her face having settled into a curiously inhuman, characterless mask, so pale as to be almost translucent. Against the far wall is a hydraulic hoist and steel doors polished to a reflective gleam. To his right are sinks and hoses, a cutting board and specimen bottles. Next to McAvoy is a large whiteboard, the names of the recently dead scrawled upon it in doctor's handwriting. The numbers scribbled in the various columns record the weight of heart, brain, kidneys, lungs, liver, spleen. McAvoy takes them in, and wonders what he should feel. Cannot help but picture himself, on the slab. Cannot help but imagine Dr Woodmansey leaning over him, slicing the scalpel around the crown of his skull, lifting his hair away as if he has fallen to a tomahawk blow . . .

As he works, Dr Woodmansey wears a green apron over green surgical scrubs, topping off the outfit with white welly boots and rubber gloves. As she was brought in, Philippa Longman's body was wrapped in plastic sheeting, evidence bags secured over her hands and feet to preserve any microscopic evidence contained within. As he watched, sombre and silent, McAvoy wondered how it felt to be a policeman a half-century before. Wondered how he would have fared were he asked to catch a killer without knowledge of skin cells, hair fibres, DNA. As ever, he felt he would come up short.

Dr Woodmansey is a short, portly man with close-shaved hair and unashamedly old-fashioned glasses. He is businesslike in his dealings with both the living and the dead. He is not one for small talk. He makes no jokes over the body and appreciates silence as he works. McAvoy likes his manner. Likes that he knows nothing more about the man than the fact he is good at his job.

'Swing me, Daddy.'

The vision disappears as Fin gives his father an attention-grabbing kick on the ankle. He smiles indulgently at his son, who is a miniature version of his dad – all broad shoulders, red face and russet hair. McAvoy picks him up and gives him a quick spin around, enjoying the laughter it brings from his wife and his child. The boy is sticky with sweat, and McAvoy can see problems this evening when they try and get him to change out of the Ross County football strip he has worn every day since it arrived in the post on his fifth birthday. As presents go, McAvoy is not sure that turning a youngster with his whole life ahead of him into a Ross County fan is a tremendous gift. Still, Fin had been pleased, and is busy working on an elaborate thank-you card for his uncle in Aultbea. McAvoy wonders if the boy will still be as grateful as an adult, when he is nursing a consoling pint and wishing that he'd been raised to support Celtic.

Fin runs off, back to the wooden timbers. McAvoy reaches out for Roisin's hand. It's delicate and cold, despite the heat of the evening, and he takes it in his great warm paw, pulling her in. She rests her head against his chest and as one, they sink down onto the pebbles. It's still horribly muggy and warm and the sky is the colour of the pathologist's cutting tools, but at least here there is enough breeze for them to be able to hold one another without their clothing sticking to their skin.

'Every night,' says Roisin, raising her head and turning to look back at the row of properties 100 yards away across a strip of grass and a quiet road. 'We can do this every night, Aector.'

McAvoy kisses her on the forehead. 'You don't think you'll get bored with the view?'

'It changes every day,' she says, looking back at the water. 'I've never seen it the same twice.'

She's right. The Humber is one of the most dangerously unpredictable waterways in the world: a mess of contrary tides and shifting sands. Two millennia ago, the estuary managed to hold the Romans back as they marched north; a procession of slaves losing their lives as they failed to find a safe channel through the mud and waters. McAvoy has never worked out why they didn't just go inland fifteen miles and turn right at Goole.

'And you're sure it's what you want? There are those apartments in the Old Town. You'd be near the shops, the museums . . .'

She reaches down and nips his thigh, then slaps him across his chest. This is her way of telling him to shut up. She has told him endlessly how much she wants this: this house, with its views and big back garden; this place, this life. He believes her. The only part he struggles to comprehend is why she wants to share it with him.

McAvoy stretches out his leg and gives the baby-carrier a little rock. Lilah is sleeping soundly at last. The heat has been too much for her, and every time McAvoy opens her bedroom window, flies, moths and wasps begin to circle her cot. Her crying had been a torturous and heartbreaking thing and they had decided to all go for a drive. To get some fresh air. To head for the new house, and indulge in pleasant daydreaming about how their lives will be when they move their stuff in next weekend.

'Mel says she'll come,' says Roisin, into his chest.

'To what?'

'The housewarming, Silly. Suzie too. And a couple of the mums.'

McAvoy nods. He doesn't know what to say. He doesn't want a housewarming party. Doesn't want strangers in his home. But he will have one, and smile as wide as he can muster, to please his wife.

'The shop's doing well, apparently. Slow, but it takes time, doesn't it? And there are loads of shops closing down, so she's doing well even to be in business, you know?'

'Aye, it can't be easy.'

'She got a big order while I was there. Big bag of suits that needed taking in. I think the bloke had been on some sort of extreme diet. He looked thin but green, and his breath smelled like cat food.'

'Lovely.'

'Aye. She'll be good. She doesn't mind working hard. I just wish there was somebody to keep an eye on her. It's rough up there, and she's not really tough, is she? I might spend a bit more time up there until she's a bit more settled. I don't like thinking of her on her own.'

Roisin met Mel a few months before at a salsa class and the two have quickly become close friends. McAvoy finds her pleasant enough company, though is never truly pleased when he comes home to find her in his living room, three-quarters of the way through a bottle of red wine and planning to spend the night on his sofa. Roisin always asks him whether he minds her friends staying over. He always tells her it's fine. Tells her to do whatever she wants. Tells her to enjoy herself, and then he goes upstairs to read a book or fiddle with some new software on the computer in the bedroom. Lets her be. Lets her do whatever the hell she wants as long as she continues to love him.

'I had a look in the hairdresser's next to her shop,' she says. 'Nice people. They don't do nails. I was thinking I might see about offering my services.'

McAvoy has to force himself not to visibly react. In his mind, Roisin has already started work at the salon. She is chatting. Laughing. Living. A sales rep comes in to offer samples. Makes her giggle. Touches her bare shoulder as he leaves. Slips a business card into her hand. She looks at it, longingly. Weighs up her options. Pictures her daft, hulking husband and his big stupid face and picks up her phone.

He feels his heart, disintegrating, in his chest.

'That's a good idea,' he says, as brightly as he can muster. 'Would do you good. Would you be able to do just a few hours, either side of school runs and stuff?'

'It's only a thought at the moment. We'll see, eh? Anyway, they might want me to have all the certificates and stuff. I'm self-taught, aren't I?'

McAvoy squeezes her. 'You're naturally brilliant,' he says.

'You think?'

'I think.'

They sit in silence, just loving each other, and for a time, McAvoy manages not to picture anything dispiriting or gruesome. Manages not to fill his imagination with Philippa Longman, or the things he has seen being done to her corpse. Manages not to picture what was done to her in her dying moments, in the darkness, on a mattress of cracked stones and smashed glass.

He lets his mind spin. Presses Roisin closer to him. Tries to be a better man. Suddenly sees himself outside the mortuary, leaning against bare brick, fringe plastered to his forehead, strong mints wedged between teeth and cheek, phone to his ear and telling Pharaoh the pathologist's findings.

'She had a heart attack while it was happening, Guv. Her arteries were furred up and her cholesterol was above average so the shock of it all sent her into cardiac arrest. By that point though she was on the ground and she was getting hit in the chest. There's a bruise to the back of her head. She went down hard but not hard enough to knock her out. There's bruising around the hinge of the jaw that suggests pressure to the lower half of her face. Perhaps a hand, holding her mouth shut. Dr Woodmansey says she was pummelled with a large flat implement with a soft surface, whatever that may mean. Repeated strikes to the ribs and chest. Ribs broke under the stress and punctured inwards. Eventually the ribs punctured the lungs and then finally the heart. He says twenty minutes all in. Twenty minutes, pounding on her chest. No evidence of sexual assault. A few fibres, under her nails. Red and black threads, soft cotton. Some substance, as yet unidentified, but organic. Could be anything, but he's sending it off for analysis. Should have it back in a couple of days if we fast-track it. Dr Woodmansey says that it was furious but sustained. Whoever did it would have had blood spray on them, but wouldn't have been covered. Her breath was full of blood particles and the killer would have been in close.'

Here, now, McAvoy closes his eyes. Tries to put the day's findings into some kind of order. Tries to work out why somebody would kill Philippa Longman so brutally. Whoever killed her, it was important to them that she suffer. Somebody hated her. Was it a random stranger, hating the world? Or has she done something so terrible that her murderer wanted her to endure that much agony in her dying moments? He thinks of Darren Robb. Tries to imagine the pitiful fat man having that much rage inside of him. He struggles to see it. But he has been wrong before.

'Did I tell you I met your friend Helen? She was up by Mel's shop.'

'Helen Tremberg? Detective constable?'

'Yeah. Big girl. Nice. Got hurt when you were both in Grimsby . . .'

'Yes, DC Tremberg. Did you say hello?'

'Just briefly. She was with some snooty cow.'

'Detective Inspector Sharon Archer?'

'I dunno. She just sat there with her hand on the horn.'

'Yeah, that would be her.'

McAvoy wonders how he feels about his wife chatting to his work colleagues. Unbidden, a blush rises from his shirt collar up to his cheeks. He imagines her telling Tremberg about their new home. Their plans. He imagines her inviting her to the housewarming. Telling her to bring a friend. Imagines Archer asking her junior officer whom she was talking to. Sees Tremberg, spilling her guts. Telling her about Aector McAvoy's traveller wife. About what he did to the men who attacked her when she was young. Fuck. Fuck!

'The lady who died,' says Roisin, shifting position so she can look up at her husband. 'Why did they kill her?'

McAvoy gazes into her for a few seconds. Her eyes are innocent and guileless.

'We've got a few ideas. It may just have been a random nutter, but it doesn't feel that way.'

'Had she been putting it about or anything? Any affairs?'

McAvoy shakes his head. 'We don't think so. She was just a nice lady. Mattered to people. Did her bit. And somebody caved her chest in. Splintered her ribs like she was made of twigs.'

'What with?'

'We don't know that either.'

Roisin makes a face, mildly disappointed in the detectives of Humberside Police. 'They break easy, ribs. Even when you're doing CPR, you can break ribs. I think I saw that in an episode of *Holby City*, actually . . .'

McAvoy has gone still. He breathes out, slowly, through his nose, and without saying anything, sits up and rolls Roisin onto her back. He places one hand on her chest and the other on top of it. Roisin looks up at him, happy, but confused.

'We trying something new?'

He gives the slightest push. She winces, but doesn't stop smiling.

McAvoy rocks himself back, onto his toes. He stares at her, eyes unfocused.

He stands and pulls out his phone.

'Guv? I've had a thought . . .'

11.58 p.m. Barton-on-Humber.

The last town before North Lincolnshire hits the water. A decent, likeable place. Pleasant. Arty. A mingling of sturdy, centuries-old merchant homes and newly built estates. A place where cosy restaurants sit comfortably beside kebab shops; where slick Mercedes park next to rusted hatchbacks while the owners of both drink happily in real-ale pubs.

This wide road leading out of the town centre, up towards the roundabout and the last stretch of motorway that leads across the bridge.

A modern, detached house with neat front lawn and a sensible car parked on a newly tarmacked drive . . .

Yvonne Dale. Forty-six. Mother of two and gratefully divorced. She's lounging at the apex of an L-shaped sofa in a long, white-painted living room. The walls serve as a timeline of her children's lives. Above the flat-screen TV are baby pictures. Jacob, restless on the photographer's cloud of tousled silk. Andrew, two years later, placid and uncrying as the same photographer manipulated his chunky limbs and soft curls into a more pleasing pose. Above the fireplace, their first holidays, all muddy welly boots and rain-streaked cheeks. First days at school. Almond-coloured skin between grey socks and shorts. Their trip to Kefalonia three years ago. Jacob then six, Andrew four. Yvonne in some of these pictures, lounging by the poolside in the rented villa, large floppy hat casting a shadow on rosy cheeks and ample skin spilling out of a black swimsuit. Behind her, pixelated on a huge canvas, both boys laughing, Jacob's arm thrown carelessly over his little brother's shoulder as they sit cross-legged and side by side on Cleethorpes seafront reading the same book; Jacob patient with his younger sibling when he struggled with longer words.

Here, now, Yvonne is wearing a baggy American football vest and pyjama trousers. She is a large lady. Always was, even when she was slim. She stands nearly six feet tall and would be considered formidable by the primary school children she teaches were it not for her big smile and silly sense of humour. She has been a teacher most of her life. Had been working with kids for thirteen years before she had one of her own. Had been content enough, too, before a supply teacher took a fancy to her. She was wooed, wed, knocked up twice, and then divorced before Andrew's first birthday. Her ex is abroad now, teaching English as a foreign language to uncomprehending teens in Jakarta, the Child Support Agency proving bloody useless in making him cough up his maintenance payments with any kind of regularity. He phones the kids once in a while. Carries their pictures in his wallet. But they haven't seen him in over a year, and the weekend he visited had been awkward, full of stilted conversation and stored-up arguments.

She pushes her scruffy blonde hair back from her face and drinks the last of her hot chocolate. At her feet are the crusts from a meat-feast pizza. She has some garlic mayonnaise left in the fridge and half-heartedly thinks of going to get it. Then she imagines sitting up in bed dipping cold pizza crusts in a pot of fattening gunk, and doesn't like the image of herself, so decides against it.

A sigh: 'Bloody carbs.'

She takes another look at her phone. Decides it's time for bed. She put the kids down just after nine. They'd watched a few episodes of some light-hearted American drama, eating popcorn chicken and spicy fries, drinking pint glasses of orange squash, wriggling in their matching cotton pyjamas until the fleece blanket that covers their half of the sofa looked like a whirlpool. Yvonne hadn't given the show her full attention. The story on the local news kept slipping into her thoughts. The picture they showed. Older, certainly. A few more wrinkles. Shading beneath her eyes. But unmistakably *her*. So sad. Such a shame.

She looks again at her phone. At the address book on the arm of the sofa. It's an old one, as full of crossings-out and amendments as useful information. She uses her phone for such things now, but the number she sought earlier this evening had not made the transition from paper to memory card and she had been forced to dig through her old diaries and papers to find it. In all honesty, she had never expected to call it. She had only taken it for form's sake and because she is a nice person who favours the old-fashioned way of doing things. She likes sending Christmas cards and birthday cards. Likes little notelets and writing with a fountain pen. Makes jam tarts and maids-of-honour and hangs proper paper chains each December. Says 'fiddlesticks' when she is cross and 'gee whiz' when the kids show her something impressive. Sometimes in the staff room they tease her about such things. Suggest that she would have felt more at home in the 1950s, teaching lacrosse or hockey in an all-girls boarding school.

Yvonne reaches again for the address book. Stares at the old address, neatly scored out with a line of black ink. At the new number, scribbled in the margin. The Hull area code.

'What a waste.'

She chides herself for never thinking to pop over and say hello. To make the kids a flask and some sandwiches and plan a nice Sunday walk across the bridge. To arrange a play date at the Country Park, perhaps. To sit on a bench while children played with grandchildren and she and her old comrade could let their conversation drift to the night they met, to that evening of blood and adrenalin, of crimson splashes on virgin snow, beneath colourful bulbs and against the whispered threats of the waves . . .

Too late to try again, she decides, putting the phone back down on the arm of the chair. She wasn't even sure whether she should have rung. Poor lot will have been inundated with real friends, she thinks. Real family. What would I have said?

Making the grunt of effort that the kids tease her over, Yvonne pulls herself from the chair. Starts the little ritual she performs unthinkingly every night. Pulls the plug out the back of the TV. Closes the living-room door. Checks the front and back door, rattling the handles and moving the kids' discarded shoes from the bottom of the stairs so they don't trip during the rush to breakfast. She walks to the kitchen, bare feet on plum-coloured carpet. Puts an aspirin in a shot glass and adds two inches of water. Stirs it and listens to the fizz. Drains the glass and pulls a face. Takes a gingerbread biscuit from the biscuit barrel beside the microwave and pulls the kitchen door closed. Puts her right hand on the banister and hauls herself up two stairs. Carries on up the steps, biscuit now just a crumb on her lower lip. She visits

Jacob's room first. Takes the book from his unresisting hands and smooths his hair down. Kisses him on the side of the head and fans him a little with his summer quilt. Visits Andrew next. He's the wrong way round in bed, his feet on the pillow, a wrestling figure clutched in one hand, another protruding from beneath his face. She leaves him as he is. Blows a kiss, knowing that he'll wake should she disturb him further. She switches his bedroom light off and pulls his door half closed.

A whisper: 'Sweet dreams.'

Yvonne heads to her own bedroom. It's untidy, with half-unpacked luggage and unsorted laundry. The bottom of the bed is covered in loose socks, still waiting to be paired a week after being spat from the tumble drier. Carrier bags from discount stores litter the dressing table, full of labels and receipts, discarded packaging from hastily bought vests and underwear. The half-dozen books she has on the go are scattered loose by the bed and behind the curtains, the windowsill is covered in empty pop bottles and dusty DVDs, as is the top of the TV that sits precariously on a wall-bracket she put up herself and doesn't fully trust. It's the untidiest room in the house because nobody else ever comes in here, and Yvonne doesn't mind.

She pushes open the door to the en-suite bathroom. Slides down her pyjama trousers and sits on the pink plastic. Looks at her feet. Spots a place on her right knee that she missed while shaving. Reminds herself, again, to take the mound of toilet-roll cardboard to the recycling bin from its place beneath the sink.

She hears the familiar creak as the door swings closed. Looks up.

Had the situation been described to her, Yvonne Dale would have expected to scream. Perhaps to physically react. To leap up or shuffle back or reach for the glass she uses for rinsing her mouth after brushing her teeth and smash it into the intruder's face . . .

There is no time. Her heart does not find the opportunity to beat between her noticing the figure, two steps away, against the tiled wall, and their moving forward to where she sits, still pissing, face turning grey.

The intruder grabs her by the hair. Pulls, hard, and instinctively she stands – one hand upon her scalp and the other trying to pull up her trousers. Something slams up beneath her jaw and her teeth mash together. Her eyes fill with tears from the pain and then she is being pushed back, onto the windowsill behind the toilet; bottles falling, glass smashing. A fist slams into her left eye and then her head is being smacked against the tiled wall. She sinks forward, falling against the intruder. Her vision swims. What she sees and what she feels merge before her. And she sees her boys. Feels them. Lashes out with a mother's instinct, suddenly desperate to fight, to flee. To live.

A weight drops on her back. The attacker pushes her down to the linoleum floor, her face scraping against the wooden door, the wall, into the dust and the cobwebs of the skirting board.

And then she feels it. The sharp, cold, metallic agony at the back of her left thigh. She roars in agony; a masculine, guttural howl of pain, and then a hand is across her mouth. She bucks. Pushes back. Claws with her right hand at the figure that presses her down. Bites at the warm, gloved hand inside her mouth. Tastes plastic. Chemical. Feels wetness at her thighs and shame at having pissed herself.

Clarity, suddenly. A moment of comprehension. Feels the stickiness. The warmth on her bare skin. Feels blood, not urine.

Rolls, left and right, trying to dislodge the weight upon her, even as her strength begins to fade. Her hand slips in blood. Head hits the ground. And then the weight is rising. She is free to move. Free, yet unable. She has no strength. She feels empty. Hollow. Unchained and weightless.

In her last moments, her eyes focus on the figure on the side of the bath. Through the tears, she sees colours. Shapes. Red mixed with black; blood and dirt. Sees the perfect exclamation mark of steel. Sees a face that she half knows; features blurred, as though a child has dipped their fingers in a still-wet portrait and swirled the eyes, nose and mouth into insensibility.

And now her mind is all children. Little palms in her big warm hand. She sees Jacob, looking down on her, eyes of concern, stroking her hair back from her face. Sees Andrew, holding out a picture he has drawn. She tries to say 'gee whiz'. . .

Her lips flutter, but no words emerge.

'Sshh,' says her killer, watching. Then: 'Sweet dreams.'

Silence, here, in this room.

A dead woman on her bathroom floor. Her killer, head in palms, shoulders shaking and fists tugging hair.

Blood seeping into every corner, intractable as night.

7

'This is yours?'

Helen Tremberg waves her hand. 'Ssh. They're all quite old. The neighbours, I mean.'

He smiles, the street light adding shadow to his high, attractive cheekbones. 'I'm not surprised.'

Tremberg pretends to be offended and opens her mouth wide. 'This is a very desirable neighbourhood,' she whispers, a slur to her words. 'Handy for the shop. Good parking. Easy access to the main road . . .'

'Meals on wheels, ambulances available if you pull the orange cord in the bathroom . . .'

She slaps him, playfully, across the arm. Feels the definition of his muscles. Starts to pull a sulky face but is too full of wine to do it properly.

'I grew up here,' she says, as she pushes open the gate and closes it again behind them. 'I told you, didn't I? When Grandad went into care it came up for sale and I got it for a steal.'

Mark slips his arm back around her waist as they walk up a red-brick driveway to the back door. They have walked this way from the restaurant. She has rested her head on his shoulder and felt his breath behind her ear and on her neck. He kissed her on the crown of the head when she said something funny. She has yet to taste his mouth, but knows that she will do that and more when she gets them inside her bungalow home.

It has been a tender, romantic evening. She had been unsure whether to agree when he suggested the restaurant only half a mile from her own front door, but she remembers them discussing it in a previous email chat, so it made sense and hadn't felt like he was trying to manipulate her into going somewhere within easy reach of her bedroom. He doesn't strike her as that kind of man. He could be, if he wanted. He's handsome, charming, and has spent all night making her laugh, but he seems too easy-going to be duplicitous. She can't remember a time when she has felt so pretty. She hadn't been sure whether or not to wear the tennis dress that shows off her legs, or whether to pair it with the high, wedge-heel sandals, but she has received nothing but compliments and admiring glances all night and Mark had said she looked 'stunning'.

Of course, it had taken a couple of brandies to get herself out of the house and to walk past her neighbours in the uncharacter-istically revealing outfit. She had got through two more while waiting in the bar for him to show up. By the time he walked in, five minutes late and dauntingly handsome in cream linen suit and black shirt, she was pink to her earlobes and flushed from both the walk and the booze. But he had put her at her ease. He'd taken her hand as if to shake it, then turned it, delicately, palm side down, so he could kiss her knuckles. He'd looked at her, over the top of her hand, and she saw it tremble. Then he gave a grin and made a joke of the action and himself, and they had giggled together, setting the tone for the next few hours.

Tremberg fumbles in her little sequinned handbag and pulls out her keys. At the second attempt, she gets them in the lock and pushes open the back door that opens straight into the kitchen, switching on the light as she goes. The sudden illumination hurts her eyes and she raises a hand to shield her vision, stumbling back a little as she does so. Mark catches her, hands upon her waist, and helps her inside, laughing. He doesn't seem drunk, though he matched her drink for drink. Ordered the best booze, but didn't argue when she said she wanted to split the bill. He seems to know her. Seems to know how she likes to be treated. How she likes to think of herself. Didn't ask her about the scar on her arm. Waited for her to volunteer the information. Didn't push or try too hard. Just spoke to her as if she was interesting, and stared into her eyes in a way that made her blush. Even when she'd invited him back, he'd been a gentleman about it. Insisted that she think about it. That she decide whether she was sober enough to make that kind of decision.

'Don't be afraid to change your mind,' he'd said, stepping from the restaurant into the warmth and dark of the evening. 'I don't want to spoil things. It's been perfect. You've been perfect.'

As they walked, Helen had done most of the talking. She has done for most of the date. She'd recognised almost every other diner in the restaurant, and they had all given her encouraging looks as she sat opposite her good-looking companion and devoured her blade of beef. It had been a nice feeling, and helped her let go. She knows almost everybody in Caistor. She grew up here, twelve miles from Grimsby, on the road to Lincoln. She went to the local school. Used to walk her dogs in the vale. Got stranded, like everybody else, each winter. The town sits in one of the few valleys in the county, and whenever it snows, the roads become impassable. Her childhood memories seem to involve endless snowball fights and sledging down the sloping playing fields in the school grounds. She had her first kiss behind the Chinese takeaway. Once got knocked over in the Market Place as she crossed the wide road while engrossed in a bag of chips. Her dad had belted the driver. Given her a bloody good telling off, too, as he took her to hospital to have her leg plastered. She stacked shelves for a while in the Co-op, in her teens. Got drunk in the park on cans of Strongbow and let a county cricketer take her virginity on a friend's sofa at sixteen. It's home, and only half an hour from the city where she now tries to catch villains. She has no plans to move over the water to Hull. This is where she belongs. It's a town that likes her, and she lost no friends when she decided to become a copper. It's a town where the police are appreciated.

Here, now, she feels absurdly pleased that she has shown Mark where she is from. She likes that he has listened. She has told him her best stories. Told him a little about being a detective. She is proud of her job, and does not mind talking about work. She has asked him a few questions about his own job, but each time the conversation has steered back to her. She has rarely felt as interesting or desirable.

She giggles as Mark closes the door behind them, then puts a hand to her mouth. 'I'm not a giggler,' she says, primly. 'I hate those giggly girls. That just slipped out.'

Mark turns her towards him and gives her a warm, forgiving smile. 'It's nice,' he says. 'You can do whatever you want. Be whatever you want. I like whoever you are.'

Helen looks away, embarrassed. Thinks about making coffee, then decides to stop the charade. She pulls him to her, and opens her mouth for his kiss, eyes closed. When she opens them again, Mark's face is an inch from her own. 'Are you sure?'

She grabs him by his short, brown hair, and pulls his mouth onto hers, kissing him hungrily, wetly, drunkenly. She is ferocious and rough with him, forcing his mouth onto her neck, her shoulders, grabbing his hands and forcing them onto her breasts. She feels outrageous and wanton, wildly happy. He pauses, grabbing her wrists so as to be able to look at her properly. 'You're beautiful, Helen. Not here. Bedroom?'

She holds his gaze. Nods. Takes his hand and leads him to her room. It's not much different to when she used to stay here as a teenager. The walls used to be patterned with Formula one posters. Now the prints are in frames, and there is a little more order to her wardrobe, but it is still an unashamedly teenage room.

Mark doesn't comment. Just turns her to him and presses himself against her. She tears at the buttons of his shirt, but he smiles and does it himself. Lets the garment fall to the floor. Stands there, muscled and perfect. Tattoos, artful and expensive, upon his shoulders and chest; a mayoral chain of Italian lettering inked into his skin.

She presses her face to it. Traces the outline with her mouth. She doesn't care what it says. Just wants to consume it. To consume him.

Mark pushes her back onto the bed. Pushes up her dress. Kneels before her and pulls down her knickers. Smiles at her. Tastes her. Doesn't even wince as she digs her nails into his skin and wraps her strong thighs around his head.

Panting, breathless, he turns her over. Plants soft kisses on the back of her thighs.

She hears him removing his clothing. Feels tiny, delicate touches on her skin. Feels his warm hands upon her hips.

'Are you a bad girl?'

The words make her wriggle. She turns back to him. He reaches forward, puts his fingers to her lips. Lets her taste herself. She sucks on his fingers. Tastes something else, too. Bitter. Unpleasant. But it is gone in a moment, replaced by fresh pleasures as he uses his other hand on her.

'I'm such a bad girl.'

She hears him breathe deep. Inhale. Slide inside her. And then she is lost in pleasure. In his movements. In the warmth in her belly and the sloshing pleasures in her skull.

She doesn't see the camera.

Doesn't see the tiny lens, busily recording it all.

Doesn't imagine, as she loses herself in another climax, that she is being watched. Filmed. Immortalised electronically, having cocaine snorted off her arse and rubbed into her gums by a man who works for the very gang she is supposed to be trying to put away . . .

4.36 a.m. The A180. Five miles from Barton and two screaming boys.

She's doing 80 mph in the outside lane, Soul II Soul on the CD player and a mug of black coffee rattling in the holder; police radio on the passenger seat and a satnav set barking lefts and rights.

Detective Superintendent Trish Pharaoh, putting on make-up in the rear-view mirror and steering with her thighs, trying to remember the right word for what has been done to Yvonne

Dale. Ex-something. *Excoriated*? No. *Excommunicated*. Don't be fucking daft.

The glass of the convertible is misting up so Pharaoh swipes a hand across the glass. She clears a porthole, jewelled with droplets and streaks. Peers through at the pissy yellow street lights and the damp grey motorway; at the distant line of pyrite glow and the beginnings of a sepia sunrise through a sky of wire wool.

She snaps her fingers. *Exsanguinated*. Bled out. Emptied. Cut to the femoral artery and left to empty on the lino.

Pharaoh is too drunk to drive, but she's driving anyway. She does, sometimes. She lives an hour from her office and downs a bottle of wine and a few vodkas every night. Sometimes she's still over the limit when she leaves the house in the morning, though she gets her kids up, dresses them, feeds them and makes packed lunches, without any noticeable sign of intoxication. She doesn't plan on stopping drinking, doesn't think she would be able to if she tried. She's a drinker. Always has been. And she has to drive. She makes no excuse for it. If she gets caught, she'll take her punishment. She'll accept the headlines and the loss of her rank. That's life. You do what you want to do, or what you have to do, and you deal with the consequences. That's justice. That's police work. That's what she is for . . .

The radio crackles. A voice asks her whereabouts.

'I'm ten minutes away. See you in three.'

She's up two hours earlier than usual, so reckons there is no doubt that she is still technically over the limit She feels fine though. Better than she should.

Pharaoh was the first senior CID officer to answer the phone.

The uniformed constable who attended the house in Barton had immediately called in the duty inspector, and he in turn had alerted CID. The duty detectives had passed it up the line, and ACC Everett was woken at home. He bumped it back down again, and within half an hour of Yvonne Dale's body being discovered, the three most senior officers in CID were getting calls on their mobiles. Pharaoh answered on the second ring. Said she'd be there within half an hour. Pulled on leggings, boots, a smartish jumper and a light suit jacket. Phoned her mum and asked her to come sit with the kids. Made a strong coffee, took her anti-depressants and her antacid tablet, and jumped in the car.

Pharaoh lives in Scartho in Grimsby. She pronounces the word properly, though true locals insist on 'Scather'. It's happily middle class, with a couple of foodie pubs and the kind of swimming pool where people actually get out of the water if they want to go for a piss. A lot of the properties are set back from quiet side streets, all white paint and neat hedges. Pharaoh does not have the funds to even dream of such a home. She earns a good wage on a superintendent's salary but historic debts, costly childcare and her husband's condition mean she is grateful to scrape together enough each month to pay the mortgage on their three-bedroomed semi in the circle of a quiet cul-de-sac. Her name and hers alone is on the mortgage. Her husband lost everything when his business went bankrupt. Lost their big home on the outskirts of town. Lost their fancy 4x4s and Florida holidays. Paid the price for thinking too big, and then let the stresses and guilt squeeze his brain like a fist.

Five years ago, aged just forty-four, he suffered the stroke that has left him crippled down one side and a stranger to his children. Adapting their house to his needs took the few savings Pharaoh had kept back when he was trying to keep his business afloat. Her home life is hard. She feels half-widowed. She still has her man; still sleeps next to him in their remote-control, adjustable bed. But he struggles to make himself understood. Can't hold her. Can't get his lips to form the right shape for the word 'love'. The children know him as little more than a living ghost; some grunting, malevolent spirit of a man they half remember. They struggle to know how to love him, and she does not know how to teach them. She feels the loss of who he was more keenly than her kids. She remembers their life. Remembers the fire in him. The fight. The way he grunted, animal-like, as he moved inside her. Remembers, too, his temper. His hands on her throat. His spittle on her face. Remembers loving and wanting and hating him all at once. She never expected to pity him. And yet that is the emotion she now feels most keenly. Sorry for him, to be so reduced. Sorry for herself. Sorry that nobody kisses her properly. Sorry that while the bitches at work put about the rumour that she's some kind of slag, she hasn't been fucked yet in her forties.

Pharaoh spots the house as soon as she turns off the motorway and drifts down the steep hill into the town. There are two patrol cars on the road and a third in the drive. An ambulance is parked across the road and a police constable is wrapping blue and white tape around a lamp post. Lights are on in windows all the way down the road. Faces peer out through glass. Some doors are open: householders on doorsteps, wearing dressing gowns and drinking tea. The properties here are worth twice what Philippa Longman paid for her place, but the reaction of neighbours to death in their midst is the same in any postcode.

Pharaoh pulls up against the kerb, one alloy hubcab scraping the stone. She flashes her badge at a slim WPC and ducks under the tape. She spots a familiar face over by the garage.

'Guv.'

'Morning, Lee.'

'We got a call from DCI Barclay from Grimsby CID. Seemed to think this was his . . .'

'I'm sure he did. So, what have we got?'

Detective Sergeant Lee Percy is a twenty-year veteran, who started as a uniformed constable around the same time as Pharaoh. He made it into plain clothes before she did, but when she finally got the call into CID, her career took off, while his did not. They were sergeants together, and were both up for the same inspector job. It went to Trish. He took it okay, but Pharaoh fancies that after a few drinks he will lance his spleen and spew bitter rants about how he lost out to a token woman who shagged her way into the job. She hopes she is wrong, of course, but has been right too many times to hold out much hope.

Sergeant Percy weighs things up and then shrugs. Decides that all the arguments will be among people well above his pay grade. He started his shift at 6 p.m. and had been planning an easy night writing up statements and trying to persuade a reluctant eyewitness to a hit-and-run to make a statement. He hadn't been prepared for this. Hadn't been prepared for what he saw in Yvonne Dale's bathroom. He stands against the brick of the flat-roofed garage, hands in his pockets, short-sleeved, pale-blue shirt flapping around arms that lack muscle or definition. He's got the slightest of pot bellies and a weak chin, but has caught his share of crooks.

'Bloody horrible, Guv.'

'Tell me everything.'

Yvonne Dale's body was discovered not long after she took her last breath. Her neighbours had been woken by a furious banging on their door and had come downstairs to investigate, expecting to find a drunk or gang of difficult teens. Instead, they found the glass in their uPVC front door had been smeared in what they took to be red paint. They did not take it to be so for long.

'Tried to wash it off, Guv. Old couple they are. The sort who don't leave a job until morning. Filled a bucket of warm water and started soaping it off. It was only when they started doing it they thought it might be something a bit more sinister. Old boy licked some off his finger. Threw up in the azaleas.'

'How did it get there? Does that mean the killer banged on the door? Why? Did he want us to find her?'

'Your guess is as good as mine, Guv.'

Pharaoh presses her lips together and scratches her nose. 'Better, I would say. And then?'

'They phoned 999. Uniforms started an immediate search of the area. One bright spark found a footprint in the mud of next door's garden. Found another outlined in the gravel of the drive. Followed the trail next door and banged on the door. Got no answer so tried to get the householder's details. Phone rang for ages. Then a little kid answered. PC persuaded him to come open the door and the poor little sod did. Uniform went inside and did a search for Mum. Found her in the bathroom in more blood than I've ever seen in my life.'

Pharaoh screws up her eyes. 'Two kids, they said on the way over . . .'

'The youngest didn't wake up until one of the uniforms came and scooped him up. Little bugger went nuts. There was proper screaming. They're with one of the uniformed sergeants now,

down the street at a neighbour's house. We're trying to get hold
of any other family.'

'Dad?'

'Lives abroad. They're divorced.'

Pharaoh nods. 'How much did they see?'

Percy shrugs, but not unkindly. He just doesn't know.

Pharaoh says nothing for a moment. She turns, as if to say
something to somebody behind her, then remembers he isn't
here. She gives a nod to Percy and pulls out her phone. She is
scrolling down to McAvoy's number when she stops herself.
Thinks of the bags under his eyes and the teething, red-faced
baby he keeps trying not to mention at work. She decides he
deserves another couple of hours. Sometimes, when the world
seems more ghastly than usual, she likes to think of him asleep.
It soothes her. When she pictures him, he is peaceful, bare-
chested and flat on his back, baby in one arm and Roisin in the
other. She enjoys the vision for a second, then puts her phone
away. She gives a wave and tells Percy to lead on. She pulls a pair
of blue plastic bags from a pocket and slips them over her boots,
then tucks her hands into her pockets to avoid the temptation of
touching anything. Then she follows him into the house.

As she steps inside, she hears sirens, growing closer. She hears
more tyres grinding to a stop by the road. It's beginning, she
thinks. Won't be long until the press are here, waking up any
neighbour still lucky enough to be asleep and asking them
precisely how sad they are that a neighbour has been bled out
on her bathroom floor.

'Body's upstairs. You need to see?'

At the foot of the stairs, Pharaoh pauses. She can already
imagine the scene. She has seen scores of bodies in her career

and accepts it as part of her job. She no longer shudders at the thought of flesh and bone torn open, and the only time she can't stop her eyes from filling with tears is when the corpse before her is that of a child. But this is a *mum*. A woman only a couple of years older than herself, who put her kids to bed, sat up for a while, then walked up these stairs for the very last time. She feels herself grow warm across her back and shoulders. Feels her cheeks flush.

Too much wine, she thinks. *For God's sake, don't cry.*

'I'll have a look downstairs first,' she says, running her tongue around her lips and scrubbing her mouth with the cuff of her jacket. 'Get the lay of the land.'

'Okay, Guv. I'll be around.'

Pharaoh enters the living room and the sheer normality of it all nearly brings her to her knees. The pictures on the walls break her heart, and it is all she can do not to mentally superimpose tears and open mouths onto the smiling faces that stare down at her.

She breathes out, slowly. Rubs her hand over her face and opens her mouth as wide as it will go. There is a satisfying click from her jawbone, then she shakes her head and gives an elaborate stretch. All of these movements represent a transformation: the putting on of another form. She is getting dressed. Becoming who she needs to be.

From the pocket of her coat, she feels a vibration.

'Pharaoh,' she says, into the phone.

'Detective Superintendent, this is Ken Cooper from the Press Association. We understand there has been a major incident—'

Pharaoh cuts the call. Switches the phone off. Looks at the wall and the pictures of Yvonne Dale with her two happy lads.

Feels a warmth for the woman. Decides this will be the picture she gives the press. Decides too that it will be the one she keeps in her mind, whatever she sees when she goes upstairs.

She turns, and sees the address book on the arm of the chair. The mobile phone, plugged in by the wall. Forensics will get to it eventually. Everything in the damn house will be printed and catalogued, photographed and entered into the system. Everything will be done properly, in time. Court cases are won and lost on whether the right serial number is entered into the right evidence bags. Murderers have walked free because the police have been unable to prove that key forensic evidence never left their sight on its way from the crime scene to the lab and the storage room. She takes a pair of polythene gloves from her inside pocket and rolls them on. Were McAvoy here, she would make a crack about him enjoying watching her do it. Might even insist he picture her wearing nothing but these and a pair of welly boots. She does it to get a reaction. She does it to warm him up. She does it because she knows that even for a fraction of a second, the image appears in his head. And she likes that. Likes it more than she should.

Pharaoh picks up the address book. It's full of scribbles and crossings out, probably only legible to the author. She puts it back down again and squats down by the phone. It's a similar make to her own, so she navigates its complex settings without too much difficulty. She finds the call log. Hull area code. She screws up her eyes, somehow already knowing what will happen when she hits redial.

The phone rings nearly a dozen times. Then a voice she recognises answers the call.

'Family Liaison. Longman household. This is PC Bob Tracy.'

'Bob?'

'Who's that?'

'This is Trish Pharaoh.'

'Sorry, Guv, didn't recognise the number. Half asleep, actually. What's happening?'

Pharaoh pauses. 'Have you had any phone calls this evening from an Yvonne Dale?'

'No, Guv. I've answered every call. But there have been loads of people ringing. Condolences, you know. Hang on . . .'

In the background, Pharaoh hears the Family Liaison Officer telling somebody not to worry. Tells them just to go back to bed. This is what the FLOs are for. It's what they're damn good at. They provide a little comfort and a lot of help. They answer the phones for a couple of days. They keep the press away. They sleep over and make tea and try to help the household forget that one of their number has had their chest caved in while walking home from work.

'Sorry about that. No, there's been no Yvonne. But like I said, the phone's barely stopped ringing. Why?'

Pharaoh doesn't answer. She's staring at the mantelpiece and the picture of the woman who lies dead and bled out in the bathroom above.

'I'll call you back. Don't worry.'

Pharaoh sits down on the carpet and leans against the wall, thinking hard. Two women. Two apparent innocents. Mums. Average, likeable, decent. Her mind conjures connections. Links. Bonds. She purses her lips, closes her eyes, then switches her phone back on. Her call is answered on the second ring, and in the background, a baby is crying. It sounds like it has been for some time.

'We've got another one,' says Pharaoh, by way of greeting. 'And they knew each other.'

8

Tuesday morning. 8.14 a.m.

Sky the colour of damp stone. Air fizzing with static, thick with dirty heat.

Aector McAvoy, both hands on the steering wheel, face and neck shaved and sore.

Buttoned up to the throat.

Sweating through grey shirt, old school tie, navy blue waistcoat and trousers.

He's pressing buttons on the dashboard to try and make the air conditioning blow out something other than this recycled warm air.

50 mph on Beverley Bypass. It's a 60 zone, but nobody else in East Yorkshire seems to know that, so he has to go at the pace of the Volvo driver in front. He takes a slow left into standing traffic, crawling past roadworks and cones. Drifts around three roundabouts. The windows are open but there isn't a breath of breeze to cool the gloss of perspiration that is already sticking his cowlick of ginger hair to his forehead.

Finally, a left turn, into a pretty village of old-fashioned, white-painted cottages and detached five-bedroomed homes: Audis in the driveways and Fiat 500s nose to bumper at the kerbside.

McAvoy likes Kirk Ella. It's a dainty, old-fashioned sort of place that looks as though it would be more at home thirty miles to the north. It feels like a suburb of York or Harrogate, but is only eight miles from the centre of Hull.

Elaine Longman lives on Hogg Lane, a tiny little street a stone's throw from St Andrew's Church and the centre of the village. It's a white-painted property with chunky sash windows and a red front door – one of a row set back from the road and which all share the same long picket fence. Elaine's has a hanging basket at the front, which looks well cared for.

McAvoy gives his policeman's knock; brisk and efficient, a pause between the fourth and fifth beats.

Elaine opens the door. She's wearing a simple white vest and a pair of linen trousers. Her eyes are so swollen and dark that it looks as though she has smeared coal dust beneath them, and the burst blood vessels and capillaries in her cheeks betray the fact she has been vomiting. McAvoy wonders if she opened a bottle or two last night, or whether grief just gnawed at her guts until she gagged on it.

'Aector,' she says, quietly. She manages a half-smile. 'Did I say that right?'

McAvoy nods. 'Very good, Elaine. Shall I try a Hull accent in return?'

'Order me a dry white wine,' she says, stepping back into the house and gesturing for him to follow. 'Or a vodka and coke.'

'Drar whart wharn,' says McAvoy, his mouth forming the syllables like a goldfish. 'Vodka and curk.'

'Perfect,' says Elaine, leading him through the homely living room and into the kitchen, where a laptop and loose paperwork sit on a long pine table. 'Now if you can just tell me there's snow on Frome Road . . .'

'That's beyond me,' says McAvoy. 'It's harder than Gaelic.'

He gives the kitchen a quick once-over. It's long, with large terracotta tiles underfoot and glass doors that open onto a small patio and garden, littered with children's toys. The fridge is covered in letters from school and a child's many drawings, all held in place with magnets bearing place names. London Zoo, Malta, Bridlington, Verona . . .

'I'd love to go there,' says McAvoy nodding at the fridge. 'Verona.' He corrects himself. 'Well, my wife would. Same thing, isn't it?'

Elaine follows his gaze to the fridge. 'I haven't been,' she says, giving a little shrug. 'Mum brought it back.'

McAvoy closes his eyes. Curses himself.

'The Family Liaison Officer said you didn't stay at the house last night,' he says, trying to brush over his stupidity. 'You didn't want to be there?'

Elaine shakes her head. 'Too much drama. Too many tears. I came home. Phoned Dad this morning. He seems okay, I guess. He just doesn't seem to be, well . . .'

'Go on.'

'He seems a bit vacant,' says Elaine, distracting herself by fiddling with her paperwork. 'Suppose it will take time, won't it? I mean, he's not really feeling anything yet, other than shock. The Internet says there will be anger before the grief. I don't know where I'm at yet. I don't have the energy. I didn't sleep much last night. Threw up half the night, though I don't know why.'

McAvoy sits down on one of the kitchen chairs. 'It's a purging,' he says. 'You need to get out what's inside you. You want to let the darkness out. It's like people who self-harm and think their pain leaves with the trickle of blood. For centuries, surgeons used to drill holes in your head to let the demons out, or bleed you so the ill humours left your system. Sometimes our bodies aren't operating in our best interests.'

Elaine looks at him for a spell, a strange expression on her face. 'You're not like other policemen,' she says, with a little smile. 'You're not like other people, now I think about it.'

McAvoy looks away. Fights down the blush. 'I'm sorry . . .'

'No, I like how you talk. I like how you think.' She gives a firm nod. 'That's it, isn't it? You actually *think*. That's a rarity these days. People just come out with the same clichés and platitudes, don't they? It's all small talk and nonsense. I've had so many "thinking of you" texts I'm going to scream. What does "thinking of you" mean? Of course they're thinking of me. My mum's just been killed. Something exciting has happened.' She pauses, and fresh tears prick at her eyes. 'I shouldn't obsess, should I? Not over things like that. My brain's not helping me out at all.'

McAvoy puts a hand on her shoulder. Gives a squeeze. 'Tea?'

She nods. 'I've drunk litres of the stuff but I can take another.'

He stands and begins looking in cupboards, filling the kettle, dropping teabags in two white mugs patterned with different-colour polka dots. As he looks back over at her to ask if she takes milk, he spots a Humberside Police letterhead on one of the documents on her table. She sees him looking, and gives a rueful smile.

'Three points and sixty quid,' she says, rolling her eyes.

'Sorry?'

'Arrived this morning. Talking on a mobile while driving. That's me up to nine points. One more and I lose my licence.'

McAvoy doesn't know what to say. 'It arrived this morning?'

She nods, then turns the action into a shake of the head. 'Just what I need, isn't it? I thought it was something to do with Mum . . .'

'It will have been sent out last week,' says McAvoy, aware that he is gabbling, unsure whether to defend the police or commiserate with her for the shittiness of the situation. 'They come second class. It's all automated. They wouldn't have known . . .'

Elaine shrugs and picks up her pen, filling in her details in the automatic guilty plea section. 'We weren't even moving. I was in a traffic jam. I phoned Mum to ask her to pick up Lucas.'

McAvoy says nothing. Just goes back to the tea and listens as she sniffs. When he returns to the table, her eyes are red and the backs of her hands are wet. He wishes he could make a phone call and tell her he will take care of it. Wishes he had that power, then realises that he wouldn't know what to do with it even if he did. Can imagine driving himself crazy trying to decide what is right and what is wrong. Here, now, he doesn't know whether giving Elaine a fixed-penalty notice for a minor driving infraction is *just*. But were he sitting in the kitchen of somebody who had lost a loved one in a road accident caused by somebody talking on a mobile while driving, he would be agreeing with their contention that blasé motorists should be strung up. He knows this about himself. Hates it, too.

Elaine gestures at herself and creases her face into a damp, half-hearted smile. 'Mess, aren't I?'

'You're doing great.'

'You think?'

'You're the one that Detective Superintendent Pharaoh and I thought we should see about this. You're the one holding it together and best able to assist in the investigation.'

Elaine gives him a puzzled look. 'There's been a development? Do you have someone?'

McAvoy raises his hands to slow her. Takes a sip of tea. After yesterday's meeting with Darren Robb he had called her and informed her that at this stage, her ex-partner was not being treated as a suspect. She had accepted the news with some relief, though she had immediately begun to ask where that left them. McAvoy had promised to keep her informed, even before he got the call from Pharaoh in the early hours and an instruction to get his arse over to the Longman house as soon as the sun came up. A call to the FLO suggested that nobody there was in any fit state to be any use to anybody, so he had elected to speak to Elaine instead.

'We haven't got anybody yet, no,' he says. 'But yes, there's been a development. Can I ask you if you know somebody called Yvonne Dale?'

Elaine squeezes her fist with her palm, thinking hard. 'Rings a bell, maybe. I don't know. Why?'

McAvoy takes a breath. 'She was murdered last night in her home in Barton. Cut with a knife. Bled to death.'

Elaine closes her eyes and puts both hands to her mouth, steepled at the fingertips. Her voice catches as she speaks. 'That's horrible.'

'Yvonne tried to call your mum's house last night, Elaine. Shortly before she died.'

There is silence in the room. Elaine simply looks at McAvoy, her bottom lip trembling, before she throws her hands up. 'I don't know! Were they friends? Why did she want Mum?'

McAvoy puts his hand on her shoulder again, as if trying to soothe a skittish horse. 'Ssh, just breathe for a second. Elaine, I need you to think hard about this. Here, I have a picture . . .'

Elaine pushes her chair back. 'I don't want to see. I can't let any more of this inside me . . .'

Fresh tears spill and McAvoy finds himself putting the picture away. He forces himself not to. Insists that he does his job as a police officer before he allows himself to become a human being.

'Please, just take a look.'

Despite herself, Elaine examines the image on McAvoy's mobile phone. At the large lady in the black swimsuit, floppy hat and sarong.

'She looks nice,' says Elaine, sniffing. 'I'm sorry, though, I don't know her. I don't know why she'd want Mum,'

McAvoy tries not to let the disappointment show on his face. He drains his tea. Begins to stand, then stops as he remembers the other thing that was bothering him.

'Elaine, last time we spoke you mentioned your mum was a lifesaver. Can I ask what you meant by that?'

Through the tears, Elaine gives a proud little grin. 'Means a lot of things, I guess. Means she was always helping people when they needed it most. She would do anything for anybody.'

'Oh.' McAvoy looks away. 'I thought you meant . . .'

Elaine opens her mouth. 'You mean actual lifesaving? Oh yeah, she was trained. Part of her job, I think. She went on a course, years ago. Came in handy, too.'

'Go on.'

'She never really told me much about it. She gave CPR to somebody though, on a long weekend in Bridlington. I think it was some drunk bloke bumped his head. She didn't speak much about it, to be honest.'

McAvoy's lips have formed a tight line. 'Do you know when this was?'

'Maybe fifteen years ago? A bit less? I'll have been at college, I think.'

'Would your dad know more?'

'Maybe.' She rubs a hand over her face. 'Why, is it important?'

McAvoy looks away, scratching at his cheek, tongue clicking at the back of his teeth. 'Did she save the person?'

Elaine nods. 'Oh yes. Apparently it took a while. That's all she really told me about it. Broke a few ribs . . .'

She stops herself. McAvoy sees goose pimples rise on her forearms, the colour bleaching from her face and neck.

'Is that . . . no . . . is that something . . .?'

She dissolves, all ghastly thoughts and half-imagined memories. McAvoy pulls her to him and holds her, her sobs trapped within his embrace. He closes his eyes, angry at himself, unsure how much he should have said, how much he should still say. He disentangles himself and tries to get her to look up. She fights like a child, one arm beneath her chin, another behind her head, face pressed into the grain of the table. He excuses himself and walks into the living room. Makes a quick call to the control room. Comes back to sit at the kitchen table. Answers his phone before it has a chance to ring.

He listens as the civilian officer relays the information he had sought. Hangs up, eyes closed. Insides churning.

'Elaine,' he says softly.

She looks up, eyes full of so much pain that McAvoy feels his stomach lurch.

'Elaine, we can't say with absolute certainty but it looks like your mum did know Yvonne.'

She blinks, twice, to clear her vision. 'How?'

'If the dates are right then your mother was an even more impressive person than we first gave her credit for. December, fourteen years ago. Bridlington seafront. Your mum saved a man's life. She gave heart compressions while another bystander applied a tourniquet to another serious wound. That person was Yvonne Dale. They both gave witness statements. The man didn't die so there was no inquest, but the person they saved was later charged with an incident and they were called to court to give evidence. As it happened, they didn't have to go into the courtroom, but I can only presume that is how they got to know each other.'

'So why was she phoning last night?'

McAvoy looks away. 'She probably heard what happened to your mum. Was ringing to offer condolences . . .'

His phone bleeps, alerting him to an email from control. The files he has requested are being electronically downloaded and will be with him inside the hour. The officer involved in the Bridlington incident is now retired, but still lives in the area. His phone number and address are included in the message.

McAvoy looks up. Locks his jaw.

'Your mum went to Bridlington a lot?'

Elaine gives a little nod. 'She was from West Yorkshire, wasn't she? They love it, the Westies. Look, should I phone Dad? Ask him about this lady? That night? I mean, her chest. Mum's chest. That's how she died, isn't it? And this other lady who died? You said she was cut. Did they say where she applied the tourniquet? Years ago, I mean.'

McAvoy shakes his head. They didn't say. But he reckons he knows anyway.

Elaine stands up, pulling at her hair. 'But somebody killed her. Hours after Mum. That can't be . . . I mean, it's too much of a coincidence. I don't understand,' says Elaine, lost and tearful.

McAvoy stares at his phone, a picture, all blurred edges and uneven patterns, swimming in his vision.

'Nor do I.'

'It should be a costume party,' says Mel, over the top of her takeaway iced coffee. 'Cops and robbers! Or tarts and vicars, maybe. No, no, Disney characters. I could make the costumes.'

Roisin laughs at the thought. 'Can you see Aector agreeing to that?'

Mel blows a raspberry derisively. 'He'd agree to whatever you asked. If you told him to run to bloody Land's End and bring you back a pebble he'd be out the door before you could tell him what type you wanted.'

Roisin pauses before smiling. She isn't sure if her friend is making fun of her husband. 'Just because he would do it, doesn't mean it's fair to ask. He'd hate it.'

'Who hates costume parties?'

'Giant ginger policemen,' says Roisin, grinning. 'He doesn't like being the centre of attention, you know that.'

'But we'd all be in costume. Oh go on, Ro, it would be awesome.'

Roisin shakes her head. 'No, he'd hate it. We'll have fun anyway. Just wear something nice.'

Mel pouts. 'Wouldn't get anything to fit him anyway,' she says, trying to get a laugh.

'Don't,' says Roisin, with a little shake of her head. 'Don't make fun.'

Mel opens her mouth to speak, but closes it again. Sips her drink.

They are sitting in Mel's alterations shop on Southcoates Lane, bakingly hot in the glass-fronted, airless room. To Mel's left is a rail of clothes in polythene covers, labels pinned to cuffs and lapels. Mel is sitting behind a sewing machine, looking pretty in a short skirt and a floaty poncho patterned with butterflies. She has her feet up on the desk, pieces of tissue paper stuck between each freshly painted toe. Roisin is sitting on the windowsill, lifting up her purple vest top to feed Lilah, the baby suckling contentedly on her left breast. Her beauty kit is open beside her, a rainbow of varnishes and treasure chest of files, clippers and emery boards. She's warm, but has not yet had to reapply her mascara, or stuff any loose and frizzy hairs back into her ponytail. Still, she's regretting her black leggings and wishes she'd gone for a skirt or pair of denim shorts. She feels sticky and a little irritable.

'Coffee's nice,' says Mel, to break the silence.

Roisin smiles. 'Place on Newland Avenue that does the good cakes. Took ages to get parked. You have to go in at such a funny angle.'

'I heard they got the plans the wrong way around,' says Mel, leaning forward to check whether her toes are still tacky. 'It's madness. You have to reverse into the space but there's never a moment when the cars aren't nose to tail. You go forwards, it's . . .' she counts on her fingers. 'It's like a 260-degree maneuver. Mental.'

Roisin nods. She'd parked on a side street because it was easier. Had thought about leaving Lilah in the car as she popped in to

Planet Coffee but decided the car was too hot and there were too many odd-looking people around to risk it. Besides, if Aector found out, he would want to go spare. He wouldn't actually do it, but he'd want to, and Roisin hates her husband suffering as much as she loves his flickering moments of true happiness.

Mel is about to suggest that they close for lunch and head to the pub near the fire station, but she stops herself when she sees the shape of a customer at the frosted glass door.

'Put it away,' hisses Mel at Roisin.

Roisin looks puzzled. 'What?'

'Your boob.'

Roisin laughs. 'Bugger that.'

The door opens and a good-looking lad in his early twenties steps into the shop, bringing with him the sound of the street and the whiff of liberally sprayed deodorant. He's wearing slouchy jean shorts and a white T-shirt with a slashed neck. He's in good shape, with a pop-star look; a diamond earring in his left lobe and three stars inked on his skin. His hair is neatly tapered at the back and stylishly ruffled at the front, and the headphones that he has taken off and looped around his neck are the most expensive model Roisin knows of.

'Hi,' he says, approaching the counter and enjoying Mel's legs as she hurriedly removes the tissue from between her toes. 'I was hoping for air conditioning.'

'We had a fan,' says Mel, hopping on one leg and blowing her fringe out of her eyes. 'It was blowing everything around.'

'I know girls like that,' he says, turning to Roisin. He gives her a quick once-over, sticking out his lower lip in a sort of gesture of admiration when he notices the feeding child at her breast. 'They do that in Amsterdam too, y'know.'

'What?'

'Shop window. Goods on display. You know how it is.'

Roisin stares at him, a half-smile on her face. 'You in here to have a few inches knocked off something?'

He grins back, playing ball. 'Nothing needs lengthening, I'll tell you that.'

Mel looks between the two of them, a little confused. Roisin is always better with the customers than she is. She has a way about her. She knows what to say. Mel always feels like she's a couple of sentences behind the conversation.

'Are you picking up or dropping off?' asks Mel, and he turns his attention back to her.

'Picking up. I've got my ticket here somewhere.' He starts patting pockets. Finds a couple of receipts in his T-shirt pocket and puts his car keys, complete with BMW keyring, down on the counter.

'When did you drop it off?' asks Mel, quizzically. 'What was it?'

'Puffer jacket,' he says. 'Dark blue.' He nods at the rail. 'That one?'

Mel turns. 'No, that was another man. He was wearing 501s. Proper Levi's. I remember because we talked about them. I think he was foreign. Turkish or Kosovan or something. Are you picking it up on his behalf?'

'Yeah,' he says. 'Mate of mine.'

Mel looks apologetic. 'I need to see the ticket. Otherwise . . .'

He shrugs. Checks his back pocket. 'I can tell you all about him, if that helps. Can give you chapter and verse.'

Mel looks at Roisin and receives a tiny shake of the head. 'We're a new business. Rules are rules. If he turns up tomorrow and I've given his coat to a stranger . . .'

The young man's face hardens. He pulls out a mobile phone. 'I can call him.'

'No, that wouldn't—'

'Look, I'm sure we can sort this out. His ticket must just be in another pair of trousers, or something.'

Mel tries her most ingratiating smile. This is becoming awkward and unpleasant. 'It's the same for everybody.'

The man stares into her eyes, hard. Runs his tongue around the inside of his mouth and bites his lower lip. He's getting pissed off. 'Come on, love. It's only a coat.'

Roisin interjects, her voice empty of patience. 'She said no.'

He gives a perceptible twitch. He's getting edgy, his gestures tense and nervous. Angrily, he reaches into his back pocket and pulls out a roll of notes, neatly bound. He throws the wad down on the table.

Mel's eyes flicker to Roisin, who is busy putting Lilah back in her stroller and tucking herself away. She looks at the pair of them, and the money on the counter.

'Your horse come in?' Roisin asks, her Irish accent suddenly more marked.

'Yours has, love. Now give me the coat.' He pauses. Adds, unpleasantly: 'Please.'

Roisin gently holds up her left hand, to indicate that Mel should do nothing. Her friend is looking at the money, and Roisin can see she is weighing up the offer. It's only a coat. She could buy the real owner a new one. It doesn't matter . . .

'I'm sorry,' says Roisin, leaning back against the wall. 'It's not worth the risk.'

He double-takes. 'What fucking risk?'

'Come on, fella, you want this coat that badly? Go buy yourself ten of the bastards. You could with that much cash. Don't be bothering us. My friend here's trying to run a business. I don't know what you want, but I'd go while you have the legs to carry you.'

As she speaks, her accent becomes so thick that Mel misses a few words. The man doesn't. He snarls.

'Who the fuck do you think you are? Do you know who I am?'

Roisin laughs, softly. 'I know what you are.'

He spits on the floor. Licks his lips.

'Out of the way.'

Without another word, he walks behind the counter. Mel gives a little squeal and tries to block his way, but he puts one hand on her face and pushes her backwards, hard, against her desk. Threads and needles and £20 notes fall to the ground.

'Silly fucking bitches,' he says, grabbing at the puffer jacket on the rail. He gives it a squeeze, as if testing fruit for freshness. Nods. Turns to Mel, who is pulling herself up. 'Didn't have to be like this,' he says. 'I just forgot the ticket. Nobody else is coming for it. Why did you make a fuss?'

He bends to her face.

Hisses: 'Bitch'.

Punches her in the stomach so hard that her feet leave the floor.

'You fucking bastard.'

Roisin is standing between him and the exit, a nail file in her hand and Lilah on her hip. She doesn't look scared. She looks like she wants to stick it in his eye.

'What you going to do with that? File and polish?' He laughs at her. 'What are you, seven stone wet through? I could throw you through the fucking window.'

'You could try.'

Mel gasps behind him. 'Her husband . . . he's . . . a policeman.'

The man laughs out loud. 'Coppers don't marry pikey slags, love. Well-known fact.'

'You're not leaving,' says Roisin, matter-of-factly. She reaches into her waistband and pulls out her phone. 'I've already called them. They're on their way.'

He peers at the screen. Can see she is connected to the emergency services. He gives a mirthless laugh and moves forward, ready to shove her bodily from the door. He does not think she will swing the nail file. Does not think for one second she will get in his way.

Roisin swings the nail file. The man sees it coming and instinctively raises his arms, still holding the coat. The file rips into the material of the jacket, and as he pulls away, a cloud of dust billows up from between him and Roisin.

'You stupid, stupid bitch!'

The man is frantically examining the coat, trying to find the patch of quilting that tore. He spins it around and a large white packet falls to the ground, spilling powder like a bag of flour.

'Jesus, no . . .'

He throws himself down, scooping the powder into pockets, looking up, sweat and fear on his face as he hears sirens.

'You don't . . . you don't know what you've—'

Roisin kicks him in the balls and he doubles over, mewling like a child, powder in his hair and on his clothes.

Behind the counter, Mel pulls herself up. 'What's happening, Ro . . .'

Through the glass, they see a patrol car pulling up beside the bread delivery van. See two officers running towards the shop, barking into radios.

Roisin only has a second to react. She bends down, and scoops up the fallen money from the floor.

Then she kicks Adam Downey in the balls again, grabs the stroller, and heads for the back door.

Part Two

Part Two

9

Two days later, 10.44 a.m.

The health centre on Cottingham Road. The same, airless room. The same hum of traffic and the dark shadow of the rowan tree at the window.

The same school chair.

The same reluctance to talk.

Aector McAvoy, jiggling his leg like he's playing boogie-woogie piano.

Sabine Keane. Sweating like she's just finished dancing a flamenco, but trying to keep professional. Her legs are sticking together as she tries to shift them. Her high heels are sweaty and slippy, crushing her already painful toes. She wants to reach into the bag beside her and pull out her flip-flops. Wants to open her litre bottle of water and pour it onto the back of her neck, to shake her head in a mountain stream like she's advertising shampoo . . .

'Aector, would you like some water, perhaps? It's still so muggy, isn't it? I thought there would have been a storm by now. I thought I felt rain on the way in but no, it's holding back. The sky's so ominous though, isn't it? Just really eerie.'

McAvoy gives her a polite nod. 'So psychologists are as irrational as the rest of then,' he says, trying to make his voice light. 'You still see signs and symbols where there aren't any.'

'Human nature,' says Sabine, returning his look and tone. 'We have to accept some things about ourselves, don't we? We may want to be the best versions of ourselves and have good mental health, but you still can't look at a sky like this without expecting a wolf to howl.'

McAvoy considers it. Pulls his clammy pinstripe shirt from his skin and wafts it. 'Last wolf in Britain was killed in 1743,' he says, studying her to see if she's interested in the story or in what it says about him. 'Shot near Inverness. Everybody was delighted. Big celebrations and the hunter was a hero. Funny thing is that since then, the number of deer has exploded. Half of Scotland is barren and treeless because the deer just eat through everything in their path. Scotland doesn't look like it should and it's because the wolves have gone. There are people want to reintroduce them. Can you imagine? Reintroducing wolves. I guess that would mean reintroducing hunters as well. It all goes round and round, doesn't it? Interesting idea, though.'

Sabine taps her chin with the nib of her pen, leaving a tiny blue dot. 'What do you think?'

'Me?' McAvoy looks surprised. 'I don't know enough about it. Dad thinks it's a good idea.'

'People have opinions, even when they don't know all the facts.'

McAvoy pulls on his nose, as if it will help him articulate the thought better. 'I don't have many opinions worth listening to. Maybe if I read all the reports . . .'

'But what does your gut say, Aector?'

He sighs. 'Why does it matter?'

'Gut instincts are important. Do you never act upon them?'

'I have them, yes. But I don't have to give in to them. They're suggestions, not impulses. A lady told me she likes how I think the other day. What do I make of that? It's not like I can take pride in it. I didn't choose to be this way. It's just how I am.'

Sabine smiles. She's fanning herself with her notes and her blonde hair is clinging to her forehead. When she reached up try the sash windows, she had exposed unshaved armpits and the label on a Primark bra. McAvoy had looked away. He doesn't want to judge his psychologist any more than he wants her to judge him.

'You seem to hold yourself in quite close control, Aector. There must be times when you have given in to those suggestions. When you've let go. Your file suggests—'

A sudden buzzing interrupts the conversation. Somewhere between embarrassed and grateful, McAvoy pulls out his phone. He holds up a finger to suggest he will be quick.

'Sergeant McAvoy? This is George Goss. You've been ringing me. Can I help?'

McAvoy gives Sabine an apologetic glance. Decides to follow her advice and act on impulse. Gestures that he will call her to set up another appointment, and bolts for the door. He hears the psychologist calling his name, but tells himself that he doesn't.

'Mr Goss, yes, I wondered if I could come and see you . . .'

An hour later, McAvoy is pulling into the driveway of a terraced property on North Road, at the centre of the Gypsyville estate. It hasn't got the greatest of reputations and the house prices are through the floor, but McAvoy has always rather liked this little network of quiet roads a stone's throw from the old trawling hub. There's no litter in the gutters or dog shit on the pavement and the people who live here strike him as the sort who would take it upon themselves to scrub a neighbour's wall if somebody had spray-painted graffiti on the brickwork.

George Goss's house is the neatest in the row. There are roses in the front garden, the exact variety neatly labelled in blue ink on white labels, and there are no weeds growing in the cracks between the paving slabs that lead to the front door.

McAvoy is fumbling in a pocket for his warrant card when the door swings open.

George Goss is in good shape. He's mid-sixties, and though his face has the waxy jowls of a man who likes a cheese course after his dessert, he's not overly portly and has a full head of grey-black hair. He's wearing a pair of polyester trousers with a neat seam down the front, with a short-sleeved checked shirt. As he extends his hand, McAvoy notices the mottling of liver spots that starts at his knuckles and carries on halfway up his arm. He's a man who likes his drink, but McAvoy has never met a retired copper who doesn't.

'I phoned Tom Spink,' says Goss, brusquely, by way of greeting. 'He said you're not a dickhead.'

McAvoy gives a laugh, pleased that Pharaoh's old boss had vouched for his credentials. 'Praise from Caesar.'

'Spink's not a dickhead either.'

'I'm sure he'd be delighted to hear it.'

'Still writing, is he? Books and stuff? His house fallen into the sea yet?'

McAvoy nods. 'He's writing a book on some unsolved cases, I think. Just finished doing something for the top brass. History of

Humberside Police, sort of thing. I'm not sure about his house. That coastline's eroding fast . . .'

McAvoy follows the retired inspector into a comfortable square living room. He figures this is the family room. It's a nice space, all sand-coloured wallpaper and pictures of Whitby seafront in tasteful frames. There is a three-seat leather sofa and matching armchair, angled to view the small flat-screen TV beneath the window. Half a dozen different pairs of spectacles lie jumbled on the video recorder and DVD player on its fancy glass stand, and a picture of a boy in school uniform grins toothlessly from the mantelpiece, above an electric fire. There is a catapult on the windowsill, with some rolled-up pieces of Blu-tack. McAvoy gives the object some thought. Considers the pretty garden, with its neatly tended roses and wall-climbing ivy. Decides that either George Goss or his wife are not big fans of cats.

'Back in a sec,' says Goss.

McAvoy hears cupboards opening and closing. Water pouring on teabags. The chink-chink-chink of spoon on mug. Hears it again. Guesses he's getting a mug of tea.

'Here you go,' says Goss, handing him a giant cup. 'Guessed you took sugar.'

'I do.'

Goss spreads his arms and makes fun of himself. 'Once a detective, always a detective, eh? Sit down.'

McAvoy sinks into the sofa, careful not to spill his sloshing drink. Goss gives a tiny nod of appreciation. 'Missus is at Sainsbury's,' he says. 'Her daughter takes her once a week.'

McAvoy notes the use of the word 'her'. Goss smiles.

'Yeah, I said "her". Not mine. I've got two of my own from my first marriage. Any of that important?'

There is silence in the room for a moment while McAvoy decides how to play this interview. The old boy seems to swing between welcoming and brusque with every sentence. He wonders if it was his trademark when he was still in the force. Wonders whether the retired inspector liked to play both roles in the 'good cop/bad cop' game.

'Mr Goss, I . . .'

'George, please.'

'George, I'm attached to the Serious and Organised Crime Unit in Humberside Police. We're investigating two murders that took place within the space of twenty-four hours. Our enquiries have demonstrated—'

Goss takes a loud slurp of tea and gives an exaggerated nod. 'I know what it's about, son. You said in your messages. You want to know about Sebastien Hoyer-Wood, yeah?'

McAvoy pauses, not liking to be steered. He considers the man in the armchair opposite. Imagines his day-to-day life. Is he bored? How does he fill his days? Does he like to talk about past cases or does he hate being reminded of the things he has done and the bodies he has stood over during a thirty-year police career? McAvoy decides that he likes to talk, but likes to tell a story rather than answer questions. Sees him as a pub raconteur who doesn't appreciate interruptions. He decides to just let the chat play out. He nods, sits back in the sofa.

Goss settles back too, mug resting on his thigh, his other hand tapping on the arm of the chair.

'Hoyer-Wood,' he says, again. 'Nasty business.'

'Hmm?' says McAvoy, coaxingly.

'More people should have heard of him.'

'I read the file.'

Goss makes a scornful noise. 'File? Date of birth, date of arrest and a couple of witness statements? They don't know the half of it.'

'Why don't you fill in the gaps?'

Goss stares for a moment, then appears to come to a decision. 'Hoyer-Wood was a posh boy,' he says, sighing. 'Mid-thirties when we got him. Nearly qualified as a doctor, if you can believe that. Left university under a cloud four years into his training. Went abroad for a bit and trained as a sports physiotherapist. That's what he was doing when all this came out. Had a private practice at his nice big house out on the road to York. Nice gaff. Don't know who's got it now . . .'

'You found all this out in the background probe, did you? After he was arrested?'

Goss nods. 'I went to town on the bugger. Spoke to everybody who'd ever met him, it felt like. We thought the case was watertight.'

McAvoy waits. Drinks his tea. Listens to the silence and stares at the carpet. When he looks up, Goss is staring at nothing. Picturing things only he can see.

'We don't know how long he'd been at it. How many there were. He liked them to watch, you see. That was his thing.' He snarls. Swallows, as if there is something vile in his mouth. 'It wasn't the actual sex that he got off on. It was the look on their husbands' faces. Their kids'. Their mums' and dads' . . .'

McAvoy breathes out. 'Jesus.'

Goss nods. 'He'd wander about in crowds. Take a shine to a family. Maybe a couple. Maybe some middle-aged woman pushing her old dad in a wheelchair. And then he'd just choose. Pick who he liked, and follow them. He'd just bloody choose!'

Goss slaps the arm of the chair, then gives a joyless little laugh. 'First one we heard about was a young mum in a holiday cottage in Aldbrough. Little village on the coast there. Her and her two boys, up here for a little break. All she could afford, poor cow. Petrol station attendant reckons Hoyer-Wood was there at the same time as she was filling up her car, second day of her holidays, but they'd wiped the CCTV. Wasn't much good in those days, anyway. Reckon that's where he took a shine to her, though. Just caught his eye.'

Goss bites on his lip. 'He broke into her place the next night. Boys were sleeping in her bed with her. She said later they'd been scared. They'd heard noises the night before. Asked if they could sleep in with Mum. She woke up with a knife against her cheek. Him looking down at her. He wore a surgical mask. Can you believe that? Like he was carrying out a procedure. He woke the kids. Wasn't rough with them. Just told them to wake up. Told the oldest to put the light on. Then he raped her. Just like that. Held a knife to her throat and told the boys that if they tried to move he'd open her windpipe. Then when he was done he said that if she told anybody, he'd come back and do it again. And again . . .'

McAvoy stares at the floor. 'She reported it?'

'Not at first. Not until after. Not until we were investigating the one we got him for.'

'In Bridlington?'

Goss nods. 'This was a couple of years later. He'd got good at it by then. Perfected his technique, so to speak. Wasn't enough for just the kids to see. He was into husbands by now. Same MO. Breaking in when they were asleep. He added a bit more of a kick this time, though. Started playing with lighter fluid.'

McAvoy looks up. 'What?'

Goss nods, finding it hard to believe even as he relays it. 'When they were asleep, all curled together. He'd spray them with lighter fluid. Then he'd stand there with a lighter. Tell the bloke to stay still or he'd set fire to the three of them.'

'The three?'

'Oh aye, he'd be covered in the stuff himself. Blokes would wake up with this stranger in their bedroom threatening to set them on fire. And they'd do what he said. They'd stand against the wall and they'd cry and call him a bastard and threaten him with all sorts. But they wouldn't stop him. They wouldn't do a thing. When he was done he'd tell them the same thing – he would come back. And nobody wanted to report it, anyway. Not the blokes. Not the blokes who were too bloody scared to stop a stranger raping their woman in the middle of the night.'

McAvoy briefly imagines how the men felt. Imagines the fear and the rage and the helplessness. Then he imagines the women. Imagines their sheer, indescribable terror.

Goss gives a smile. 'I know what you're thinking, son. Thinking you'd never do what he asked, yeah? I thought that too. But these weren't cowardly blokes, lad. These were ordinary fellas. Blokes who would wade into a scrap if you asked them to. But there's something about fire, isn't there? Something that stops you dead. Hoyer-Wood knew that. He would have kept going if he hadn't messed up.'

'Bridlington, yes?'

Goss nods. 'Picked the wrong family, I'll tell you that. Locals, they were. Not holidaymakers . . .'

McAvoy sits forward. 'Sorry George, can I just ask, were these cases all seaside towns? Was that part of his thinking?'

'No, there were a couple in little towns as well. Or at least, we think there were. Half of this is guesswork, son. We put this together afterwards, based on where we knew he had been, and with a lot of promises that none of the information we received would ever be shared. No, we think he liked the seaside because it's where families and couples spend happy times. You know how it is when you see a family enjoying themselves at the beach. All that candyfloss and kiss-me-quick hats. That's what he liked.'

'But this happened in December, yes?'

'You can get cheap breaks in places like Bridlington in winter. You still find holidaymakers. Maybe he'd seen this family before and got a taste for them then and couldn't wait until the snows thawed. We don't know.'

'What happened?'

'Same thing,' says Goss, wearily. 'Woke a family up. Cromwell, their name was. But he hadn't done his research properly. Didn't know the Cromwells like we did.'

'Bad news?'

Goss opens his eyes wide to demonstrate his strength of feeling.

'He didn't cooperate? The dad?'

'Did for about five seconds. Did as he was told. Stood against the wall and watched Hoyer-Wood stick his cock in his wife, holding a lighter to her hair.'

'He intervened?'

'He hasn't got many gears, Johnny Cromwell. He's not one of life's thinkers.'

'And Hoyer-Wood dropped the lighter?'

'We don't think he'd ever have done what he threatened to. He just liked having the power. Soon as Johnny-boy came at him he panicked. Tried to flick the wheel on the lighter and dropped the thing. Johnny threw him around like he was made of straw. Beat the shit out of him.'

'There was a fire, though, yes? The reports I read—'

'Johnny told us that Hoyer-Wood did it himself. Flicked the wheel on the lighter. That's bollocks. It was Johnny. Set the bastard on fire.'

McAvoy purses his lips. 'Was he naked? Hoyer-Wood? During the attacks?'

'Aye,' says Goss. 'Just the surgical mask. We found his clothes outside Cromwell's house. We reckon he used to get changed before and after.'

'Condom?'

'Yeah. Put it on before he came in.'

McAvoy considers it. 'That rather suggests—'

'That the anticipation of it got him hard? Yep. Sick bastard, like I said.'

'What happened next?'

Goss gives a laugh. 'Threw himself out the bloody window, didn't he? First floor, straight through the glass. Tore himself to bits and hit the ground like he'd fallen from an aeroplane.'

'Bloody hell.'

'He got up, though. Was thick snow that night. That took some of the impact out of his fall and put the flames out. Staggered a few hundred yards before Cromwell caught up with him again.'

'This was on the seafront, yes? There were people around . . .'

'That's what saved the bastard. People in pubs and chip shops, looking out as this battered and burned naked bloke stumbled past the window.'

'They stopped Cromwell? Stopped him from killing him?'

'Couple of blokes held him back. They didn't know what was happening.'

'And Hoyer-Wood?'

'Went into shock. Heart stopped. His leg had been cut coming through the glass. He'd fractured his skull, too.'

'And Philippa Longman? Yvonne Dale?'

Goss breathes out, slowly. 'I didn't realise when I heard about the poor woman in Barton. But yeah, I remember Philippa. She was up in Bridlington for a mini-break or something. Over from West Yorkshire. She pumped his heart. Blew in his lungs. Brought him back.'

'Yvonne?'

'I've brought her to mind since I got your message. Quick thinker, that one. Pulled off her tights and tied them around the wound. Tourniquet, it's called, yeah? Then she sat there in the blood and snow holding his hand until the ambulances arrived. They say you shouldn't do that now. Guidelines have changed. You should just hold a compress over the wound. But back then, she did the right thing.'

'They saved him?'

'For a while. His heart stopped again in the ambulance. They brought him back. Then they operated. Saved him, though.' He shakes his head. 'They should have let him die.'

McAvoy finds himself nodding and then stops himself. 'They didn't know. And even if they did—'

'The local uniforms turned up to arrest Cromwell. He told them everything. That's when we got the call. CID.'

'And?'

'And it unfolded, lad. What he'd done. What he liked.'

'How did you find out about the other incidents?'

Goss points with his chin, as if Hoyer-Wood's home is at the end of the garden. 'Searched his place. Found his appointments book. Had a look at his magazine collection. Proper police work, lad. Appealed for witnesses and got a call from the Aldbrough lass. She said she could never give evidence, but thought we should know what he did to her. I think she wanted to know, more than anything. Wanted to know if it was the same man. Why he'd done it. Who he was. Just couldn't bring herself to give a statement.'

'And the others?'

Goss closes his eyes. 'Hoyer-Wood liked to write. In court, they said it was just fantasy. It wasn't. He wrote it all down afterwards. Described every bloody moment of it.'

'What did he say? When he came out of surgery, I mean?'

Goss laughs. 'He didn't say much, lad. He was a wreck. Paralysed down one side. Couldn't walk. No motor skills in one half of his face.'

'But he was charged?'

'We charged him with what we knew for certain. One count of rape. Figured that when we got him for that, we could start to build a case around any others that decided to give evidence. The important thing was locking him up.'

'What happened?'

Goss grinds his teeth. 'His posh friends happened, that's what. A psychiatrist said he was unfit to stand trial. Judge bought it.'

'But you didn't?'

'He was an evil little bastard but he knew what he was doing. The shrink was an old university friend. They'd studied together. Half his old university chums sent the judge letters saying what a super chap Hoyer-Wood was. They said they didn't believe he had acted maliciously but was suffering from some mental disorder or something.'

McAvoy squeezes the handle of his empty mug. 'He was sent to a mental facility?'

'He was sent to his mate's place. Private healthcare facility, licensed by the Home Office to look after dangerous patients.' Goss sneers. 'Got the licence about a week after Hoyer-Wood was arrested. It was a holiday camp! Went to live there in bloody luxury.'

McAvoy rolls his head from side to side, his neck suddenly stiff and sore. He becomes aware how cool it is in here. Wonders where the chill is coming from. What is raising the goose pimples on his skin.

'And he's never stood trial? Never been brought to account?'

'No.'

'Cromwell?'

Goss shrugs, suddenly looking a little older. 'Got sent down a couple of years later for attempted murder. Row in a bar. He never did control that temper. Still inside.'

'So where is Hoyer-Wood now?'

'Went to stay at his pal's asylum, not far from here. Was there a couple of years then moved to another facility. He's still classified as unfit to stand trial, and there's no hunger to change that. I heard he suffered a major stroke a few years back that left him worse than ever. He's a cripple. Can't do anybody any harm and has to piss and shit in a bag. The thinking is that for a man with appetites like his, that's punishment enough.'

McAvoy considers it. 'No, it's not,' he says, finally.

'Tom Spink was right about you.'

They share a tired smile and McAvoy scratches at his eyebrows, trying to formulate his thoughts.

'The murders I'm investigating . . .'

Goss holds his gaze. 'Bloody big coincidence if it's nothing to do with this, but I don't know how it could be. How, or why . . .'

'They saved his life. Saved the life of somebody who did terrible things and ruined the lives of others.'

Goss nods. 'I don't envy you,' he says, ruefully. 'Bloody shame, all this. I only spoke to Yvonne the once and Philippa not much more than that, but they were nice ladies. Didn't deserve that. If somebody is punishing them, whoever they are, then they're as bad as Hoyer-Wood. And he was the fucking worst.'

McAvoy stares into the bottom of his mug.

Goss softens his voice. 'I made it with a bag, son. You won't find answers in your tea leaves.'

McAvoy runs his hands through his hair, wishing he had started taking notes when the conversation began. It would help him, now, to be able to read back through what he has discovered. To busy his mind, his eyes, his fingers, with something other than the thoughts banging like heartbeats in his head.

'The facility. The one his friend ran . . .'

'On the way to Driffield.'

'You ever go?'

'Tried to. His mate wouldn't agree to the interview. Said it would interfere with his treatment.'

'You push?'

'Had to apply to the Home Office. Orders came down to leave it alone.'

McAvoy reaches into his pocket and pulls out his notebook.

'I'll need some names and addresses. Whatever you can remember . . .'

Goss considers. 'I promised the people who came forward I'd never share.'

McAvoy says nothing. Lets the old man consider it.

He shakes his head. 'I'll see what I can rustle up. First thing you want to do is visit the shrink who got him off.'

McAvoy raises an eyebrow. 'You think?'

'There are questions to be answered, lad.' He stares hard at McAvoy.

'On the road to Driffield, yeah?'

Goss reaches into his shirt pocket and pulls out a scrap of paper. 'I wrote the address down before you arrived, lad. Figured it would be your next stop. I think it's in new hands, but there are some ghosts at that place worth exorcising.'

McAvoy starts to stand then stops himself.

'Does it get easier?' he asks, softly. 'Living with it. The ones that beat the system? Got away with it?'

Goss is silent for a second then lets out his breath in a hollow laugh. Shakes his head apologetically.

Come on, Mark, please, just a text, just a trio of kisses or a promise to call later . . .

Helen sits at her desk, staring at the screen, desperate for her email inbox to light up. She hasn't heard from Mark since he slipped away from her home in the middle of the night. She woke unsure if he had ever been there. The warm residue of pleasure and the stickiness between her legs were the only evidence that they had made love. That they had made love the way they do in the movies and in a way that she wants to be made love to again.

Her inbox flashes and she clicks on the screen. It's not him. Just a message from another police force about Adam Downey:

the little shit who's been saying 'no comment' for two days and who they are about to charge with possessing a large quantity of cocaine.

Colin Ray's team were among the last to hear about what had happened at the alterations shop on Southcoates Lane. The incident went to Drugs Squad, who held on to it for as long as they could. Their detective inspector, a fast-track university graduate by the name of Rick Breverton, had done the first interview with Downey. He had done some decent work on the basics. Got his name. A list of known associates. Even persuaded the lass from the shop to give a statement. Breverton didn't deserve to be called the names that Colin Ray threw in his direction when they both met with the Assistant Chief Constable and the head of CID to decide who was going to be given the case. Ray was adamant that it fell within his remit. He had no doubt that the lad was involved with the drugs gang he had been tracking for months. Breverton believed the young man was more likely linked to an older, more established outfit within the city, and therefore nothing to do with Ray's wild imaginings about the elite new organised crime outfit outmuscling the old guard. For an easy life, ACC Everett had given the case to Ray, who had briefed his team immediately. Given them chapter and verse on Adam Downey.

Downey is twenty-four, and lives on the Victoria Dock estate by the waterfront. The area was built with London's Docklands in mind and marketed as an 'urban village' but has failed to draw the middle classes away from the West Hull villages, and large chunks of the area have been bought up by private landlords to rent out at reduced rates. It's a mixture of hard-working families and dodgy bastards. Downey falls into the second category. He did his first stretch in a young offender institute

at sixteen, having been caught using stolen credit cards. None
of the other incidents on his record include violence, but he's
no stranger to drugs. A year ago, he was arrested when a van
on board the *Pride of Rotterdam* ferry was found to have packets
of pure cocaine stitched into the upholstery. CCTV showed
Downey getting out of the van when it boarded. He and the
driver were both charged, but the case collapsed before it got
to court. Downey had done a few months on remand in Hull
Prison. Ray told his troops that he believed it was during his
time inside that Downey joined the new outfit. The old punk
rocker who used to have a hand in local supply and demand
had disappeared not long afterwards.

'He's in the big leagues now,' Ray had barked, tugging at his
tie as if involved in some auto-asphyxiation sex game. His face
was greasy with sweat and his hair, slicked back from his ratty
face, had only been combed at the front. It stuck up on his crown
like an antenna and gave him the look of a crazed preacher as he
stomped about in front of the whiteboard and scribbled illegible
theories and scrawled lines between suspects' names.

'It was a handover, plain and simple,' he'd snorted in a spray
of spit. 'They were trying something. One lad drops the coat off,
pockets full of coke. Passes the ticket to our boy. Our lad's a thick
piece of shit and loses the ticket. Reckons he'll charm the coat
out of the shopkeeper. She says no and the next thing it turns
nasty.'

Shaz Archer had chipped in next, sitting directly in front of
the fan so her hair billowed theatrically around her and the lads
could see her nipples through her white sleeveless blouse.

'The call to emergency services came from an unregistered
mobile phone. The shopkeeper says she has no idea who called

it in. Must have been somebody passing by the window. We have our doubts. I think she has a friend who didn't want to hang around. We'll look into that. For now, Adam isn't talking and we're going to charge him. See who he calls. What he does next. We've got a chance here, people. They've fucked up. They've hired themselves a right bloody monkey, and if they don't want their operation going tits-up, they'll want to get him out of custody before he can talk to us. Col has a few friends inside who are going to make sure he doesn't enjoy himself too much. Let's shake the tree and see what falls out, yeah?'

Helen had registered only mild surprise that the incident had occurred in the shop she had stood outside only the other day. She had barely taken anything in. Her mind had been elsewhere. Had she gone too far? Should she have slept with Mark on the first date? She can't concentrate. Her mind is screeching with fears and uncertainties. Is he playing it cool? Should she play it cool too? Should she just write it off as one great night?

She is staring blankly at the PNC database. She can't find any connection between Downey and the driver who chucked piss over Shaz Archer, but she's hardly concentrating on the task.

Her email lights up. It's a message from an address she doesn't recognise.

Subject: 'Thought you might like to see this'

The email contains a video clip. The file size suggests it's only a few seconds long, so she mutes the sound and opens it up.

She sees herself. Herself on all fours, bare arse and curved spine: her sex pointing catlike at the sky. Sees Mark. Naked. Face in shadow. He's drizzling a line of white powder onto her buttocks. Lowering his face. Snorting it up. Rubbing his fingers on her gums. She's looking back at him, lustful and dreamy, mouthing 'do it, go on' and then losing herself in pleasure, powder sparkling in her smile . . .

Here, now, she starts to shake. Feels her whole body tremble. Can barely control her fingers for long enough to close the video down before anybody else can see. Just stares at the blank screen, as sickness crawls up her throat.

Another email flashes up, from the same address.

With fingers that quiver, hands that do not feel like her own, she opens the message.

Blinks away hot tears as she reads the words.

We will be in touch. x

10

Friday. 9.46 a.m. The sky a dark shroud: crumpled and creased above a landscape of dying greens and browns.

Aector McAvoy's people-carrier heading north; dead flies on the windscreen and fluffy toys in the boot. A local DJ talking nonsense on the radio, and sweat on the inside of the glass.

'She was brave,' says Pharaoh, fanning herself with her notes. 'Standing up to him. Saying no. Lot of people would have filled their pants.'

McAvoy gives a grunt of agreement. 'You never know, do you? How you'll react?'

'She gave him a couple of good ones, according to Colin Ray. Was my grandma taught me that, as a kid. Go for the soft places. Eyes and bollocks.'

McAvoy watches the road. Nods along to the song playing in his head. It's a salsa number and always arrives, unbidden, in his skull, when he thinks of Mel. He'd been shocked to hear what had happened at her shop. Relieved, too, to hear that Roisin hadn't been there. More than anything he'd been impressed. He didn't think Mel had it in her. Apparently some drug pusher had turned up at her shop demanding a coat containing a bumper stash of pure cocaine, and she had refused to let him take it because he hadn't got his ticket. It had all got nasty, and according to Roisin, Mel had managed to call the police in her pocket then give him a couple of swift kicks to his tender places. He'd been crying like a girl when the uniforms arrived.

'Never said a word in the interviews,' says Pharaoh. 'Colin's doing his nut.'

Bored, listless and too bloody hot, she stares out of the window. There's not much to look at. It's all green fields and sparse woodland, overgrown footpaths and villages with names that were recorded in the Domesday Book. She's seen half a dozen lay-bys where swingers could get their kicks. Took great pleasure in pointing them out to her favourite sergeant.

'Detective Inspector Archer gave it her all, apparently.' McAvoy's voice is unreadable, his expression to match. 'In the interviews, I mean.'

Pharaoh turns to him, licking her lips. 'You could be a politician, Hector.'

'Guv?' he asks, innocently.

Pharaoh lets it drop. Were she to start criticising Shaz Archer, she would never stop.

For a time, she considers the Adam Downey case, and what a good result would mean for her unit in general, and her own position within it. Were Colin Ray to bring the new outfit down, she would be hard-pressed to justify remaining head of Serious and Organised. She and Ray have fought like cat and dog ever since she got the job. He had expected the unit to be his, and had planned to make Shaz Archer his second-in-command. Pharaoh got it instead. They have very different styles, but Pharaoh at least knows that her rival's style is effective and respects his record.

He, on the other hand, thinks Pharaoh is little more than a nice pair of tits in a stab vest.

'You all right, Guv?'

Pharaoh shakes it away. Concentrates on what she had learned in this morning's briefing.

'He's shit-scared,' she says. 'Downey. I reckon they'll charge him before the day's out, whether he talks or whether he doesn't. He won't get bail, so the next few days should be interesting for the lad. Pretty bloody obvious he works for the new outfit in some capacity, but it's all guesswork. Colin Ray's going to pop a vein.' She gives the matter some thought. 'Could be worse.'

'You don't want a crack at it yourself?'

Pharaoh raises her hands to point at herself and mouth the word 'moi?' Her bangles give a clank. 'I can't be everywhere,' she says, sighing. 'Ray brought in the only significant victories we've had with this lot. He's earned the right to run with it, and to fall on his face if he does it wrong. My only contribution so far has been getting one of the units firebombed down at St Andrew's Quay. I don't think it would be well received if I marched in and took over, no matter how much I'd like to. I've got some questions I'd like to ask that shopkeeper, I know that much . . .'

McAvoy says nothing. He finds himself uncomfortable talking about what happened on Southcoates Lane. It was pure good fortune that Roisin wasn't there when Downey tried to muscle Mel. He imagines his wife in danger. Pictures her, helpless and afraid. The thought makes the hairs on his forearms rise. He imagines her giving a statement to Colin Ray. Imagines the look on the bastard's face. Passing judgement on her. On him. On his family. McAvoy is not ashamed of his wife, or her heritage. He just doesn't want to give the people that he knows to be bastards any more sticks to hit him with.

'That's nice,' says Pharaoh, nodding at his left wrist.

'Thanks Guv,' he says, and can't keep the smile from his face. Roisin had given him the new watch in bed last night. She had told him it reminded her of him. 'Precious, with a big face,' she had said, giggling and sitting cross-legged in front of him, their bedroom piled high with boxes and bags, ready for the move to their new home, their new lives. He had hugged her and stroked her hair, said thank you time and again, even as the policeman's voice in his head screamed.

Where had she got it? Where had the money come from? Christ, we're up to our eyeballs in debt and she's splashing out on a watch for me, a new mobile phone for her, football boots for Fin . . .

'Thought you were skint,' says Pharaoh, guilelessly.

'I think she'd been saving. She's been doing nails . . .'

Pharaoh nods again, losing interest. She hums a song that sounds a little Motown in origin, then begins to root through the glovebox of the people-carrier. She is worse on long journeys than either of his children. She's a terrible passenger and can't seem to help giving him directions, urging him to slow down, speed up, change gear or indicate, even though she drives like a madwoman herself.

'How do you keep it so neat?' she asks, her tone critical.

He takes his eyes off the road for a moment and glances in her direction. She's wearing black today. Head to toe. Trousers, boots, blouse and biker jacket, which she is steadfastly refusing to remove, even though she is clearly far too warm. Her hair is sticking to her forehead and clinging to her hoop earrings, and she has a sheen of perspiration on her upper lip.

'Eclectic tastes, Hector,' says Pharaoh, examining his CDs and not waiting for him to answer her previous question.

'Some of them are Roisin's . . .'

'Yeah, I can see that. Shakira. Pink. Lady Gaga.' She eyes him. 'You sure you're not a closet pop fan?'

He gives a laugh. 'Mine's the depressing stuff. That's what Roisin says.'

Pharaoh holds up a CD with a picture of a woodland clearing on the case. 'This any good?'

'Emily Barker? Superb.'

Pharaoh puts the CD in the player. After a few seconds the car is filled with mournful accordion and sad guitar, vocals about love and loss, bleeding knuckles and flying crows. The song always hits McAvoy in the heart. He can't listen to it with his eyes open, which is why he rarely plays it in the car. Pharaoh gives it a minute, then switches it off.

'Fucking hell, Hector.'

'She's amazing.'

'That your thing? Folk?'

'It's not folk. Not really. And no, it's not my thing. I don't have a thing . . .' He stops himself, chewing his lip, embarrassed. 'There's some U2 in there. Oasis.'

Pharaoh holds up another CD. 'Prodigy?'

McAvoy shrugs. '"Firestarter" was a big hit when I was at university.'

She considers the image in her mind. 'I'm not sure I can imagine that without going insane, Hector. I can't see you dancing. Not properly. Maybe a Highland fling. In a kilt. Eating haggis. On the back of the Loch Ness monster.'

McAvoy pulls a face, scowling at the road, saying nothing as Pharaoh stuffs the CDs back into the glovebox with no consideration for the careful order in which they had previously been stacked. She goes back to staring out of the window, occasionally referring to the notepad in her lap. After a while she gets bored again. 'Are we nearly bloody there?'

McAvoy had been pleased when Pharaoh had told him she was coming with him to the mental facility on the road to Driffield. She had been interested in what he had told her about Sebastien Hoyer-Wood. She even remembered hearing about the case, though she had been a young sergeant working in another patch at the time of his crimes. McAvoy's discoveries are being thought of as a lead, though the exact direction is unclear. Back at the station, Ben Nielsen is trying to find a current address for the shrink who did the medical report on Hoyer-Wood and who worked at the private asylum that McAvoy and Pharaoh are on their way to visit. They have requested the old case files and already discovered that the psychiatrist was a man called Lewis Caneva. A Google search came up with a few old academic papers and a profile in some long-defunct medical periodical, but he has clearly not been thought of as a rising star in a long time. A quick check with his professional association showed Caneva is no longer practising, and as such, the association has no record of his current whereabouts. It had all struck McAvoy as worthy of some further digging, and he had suggested a trip to the facility, which has lain dormant and for sale for the best part of a decade. Another quick sweep of some property websites revealed that Abbey Manor had just been snapped up by some multinational healthcare giant, which is seeking planning permission to transform it into a luxury home for the rich and dying.

'It just all seems to point to something,' McAvoy had said, when he filled Pharaoh in. 'I don't know what.'

Pharaoh had agreed with him. She'd phoned him in bed last night and spent twenty minutes listening to his theories. It was a bizarre conversation because she was on his TV at the same time, busy appealing for witnesses to Yvonne Dale's death to come forward. Roisin had made a gun of her forefinger and thumb and pretended to shoot herself in the head. Sometimes, there is too much Trish Pharaoh in her life. By the time McAvoy hung up, Roisin was making a noose out of her dressing-gown belt. Still, he's pleased she's here. Her presence suggests he is doing things the right way. He is following the trail correctly. He has investigated murders on his own before and found himself constantly riddled with doubts and questions. Having Pharaoh here makes him feel like a policeman.

'Here,' she says, suddenly. 'Right.'

Dutifully, McAvoy turns the vehicle down a barely visible side road, hemmed on both sides with sycamore and ash trees. They follow the deserted road for half a mile, past a row of half a dozen houses whose occupants will probably be the last to hear about the end of the world.

'Pretty,' says Pharaoh appreciatively, as she glimpses the old church to her left. She succumbs to impulse and winds the window down, sticking her head out like a happy dog.

'Have I told you the story?'

'Yes,' says Pharaoh, abruptly. 'You have.'

They have arrived in the tiny hamlet of Watton. The nearest place with a post office or somewhere to buy milk is four miles away in Hutton Cranswick. The larger town of Driffield is a little further up the road. After that, East Yorkshire starts to become

North Yorkshire, and the house prices go up. McAvoy has never been here before, but plans to bring Roisin and a picnic. 'Bloody hell,' says Pharaoh, as they drive slowly through ornate brick gates and into a vast drive coated in round, shiny pebbles. 'Rather swish.'

The manor house is magnificent: all stone vaulting and turrets, tippy-topped towers and rounded, mullioned windows. In this light, it appears timeless, though McAvoy finds it hard not to imagine some medieval princess sitting at one of the dark windows, weeping and working on her tapestries as father and brothers practise swordplay in the grounds.

'Cost more than three million,' he says. 'I've requested a brochure.'

McAvoy parks the car in the shade of some tangled elderflower trees. He makes a note to tell Roisin the berries are coming early this year then steps from the car and listens to the silence. Wonders how one should knock on a door of this size. Whether he should go the kitchen entrance, like a tradesman.

Christ, Roisin would love this, he thinks.

It's a beautiful home, and yet carries with it an air of something vaguely unsettling. It is not so much the quiet, though the absence of noise is noticeable. It's the air. The heat seems more oppressive here. There is a whiff of something McAvoy recognises as rotting vegetation; like the bottom of a compost bin when it has been cleaned. Something remains here. Something lingering and powerful. McAvoy listens hard and can hear the sound of rushing water somewhere nearby. He hangs on to the sound. It seems to represent a place beyond the mansion walls. It represents escape.

As they approach the big front doors, a figure comes into

view. A young man in overalls and a lumberjack shirt is spraying the paved area in front of the giant front portico with what McAvoy takes to be weedkiller. A large canister of the stuff is strapped to his back and he has a hose in his right hand. He's whistling to himself, the wires from a pair of headphones dribbling out from underneath a dark baseball cap. McAvoy doesn't want to come upon him unaware so makes as much noise as he can as he approaches. Pharaoh has no such qualms, and merely yells 'Oi'. The man turns, startled. He's in his late twenties. Not bad-looking, but could do with a scrub. He pulls an earpiece out of one ear but leaves the other one in. He gives them a smile.

'Not open yet,' he says, and his accent is local.

Pharaoh pulls out her warrant card. Crosses the space between them. He gives her a quick once-over and his eyes linger on her breasts for no longer than anybody else's do.

'Superintendent,' he says, reading the card and looking impressed. He smiles, friendly and open. 'What's he?'

Pharaoh turns to look at McAvoy, trying to get his warrant card out of his waistcoat pocket and dropping his car keys all at the same time.

'Him? He's a defective sergeant. Don't try and pronounce his name. He's Scottish.'

The man looks at McAvoy, who is straightening his clothes. 'Rangers or Celtic?'

McAvoy pushes his hair back from his face. 'Ross County. I can only apologise.'

The man laughs. 'Better state than Rangers these days, at least. How the hell did they let that happen, eh?'

Pharaoh gives a wave of her hand, telling both men to stop talking about football. She looks up at the imposing building. 'Lovely place,' she says. 'You the groundsman?'

The man sticks out his hand and withdraws it when he sees the dirt on his knuckles. 'Groundsman? Nah. I'm a contractor. New owners have got a whole crew coming in next month to do the place up. I'm keeping it nice enough so that the MD can show his investors around as it stands. They're not short of cash, I'll tell you that.'

'I read on the Internet it had been sold . . .'

'Yeah, big company with a base in Sweden. Or Norway. One of those—'

'Sweden. Sceptre Healthcare.'

The man rummages around in the pocket of his overalls and finds a grubby card. He reads the name on it. 'Yeah, Sceptre.' He shows them the card. 'Bernt Moller,' he reads. 'He's my contact. Just told me to keep it nice, really. They've only been up here a couple of times but they had people in expensive suits with them. It's going to be fancy. I've seen the plans.'

Pharaoh looks at the card, and in the corner of her eye sees McAvoy taking down the name and number in neat handwriting.

'It's not going to house nutters any more, then?'

The man gives a laugh, showing slightly crooked teeth and silver fillings. 'Last of them were long gone by the time I got this contract.'

'And it's going to be an old folks' home?'

'Don't let them hear you say that! I've seen the brochures. They love their marketing speak, it's all respite care and quality of life and fancy words to try and get you to part with your cash.

Going to be lovely, though.' He gestures at the house. 'Couldn't not be, really. Gorgeous place.'

McAvoy looks around him. Through a line of lime trees he spots an outbuilding with a red slate roof. He can see a faint line of what looks like barbed wire above loose brickwork.

'Outbuildings come as part of the sale?'

The contractor looks puzzled. 'I just stop the weeds growing through the cracks and pull the leaves out of the gutters. Why do you ask?'

McAvoy shrugs, and then realises he doesn't like being the sort of person who answers a question without words. 'I heard there had been an incident here. When it was still in the hands of the old owners.'

'No idea, mate. Is that what you're here for?'

Pharaoh kicks a pebble with the toe of her biker boot. She seems to be mulling something over.

'I'm Trish, by the way,' says Pharaoh, with the practised ease of somebody who knows how best to get men on her side. 'You are?'

'Gaz,' he says, with a smile. 'Gary. Reeves.'

'A pleasure, Gaz. We were rather hoping to speak to somebody who used to work here. A psychiatrist. He was a very senior figure here a few years ago.'

Gaz rubs a hand over his jaw. His face implies that he would love to help but can't.

'There's still some of the old stuff in boxes,' he says, after a pause. 'Belonged to the old owners. May be some names and addresses. If you ring that Swedish bloke he would probably say to help yourself.'

Pharaoh looks at him for a moment, then swallows, letting a smile creep onto her face. 'Already phoned him, Gary. Just now. Nice chap, isn't he? Loves pickled herring, apparently. Got a poster of Freddie Ljungberg on his desk. Reads a lot of Wallander. Says it's fine. Just to go right in. You probably heard me.'

Gaz's smile matches Pharaoh's. He looks like the sort who enjoys giving the rules a slight tweak. He looks as though he had been expecting a boring day and now has the opportunity to give himself a story to tell in the pub tonight.

'Was he sitting in an Ikea chair?' he asks, enjoying this. 'Blond. Drives a Volvo . . .'

'That's the chap,' says Pharaoh. 'We good?'

Gaz nods. 'I'm going for a bacon roll in a bit anyway. Door's open. Load of cardboard boxes in the second office to your right. I'm sure he told you that.'

Pharaoh reaches out and puts a hand on his forearm. 'Word for word.'

Gaz crunches away across the gravel, towards a small blue Transit van parked in the shade of the far wall. A moment later, he's reversing out and heading through the gate.

'Coming?'

McAvoy has a finger in his ear and his phone to the side of his head. He's reading the dirty business card in his hand and having no luck getting in touch with Bernt Moller. He leaves a message with a secretary with a better English accent than his own and mentions that Gary Reeves had told them to go right ahead.

Pharaoh is standing in the doorway of the great stately home, leaning against the cool stone. 'Does it suit me?' she asks, gesturing at the mansion. 'Think I would fit in here?'

McAvoy stands beside her and turns to take in the view.

Examines the grounds, the church, the tumbledown outbuildings and the lime trees that veil the barbed wire.

'Lady of the manor,' he says, nodding. 'I can see it now. You married the owner and he died on your honeymoon night. Now you offend all the old-money posh nobs and have elaborate parties here with your husband's money.'

Pharaoh laughs appreciatively and plays along. 'And you can be a Scottish laird, visiting from the Highlands. You're here to persuade me to buy five hundred acres of quality sheep-farming land. This evening I'm going to get you drunk on old wine from the cellar and persuade you to do a handstand in your kilt.'

McAvoy busies himself putting his notebook away. 'It's always the kilt with you, isn't it, Guv?'

Pharaoh turns her back and enters the cool of the porch. 'You should wear one for work. Would be something to threaten the villains with during interviews. Can you imagine? "For the benefit of the tape, Detective Sergeant McAvoy just waggled his bollocks at the suspect. The suspect is crying."'

They cross a wooden parquet floor past the deserted reception desk. It's a cool, airy place with high ceilings and dangling chains that have clearly been used to support chandeliers. It has the air of a Tudor castle: its owner imprisoned for heresy and his buildings left to fall into disrepair. The light does not extend much beyond the open doorway but there is enough of a glow for McAvoy to investigate the black and white photographs that still hang in brown wooden frames upon the drab magnolia walls. He and Pharaoh spend a few minutes using the lights from their mobile phones to stare into crowd scenes, to examine pictures of agricultural workers long dead, standing by hay bales and scowling below hats and moustaches. The images are a joyless jumble, all pixels and dead eyes.

Pharaoh pushes at a pair of mahogany double doors that swing open as she twists the brass handle. It's dark and cold inside, and smells old.

'This place would drive you mental even if you were sane,' mutters Pharaoh, shivering. 'Shut down for years, you said. How come I can still smell cabbage and disinfectant?'

She reaches up to the long panel of light switches and flicks half a dozen of them down. After a slight pause, the chandeliers crescendo into life, pitching a yellow puddle into the chilly space, spreading in a flood down the corridor.

Pharaoh carries on down the hallway with its chessboard floor and burgundy walls, to the staircase, which sweeps elegantly upwards.

Peaches-and-cream little girls in velvet dresses.

Stern patrician types in curled wigs and uncomfortable robes.

The place may have been a hospital but it feels like an abandoned stately home. Pharaoh looks as though she is considering sliding down the banister, then gives a shiver and comes back down, heading businesslike to the door she had been directed to.

'This one,' says Pharaoh, twisting a door handle. 'Oh bloody hell.'

'Guv?'

Pharaoh pulls a face. The door that Gaz had directed them to is locked.

McAvoy lets his disappointment show. He wants to try the handle himself, just to feel involved, but forces himself not to.

'Worth looking around?' he asks.

Pharaoh angles her head to peer up the stairs. She doesn't

look keen to spend any more time here. It feels old. The walls have soaked something up over the centuries and seem to be silently screaming that this building will be here long after they, and everybody else, has gone. McAvoy wonders what the patients thought when they were brought here. Some were willing, asking for help. Others had been sectioned by their families. Half a dozen had been sent by the courts, trying to ease the workload of busier and better-known facilities like Rampton.

Pharaoh screws up her face. 'Load of empty bedrooms and the lingering smell of cauliflower farts? No thanks. It's okay, we weren't sure what we were looking for anyway, were we? We're just bloody fishing.' She looks a bit dejected, suddenly. 'Let's go, eh? Ben Nielsen will have an address for the shrink by now anyway. And it won't be hard to find out where Hoyer-Wood is a patient, even though I don't know what we're expecting to find there either. Bloke's a cripple, you said.'

Discreetly, McAvoy gives the door handle a shake, for good measure. Were he to allow himself to try, he would be able to kick the damn thing off its hinges. But he knows he will not try.

A sudden vibration in his pocket causes McAvoy to give a tiny shout and Pharaoh begins to laugh as her sergeant retrieves his phone and blushes furiously. He speaks softly and quickly. Lays on the charm. Hangs up, smiling.

'Bernt Moller,' he says, by way of explanation. 'Very polite man, but asked if we would mind submitting our request through the proper channels. Told us that our new friend had overstepped the mark a little.'

'Reeves?'

'Yeah. Moller employed him by pure luck when he was on a site visit. I hope we haven't got him in trouble. Seemed a decent sort.'

'Well, we better hadn't upset the Scandinavians any further,' says Pharaoh, and threads her arm through his own. 'Come on.' He feels the heat of her, the closeness. Smells her. Hairspray and wine, perfume and perspiration.

He doesn't know what to say. What to do. Just feels himself colouring, and the hairs on his arm rising to scratch the strap of his watch.

'Excuse me, this is private property.'

McAvoy looks up as the double doors swing open. Two men in uniform stand outlined in the soft light.

'We're police,' says Pharaoh, pulling out her warrant card. 'Sorry. The gardener said to go straight in . . .'

The nearest man takes the warrant card from Pharaoh's hand and looks at it closely, then at her. He's young. Too young to scare anybody but not old enough to realise it.

'I've grown my hair since then,' says Pharaoh, pointing at the picture on the ID. 'You like it?'

'You be quiet,' says the second man. He's got a round belly and receding hair and there are short bristles sprouting from his red nose. Up close, there is enough of a similarity about the two men's eyes for McAvoy to think that they may be father and son. The logo on their uniforms is a bearskin hat, and the words 'Tower Security' are stitched in yellow onto their grey short-sleeved shirts.

'Easy now,' says McAvoy, stepping forward. 'We were just hoping to speak to somebody in charge . . .'

'There's nobody here yet,' says the older man. His face softens a bit. He's clearly relieved that the intruders are nicely dressed and aren't carrying anything that could be used as a weapon. He instructs the younger man to give Pharaoh her warrant card back. 'Sorry, we get no end of bloody trespassers.'

Pharaoh is sucking her teeth, unsure whether to accept the apology or beat the man to death for telling her to be quiet. She nods.

'We'd best get some air, eh?'

The four of them walk back into the light, the heat feeling like a physical barrier as they emerge from the cool of the reception area. As one, they stare up at the grey clouds. They are shifting. Rolling. Taking shape. Taking on the hue of rotten fruit and crackling with barely contained energy.

'Going to be one hell of a bloody storm,' says the younger security guard, breathlessly. 'Will give us an easier life though, eh?'

'You get much hassle, do you?' asks McAvoy, showing his own warrant card and finding that nobody cares.

The older man blows out demonstratively. 'Ramblers are no bother. There's a public right of way past the church, even though it's all bloody nettles and thistles and cow shit, so you wouldn't head up there for a picnic. It's the house itself that brings the nutters out. You know how it is. They read on the Internet about this abandoned asylum and get all these images in their mind. We've had loads of photographers trying to get in. Lick of paint and it could still be a mansion. You should have seen it back in the day. We just chase them away.'

McAvoy considers. 'You're on site all the time, then?'

The older man shakes his head. 'Head office is York but we have regional offices here and there. Two-man teams look after a few different properties. Me and the lad are based in Driffield. Got a call on the radio about a couple of intruders. We weren't far off so shot on over.'

Pharaoh and McAvoy exchange a look, picturing Gary Reeves. *Little git.*

Something occurs to McAvoy. 'You saw this place in its glory days, then?'

The older man nods. 'We've had the contract to look after it for years. Tower has been in business for decades. You've probably heard of us. We try and help the police where we can –'

'Did you work here fourteen years ago?' McAvoy breaks in.

'Boy was at school,' says the older security guard. 'I was still working the oil rigs.'

McAvoy gives up. He is about to thank them for their time when the older man speaks again.

'I live just up the road though, mate. Hutton Cranswick. If you're talking about the fire, I know a bit.'

McAvoy scratches his face. Controls his breathing. Stares at the grey sky and the bare brick, the barbed wire and the lime trees.

'Fire?'

'Yeah, not a big one. Just the old groundsman's cottage. The doctors had access to it, you see, for when they stayed over. Not much of a place to live, in the grounds of a nuthouse, but the shrink who had it seemed happy enough. Was a shame what happened.'

McAvoy coughs, knowing that when he speaks next, he is at risk of sounding feeble.

'A shame?'

The older man nods. 'One of the nutters went nuts, mate. Held one of the doctors and his family at knifepoint. The owners called security instead of the police, but by the time our lads got here it was all over. Horrible for the family, though. I got all the gossip from one of the old boys in the village. Was a bit of a balls-up all round, apparently . . .'

'The doctor had family with him?'

More nodding. 'I can't remember much more than that. Was amazing they kept it out of the papers, really. That was the beginning of the end, I think. Old owners put it up for sale not long after. Took years before this Swedish lot showed an interest.'

Pharaoh nudges McAvoy. Indicates he should shut up. 'How did it end?' she asks. 'The hostage situation?'

'Don't really know,' says the older man. 'Nobody really wanted to go into it. Was all very embarrassing. Mental units are supposed to have strict security measures, you see. Tower were the outside contractors. The owners' own psychiatric nurses would have been the ones in the firing line if it had got out. I'm just surprised it's taken you so long. Bit late now, though, I reckon. Shrink's long gone. I reckon the locals will like the place more as an old people's home, don't you think?'

McAvoy closes his eyes. 'The incident,' he says, softly. 'The night it happened. Could you tell us everything? We're investigating a murder. Two.'

The older man whistles. 'More than my job's worth, mate.' He looks at the younger man, then the two detectives. Gives a naughty smile. 'But it's lunchtime in a couple of hours. We drink in The Wellington in Driffield. Mine's a pint.'

Pharaoh smiles, and McAvoy breathes out. He watches the other two walk away. Stands here, on the steps to the manor house, his back to the forbidding structure where Sebastien Hoyer-Wood was a patient because his university friends convinced a judge he was crazy.

'Sebastien Hoyer-Wood,' he shouts, at their backs. 'You know the name?'

The security guards looks baffled. Shrugs. 'I'll check with the lads who worked here.' He looks at his watch. 'Pint. The Wellington.'

And they are gone.

McAvoy nods. Tries to walk down the steps to where Pharaoh is waiting, looking at him strangely. Behind her, he sees the dark clouds of the coming storm.

Detective Chief Inspector Colin Ray turned fifty last night. He celebrated at home, alone, in his flat in Hull's Old Town. There were two cards on his mantelpiece, both from mail order companies that valued his custom and wished him a very happy day of celebration. He drank four cans of beer, ate a chicken bhuna, texted a filthy joke to Shaz Archer and then masturbated half-heartedly over a picture in the *Hull Daily Mail*. The lucky recipient of his attentions was a local MP, fronting a campaign for better street lighting, and there had been something about her smile for the camera that had struck him as mucky. Not mucky enough, as it happened. He had gone to sleep half-pissed and frustrated, fingers coated in garlic and grease, cursing the MP, his mobile phone discarded next to him on a yellow-stained pillow. The call he had been hoping for never came.

Here, now, he can still taste the curry on his skin. Can pick out the flavour of spice and cardamom, in among the heavier aromas of nicotine and old booze. He's chewing on the fat of an index finger, gnawing on it, like a dog with a bone, squinting at a computer screen and breathing noisily through his nose. When he sat down at the desk there were half a dozen other officers in the room. They have gradually drifted away, to speak to witnesses or check in with informants, or go for a walk around the car park. Nobody wants to be near Ray when he's in this mood. Even Shaz Archer is giving him a wide berth.

He should be pleased, of course. They've just charged Adam Downey with conspiracy to supply a large quantity of Class A drugs and the evidence is pretty damning against the pretty boy in cell 4. He'll be denied bail, come the hearing on Monday morning. He'll be found guilty, should he have the temerity to deny the charges. Should he plead guilty, he'll still get hit with a few years in view of his previous offences. Ray has got a scumbag off the streets. He's put away a villain. He should be drinking the cheap whisky in his desk drawer and slapping backs as people tell him he's ace.

Instead, Colin Ray looks like he is about to tear his own skin off and start throwing it at people in great wet clumps.

Adam Downey isn't enough. Not nearly enough.

A few months ago, Ray spoke to one of the senior figures involved in the new drugs outfit. At that time, the group had just taken over all cannabis operations on the east coast, and successfully outmuscled the Vietnamese gangs that had previously been responsible for growing the crop. The new lot had simply moved in, and told the Vietnamese that they now worked for them. Even more remarkably, the Vietnamese bosses had complied. The foot soldiers and farmers who did not like the new arrangement were dealt with swiftly: hands nailgunned to their legs, chests turned to tar with a blowtorch. A few physically imposing enforcers kept an eye on things, and a handful of bright young chancers looked after deliveries and shipments. During his conversation with the voice at the other end of the phone, Ray had realised that the new outfit had plans. They were never going to content themselves looking after a bit of cannabis production. They had moved in without any real resistance, and in Ray's mind that kind of victory could make an ambitious man feel invincible. The voice on the phone had warned Ray that it was in nobody's interests to look into their operations too carefully. He had made it plain that they were well informed, well connected, and had half of the Drugs Squad in their pocket. Ray hadn't given a damn. He'd ignored their bribes and gentle threats, and given the go-ahead on an operation that led to the unit's first significant arrest. Now he feels he has made another. It just hasn't had the domino effect that he'd hoped.

Last night, sitting in his boxer shorts and mismatched socks, he had expected his mobile phone to ring, expected threats or promises from a mysterious voice. But nobody had called. He is not given to self-doubt, but his conviction that Adam Downey is connected to the operation is starting to waver. Ever since the lad was brought in, he has been convinced that Downey is a mid-level operative for the new group. He's young, bright enough, and has met some proper villains while inside. He's been dealing in drugs since he was a teen, and the sheer quality and quantity of the cocaine found in his possession suggest to Ray that he is part of something big. But the bastard isn't giving them anything other than 'no comment'.

Ray pushes back his greasy hair and scratches at the psoriasis on the back of his neck, sending flakes of dead skin into the air. He sniffs and swallows the phlegm that appears in his mouth. He's fighting his instincts. Fighting the urge to go down to the cells and beat some answers out of Downey with his own shoes.

He is so wrapped up in his thoughts that it takes him a moment to register the vibration coming from his shirt pocket. At his age and with his diet, any trembling by his heart should be a cause for concern, but Ray is smiling as he pats at his chest, and removes the old-fashioned mobile. Number withheld.

'Colin Ray.'

There is silence at the other end of the phone, and then a familiar voice: accentless and perfectly enunciated.

'Mr Ray. A pleasure to speak to you again. Allow me to apologise for the unforgivable delay between our last conversation and this one. We have been extraordinarily busy and there has been no opportunity for indulgences.'

Ray sits back in his chair, a broad smile on his face. He's remembering their last chat, sitting in the front of an umarked car down Division Road, rain beating on the roof and steam rising from his clothes, Detective Superintendent Adrian Russell shitting himself in the driver's seat as Ray took the phone from his hands and put the call from his colleague's paymaster on loudspeaker.

'Now then, lad,' says Ray, warmly. 'You're right. It's been a while. And yeah, you've been busy. Onwards and upwards, I see.'

'A business has to expand or it stagnates, Mr Ray. Running water is so much fresher and more vibrant than a static pool, would you not agree?'

Ray sticks a finger in his ear and inspects what he finds, rubbing it on his suit trousers. 'Never thought about it, son. My mind's a bit busy right now. Just charged a young lad with conspiracy to supply. Seriously good quality, the stuff he had on him. Must be worth a fortune.'

There is a silence at the other end of the line. Then the slightest suggestion that the caller is taking a discreet sip of liquid. In the background, the softest of sounds – china on china, cup on saucer; the extinguishing of a cigarette into a clean ashtray.

'You have probably never seen the like, Mr Ray. Even during your time working in the Met. Even when you lived in that flat in Maida Vale with the Polish lady whom your senior officers did not know about and whom you met during a six-year undercover operation that ended in disaster. Not even when they moved you up to Newcastle to keep you out of the way and you beat a suspect half to death in the custody suite. Even then, you will not have seen a product like the one that was spilled all over the floor of the premises on Southcoates Lane.'

Ray shrugs, though nobody can see. 'My CV has its ups and downs. Like your lad. Downey.'

'Yes, indeed. My associates are of course aware of the young man to whom you are referring . . .'

'Whom?' says Ray, mockingly. 'Public schoolboy, you, I reckon. Definitely got breeding. That narrows it down a bit . . .'

'Mr Downey,' continues the voice, as though there has been no interruption, 'is a young man for whom we had some hope of future advancement. This week's development was most unfortunate.'

'Yeah, that's the word. Unfortunate. If I'd lost one of my main guys and a packet of pure coke, I'd call it a bit more than that, my lad.'

There is more silence. Ray wonders if this will be it. Whether there will be more. He suddenly feels empty at the thought of the call being terminated. He wants to talk. Wants to tell this supercilious bastard with his perfect vowels that he's worked it out.

'Shall I tell you something?' he asks, suddenly sitting forward in his chair. 'I've been thinking about you lot. Thinking about you a lot. Where you came from. What you do. I've been thinking about the way you marched in and turned every Vietnamese cannabis factory into your own personal operation. The way you kept the workforce. I've been thinking about what you did to those poor bastards who said they were going to talk. And I reckon I know how it works. It's a hostile takeover, isn't it? And you can carry those out with only a few guys. I reckon you look at which organisations are profitable, and instead of setting up a rival business, you just take over the one that works. You scare the shit out of the top dogs, and tell them they can carry on and pay you a handsome cut, or you can put them in the ground. It's a beautiful system, matey. I reckon with the right information and a few good lads you could have half the established gangs in Britain paying you protection money. How am I doing?'

There is a lengthy pause before the man speaks again. When he does, there is a note of humour to his voice. 'That sounds like a great deal of conjecture and guesswork, Mr Ray. But I admire the scale of your imagination. I'm sure my associates will too. However, if that is indeed the case and they are only a few individuals with vision and guile, why would they show any interest in the young man in your cells?'

Ray spits in the mesh waste-paper basket. Watches the phlegm slide down the inside of a polystyrene food carton. Sniffs, and scratches at his neck.

'I'll tell you that when you tell me why you are ringing,' he says, wetly, into the phone. 'If you're ringing to suggest that we somehow lose interest in Adam Downey, then I reckon it's because your organisation is bright enough to know that loyalty has to be earned. We already know that Downey worked for a dealer around here for years. He supplied on street corners then got a bit more of a reputation and started dealing wholesale. If your outfit has taken over the gang he used to work for, Downey will know about it. He might even have done the killing himself. I reckon his old boss is in the ground. I think during his last stretch inside, one of your bright things got in touch with him and promised him the earth if he showed a little ambition. That's how you lot work, isn't it? You look at the individual. You look at what they want. And you find a way to give them it. That's how it worked with Aidy Russell, I'm guessing. You realised he was an ambitious officer and you gave him enough information to get him some good headlines, and the price was that he left you alone.'

The caller breathes out, slowly. 'There are so many more people willing to assist us in our endeavours than your friend the detective superintendent, Mr Ray. As you say, my associates have an uncanny ability to find out what matters most to people. We are all about the individual. And Mr Downey is an individual who has demonstrated loyalty. We would not be particularly effective employers were we to then turn our back on him for making an error of judgement.'

'Storing his gear in a sewing shop, you mean?'

Another pause, then: 'He was demonstrating original thinking. We prize that, even when the results do not go as hoped.'

Ray taps his fingers on the phone at his ear, slowly, deliberately. He fancies it will be irritating to the man at the end of the line.

'So you're ringing to ask me to go let him out?' asks Ray, smiling wide enough to show the pastry crumbs in his back teeth.

This time, the man allows himself what could almost be called a laugh. 'No, Mr Ray. I am ringing to tell you that Adam Downey will be released within the week. He will not talk to you. Nothing you can do or say to him will change that. I am aware of the conversations you have had with some local hooligans with regard to Mr Downey's incarceration. I can assure you that Mr Downey's brief time at Her Majesty's Pleasure will not be the purgatory you envisage. Nobody is going to threaten him, Mr Ray. Nobody is going to lean on him. If you check your call log in around twenty minutes, you will see that two members of your CID will be on their way to Hull Prison, where one of the inmates of your acquaintance was found, moments ago, in the shower block, with nails through his hands and knees. A most unfortunate incident. I am ringing to tell you that while some people are resistant to change, others embrace it. These are changing times, Mr Ray. I am ringing out of courtesy, because there is something about your intractable demeanour that some of my associates find charming. More than anything else, I am ringing to apologise for not sending you a birthday card. You made a sad sight, sitting there alone. I do hope that by next year, you have somebody to share it with.'

Ray's smile fades. He clears his throat.

'Do you think I'm scared of you, son?'

The line goes quiet. There is a suggestion of a cigarette being lit.

'No,' comes the voice, finally. 'You have nothing for us to threaten. You have no money and no children. You have your pension and will be dead by the time you are sixty even without our intervention. You would not respond well to promises of remuneration and you treat your body far more poorly than anybody in our employ could.'

'So what are you going to do with me, eh, son?' Ray asks it with a laugh, but it sounds weaker than before.

'Nothing, Mr Ray. We will simply tolerate you. You are not important enough to care about.'

Ray's fist slams on the desk. The computer shakes, a coffee mug falls. The sound bounces off the walls of the empty room.

The call is terminated with a click.

Ray shouts expletives until he can think of nothing else to say. Then he throws his phone at the wall. The smash isn't enough. It hasn't made a dent in what he is feeling. He picks up the swivel chair and knocks his computer from the desk with it in a shower of glass and crumbling plastic. He pants, hands on his knees. Feels the demon sloshing around in his belly.

Makes up his mind.

Then he heads down to the cells.

He heads for Adam Downey.

Ray manages to look sane for the briefest of moments. He winks at the desk sergeant and grunts something about needing to ask a few extra questions.

The uniform hands him a bunch of keys.

Here.

Now.

Cheap shoes, clip-clopping on green linoleum. Pausing at a metal door. A stained hand pulling down the grille. A yellow, bloodshot eye staring at the handsome little bastard who has refused to talk for three fucking days . . .

Ray opens the door. Enjoys the look of panic on the young lad's face. Then he wraps the key-chain around his fist.

A moment later, the silence of the custody suite is broken by a guttural, agonised shout. There is the sound of skin on skin. Boots on flesh. There is the rattle of a key-chain, the wet thud of metal striking something soft and vulnerable.

And then the desk sergeant and half a dozen uniformed officers are running into Adam Downey's cell, dragging a bloodstained, sweat-streaked Colin Ray into the corridor by his arms and legs. Somebody presses the alarm; a high-pitched wail shrieks from the speakers on the wall. The prisoners in the adjoining cells start to shout. To bang on their cell doors.

Adam Downey lies on the floor in a pool of his own blood, arms wrapped around his head, lacerations to his arms and chest; his expensive T-shirt ripped to the waist, his diamond earring dangling from a shredded earlobe.

And above the shouts and the alarm, Colin Ray's voice, filled with bile and madness:

'Tolerate that! Fucking tolerate that!'

11

Monday morning, 9.18 a.m.

The same room in the same health centre on the same road.

Too hot to breathe.

Aector McAvoy: bone-tired and unshaven, aching across his shoulders and back. He has bags under his eyes and plasters on the backs of his hands, and the blue suit he is wearing was chosen because it has the fewest creases rather than none at all. He's spent the weekend lifting furniture in and out of a removals van. Has carried mattresses and bed frames up flights of stairs and climbed in through a first-floor window with a wardrobe on his back while a crowd gathered on Hessle foreshore and shouted encouragement. He has spent two days struggling with cardboard boxes full of books and shoes and pots and pans, wrestling with a sofa that wouldn't fit through the bloody front door, despite the careful measurements he had taken when they viewed the place. Spent an hour with his fingers in an ice bucket borrowed from the Country Park Inn, after Fin decided that tickling Daddy while he carried a washing machine would be incredibly funny. This morning he selected his clothes from a suitcase and a variety of bin liners.

He is trying not to dwell on the fact that his socks don't match. He has already made up his mind never to move house again. He's exhausted and sore and doesn't want to be back here. Not back in this airless room, with its traffic sounds and buzzing flies and stupid plastic chair.

'It went okay, yes? The move? It was this weekend, wasn't it?'

Sabine Keane is giving him an encouraging smile. He tries to return it. This could be his last session, if he plays nicely.

'Hard work,' he says. 'I didn't know we had so much stuff.'

'You didn't get removal men in?'

'Sort of. A man with a van. I thought he'd be more help than he was. He was very good at drinking tea and smoking cigarettes.'

'So you did it all yourselves?'

McAvoy gives a laugh. 'Roisin was more of a foreman. She's not built for lifting sofas. She and Mel kind of directed . . .'

'Her friend, yes? You've mentioned her before.'

McAvoy clears his throat. Stares at his tie for a while. 'She's been through a bit of an ordeal. There was an incident at her shop. Had a bit of a set-to with a drug dealer and helped the police nab him.'

Sabine looks impressed. 'So you're tolerating her more readily?'

McAvoy wonders if his answer will lead to another note in his file. 'I don't dislike her. I never said that I did. And Roisin thinks she's great. Is that important?'

Sabine shakes her head. She looks up at the ceiling. Looks down, into her open handbag. Appears to be working out what to say.

'This could well be your last session, Aector. If I count the last one.'

She says it with a smile. Warm and friendly. McAvoy nods, hopefully.

'Yes?'

She sighs. 'I'm not sure you've really told me anything.'

McAvoy looks frustrated. He opens his mouth and makes gestures with his hands, then breathes out as if this is all too much. 'What would you like to hear, Sabine? I'm fine. I'm investigating two murders. I'm doing my job.'

'But you feel better *because* you are investigating murders, Aector. What if there were no murders to investigate?'

He looks at her, perplexed. 'I don't think we need to worry about that. This is Hull. And people will always be horrible to each other.'

She persists. Sits forward in her chair. Adjusts the strap on her sensible sandals then gives him her full attention. 'How would you define yourself if not for your job? That's what I mean.'

He doesn't understand. 'But I *am* a policeman.'

'And what does that mean?' she asks, probing deeper. 'What does being a policeman mean to you?'

McAvoy wants to stand up. Wants to pace. 'Is this about duty again, because we've talked about that—'

'What I want to know, Aector, is whether you are a policeman first and a human being second, or whether there is room inside you for both.'

McAvoy turns to her, wondering what she is trying to get him to say.

'You've broken the law, yes? You've hinted at doing something bad when you and Roisin met. You have been present when people have been killed. You can talk about these things in here, Aector. You're safe.'

He looks at her, hard. Looks at this middle-aged woman in her cream dress and frizzy hair, her visible panty-line and her untended nails. He does not see her as a safe repository for his secrets. Were he to meet her in the street he would not take it upon himself to tell her what he did to the men who attacked Roisin as an adolescent. And yet, she is right in what she says. This room is safe. Her report to his senior officers will only declare that he is not suffering from any mental illness and is fit for duty. Were he to unburden himself, he would not lose a friend. He does not mind if she judges him harshly. This is a confessional. A place to give voice to the thoughts and feelings of guilt that sometimes threaten to eat him up.

'Aector, you're safe. I don't want anything from you. I want to help you. This case you are investigating now must be taking its toll. You have so much to think about. You can't rely on Roisin for everything.'

McAvoy looks away. She is right, of course. He expects too much of his wife, though she never fails to give him what he needs. She is his confessor. She is his sounding board. She is his whole soul. And yet he cannot tell her everything, for fear of reminding her of darker times. Cannot discuss how he feels about the day he found the farm boys raping a twelve-year-old traveller girl. Cannot tell her what he did to them for fear of changing the way she views him.

He rubs a hand through his hair. Sabine has begun talking again but he is not listening. He finds his thoughts turning back to Friday's meeting in The Wellington in Driffield. His chat over a couple of pints of real ale with the two security guards. The older man had introduced himself as Jimmy Forsythe. Taken a pickled egg from the jar on the bar and devoured it in a bite.

Took his pint, found a table, and gave McAvoy and Pharaoh the lot. Told them what the lads at Tower Security knew about what happened at the facility. There had been no dazzling revelations, but Pharaoh considered the cost of a couple of pints to have been money well spent. They are building up a picture of Sebastien Hoyer-Wood and his friend Lewis Caneva. It is becoming clear that the rapist was neither as injured nor as mentally ill as his old university friend claimed. He seemed to have lived with Caneva and his family more as a house guest than as a patient at the neighbouring asylum. And something had happened that had broken up this cosy arrangement and sent Caneva into a tailspin.

Caneva is the man they want next. Ben Nielsen has found an address for him and McAvoy will be heading there as soon as he has got this last session with Sabine out of the way. He's going alone. Pharaoh is back at the station, fighting fires. ACC Everett is attempting to suspend DCI Colin Ray from duty for beating the shit out of Adam Downey in the cells. Downey has spent the weekend in Hull Royal Infirmary and has a bail hearing this morning. The top brass are doing their damnedest to keep quiet what happened, but Downey's solicitor is threatening to blow the whole lot in his address to the court unless bail is agreed to. Ray has made an almighty balls-up and played into the hands of whoever pays Downey's wages. The case is likely to collapse before it ever gets before a judge.

'Aector?'

McAvoy sighs. Closes his eyes and tries to keep his breathing steady.

'She thinks I killed them,' he says, and is surprised to hear himself speaking. 'Thinks I put them in the ground.'

Sabine's eyes widen.

'And did you?'

McAvoy looks at the floor. Gives the slightest shake of his head.

Confesses his greatest sin and is surprised to discover that he still has tears to shed.

It's just before one o'clock, and on Hull's Princes Avenue a blue Peugeot 306 is sitting in stationary traffic, waiting to turn left. On its roof is a large sign, advertising the services of the man at the wheel. It boasts of a 90 per cent first-time pass rate and promises that the first two lessons are free. Godber Driving School is written in a sporty-looking font, though to call the company a 'school' may be an overstatement. Allan Godber has no colleagues, though he has plenty of students. Allowing himself this hour for lunch is a luxury.

As he sits waiting for a gap in the traffic, Allan Godber hits himself in the chest with the flat of his hand. He swallows hard, neck bulging like a bullfrog's. He makes his hand into a fist and strikes himself in the ribcage. Manages half a belch. He screws up his face at the taste and spits like a baby trying solids for the first time. He reaches into the pocket of his jeans and finds a loose antacid tablet among the coins. He takes his eyes off the road for a moment, checks the chalky pill for any obvious fluff, then pops it in his mouth. He chews it up and swallows, wishing he had a glass of milk to chase it down with. Then the weight settles back on his chest.

During his last visit to his GP, Allan had been told he was suffering with gastro-oesophagal reflux disorder. It was a more satisfying title for the condition than the 'heartburn' that his wife had diagnosed him with. Allan also discovered that he more than likely had something called a hiatus hernia as well. They won't know until next month, when he goes to Castle Hill Hospital for an endoscopy. He's not looking forward to the procedure. He still knows a lot of the staff at the hospital, and doesn't want to know which of his mates will be knocking him out and sticking a tube down his gullet. He knows them too well to believe that they won't take a liberty or two while he is unconscious. He imagines himself coming round from the procedure to find himself naked in a corridor with the name of his least favourite football team scrawled in permanent marker on his chest.

Allan misses his old job. Misses the camaraderie and his mates. He gave seventeen years to the Ambulance Service, but when the last voluntary redundancy scheme was announced he saw a chance to get out and retrain in something that didn't involve quite so much blood, guts and night shifts. He's been a driving instructor for four years now and doesn't hate it. The money's okay, he's patient enough to tolerate the pupils, and he hasn't had to pick up any body parts or restart someone's heart in an age. The only downside is the rather sedentary nature of his job. He spends all day sitting down. He's put on three stone since quitting the service, and the gastric problems are clearly linked to his increasing waistline. Still, he's not a bad-looking guy. Despite being bigger than he was, he's not noticeably fat and has most of his hair, which he keeps in a short and fashionable style. He wears T-shirts with the right logos and buys the kind of jeans that his two teenage sons don't sneer at. He's in okay condition, and smells of an aftershave that his female students have admired from time to time, while his prescription sunglasses carry the same designer emblem as his underpants. He looks like he's doing alright, generally speaking, though he does not see himself as any kind of catch or Romeo. It's hard to woo women or charm your way into somebody's pants when there's a risk of you burping sick every thirty seconds.

Allan turns the car onto Park Avenue, his back to Pearson Park. On a hot, muggy day like this, the park will be full of foreigners playing football and students lying on towels, drinking bottles of pear cider and trying to feign interest in textbooks. Kids will be taking it in turns to laugh and cry in the swing park, grazing their knees on rocks, coming off the slide too quickly and spraining their ankles, bumping heads or falling from railings onto the woodchip floor. As a paramedic, he has been called to that park too many times to think of it fondly. He once had to pop a three-year-old girl's shoulder back into place after she grabbed hold of a spinning roundabout. He'd tried to be as gentle as he could but she had still screamed. Her dad had still stood there crying in front of him and saying it hadn't been his fault, it was just an accident, these things happen . . .

Allan burps again. Grimaces. Rubs his chest.

It's been a normal morning. He's given three hour-long lessons and navigated his way through the traffic from one side of the city to the other without messing up his schedule by more than a couple of minutes.

The car glides past the shabbily grand houses on the wide, tree-lined street. The Avenues is the Hull address that everybody wants if they choose to remain inside the city boundary and not head for the suburbs. The parking's a bloody nightmare and a few too many of the three-storey dwellings have been converted into flats, but these are still mightily impressive homes and he is proud to call one his own. Allan lives on Ella Street, which is not, technically speaking, an Avenue. But it's close enough for him to share a postcode with those in the slightly larger properties that run parallel to his own.

There are no other vehicles around, but Allan indicates his intentions anyway. He checks his mirror and his blind spot, then slowly turns, in first gear, past a large detached house and into a row of lock-up garages. On foot, he is three minutes from home, and believes the lock-ups are well worth the tenner a week he pays by direct debit to a landlord he has never met. His car is his livelihood, and while there is on-street parking on Ella Street, there is also the occasional gang of on-street teenage wankers to worry about, and he can't relax worrying that somebody will rip the wing-mirrors off or write 'knobhead' on his advertising boards.

Allan swallows again and gives another little shudder. He's sick of tasting his own insides. He had always presumed that the condition was a result of stress, but his current job is considerably easier than the one he did for seventeen years. He has a pretty easy life. He only has another nine years to go on the mortgage, his children are doing okay at school, he gets a fortnight in Majorca every August and he doesn't dislike his wife. They'll still get away at Christmas too, having recently earned a minor windfall. The money they had been saving up to repoint the brickwork at the back of the house had turned out to be far more than was necessary, after Allan found a contractor who would do the job for next to nothing, cash in hand. If Liverpool would buy a decent centre forward and Cheryl Cole could be persuaded to send him a picture of her in her knickers, he would have everything he could ask for.

The row of garages is deserted, as ever. There are half a dozen on either side of the central area, all with rusty blue doors and

their numbers spray-painted freehand in their centre. Allan
pulls up next to his own garage. He looks out and decides, once
again, that the tenner a week is worth it. Sure, there are a few
potholes in the tarmac and somebody has dumped a mattress
on top of the industrial bin at the far end, but it's nice to have
a little space to call his own and where he knows the car is safe.
Sometimes, when the kids have friends over and the noise is too
much, he'll come and sit here and read the paper, alone in the
cool and the dark.

He steps out of the car, giving a grunt of exertion as he moves
his right leg for the first time since he got in the vehicle at 8.30
a.m. He crosses the small patch of tarmac, pulling the garage key
from his pocket. Puts it in the padlock and turns. Unhooks the
padlock from the rusted metal loop. He raises the garage door,
up and over, then reaches inside to pull the cord that brings the
bare bulb on the far wall to life.

As he turns to head back to his vehicle, there is a movement
in the periphery of his vision. A crunch of boot on broken stone.
There is a moment in which he feels unbalanced, half-turning,
feet in opposite directions, knee twisted, hands flailing. And
then he feels a blow to the back of his head.

Allan pitches forward, into the empty garage. For a moment
he wonders if the door has come down and struck him, but he
cannot remember hearing the metallic clang. He wonders why
he is considering this. Why here, now, he is giving it any thought
at all.

There is another blow, and suddenly Allan is not thinking
about much any more. He is on his face on a cement floor,
smelling dust and diesel. Over the rushing of blood in his ears,
he hears the distinctive grating of the garage doors closing. He

tries to right himself, but his limbs don't seem to be responding to his commands. He feels fingers in his hair then hands upon his shoulders. Feels himself being turned over onto his back. His eyes flutter open, but then a fist closes around his short hair and his head is cracked back onto the floor. After that he keeps his eyes closed.

Allan feels as though he is swimming inside his own skin, oblivious and helpless. He feels his shirt being torn away, ripping from the buttons through the expensive logo. There is a pause. Nothing. No sound, no sensation, and then he feels a tightening of the skin on his chest. He wants to raise his head. Wants to see what is happening to him, but he can taste blood and his head feels too heavy and his body is not his own any more.

Suddenly, in the darkness, there is a voice. A robotic, inhuman thing. He cannot make out the words, but they seem familiar, somehow. He struggles up. Raises himself on his elbows. Sees a figure, crouching at his side, an open plastic box beside him. The figure is raising its arms, frustrated and angry. The metallic voice is calling for medical assistance.

Allan tries to speak, and the bubbling sounds that come from his lips cause the figure to raise its head. For an instant, the merest fraction of a second, Allan sees a familiar face. Sees features he knows, twisted into anger and madness.

Then words, bestial and screeching, echoing off the bare brick walls.

And the figure is upon him, the plastic box gripped in its hands, the weight and the cold and the tight sensation still upon Allan's skin.

Allan looks up, and sees the figure raise the object over their heads. For a second, he sees an image from a movie, playing in his mind. Sees an ape, holding a club in front of a blue sky, smashing a skull against uneven rocks.

The impact of the first blow breaks his nose and fills his eyes with blood.

After that, he is not really Allan any more.

Part Three

Part Three

12

It started raining as McAvoy crossed the Pennines, a sudden downpour hitting the glass a mile before the Lancashire border. He passed into the storm as if driving into a waterfall, watching in his rear-view mirror as Yorkshire's green and brown slopes were abruptly snatched away.

The rain felt wonderful. It was good to open the window and let the droplets run in. He has baked in oppressive heat for weeks and the cool breeze and damp air had felt both cooling and healing as they touched his flesh and drenched his clothes. By the time he reached the Chester city limits, the novelty had worn off. The car was steaming up, he was shivering inside clothes soaked with both sweat and rain, and he had the beginnings of a headache from squinting through the wall of water at the brake lights of the car in front.

He rubs his temples. Kneads his forehead. Pinches the bridge of his nose. He looks like a Plasticine man trying to disguise his identity.

On the passenger seat, his mobile phone is barking out lefts and rights, and he is grateful for its help. With the windscreen made opaque by the deluge, he would have no chance of spotting the road signs without the metallic tones of the satnav. He's only been to Chester once before. Fin was still in a pushchair and he and Roisin had thought he might like to see the elephants at the impressive city zoo. The boy had slept the entire time. Roisin and McAvoy had enjoyed it just the same. They'd had a picnic in the bat cave and gone home owning one more okapi than they did when they woke up. Roisin had fallen in love with the curious striped creature, half-giraffe, half-zebra. She'd felt compelled to adopt one, and still receives monthly updates on its well-being. All in all, it had been a nice day.

'In 100 yards, turn left . . .'

The row of shops is a jumble of damp colours and swirled shapes. He glimpses a convenience store and a takeaway then turns the car abruptly into a quiet side road. He cruises past a school at less than 5 mph, nosing the people-carrier over a speed bump, then turns right twice more and finds himself edging down a quiet street of semi-detached homes. It's early afternoon, so most of the homeowners are at work, their empty driveways and unlit front rooms testament to the emptiness of each property. McAvoy squints and makes out a house number on the brick wall by a white-painted front door. Consults his notes and follows the curving road another hundred yards. He pulls in outside number 17 and leans across the passenger seat, opening the electric window as he does so. He stares through the rain at Lewis Caneva's home.

It's an unremarkable property. Three bedrooms, a small front garden screened by tall green trees, and a boxy Fiat on the brick drive.

Craning his neck he sees a face appear at the downstairs window.

Sees peach curtains moved by a timid hand.

Sees the bone-white of Lewis Caneva's skin.

McAvoy puts the window back up and switches the engine off. He looks at his phone, half-expecting there to be a message. There is none. Everybody back at the station is too bloody busy, fighting fires or trawling databases. Nielsen and Daniells have spent the weekend going goggle-eyed in front of computer screens, trying to come up with a list of anybody and everybody who had some involvement the night Sebastien Hoyer-Wood went through the window. They have managed to track down all the witnesses who gave a statement to the uniformed officers at the scene, and at McAvoy's suggestion, persuaded the Ambulance Service to give them the names of the paramedics who saved Hoyer-Wood's life. One is now living abroad and the other is a driving instructor in Hull. Daniells is trying to get in touch with him and two uniforms have been sent to his house, but so far he's off the grid. Were Pharaoh around she would no doubt be able to rustle up some extra resources, but Pharaoh is still locked away in a meeting room with ACC Everett, the Police Federation rep and Adam Downey's slick lawyer, trying to thrash out how best to play the case in the wake of Colin Ray's decision to beat the shit out of his client.

Downey is still in Hull Royal Infirmary and the legal situation is a mess. He has already been charged, but without a bail hearing he is in a state of limbo. It's likely that before the end of the day, magistrates will be instructed to give him bail, allowing him to walk free as soon as his injuries are healed. Where that leaves the case against him is anybody's guess. Pharaoh is trying to persuade Everett they should go ahead with the prosecution of Downey. Even Colin Ray has told them he is willing to take his punishment rather than let the little bastard go free. But Everett is unsure. He can see the headlines. He knows that Downey's legal team will tell the court all about what one of his senior officers did to him in the cells.

McAvoy steps from the car, his battered leather satchel above his head to try to block the rain. He slams the door and runs up the drive, sheltering against the wall as he raps on the wood. The colours change behind the opaque windows of the door and a moment later, Lewis Caneva is peering out.

From his file, McAvoy knows that Caneva is fifty-six years old, but the man in the doorway could be two decades older than that. He has a slightly Mediterranean look, but if he is as Italian as his name suggests, he has not aged like a Pinot Noir. He is bald on top, with a short horseshoe of white hair running from just behind his large ears. He's wearing dust-speckled glasses, and there are broken blood vessels and purple mottling across his cheeks. His skin puts McAvoy in mind of church candles. Small patches of grey hair sprout below his nose and below his jawline, and it looks as if he has shaved haphazardly or in the dark. For a moment, McAvoy wonders if this is true. Wonders whether Caneva struggles to look at himself in the mirror for any length of time.

'Sergeant McAvoy,' says Caneva, closing his eyes and sighing. 'You made good time. Please. Come in.'

There are long pauses between Caneva's words and he sounds breathless, his chest and throat bone dry. McAvoy rubs his boots on the plain welcome mat then follows Caneva down a short corridor with varnished wood underfoot. To his left is a staircase, a waterproof coat slung over the banister and two pairs of shoes on the bottom step. Caneva leads him into a small square living room. There is a two-seater leather sofa against one wall, facing an elaborate fireplace that houses an unlit, furnace-shaped wood-burner. The walls are decorated with what appear to be quality lithographs and sketches, all fine detail and pen-and-ink contours. There is no TV, but a variety of books lie scattered on the coffee table. As he stands in the doorway, McAvoy tries to glimpse their titles. They appear to be poetry books, though some of the text is laid out like prose. Caneva follows his gaze.

'Bit of a hobby,' he says. 'Analysing a few of the old Beat poets. Keeps me busy.'

McAvoy nods, unsure what to contribute. He vaguely remembers reading some Allen Ginsberg while doing his 'A' levels but fancies any attempt at demonstrating wisdom on the subject would end in tears.

'Please,' says Caneva, pointing to the sofa. 'Take a seat.'

McAvoy sits down awkwardly, watching as Caneva lowers himself painfully onto the seat next to him. It's an awkward position and McAvoy has to half-turn to look the man in the eye. This close, he can tell Caneva is not well. He's wearing two sweatshirts over a padded lumberjack shirt and still appears to be shivering. McAvoy wonders why he has not lit the fire. Notices, as he opens his mouth to speak, that his breath has begun to form crystals in the air.

'Dr Caneva,' he says. 'I'm grateful to you for agreeing to see me. As I explained on the phone . . .'

Caneva nods, telling him it's okay. 'You mentioned it was to do with a case I assisted with? As I explained to you, I am of course constrained by doctor–patient confidentiality . . .'

Now it is McAvoy who interrupts. 'I am fully aware, Dr Caneva. I appreciate you are in a difficult position and anything you say that breaches those rules would of course be inadmissible in court. However, I understand that you are no longer a practising psychiatrist, so at least you won't have the fear of breaching any professional code of ethics.'

For a moment there is silence in the room. McAvoy has decided not to make up his mind about the man who declared Sebastien Hoyer-Wood mentally unfit to stand trial. He does not want to prejudge him and therefore colour any information he gleans from this interview.

'It's very cold in here,' says Caneva, at length. 'I would have made up the fire but it wears me out. I'm not in the best of health, Sergeant.'

McAvoy looks at him, as kindly as he can.

'I could do it,' he says, shrugging.

'Could you?'

'No problem.'

McAvoy pulls himself off the sofa and kneels down in front of the fire. He does not speak as he twists newspaper into cones and assembles a triangle of kindling in the centre of the grate. He takes larger logs from the stack by the fireplace and a couple of pine cones, which he knows will burn like the devil as he touches a match to the paper. He wishes he had a little dried ragwort to add to the pile, the way his father taught him. The poisonous plant is one that fascinates him. Though it can kill horses, they seem to seek it out, nosing aside any quantity of verdant grass to nibble at the yellow-headed flower that can cause them an agonising death. McAvoy wishes he knew its Latin name, but never did that project at school. He makes a note to ask his dad.

'Lovely,' says Caneva, a slight smile on his face.

He sits back against the sofa cushions and watches the yellow flames take hold. Though it is not yet giving off warmth, the light in the room seems to have energised Caneva a little, and there is a healthier colour to his cheeks.

McAvoy returns to the sofa and prepares to speak, but Caneva beats him to it.

'Bowel cancer,' he says, unexpectedly, turning his head to McAvoy. 'Diagnosed six years ago. Two operations and a bout of chemo. They say I'm better now. Not cancerous, anyway. Not sure I feel it.'

'I'm sorry to hear that.'

'You imagine that once they've cut the cancer out everything will be back to normal, don't you? It's not like that. They messed about with me so much that my old life is gone. I don't mean to be rude here but I'm never off the toilet. Seriously. That's where they'll find me, when I go. I'll be on the toilet.' The smile drops. 'Not that anybody will be looking.'

McAvoy brushes the raindrops off his trouser legs. Rubs his hands through his hair. 'You don't get many visitors?'

Caneva shrugs. 'My daughter, couple of times a month. My son every few months. They'll ring. Birthday or Father's Day. But they have their own lives, I suppose.'

'Grandchildren?'

Caneva shakes his head. 'Not yet.'

They both sit and watch the fire, as if waiting for the other to spoil the nice warm glow that the policeman has brought to the room.

'You want to talk about Seb,' says Caneva, with a sigh.

'What makes you say that?'

'Just a feeling, I suppose.'

McAvoy looks at the older man. 'Is that something that psychiatrists believe in? Intuition?'

Caneva looks away.

'None of us are as clever as we think we are.'

After a moment, McAvoy nods. 'We're investigating two murders within the Humberside Police boundary. Both victims assisted in saving Sebastien Hoyer-Wood's life almost fifteen years ago in Bridlington. Our enquiries have led us to believe that Hoyer-Wood was a very dangerous man who was responsible for some very serious crimes. However, he has never been tried and never been jailed, and that was due in part to your testimony that he was mentally unfit to stand trial. At the moment, none of this makes a great deal of sense and we have no suspect and only half an idea, but I am of the opinion that you have some things to tell us about Sebastien Hoyer-Wood that may help. So, in essence, we're in your hands. It's very much a question of what you would like to tell me.'

Caneva looks away. Stares, through the net curtains, at the dark skies and the wall of water that beats against the houses and pavements of this quiet street. He looks back. At McAvoy. At the glow of the flame. At his books upon the coffee table, then down at his slippered feet on the peach carpet. His eyes close. He breathes, slowly, painfully. It is as if he is coming to an end.

'Dr Caneva?'

The older man turns to him.

'We were university friends,' he says, and has to cough when his voice comes out weak and reedy. 'Both studying medicine. Early Seventies, this was. I can't remember how we got talking. I think I was reading a book that he'd just seen the film of. Don't ask me what it was. But that was kind of typical of the pair of us.

Me, reading. Him enjoying the bright lights. Seb was kind of a big personality. He was a couple of years younger than me. I'd seen a bit of the world after finishing school and started university a little later than everybody else. Even so, we hit it off. We lived in different dorms for the first year but got a house together in our second.'

'And this was London, yes?'

Caneva nods. 'Yes, sorry. We're both southerners. I only moved up here to be near my son, after I retired and sold the house. I just live off the equity nowadays. The difference in prices . . .'

McAvoy waves a hand, and immediately regrets it. He should just let the man talk. To rattle on the way he wants. 'I'm sorry,' he says.

'No, no, you're right. You want to know about Seb. Well, we were friends. Best friends, if you can imagine such an old-fashioned concept. I was the quiet, bookish one, and he was all buzz and big bangs. He was very good-looking. Got a lot of attention from the ladies. Could have had anybody he wanted. I just don't think he wanted them. There was the odd girlfriend here and there but he wasn't really into relationships. Had a lot of female friends but didn't take advantage. I think that was partly what caused the incident.'

McAvoy's eyebrows meet. 'In Bridlington? Seriously?'

Caneva waves his hands. Seems to send his mind somewhere else. 'No, no. While at university. A girl. A fellow student. She tried it on with Seb. He politely declined. She was a real beauty, very vivacious and lively. She wore these little hippy dresses that drove people crazy. She wasn't used to being rejected. She went off in a huff and the next day she told her modern languages tutor that she had been assaulted. Sexually assaulted. I'm not saying she hadn't been, don't get me wrong. I'm just saying it wasn't Seb. He was with me all night. But Seb was the one she pointed the finger at. She didn't tell the police. Just told her tutor and he told the faculty of the university and Seb was brought in. He was shocked. Just didn't know what to make of it. It was like his whole world had fallen in. Seb's from an old family in Warwickshire. Military men, most of them. I think Seb had hopes of maybe serving as a doctor in the military when he finished his training. His dad was one of those really strict, distant types. I was with Seb when he called him to tell him what had happened. I had to listen in as he told his dad they were thinking of kicking him out and were advising the girl to go to the police . . .'

'What happened?'

Caneva rubs his hands over his face, pushes his cheeks back so it looks as though he is moving at speed. 'We changed courses.'

'We?'

'I wasn't doing very well in regular medicine anyway. I persuaded him to take the easy route and just get the hell out of there. Seb had shown a flair for physiotherapy. I felt psychiatry was something I could do well. The faculty were pleased to have the situation brought to a quiet conclusion.'

'And the girl?'

Caneva looks away. 'I don't know.'

There is silence in the room as each man absorbs the story. Finally, McAvoy speaks.

'You stayed in touch, yes? You both graduated and went on to decent careers?'

Caneva pulls a face. 'I did a little better than Seb,' he says, almost guiltily. 'I was a good psychiatrist. Got a job with a respected London firm straight out of university and specialised in several elite fields. I ended up as a partner in a practice in Bloomsbury. I married. Had two children. The right kind of life, or so they tell me.'

'And Seb?'

Caneva stares at the flame. 'He had his problems. I don't think he put himself back together really. He did okay in physiotherapy. Worked for a decent practice, met some interesting people. But there was a bit of him missing. That spark. We stayed in touch, of course. He spent a couple of Christmases with us. He was my son's godfather, though it took some persuading to get him to take the job.'

'He didn't want it?'

'Said he didn't deserve it. By then he had withered a little. He was drinking a little too much. I don't know whether he had started using drugs but I know that whenever we met, he would make jokes about him needing to see me for more than just my sparkling personality. Looking back, I should have seen that he was in trouble. I should have done more.'

McAvoy clicks his tongue inside his mouth. Thinks again of the crimes Hoyer-Wood went on to commit. 'You didn't think he was dangerous?'

'I wouldn't have had him near my family if I did,' he says, and his voice cracks on the word 'family'. He closes his eyes, tight. Controls his breathing. 'I knew he was depressed. I knew he was single and lonely. I should probably have had him to the house more often, but hindsight is a wonderful thing.'

'Your wife?' asks McAvoy, suddenly curious. 'How did she feel about your old university friend?'

'She knew him from university too. She liked him. Thought he was fun. But she saw the change in him too. Saw what a mess he was becoming.'

'And when you heard about his crimes?'

Caneva pinches the bridge of his nose. 'You have to remember that Seb was only ever charged with one incident. Despite the investigations of Humberside Police, there was no evidence he carried out any other crimes. So, when I heard about him breaking into a house in Bridlington and being viciously beaten by the homeowner, I had a very different picture in my mind from the one you currently hold. To me it was a cry for help. In my mind, he was the victim. Seb underwent surgery. He nearly died. And while he was under the knife, the police tried to build a case against him that would have put him in prison for a very long time. I visited him in hospital. He could barely speak. He couldn't move down one side of his body. They tried him with physiotherapy and he collapsed after every step. He had to defecate in a bag. This was not a man who needed prison. He needed help.'

McAvoy nods. 'So, you helped.'

Caneva breathes in, holds it, and then lets the air out of his lungs. 'For a while, my firm had been looking to provide a facility for the mentally ill. We wanted to set up a place for calm, quiet study that would be a relaxing, soothing place for the patients. I brought that initiative forward. I found premises in East Yorkshire. At that time, there was a high demand on existing provision for the criminally insane. It seemed obvious that there was money to be made for the company by getting Home Office approval to also take mental patients referred by the courts. Thankfully, one of our other partners had some old school connections that were able to fast-track the application. I was managing director and chief psychiatrist. I planned to maintain the Bloomsbury practice and provide a certain number of days at the premises in East Yorkshire.'

'And Seb?'

'He was still in hospital. Still barely able to communicate.'

'And yet you volunteered to compile the psychiatric report that went before the judge.'

McAvoy does not mean for his words to sound like an accusation, but there is little other way for Caneva to take them. He bristles a little.

'At that time, there was nobody better qualified in the country than me.'

'How did you conduct the interviews, given his difficulties?'

Caneva looks down. Begins to speak and stops himself.

'You didn't, did you? Didn't interview him at all?'

Caneva sniffs. Takes a handkerchief from his trouser pocket, but does nothing with it other than hold it in his palm.

'I'd known him for twenty years. It was obvious to me prison was no place for him. My facility was a healing place. A place where he would get well.'

McAvoy considers taking out his notebook, but decides not to. He wants to focus his gaze on the older man's eyes. 'And the judge agreed, yes? The criminal proceedings were thrown out.'

Caneva nods. 'We had the very best facilities. We brought in specialists to help with his physiotherapy, and obviously Seb's own skills and expertise were very handy with that. Once the court case was no longer hanging over him he could concentrate on healing. He made progress. He began to speak more freely . . .'

McAvoy nods. Runs his tongue around his mouth. Cracks his jawbone.

'Dr Caneva, I'm informed that you and your family eventually moved into the gamekeeper's cottage at your facility and that Sebastien Hoyer-Wood lived with you almost as part of the family.'

The accusation hangs in the air.

Caneva looks puzzled. Then he protests.

'That is simply not true, Sergeant. Yes, we had access to that lodge when I stayed in East Yorkshire for any significant time. Yes, I brought my family on occasion. And yes, after a time, I felt that Seb was well enough to begin a course of psychotherapy with myself, and we opted to conduct some of those sessions at my private residence . . .'

'But he was sent to a secure mental facility, Dr Caneva. That was the point. You can understand why some people may have issues with the idea of him spending so much time in a nice house with an old friend . . .'

Caneva raises a hand. He bristles. Scowls. His flash of temper has added some life to his features, and for the first time McAvoy can imagine this man in a sharp suit and designer glasses, sitting in a swish London consulting room.

'I had known him for twenty years!' barks Caneva. 'I knew best! The sessions were tremendously important and a safe, friendly atmosphere was crucial to that. People should leave it to the experts. People shouldn't judge . . .'

Now McAvoy pulls out his notebook. He flicks back a page and shows Caneva the date he has underlined twice.

'What happened that night?'

Caneva waves his hand again. Looks down at the floor. 'Without checking my diary, I couldn't honestly . . .'

McAvoy reaches across and puts a hand on Caneva's shoulder.

He forces the older man to meet his eyes. 'You know the date I'm referring to, Doctor.'

Caneva rubs his hand over his head. He takes off his glasses and holds them in his lap. McAvoy takes them from him, and cleans them with this cuff of his shirt. Wordlessly, he passes them back. Caneva nods his thanks. Purses his lips.

'It was just bad luck,' he says, at length. 'Seb was at the old gamekeeper's lodge with us. Our place. Tilia Cottage. We had been meeting once a week for several months. His therapy was going well. It was clear, at that stage, he had no memory of the incident in Bridlington or the alleged incidents before that. We were talking about his childhood. His relationship with his father. His dead mother. He had no siblings and grew up in a very isolated property. It was really quite surprising he was so gregarious by the time he came to university. It was obvious there was a lot of sadness in him. A lot of pain.'

'Anger?'

'There is anger in all of us. I am sure you know better than anybody that people are capable of things that come as a surprise to them.'

McAvoy gives an accepting nod. Wonders whether Caneva Googled him after he ended the phone call to arrange this interview. Whether the man has a computer and how he spends his time . . .

'And the night in question?'

Caneva sighs. 'One of the other patients made a run for it. I don't remember their name. They had a taste for arson, I remember that.'

'And Hoyer-Wood was at your home?'

'I received a call from the chief nurse. He told me what was happening. Told us to stay inside.'

'And then?'

Caneva breathes deeply. In the fireplace, a log cracks and the ash settles. A pine cone, half aflame, falls from the pinnacle of the fire to land in the grate. It burns, brightly and alone, then winks out.

Caneva lets his gaze drift to the ceiling then back to the fire. He closes his eyes.

'The house was set ablaze. We don't know why. The patient just wanted to see the smoke and the flames, I think. Just wanted to see some firemen.'

McAvoy sucks at his cheek.

'And Hoyer-Wood? Your family?'

'We got out. Seb was moving a little better. The nurses were able to talk the escaped patient into coming back inside. The fire was put out. Unfortunately it had already burned through a supporting wall, so it was declared structurally unsound and the property has since fallen into ruin and disrepair.'

McAvoy stares at him. Waits for more.

'Dr Caneva, it would seem that since that date, your life has taken something of a turn. Might I ask what happened?'

Caneva rubs his palm across his forehead. 'I had overextended the practice financially. We couldn't afford to run the facility and nobody wanted to buy it. At the same time my marriage was in difficulty. Things were hard at home. My wife's own mental health began to take a turn for the worse. It was a difficult time.'

'And your sessions with Hoyer-Wood?'

Caneva shrugs. 'I'm afraid that despite my best intentions and our long-established friendship, I had to curtail our sessions and find him alternative accommodation. A panel of psychiatrists declared that he was no longer mentally unstable but there was no appetite for reactivating the criminal case against him, and due to his physical difficulties he went to live at a private medical facility in the Lake District. We're no longer in touch, despite my best efforts. I know he suffered a major stroke some years ago. He began to suffer epileptic fits as a result of the damage to his brain, and one caused a severe stroke that left him paralysed.'

McAvoy has not taken his eyes off the side of Caneva's head. 'You went bankrupt?'

'I didn't have to, thankfully. The business did but I did not. I sold my home and moved to Chester. My son lived here, for a time. My daughter not too far away. She's doing very well in her career. A nurse, did I say? I had hoped to build some bridges.'

'There were problems?'

Caneva looks away. 'All children blame their parents, don't they? And they had a lot to blame me for.'

McAvoy looks at him, expectantly.

'Oh I'm sorry,' says Caneva, startled. 'I thought you would have that in your file. My wife died, Sergeant. It must be ten years now. More.'

'I'm sorry,' says McAvoy, and means it. Then, gently: 'How?'

Caneva closes his eyes. 'She took her own life, Sergeant. Pills. Enough pills to kill herself a dozen times over. She did not want to go on.'

He knows that Caneva is holding back but finds himself unable to bully this old, broken man. He wishes Pharaoh were here.

'Is that it, Sergeant?' asks Caneva, looking puzzled. 'Is that any help? I don't know anything about the incidents in Humberside.

I didn't know there still was a Humberside. I thought that all went with the boundary changes . . .'

McAvoy blinks, hard. 'We just kept the name,' he mumbles. 'Us and Radio Humberside. It's East Yorkshire on one side and North and North East Lincolnshire on the other. Bit unwieldy fitting that on a badge.'

Caneva manages a tired smile. 'So much pain,' he says, sadly, then looks at his watch, as though expecting the sergeant to say his goodbyes.

Instead, McAvoy gestures at the books on the table. 'This is just for fun, is it? You must miss the analysis. The sessions.'

Caneva looks a little more animated, sitting forward in his chair. 'I like getting inside people. Understanding them. Helping them understand themselves. Poetry is perhaps the human brain at its most exposed and honest.'

'Do you ever revisit old patients? In your mind, I mean.'

'Oh yes,' says Caneva, clearly thrilled to be talking about a subject he knows a lot about. 'I used to tape-record my sessions and have them transcribed. Sometimes, I will go through an entire transcript and something new will jump out at me . . .'

McAvoy swallows. 'Did you tape-record your sessions with Hoyer-Wood?'

Caneva stops, aware that his mouth has run away with him. Then he gives a half-laugh. 'I can't let you have them. It's not about never practising again. It's about your own code of ethics. Besides, I don't know if I could even find them . . .'

A sudden vibration in McAvoy's pocket alerts him to a text message. He opens his phone. Reads about the fate of Allan Godber. Beaten to death in a garage down the Avenues. A defibrillator machine found at the scene. Nothing left of his features save gristle and bone.

Suddenly, McAvoy's pity deserts him. His face becomes hard, his voice soft. Were Pharaoh to see him, she would not recognise him. Roisin would. She has seen him like this before. She was twelve, and bleeding, and the handsome constable with the ginger hair was smashing a wooden plank across the skull of a dying man . . .

'Dr Caneva,' he says, his jaw locked. 'Dr Caneva, it would be a tremendous help to me if you were to send the transcripts to the address on my card. I am not going to threaten you or appeal to your better nature. I am merely going to say that the doctor–patient privilege only extends so far. Sebastien Hoyer-Wood is alive. I am on my way to see him this afternoon. I feel he will make it clear that he has no problems with you sharing the transcripts with me. I know you have not been honest with me and I know that you are hiding many things, and I may never find out what they are. But people are dying and I feel that whatever sin you need to atone for could be atoned for now.'

McAvoy stands, placing a card on the coffee table. He towers over Caneva. Stares at the man until he looks away.

'Another man has died. The paramedic who saved Hoyer-Wood's life. This is no longer a theory. I know something happened that night and it cost you everything.'

He leans forward, his face in Caneva's, his breath upon his lips.

'Don't let it cost you anything more.'

Helen Tremberg has almost managed to persuade herself that she is suffering from a genuine virus. She has all the symptoms.

Sweats. Upset stomach. Sudden chills and uncontrollable shaking. She had felt almost unfairly treated when she phoned Shaz Archer this morning and said she was too ill to come in, only to hear her line manager give a snort of derisory laughter and tell her she was letting people down. It was only as she opened her mouth to defend herself that Helen remembered that her sickness is self-inflicted. Her mind, her heart, her conscience, are what is making her sick. She has spent the weekend crying, drinking, unsure who to tell or what to do next. Her thoughts keep turning to McAvoy. She wants to call him. Wants to tell him what she has done. Wants to ask for help. But McAvoy looks disappointed in her when she admits to taking the last chocolate biscuit. What the hell would he look like if he knew what she had done? The detective in her wants to send the footage to the science unit and have their boffins trace the origins of the email. But her face is clearly in shot. There is no denying that it is her in the film. It's her, gasping and moaning and slurping at the cocaine on her lips. It is her pushing back against the toned, tattooed man who never shows his face to the camera.

Helen has emailed him several times. She has asked him why. Asked him what he wants. Has called him every name she can think of. The emails have bounced back. The address she sent them to, and with which she shared such gorgeous flirtations these past weeks, no longer exists.

Here, now, Helen sits on her sofa, wrapped in a duvet, shivering as she drinks hot blackcurrant juice and stares at her phone. She has come up with a hundred different angles that could yet play out. Those in possession of the film could demand money. She has little, but has made up her mind to pay if that is what they want. They could demand information. She is willing to go only so far. Her fear is that they will simply keep her in their pocket. Her fear is she will become what she despises: a mole for the criminals she should be trying to catch.

Her phone rings.

Number withheld.

Helen's hands tremble as she answers.

'Hello.'

'Detective Constable Tremberg. Good morning. I am sorry to hear you are not in the best of health. Could I perhaps suggest that you take a couple of Ibuprofen and drink plenty of fluids? I am also led to believe chicken soup is good in these situations but can neither confirm or deny that from my own experiences. I have a very robust constitution.'

Helen says nothing. Just feels tears make tracks down her cheeks.

'Perhaps you are right,' comes the voice, after a moment. 'Perhaps we should not dilly-dally with pleasantries and chit-chat. Perhaps we should come to the crux of the matter. And the matter is this: I have in my possession footage of your good self, performing acts that are most unbecoming for a police officer. I have no doubt you would not wish for this footage to be seen by your superior officers, or any members of the popular press, or for that matter simply emailed to every one of your colleagues. If it is any consolation, I do not wish to see that happen either. You are not a very attractive woman and nobody really wants to open their emails to find footage of your large posterior bouncing up and down in front of them. So perhaps we could spare ourselves any unpleasantness. Perhaps you could help my associates and me.'

Helen swallows. Manages a few words. 'What do you want? Please, I don't have much—'

'Detective Constable, we know precisely what you are worth, and financially, your meagre savings are akin to the fluff in my pocket. No, I need one small favour from you, and then the footage in question will be destroyed.'

'What? What do you want?'

'At present, a young man of my acquaintance is unreasonably being held in custody. He is in Hull Royal Infirmary having suffered some rather nasty injuries at the hands of the intriguing and entertaining Detective Chief Inspector Colin Ray. I am optimistic that your ACC Everett will ensure that the charges against him are dropped. He is, after all, an accommodating man. However, there are those within the police force who will not roll over quite so easily, and to that end, it would be best if those who witnessed young Mr Downey's brief moment of embarrassment could be persuaded to alter their statements. There is a seamstress by the name of Melanie Langley who helped apprehend Mr Downey. I would be most grateful if she could be persuaded to alter her version of events. I have, of course, got many other ways to accomplish this goal, but your intercession would be least messy.'

Helen holds her stomach, feeling a fresh wave of nausea. 'I can't, I don't—'

'Please, Detective Constable, there is more. I am further led to believe that while Mr Downey was incapacitated, an associate of Miss Langley took it upon herself to relieve him of a sum of money. This money is neither here nor there, but the presumptuousness, the lack of respect, are unacceptable in light of the ongoing expansion of our enterprise. I would like the name and address of this person. If it helps, I am led to believe she is very pretty, was carrying a child, and is somewhat Romany in her appearance and deportment.'

The nausea stops. The pain halts. Adrenalin flows through Helen's body. She opens her mouth but is cut off before she can manage to speak.

'I am grateful for your assistance in this matter. I realise this is a lot to ask and it will be difficult for somebody with your sense of justice and morality. To this end we have deposited a large sum of money in your bank account. I would suggest, as you endure the sting of acting against your better judgement, that you remind yourself you are doing so to save lives. I would also encourage you to visit a general practitioner at your earliest convenience. Our mutual acquaintance is a carrier of any number of sexually transmitted infections . . .'

Helen drops the phone. It lands on the sofa without being switched off, and at the other end of the line the man to whom she was speaking hears her throwing up all over her living-room floor.

13

4.40 p.m. Chamomile House, in the heart of the Lake District: just two miles south of where William Wordsworth doomed the humble daffodil to a lifetime of overexposure.

Some 160 miles north of Hull.

Aector McAvoy is leaning on the desk in a brightly lit reception area, talking to a pretty young woman about the traffic he has endured on the three-hour drive up from Chester. He has passed through hail, rain and blindingly bright sunlight. He would not be surprised to see snow start to fall.

Here, now, the weather is dry but decidedly gloomy. Beyond the windows the clouds hang low: a damp hammock punctured by the tops of the trees that dot the woodland grounds of this expensive care home. It's a welcoming place; all slate roof and chunky brickwork, low roofs and climbing ivy. It is home to twenty-two patients with varying degrees of dependency, all of whom pay handsomely to enjoy the best possible facilities. This is a care home that smells of rhododendrons and roast dinners rather than boiled cabbage and bleach, and McAvoy, with his aching back and tired eyes, is considering checking himself in.

'I'm sure she won't be long.'

McAvoy is running out of things to say to the receptionist. She is strikingly pretty, and from his elevated vantage point he has inadvertently noticed both the tattoo on her chest, and the lace of her bra. Neither of these discoveries has helped him make small talk, or calmed him down after a difficult and tiring journey, made longer by constantly having to pull over to take phone calls from the office. Ben Nielsen is doing a superb job, following McAvoy's instructions and hunting down everything they have on the people who were patients at Caneva's facility the night of the escape. He is also seeking whatever is available on Lewis Caneva's family, and on a hunch, is doing a general search on the father of Sebastien Hoyer-Wood. McAvoy does not know what he expects to find but is certain the answers will be unearthed if they all just keep working hard and thinking positively. The thought of giving any kind of rousing speech to the troops terrifies him, but he fears that such a moment may yet be called for. Pharaoh has unofficially handed things over to him during her absence, and the two officers under his command are rising to the challenge of pleasing him.

He's pleased they aren't grumbling about being stuck in the office, giving themselves migraines in front of flickering computer screens, getting steadily unhealthier in sticky, fly-blown rooms. After all, it is McAvoy who has taken on the job that none of the others want. He's the one who has to sit down with a monster. It is a thought that scares him. He doesn't feel up to it. He has got better at believing in himself, but there are still times when he wants to run back to the office and hide in a cupboard while stronger personalities take charge.

A little shaky, a tremble in his voice, he turns his attention back to the young girl.

He is trying to think of something to say to her when a small, round-bottomed woman in her late thirties emerges from a corridor, smiling broadly. She extends a soft plump hand, which McAvoy takes in his. She is wearing what looks a little like a karate suit, but it is a livid blue and has the name of her employers stitched on the breast, next to an upside-down watch.

'I'm Evelyn,' she says, brightly. 'I'll be looking after you. Sebastien's waiting for you. He seems quite excited.'

McAvoy turns back to the receptionist, who appears to be checking that her blouse is sufficiently unbuttoned for a tall man to enjoy the view. He gives a smile that makes him look like a pumpkin lantern, and then scurries away. At six foot five, McAvoy is not built for scurrying. He looks like a giant in chains.

Evelyn leads McAvoy back out through the front door and across the car park where his people-carrier is still making a worrying whooshing noise. So far, he has driven well over 200 miles today and the car is as unaccustomed to long journeys as he is to squeezing his big frame into such a small seat for so long. Both he and the vehicle are suffering.

'You've caught us at an awkward time, Sergeant,' says Evelyn as she points him down one of the footpaths into a copse of trees. 'Problems with the drains. We have a septic tank here. Doesn't need emptying more than twice a decade, provided you use the right chemicals, but we rather forgot to inspect the chamber and it's really backed up. Not very nice. If we hadn't got it drained we would have been wading in sludge, and that isn't what you want when you're in a wheelchair.'

McAvoy, who stands a good head and shoulders above her, is surprised to find that he has to jog to keep up with her boisterous, bustling progress down the path. He can't think of what to say, so sniffs the air. Smells rhododendrons and damp grass. Smells earth. Gets a tiny whiff of Evelyn's anti-bacterial hand-wash and Avon perfume. He decides to make no comment on the septic tank.

'Sebastien's at the end there,' says Evelyn, pointing ahead. She has led them around the building and swipes a key card on a pad by the glass back door. Stepping inside, she ushers him down a wide, empty corridor, its walls illustrated with pictures of hot-air balloons and birds.

'I don't really know what you're expecting of him,' she says, neutrally. 'He can't communicate well at all. He can make emotions understood and we know when he's angry, but other than that, it depends whether you're on his wavelength or not. I've helped him write the occasional message on some website or other that has caught his eye, but you have to go through the alphabet with him for every single letter. It's very laborious, but that's what we're here for, I suppose. His computer is his lifeline. Very expensive piece of kit, but it means he gets to know what's going on in the outside world and I don't have to spend every moment reading to him.'

McAvoy stops in the corridor, several feet from the room that contains the man who used to enjoy raping women in front of their husbands. He suddenly doesn't want to knock. He turns to Evelyn.

'So you're his personal carer? Full-time, yes?'

Evelyn brushes her bobbed hair back from her pleasant round face. 'I'm his nominated staff member, if that's what you mean. Each of our patients has somebody who is specifically responsible for their well-being and standard of care. I oversee a team of nurses and health-support workers who then assist in taking care of him. Sebastien's one of our more challenging patients. A lot of our patients are relatively mobile. Sebastien needs round-the-clock care. We have a good staff though and can call on a central agency for support should we ever be short-staffed. He's well looked after.'

McAvoy nods. He's not sure he's overly concerned with how well they are looking after Hoyer-Wood.

'How much do you know about his case history?' he asks, delicately.

Evelyn appears to understand the magnitude of the question. 'To treat our patients the best way we can, it's important to know as much about them as we can. We have full access to Sebastien's case notes. He's been in the system a long time.'

'And the court case?'

Evelyn looks nonplussed. 'The file said he was charged with an offence while exhibiting mental health problems. That was when he suffered his initial injuries, I believe. Those injuries to his brain led to severe epilepsy, and I understand that in turn caused the stroke that left him like this. It was a double tragedy, really, as it appears that he was making good progress with his physiotherapy and speech therapy. Some people just have misfortune thrown at them.'

McAvoy studies the image nearest him on the wall. Admires the fine pencil strokes that have created the wicker basket, hanging below a brightly coloured balloon. It is an image that suggests freedom. Release. He doesn't want to take his eyes off it and step into the room of a man whom he cannot picture, but feels he is beginning to know.

'It's expensive here, I presume?'

Evelyn smiles. 'You get what you pay for.'

'And who pays for him?'

She spreads her hands, apologising for not being able to say. Then she leans in and whispers, as if this will be less of a breach of confidentiality: 'His father died. He inherited a lot of money.'

McAvoy nods his thanks.

Breathes deeply.

Coughs.

Blinks.

He can't put it off any longer.

He takes three steps and knocks on the pine. At his side, Evelyn turns the handle and pushes open the wide door.

Sebastien Hoyer-Wood sits in a low-backed chair at the centre of a large, green-painted room. In front of him is a computer monitor; to his right a low sofa facing a television. One wall is all glass, reflecting back the opposite wall, which is stacked with books, CDs and DVDs. The floor is linoleum, but with a wood-panel effect.

'Would you mind?' says Evelyn, pointing to a small patch of black matting by McAvoy's feet. 'You have to discharge your static on there or it can cause a fit.'

Flustered, McAvoy does as he is told, rubbing his shoes on the odd material, until Evelyn tells him he can stop.

'Do I take my boots off?'

'No, you're fine now. Anyway, this is Sebastien. Sebastien, this is Detective Sergeant McAvoy. He's come to talk to you.'

McAvoy extends a hand, as if to shake. He looks at the proffered palm. Feels appalled with himself. Drops it back to his side.

Up close, Hoyer-Wood is a melted waxwork, a handsome sculpture left too close to the fire. His face is bottom-heavy, locked open in a permanent yawn. A column of thin drool spills from his lower lip to puddle on the chest of his green sweatshirt. His clothes seem to conceal nothing but bones. McAvoy is put in mind of a pirate's skeleton. He half imagines pulling back the man's shirt to reveal bare ribs and a cutlass blade.

Evelyn beckons him forward.

'Please, take a seat. It's best if you're near him. It might help you better understand.'

Hoyer-Wood's expression does not change as McAvoy clumsily takes a wooden chair from beside the bookcase and places it next to the patient. He turns his head and looks at Hoyer-Wood's computer screen. A web page is open, the text-size triple the norm. McAvoy glances at it. Hoyer-Wood is reading an essay on a poem by Robert Browning. It is a verse that McAvoy recognises and admires; ugly language made beautiful. It is written in the voice of a jilted wife, planning to poison her husband's lover. McAvoy glimpses the words 'moisten' and 'mash'. Reads the phrase 'pound at thy powder'. It is a poem in which murder is coolly and deliberately planned and enjoyed.

'Browning?' asks McAvoy, turning to Hoyer-Wood, whose eyes are rolling back to stare at the panelled ceiling. 'I always enjoyed "Lost Leader". I like the Beat poets too. And the modern classics. Actually, a mutual acquaintance of ours is currently studying the Beat poets.' McAvoy looks at the side of the other man's face, trying to capture his gaze, before adding: 'Lewis Caneva.'

Next to him, Hoyer-Wood twists in his chair, his mouth opening and closing and a series of unintelligible noises coming from his throat.

'I don't think that's one of his favourites,' says Evelyn, sitting down on the sofa.

'No,' says McAvoy. 'I got that.'

'He's very fortunate to have this machine,' says Evelyn, indicating the computer in front of Hoyer-Wood. 'It recognises certain sounds. It has a keypad too that he can operate with his finger when the drugs have his muscle spasms under control. At the moment he's having quite a rough time. He can surf the Net quite easily. We loaded up a lot of favourite sites and he can scroll through them as he wants. He can spell out search words, though it's a hell of an ordeal. Still, it keeps him out of mischief, eh, Sebastien?'

McAvoy says nothing. He just looks at the man in the chair. The room is warm and bright, but it contains a scent, perhaps a colour to the air, that he finds unsettling. It is as though something has died in this room. He smells decayed humanity. Something nearby is rotting. It is a place of moist corruption and slow, damp death.

For a moment, McAvoy is unsure how to proceed. He doesn't know what he wants or what he expected. It is clear Hoyer-Wood is not faking his injuries. Before he entered the room he half-entertained the notion of tipping him from the chair and seeing if he put out his hands to break his fall. Now he sees how unnecessary that would be. Hoyer-Wood is a virtual skeleton. His body will not obey his commands. His mind is a prisoner in a bag of bedsores and rotting flesh. McAvoy feels a sudden rush of pity for the man. Tells himself that whatever his crimes, he is suffering punishments far greater than a prison sentence. He reminds himself that only one case was ever built against him and that the rapes he is alleged to have carried out are based on unsigned statements and guesswork. Perhaps the man in the chair was truly a victim. Perhaps he, too, suffered in his youth. Perhaps he acted as he did as a cry for help, and care facilities

such as these are a better place for him than a jail cell. He is glad
Pharaoh is not here. She would see the softening of his face.

'Sebastien,' he says, quietly. 'Is it okay to call you Sebastien?
Thank you. Sebastien, I'm investigating two murders. Three, I
suppose. I don't know whether you read the newspapers or have
much interest in current affairs, but over the past week, three
people in the Humberside Police region have been killed. You
might remember these people. They saved your life. Philippa
Longman gave you CPR the night you almost died. Yvonne
Dale applied pressure to your leg wound. Allan Godber was
the paramedic who restarted your heart. All of these people
have been killed in manners that suggest somebody is not very
grateful to them for saving you. I would ask you to think very
clearly and carefully. Now, do you have any thoughts that might
be of benefit to our enquiries?'

McAvoy licks his lips and breathes out, slowly. Behind him, he
hears Evelyn let out a little exclamation of surprise. He wonders
how long it will be before she goes and makes a quick phone call
to her superiors. When he had rung to arrange to speak with the
patient, he had been a little economical with the facts.

Suddenly, Hoyer-Wood begins to spasm. His right arm bounces
up and down and his jaw jerks forward so suddenly that McAvoy
half expects his neck to crack. His left hand clutches at his own
trouser leg and his face suddenly looks pained and wretched.
McAvoy turns to Evelyn, unsure whether to intervene. She gives
him a quiet shake of the head. This is normal.

At length, the paroxysm subsides. Evelyn crosses to his side.
She takes a pad from her pocket.

'Do you want to talk, Sebastien?'

A noise. A blink.

Evelyn confirms that he has given his assent. She starts to recite the alphabet. After he has picked four letters, McAvoy interrupts.

'Is he saying he's sorry?'

The noise Hoyer-Wood makes is clearly a 'yes'.

'Sorry they are dead?'

Evelyn looks at him, not understanding. Hoyer-Wood stays silent. Just drools onto his clothes.

McAvoy sighs. He wonders what he can possibly get from this.

'Sebastien, I spent an hour today with Lewis Caneva. You remember him, yes? Your best friend from university. The man who did you quite a good turn? He tells me that there was a time, back when you were a patient of his, that you were getting better. He tells me you were beginning to walk unaided. You could make yourself understood. I wonder, could you tell me exactly what happened to leave you in this condition you are now in?'

Hoyer-Wood's face stretches open. The top half of his head looks as though it could come off. McAvoy turns to Evelyn, and she begins the process again.

McAvoy does not want to interrupt. He crosses to the bookshelf. He examines the spines of some of the novels. There are some classics. A few thrillers. Poetry anthologies and biographies of poets. He tries to find anything useful. Any tome on voyeurism or domination. But there is nothing incriminating.

'Sergeant?'

He turns back. Evelyn is standing with her pad open.

'He says Lewis is his friend. His wife was too. He misses him. He hopes he remembers what good friends they once were.'

McAvoy waits for more.

'And?'

Evelyn gets up and walks over to McAvoy. Her voice drops to the conspiratorial whisper in which she had shared the details of his financial circumstances.

'He says I'm to tell you the rest from what I know of his files,' she says. Takes a breath. Rushes on. 'The epilepsy got steadily worse in the years after he left the home that you mentioned. The fits became so severe that even if the mental health authorities left him out, he would not be safe to live alone. Then he had what we call a "catastrophic" stroke. There was an incident involving a vehicle he was a passenger in and the stress of that event was almost certainly the trigger. He came to us shortly afterwards. It was such a shame because he had started writing. He was getting fitter. I think he entertained hopes of being allowed to go back to work some day . . .'

McAvoy crosses back to Sebastien Hoyer-Wood. It is impossible to read his expression. His face is too inhuman to convey his thoughts. But for an instant, McAvoy could swear that in that gory mask, between the damp eyes and the rictus set of his mouth, he sees a flash of life.

Unable to stop himself, McAvoy reaches out and touches Hoyer-Wood's computer screen. He takes the sensor that sits on the smooth plastic tray in Hoyer-Wood's lap, and quickly flicks back to the websites that Hoyer-Wood has been browsing before McAvoy entered the room. He looks at the screen for a moment. Swallows. Drinks in the gaudy colours. The lurid banner adverts. The image of the young girl on all fours, crying as a man in a mask holds her hair and fucks her roughly; another man tied to her bedpost with a belt and clearly begging the masked man to stop. He wonders how long it took Hoyer-Wood to blink out the word 'cuckold'. Whether his nurses allow this indulgence or if he has found a way to keep it to himself.

McAvoy flicks the screen back to the poetry as Evelyn moves back to his side of the screen.

'Erm, Sergeant, I'm not one hundred per cent comfortable with this. Would you mind if we took a temporary break while I contacted my superiors? I'm terribly sorry . . .'

McAvoy does not want to cause a scene or get her into trouble. Nor does he want to leave without understanding who the man in the chair used to be.

'You said he was writing again?' he asks, innocently.

'Yes, yes, some lovely poetry. A diary of sorts, all about his plans to get well again and the battle with his physiotherapy. It was all sent to us when he moved here, though I believe he asked for much of it to be thrown away during one of his darker days. I read a little myself. Very inspirational. He spoke about the staff at the last care home. How he imagined them at home, in their peaceful, pleasant lives. He wanted that. Wanted to share it with them. Very moving. Now, please . . .'

McAvoy turns his head to Hoyer-Wood. Slowly, softly, he bends down and places his lips by the crippled man's ear.

'You'd do it all again, wouldn't you? You'd get out of that chair and rape women and destroy lives and get off on the suffering. I know you would. Somebody else knows you would too. I think they are punishing those who saved you, Sebastien, because after you were caught, after your life was saved, you ruined somebody else's life too. They can't punish you, can they? What's to punish? There's nothing left of you. So they're taking out their rage on the people who kept you in the world. Whose life did you destroy last, Sebastien? Whose?'

McAvoy raises his head. Watches the brown of his own eyes swim in the blue irises of the man in the chair.

Slowly, as though using every ounce of his strength, Hoyer-Wood says Evelyn's name. She crosses to his side. Dutifully takes out her pen. Begins the alphabet afresh.

A moment later, McAvoy stomps from the room, moving as fast as he can. Were he to stay, he would not be able to stop any violence he began.

In Sebastien Hoyer-Wood's room, Evelyn looks quizzically at the letters on her pad. Reads again what he has told her in grunts and blinks.

'Tell me about your wife.'

Adam Downey is on his knees, spitting saliva and bile into the green water of the toilet bowl. He can taste blood. Can taste the three slurps of tea that he had managed for breakfast. He can smell the thick mucus that seems to have formed a wall in his sinuses behind his bruised nose.

He snarls as he wipes his mouth. Sneers at his own distorted reflection in the water of the toilet bowl. The act of retching has made his bruised ribs throb with pain and his already aching jaw now feels as though it has been opened with a car jack.

Fucking Colin Ray!

He pushes himself back from the toilet. Rinses his mouth and splashes water on his face. He looks at his reflection in the tiny mirror above the sink. He has cuts and bruises to his handsome face and a big scab on one elbow. The bandages and padding that cover the lacerations to his back form a slight bump in the outline of his T-shirt, but he doesn't look as bad as he feels. He uses his thumb to check, one more time, that none of his teeth are wobbly, then opens the door.

The smell of the hospital ward offends his nostrils, so his

actions are quick. He crosses to the bed where he has been a patient these last couple of days. He picks up his copy of his release paperwork, feeling a half-smile crease his face. He knew he'd get bail somehow. He just didn't expect to have to get his head kicked in to achieve it. Still, he trusts that his new employers had no alternative. He's just grateful they kept their promises. He always intended to keep his.

Downey takes another quick look at the room. He's pleased to be leaving. He doesn't like being cooped up, and the succession of uniformed constables who kept him company were not great conversationalists. Anyway, he hasn't really wanted to talk. His mind has been elsewhere. On getting out. On getting paid. On getting *her*.

The last uniformed constable has gone. Downey is a free man, for now. He can walk out the door and do what the fuck he likes. And he knows exactly what he'd like to do.

Gingerly, painfully, but refusing to yield to his injuries, he gets himself ready. The bin liner that contained the possessions he had brought with him from the custody suite is lying on the bed. The T-shirt he was wearing when they brought him in to A&E was too ragged and bloody to be kept, but he slips into the same jeans he had on when Colin Ray beat the shit out of him. The T-shirt he is wearing was torn fresh from a cellophane packet. It had been inside the bin-liner. He doesn't know if it is a present from somebody. Perhaps it is some kind of apology from the police for what happened to him. If it is, they can fuck off. He doesn't wear plain T-shirts. He likes a label.

Downey stands in the doorway to his hospital room. He takes a breath.

Young, fit and energetic, Downey would normally be able to walk the mile and a half to his Victoria Dock home, but he's feeling a bit banged up and doesn't fancy walking through the city centre wearing this T-shirt. He pulls out his phone to call a taxi. There's probably a rank of them somewhere around here, or a pay phone with a free link to a local firm, but Downey reckons there's no point running a taxi firm if you can't get yourself a lift. Besides, it will be nice to give the drivers a real job for a change. He might request Hakan. The lad will have been shitting himself these past few days and it will be better all round if his punishment comes quickly.

He opens his phone. He's surprised to find that it's already ringing. The number has been withheld.

Downey feels a tongue of nausea licking the inside of his throat. He knows himself to be able to hold his own in a fight, but his confidence has taken a little knock and he's weak as a kitten. If the call is from the man he thinks it's from, he knows he needs all his faculties, and right now, he's not himself. He's had his arse kicked twice in the past few days – once by an old bloke and once by a girl. It's the girl who's hurt him most. She took his money. Got him caught. Acted like he was a nobody. Oh, he has such plans . . .

'Hello,' he says, focusing on the call.

'Mr Downey,' comes a familiar voice. 'I hope you are well.'

Downey closes his eyes. He leans against a circular column that supports the front of the hospital, pleased to be outside. He looks around him. There are people in wheelchairs, people holding drips. On the grass, beyond the little shop, is an area where patients and visitors alike sit and smoke; some holding cigarettes in hands that are wrapped in bandages or skewered by a cannula. A husband and wife pass a cigarette between them. She's in a pink dressing gown, both eyes black. He's in jeans and a Man United shirt and his right hand is in plaster. To his left, Downey sees the maternity hospital. New life. New hopes. New customers, some day.

The vista of real life suddenly makes his head reel. He doesn't want to be a part of it. Of *them*. He's above it all. He suddenly reminds himself who he is. What he had to do to prove himself to these men. The voice at the other end of the line scares him. But he has earned their respect and they owe him a favour. He tells himself to get it together.

'I've been better,' he says, trying to sound casual. 'But fresh air feels nice.'

'Excellent. I can assure you that we had several stratagems for securing your release. The one that was successful came at a high price to your well-being. I trust that when the physical wounds heal, no festering resentment will remain?'

Downey finds himself smiling. He likes how this man talks. He wishes he could picture him.

'I'm out, that's what matters.'

'A pragmatic and sensible approach, Mr Downey. You repay our faith in you.'

There is a pause. Downey expects more, but nothing comes. Nervous again, he fills the silence himself.

'Look, what happened . . . at the shop. One of my lads thought he was going to get pulled over. He didn't want to lose the gear. The sewing shop was his idea. I did my best. It just got out of hand—'

The voice is placating and soft. 'Hush, Mr Downey. We fully understand that sometimes our employees do not represent us in the way we would represent ourselves. You have been an asset to us during your brief time in our employ. We have no inclination to rebuke you for this minor blot on your otherwise impressive curriculum vitae. I would, however, prepare yourself for some distressing news about one of your drivers. Hakan is no longer available for night shifts. Or day shifts. Or walking around and breathing. I trust you will not grieve too much for this loss to your staff?'

Downey screws up his eyes. He'd planned to give Hakan a slap. Maybe cut his take. He tries not to let himself picture what they did to him. He knows it will have involved a nailgun and a blowtorch. He knows his skin will have bubbled like sugar in a pan. *Fuck.*

A memory comes, unbidden. He and Hakan had talked about football. They'd watched a Champions League game together, Hakan's team trying to get past the group stages. They'd both cheered and laughed when they stuck one past Barcelona. They might even have bloody *hugged*. Christ, Hakan had given him a Galatasaray scarf to wear. They were never mates. But they'd laughed together. Shared a few cans of beer . . .

Downey gives a little cough, which becomes a retch. He swallows down what comes up.

'Mr Downey?'

'It's okay,' he says, and hopes it is.

'Excellent. Now, as you can see, we are calling on a mobile phone number that is open to abuses and eavesdroppers. I hope you do not distress yourself over this. We have taken steps to ensure that we can talk freely. However, there is always the possibility of the unforeseen hiccup, so I will keep the remainder of this conversation brief. You should know that Colin Ray is currently suspended and under observation by ourselves. The seamstress will soon be withdrawing her statement. The loss of our product is not of huge concern at this time. You will soon be free to resume deliveries. There remains just the one frayed thread for you to pick at.'

Downey focuses. Feels his lips twitch. 'The girl.'

'Precisely. I do not want you to feel too emasculated by her involvement in your predicament. However, you are a young man with pride and an ego, and I know you will not sleep well until you have demonstrated to this young Romany that you are not to be treated thusly. It would also be a useful PR exercise if you were to make an example of the penalty for such transgressions.'

'You've found her?'

'I am confident the information will be with us swiftly. For now, I would advise you to go and reassert your authority with your workforce and perhaps offer a little financial incentive to anybody who wishes to relieve their frustrations by assisting you in censuring the young lady.'

Downey bites his lip. Holds in vomit and a smile.

'How far can I go?'

For the first time, Downey hears the man give what might be considered a laugh. 'Mr Downey, you are a young and vigorous man, watched over by powerful friends. I should imagine that by now it has occurred to you that you can do whatever you want.'

The nausea subsides. Downey finds himself grinning. He likes this. Likes the feeling. He's untouchable. The sea of humanity may not part as he walks through, but here, now, it feels as though he can point and nod and dispense life or death as he sees fit. He matters. He's going to show his guts, that he's got what it takes . . .

'Blowtorch?' he says, softly.

The line remains silent, as if the man is weighing things up.

'Perhaps not. This is not our regular business. This is a perk. I leave it to your discretion. We will be in touch.'

Downey hears the phone being put down and stands, unmoving, for a moment or two. He looks around him. At the people. The *plebs*. He feels sick and decides he doesn't give a damn.

He decides to walk. Suddenly, he is a young man with energy and a sense of purpose.

More than anything, he is a man with a bitch to kill.

14

Everybody thinks the rain will come today. The sky is a mountain of cold ash but the sun still burns through, and the air is thick and greasy. Hull yearns for a storm. People watch the skies the way they used to watch the seas. Then, it was to glimpse a returning trawler. Today, it is in the hope that the clouds will finally part and the tensions that fizz and crackle across the city will be swept away in a flood of healing rain.

In his ten years in Hull, McAvoy has never known its residents to actively yearn for a downpour. On this flat landscape, rain is something to be feared. In 2007, the city was almost lost to floods. An extraordinary deluge left Hull half-submerged. The city had sloshed and skidded to a halt as an ocean of water tumbled from the sky onto bone-dry streets and poured into drains blocked by rubbish and leaves. McAvoy, in his last few days in uniform, had barely slept for three days as the city's emergency services worked round the clock to drain the water and help stranded motorists and residents make it to high ground. McAvoy was even shown on the local news, carrying a pensioner and her dog in his arms, the water up to his waist, a look of grim determination upon his red face. If it had happened in London it would have been a major catastrophe, but it happened in Hull, and barely made the national news. All these years later, there are still people living in mobile homes in the driveways of their houses, gradually repairing the damage to their properties. Every time it rains, there is a sense of mild panic in the city. Even so, most would risk a downpour now. It's just too hot. Too oppressive. Too bloody muggy by half. And with three murders in and around the city inside a week, Hull is feeling twitchy. It is as though the air is charged with something. People are aggressive, and scared.

McAvoy is feeling ill. He feels like he's coming down with a cold. His bones ache from yesterday's long drive, and though he made it home to Roisin by 8 p.m., there was unpacking to be done, and Lilah had not settled in her new bedroom, so there was little chance to rest and groan the way he had wanted to. The baby's cries began around five minutes after McAvoy's eyes finally closed, having spent restless hours trying to get Sebastien Hoyer-Wood out of his mind. Roisin had told him to stay in bed, to leave it all to her, but he couldn't be that kind of dad. He got up. Sat with his wife and child on the front step of their new home and watched the black waters and the distant lights. It had been nice, at the time. She had closed her fingers in his, and Lilah had been happy enough to sit in Daddy's lap and pull his chest hair. But it meant that he got little more than an hour's sleep. A breakfast of scrambled egg and home-made tomato sauce now sits uncomfortably at the top of his stomach, refusing to go down, and he doesn't know if it's sickness or the heat of the day that is making him sweat.

It's mid-morning and McAvoy is walking over to the small swing park that sits near the police station at the edge of the Orchard Park estate. The schools break up for the summer holidays in a day or two and soon the place will be packed with kids from the estate. Coppers looking for a place of quiet reflection will not be made welcome. It will be teeming with shell-suited yobs necking energy drinks, and younger kids trying to play games without appearing to act like children. McAvoy has chatted to a few of them in the past and knows the locals are far from all bad. Though some of the pre-teens can be obnoxious, most are just normal children who happen to have been born somewhere that offers more bad influences than good. There are good people here. They just seem to get swallowed up.

He couldn't have stayed in the office any longer. For the past couple of hours, McAvoy has been briefing his small team of officers on what he learned yesterday. As he spoke, he heard how half-hearted and far-fetched it all seemed, and he could see from their reactions that they were losing faith. It is clear that the victims are all linked to Hoyer-Wood, but McAvoy's half-formed idea that somebody is punishing those who saved the man's life is starting to be challenged by the team. While McAvoy mumbled and stumbled through his notes, the junior constables began to throw out fresh theories. Perhaps the victims simply *met* through Hoyer-Wood. Perhaps they became friends. Perhaps their deaths were nothing to do with him. Would it be worth checking their Internet histories to see if they were in some kind of relationship? Was there a weird three-way love triangle at the centre of it all? McAvoy had pointed out the nature of the injuries. He had tried to make them *see*. But when they asked him whom he had in mind as a suspect, he had nobody to offer. He'd agreed to let Nielsen run with the alternative theories. He told them that Trish Pharaoh would be back in charge before the end of the day and they would all meet up for another briefing at teatime. He had bolted for the exit like a frightened horse, not knowing what to do next.

He thinks, again, of the words Nielsen had so carelessly tossed into the pot.

The thing is, you might see serial killers everywhere, Sarge. After what you've been through . . . after that shit at Christmas. Not everybody is killing for cosmic reasons, Sarge. Some people are just stupid or horrible or evil little bastards . . .'

McAvoy had stood there, face so sallow and motionless as to look halfway decomposed. He'd wanted to run. Wanted to sprint from the room before he was reminded of any more bodies from his past.

While he tries to get a hold of himself and fit some of the pieces of it all together, the basic police work is continuing. Door-knocking, fact-checking, forensics and CCTV may well provide the lead that they are seeking. The Allan Godber murder had clearly not gone as the killer planned. The team are working on the assumption that the killer had planned to electrocute Godber with the defibrillator machine, but that he had not reckoned with the complexities of the device. Constable Daniells had done a quick crash course on defibrillators yesterday evening and this morning told the team what he had learned. Over the past couple of years, a charity had seen to it that thousands of the damn things were given to community centres, leisure centres and various neighbourhood groups, for use in emergencies. The serial number of the device found with Godber's body showed that it had been stolen from a swimming pool in North Yorkshire. The staff there had presumed it was still locked safely away in the cupboard they had installed for it, and nobody had looked inside for at least three months. The reason that it had not been used to stop Godber's heart was because it simply would not activate on anybody still alive. The machine is equipped with sensors that can detect any sign of a pulse, and if it can, the electric current cannot be activated. The killer had been unable to use it as they planned, and in their frustration they had used the case to batter him to death. They had left a footprint in his blood: the same kind of boot that had been near Philippa Longman's corpse. They had also been haphazard in wiping down the garage door handle. While there were no usable fingerprints, there was a smear of blood that contained an animal's fur and some other organic material. It has been sent off for testing.

The team are optimistic that this kind of detailed forensic work will lead to a breakthrough. They need one. The national press are starting to arrive, sensing something big. McAvoy knows that it will be only a day or two before some tabloid discovers the link between the victims. At present, ACC Everett is refusing to allow Pharaoh to make that link public. In the eyes of the public, the three crimes are being treated as separate murders. Everett wants to hold off on using the phrase 'serial killer' for as long as he can, even though by doing so he runs the risk of increasing the number of victims. Pharaoh wants to alert the public. Wants to tell anybody who helped save Sebastien Hoyer-Wood's life that they are in danger. Everett is insisting on softly-softly. Those who may be in danger are getting a gentle knock on the door from a uniformed officer or a phone call from Ben Nielsen. They are not getting protection; just being told to be on their guard. Those who have been contacted are not reacting to the news particularly well.

McAvoy can sense the case getting too big. Too unwieldy. Too many people, too many interfering, self-interested parties. He just wants to catch a killer and stop them hurting anybody else. He doesn't know if he is on the way to doing so, or just wasting time and resources on suppositions and hope, doesn't know if he is being a good policeman or a loose cannon. He just hopes that the answers lie in the bundle of documents that had been waiting for him on his desk when he returned from the briefing.

Here, now, McAvoy takes the envelope from his bag. Weighs it in his palm. Feels the pleasing heft of the pages within. He takes a bottle of Roisin's elderberry cordial from the bag as well. It's good for his chest and for preventing colds getting worse. He takes a swig as he empties the sheets of paper, and begins to examine the notes of Lewis Caneva's counselling sessions with Sebastien Hoyer-Wood. It had been a surprise to receive them. Despite the veiled threats he made in the ex-shrink's house yesterday, he figured Caneva would stubbornly refuse to assist. Perhaps McAvoy had scared him more than he meant to. He hopes he didn't. Although he knows Caneva is holding back, he would not like to be that kind of policeman. He would rather people just did the right thing. He consoles himself that Caneva did just that. Nothing in the file will be admissible in any court case, but McAvoy needs to better understand the mind of a demon, and fancies that he will get an unrivalled glimpse when he sees what makes Hoyer-Wood tick.

For an hour, McAvoy pores over the documents. His sickness dissipates. He forgets to feel ill. He drains the cordial, eats a Mars bar and ignores five phone calls. Then he reaches the final page. He turns it over, expecting more. He finds nothing. Checks the envelope, looks frustrated, then gathers his notes and stuffs everything back into his bag. Then he looks up at the sky, rubbing his face and breathing slowly out. He stands, as if to walk back to the office. And yet he can't face it. Can't be among them. Can't think the way he needs to when he hears them laughing and chatting and living a way he can't. He turns his back on the police station and sets off into the estate, letting his mind unravel like a kite string as he tries to make sense of what he has learned.

Hoyer-Wood had not wanted to talk at first. Even with his best friend, his oldest confidant, he wanted to keep his secrets inside. His difficulties in making himself understood only served to frustrate him, and Caneva's records of their early sessions are filled with little more than polite enquiries about health, the weather and how he is settling in. In those sessions, it is Caneva who does most of the talking. The notes are a seemingly endless soliloquy on the tiresome business of driving up from London; problems with the practice; getting the right staff. In terms of insights, the first months drew a complete blank. It was only as Hoyer-Wood began to physically improve, and became more able to communicate, that he opened up. And in the sessions that followed, he told Caneva all about how it felt to live inside a head that worked as his did.

As he meanders through the deserted streets, McAvoy tries to marry up what he already knew of Hoyer-Wood with what he has just discovered. He thinks of the broken man in the chair. Then he pictures Hoyer-Wood as a child. More than anything, he pictures Hoyer-Wood as the criminal who broke into homes, doused his victims with petrol and threatened to set them alight unless they opened their legs to him in front of those they loved.

McAvoy stops, suddenly too tired to carry on walking. He leans against the front wall of a small, semi-detached house. Next to it is a boarded-up, burned-out building. McAvoy thinks he may have been here before. He seems to recall attending a murder here. He feels compelled to laugh at his own uncertainty. Wonders if, twenty years from now, he will be unable to drive through the city without pointing out places where he has smelled blood and decay. He found a young girl here, her corpse having suffered horrendous indignities. McAvoy had been new to CID then. New to Doug Roper's super-squad. He had been eager to make his mark and impress a boss who seemed too good to be true. And then he had discovered just what kind of man Doug Roper was, and everything had changed.

He shakes his head. Pulls the papers from his bag again. Opens the envelope and hurriedly leafs through the pages. There are letters in here too, marked with the name of Caneva's private residence in the hospital grounds. Tilia Cottage. Such a pretty name for a property now broken and overgrown . . .

McAvoy finds the session he can't get out of his mind. He sits down on the brick wall. Lets his eyes pore over the confessions of a psychopath.

Hoyer-Wood: It's strange. Talking to you, Lewis. About this.

Caneva: We're past that, Seb. You're doing so well. You've made such progress. But we can't move on until we address what made you enter that house. What made you need to look into that lady's eyes. What made—

Hoyer-Wood: It wasn't her eyes. It was his.

Caneva: His? Whose?

Hoyer-Wood: His. Any 'his'. The man. Or the children. Those who cared. Who loved.

Caneva: Seb, I'm not sure—

Hoyer-Wood: My father was a weak man. Oh he was an

army man, of course. A proper old-school officer. He
drank sherry in the officers' club and knew how to fasten
a cummerbund. He'd seen service and got his scars, but
it was all giving orders rather than fighting. He was a
Rupert. That's what they call them, did you know? Posh
officers. Expensive education and a stately home. That's
what he was. I didn't know that, growing up, of course.
He was a hero to me. He was still serving when I was
born. Stationed in India, though I don't remember it.
He had an accident of some kind and was invalided out.
Mother, him and little baby me. Came back to the family
home. I don't know how much of this I remember and
how much I've made up, but he walked with a stick and
always seemed to be in pain. Mother was from good
middle-class stock as well. She'd married him when he
was home on leave. Followed him to India thinking it
would be a grand adventure. Coming back to England
was not part of her plan. Nor was looking after a listless,
injured man. I remember Mother as being sad. Angry.
Never content. She did her duties, of course. Raised me,
clothed me, sent me to the right school in the right
uniform. Dad managed some of the lands that belonged
to the family estate. I went to boarding school at seven. It
was all very formulaic and dull. It was when I came home
in the holidays that I discovered Mother had found a way
to make her life more interesting.

Caneva: She had an affair?

Hoyer-Wood: She had lots of affairs. Again, I was young, so
I don't know how much I imagined and what I saw, but
I saw enough. Dad must have known. He must have. But

he turned a blind eye. We never talked about any of this. Not after.

Caneva: After what, Seb?

Hoyer-Wood: Mother met somebody different. Before him, it was farmhands and blokes from the village. It was knee-tremblers behind the pigsty. Then there was this man. He entered our lives and nothing was ever the same again.

Caneva: Explain, Seb. You're doing so well . . .

Hoyer-Wood: He wasn't a big man. Nothing special to look at. He did a bit of work at the garage in the village, as far as I can recall. I spotted him at the house often enough for it to become remarkable. I could sense something different between Mother and Dad. I think she was considering leaving him. For this man, this exciting, virile, alpha male with his dirty hands and oil on his overalls. He wanted her to leave me, to leave Dad, to abandon the big house and go rut in poverty for the rest of her life with him.

Caneva: The atmosphere must have been unbearable. I'm so sorry, Seb. How old were you?

Hoyer-Wood: I was eight. Maybe seven. I don't remember the conversations. Just the shouting. The way the air felt. I just rattled around in the big house, wondering what the hell was going on.

Caneva: Did she leave him?

Hoyer-Wood: This is so hard, Lewis.

Caneva: It needs to come out. You know better than anybody, secrets just eat away . . .

Hoyer-Wood: If she'd left him, it wouldn't have happened.

Caneva: What?

Hoyer-Wood: She told him no. Said she couldn't leave me, though in all honesty I think it was the house and the money that twisted her arm. He didn't take it well. The man. Came to the house.

Caneva: To confront her? To confront your father?

Hoyer-Wood: I don't know what his intentions were. But it was late at night and I was reading in bed and suddenly there was this commotion in the hallway. I went downstairs and there he was: this angry ball of venom in a donkey jacket and flat cap. Mother was crying. Father was standing there in his dressing gown and pyjamas, leaning on the banister like he was going to fall down. Mother was in her nightdress. They were all screaming at one another, but somehow they heard me. Mother told me to go to bed, but the man didn't want that. He looked at me, then at Father, and told me to stay where I was. He wanted Mother to see the kind of man she had chosen. Then he hit Dad. He just punched him in the stomach and Dad doubled over. I couldn't move. Just stayed there on the stairs. And then he grabbed Mother by the hair. Forced her down and kicked her legs apart.

Caneva: Oh Seb, I'm so—

Hoyer-Wood: He raped her right there. Kept his eyes on me the whole fucking time. Dad wasn't tied up. Wasn't even that hurt. He just didn't do anything. He froze. Stayed there a few feet away from where this animal was raping his wife. And he just sat there with this look on his face.

Caneva: And you?

Hoyer-Wood: I couldn't move. Couldn't take my eyes off what was happening either.

Caneva: You can't blame yourself. You were a child, and that kind of trauma—

Hoyer-Wood: I don't blame myself. I blame her.

Caneva: How so? I don't—

Hoyer-Wood: Even as it was happening, this thought kept hammering away in my head. The thought that even though she was crying and telling him to stop, it was the same cock she'd loved before.

Caneva: No, Seb, you can't—

Hoyer-Wood: I remember when he finished, he walked over and took the hem of Dad's dressing gown and wiped himself on it. Then he spat on him and walked out the door.

Caneva: Did they phone the police?

Hoyer-Wood: No. They went back to bed. By breakfast, we were all wearing our masks again. Nothing had happened. We went back to living. Mother started having a few extra shots in her morning Bloody Mary. Started having longer naps during the day. By the time I was in my teens she was drunk most of the time. She died when I was twenty.

Caneva: But I knew you when we were twenty. We were friends. You never—

Hoyer-Wood: Never said anything? No. It didn't matter, did it? I had a new life. I'd escaped. I had friends and people liked me.

Caneva: But you must have had so much you wanted to say. So much inside.

Hoyer-Wood: I'm English, Lewis. English going back

hundreds of years. We don't say anything. We keep it all in.

Caneva: But the effects of what you saw . . .

Hoyer-Wood: Oh it took its toll, Lewis. That was my introduction to sex. That was when I saw real control. I saw a nobody, a man in a flat cap, scare my rich, army-officer dad into sitting mute while he fucked his wife. That went in, Lewis. It took root. When I had my first sexual encounters in my teens it was nothing but a disappointment. A disaster, even. I didn't get hard over the same things as other kids. When I got a chance with a girl, I wanted her friends to be watching. Her mum. Her bloody dad. I knew what I wanted to do. I just didn't do it. Honestly, Lewis, it was just that one time, when the demons in my head took over and I found myself in that room in Bridlington, staring down at this woman, and the next thing her husband was throwing me through a window and I was waking up barely able to move. I was in this chair. Lewis, I know you must have had your doubts about the stories you heard. I know they said I did more. But I'll never forget what you did for me. To be here. To be getting better, with your family, in your care, able to talk about it. I'll always be grateful . . .

McAvoy stops reading. The transcript of the counselling session ends shortly afterwards. The next page in the envelope is a photocopy of a report sent to the Home Office by Caneva, using Hoyer-Wood as an example of the good work the new facility was continuing to do. There are no more transcripts of their sessions. McAvoy leafs through the other pages, in case they have been sent out of order. He checks the dates. This was the last session, a week before the breakout and the fire. He checks the time on the document. Cross-references with previous sessions. They all took place on Tuesdays, 4 p.m. He flicks through his notes. Checks the date of the fire and discovers that it happened on a Tuesday. The escape was noticed late afternoon. He bites his lip. Caneva had told the truth. Hoyer-Wood would have been involved in another counselling session, over at Caneva's private residence, at the moment the other patient disappeared.

McAvoy frowns. Wonders if it changes what he already knows. He knew Hoyer-Wood was over there. Why else would he have been there but for counselling? Does it matter? Does it help him catch a killer of three innocents . . .

He holds the documents, loose, in his hands. Sees himself leave damp fingerprints on their pages and smudge the ink. They have only been printed recently. He raises one of the pages and examines the tiny row of black digits in the bottom right-hand corner. They were printed yesterday evening. Could they have made the last post? He looks at the envelope. Examines the postmark. He swallows, unsure what to think. The letter was posted to him in Bradford; an hour or more from Caneva's home in Chester. Why Bradford? He wonders at the significance of it. Grows frustrated. He curses the fact he is clever enough to know he is no genius.

McAvoy pushes himself off from the wall. The sweat on his back has cooled on his skin and his shirt feels cold and damp on his flesh. He feels uncomfortable and strangely angry. He can see fragments of something but cannot even conceive of how the finished picture will look. He starts to walk back towards the station, Hoyer-Wood's words tumbling in his mind like dice in a cup.

McAvoy thinks of himself at seven years old. His mother had been gone four years, disappearing with a man who offered more wealth, more excitement. He, his brother, his father and grandfather were living a simple life in their croft, halfway up a heather-clad hillside in Aultbea. They had a few cattle. Some sheep, on a nearby pasture. They ate well and laughed a lot. They told stories and watched old movies on a black and white TV with a poor picture. Those experiences formed him. His was a childhood of unspoken love and safety. At eight years old, Sebastien Hoyer-Wood saw a father he barely knew sit mute as a stranger raped a mother who didn't give a damn about him. McAvoy finds himself beginning to pity the child. But then he thinks of him as a man. Thinks of what he did. Thinks of the creature who, even yesterday, managed to assert power over a bigger, more able man, by simply mentioning his wife. He cannot pity the rapist Hoyer-Wood became. And he does not believe a word of his denials. Even through the dry black-and-white of the typed sessions, he can smell the lie of Hoyer-Wood's words. Can see when his tone changes, from the raw honesty of his childhood confession to the subtle manipulation of his friend in the closing paragraph. McAvoy doubts much about himself, but he knows he is good at reading people.

A dull headache is starting to form behind McAvoy's eyes. He feels wretched suddenly. Wonders what would make him feel well. He imagines lying on a rug in the back garden of his new home. Imagines Lilah asleep on his belly, Fin kicking a football at the bottom of the garden, Roisin sitting on the new designer swing she has ordered, reading a magazine. He finds himself drifting into maudlin thoughts. Finds himself beginning to over-analyse. Thinks of his days spent with the dead, and his nights trying to be the silly, capable, strong protector that his wife and children adore. Whether Lewis Caneva still thinks he did right by his friend in writing a report that declared Sebastien Hoyer-Wood mentally unfit to stand trial. Whether he would do the same. Whether he has a best friend. Any friends at all . . .

As he crosses the car park and heads for the back door of the police station, he stops short. Somebody has called his name. He turns, and sees a woman standing by a beaten-up old Fiesta in the car park. She looks tired. More than that.

Warily, McAvoy crosses to where she stands.

'Can I help you?'

He takes her in. Short, unnaturally red hair. Blackheads across her nose. Scarring to her hairline and below her ear. One of her teeth is markedly whiter than the others and clearly false. She's wearing a plain, round-neck T-shirt and there are home-made iodine tattoos on arms that bear scars. She has lived, this woman. Lived almost unto death.

'You're McAvoy?'

He nods. Extends a hand. She looks at it, and seems to recoil.

'I'm Ashleigh,' she says. She opens her mouth to speak again, then closes it.

McAvoy waits, then gestures at the police station. 'Would you like to come inside? We could get a coffee . . .'

'You're looking into the deaths, yes? Yvonne. Philippa. Allan.'

McAvoy stops speaking. Holds her gaze. 'I'm on that team, yes.'

She nods. 'You know about Hoyer-Wood, yeah? You know how they're connected?'

McAvoy wants to get her inside. Doesn't want this chat to take place in a car park, with sweat on his clothes and the broken glass and dog shit of the city streets on his shoes.

'We're investigating several lines of enquiry. Could I ask you to come inside, Miss . . .'

She pulls a face. Waves a hand, telling him to be quiet. She takes a breath, and he can see her shoulders shake. 'Is he doing it again? Is he well again?'

'I'm sorry, could you explain . . .?'

She puts her hands in her hair and scratches her face, leaving white lines among the broken blood vessels and acne.

'I think I know who's doing this.' She pauses, and her hand makes a tight fist. 'He tried to do it to me.'

McAvoy freezes. Then he reaches out to take her elbow. She lets him do it. Turns her face to his and lets him look into her brown eyes. Then she speaks again.

'That bastard raped me. That night in Bridlington when he nearly died. It was my bloke who nearly killed him. It was that night I got these scars. And whoever's killing these poor sods wanted to start with me.'

15

11.40 a.m.: fifty feet away.

Helen Tremberg sits in the front seat of her blue Citroën and tries not to let the tears that fall from her eyes bleed into her voice.

She's not touching the mobile phone to her ear, and she is holding it with the cuff of her blouse. It's an unconscious thing. The phone is her own. She's not trying to reduce the chances of leaving evidence. She just somehow doesn't want her skin to be tainted by this phone call. She wants as little of herself as possible to be involved.

She speaks again. Wants to bite her tongue in half as she does so.

'So, you can see why I thought you should be told.'

The young woman at the other end of the line sounds confused and afraid. Helen can't blame her. She should be.

'The other officer made it clear that I was really helping out by making a statement. I didn't want to. I just wanted it to be over and done with. It was horrible, y'know? My dad warned me about setting up my own place but I thought nobody would want to rob a place like this. And I didn't go through the pockets. I don't do that. I'm trying to run a professional business and . . .'

Helen lets her talk. Melanie Langley seems a nice girl. Helen finds it hard to imagine her kicking a robber in the bollocks. Reckons she has a friend she can rely on for that sort of thing.

'The thing is, there have been some complications. Legal issues. I won't bore you with the details, but the thing is,' Helen tries not to stumble over her words, 'Adam Downey has been released on bail. Obviously we are very keen to secure a conviction in this matter and I shouldn't even be calling you but I feel I have a duty to your safety. Adam Downey is a very dangerous man with dangerous friends. I'm deeply concerned that if you don't withdraw your statement, he may take it upon himself to ensure that you do.'

Mel stays silent for a moment, then there is a snuffling noise. 'How can this be happening? I didn't . . . I mean, it wasn't even . . . please, what should I do?'

Helen presses her lips together. She feels tears drip onto her collarbone. She is disgusting herself more every second she stays on the line. She knows she should confess all to Pharaoh. To McAvoy. She knows that she did nothing wrong. Not until now. But she cannot bear the thought of that video being seen. And more, the man who called her had known so much. He had seemed so absolutely certain when he told her how easily her career could be smashed. In the past couple of days she has told herself that perhaps she is doing Mel a favour by persuading her to withdraw her statement. She has no doubts that Downey's employers will stop her from talking one way or another. Yet she still finds herself abhorrent. She can smell the stench of corruption on her skin. It is choking her. Inside the little car, with its misted windows, her senses are full of her own vile lies and it makes her want to gasp for air.

'Miss Langley, I would get in a great deal of trouble if it was discovered I was making this call. My advice would be to call the investigation team and simply tell them you are no longer sure what you saw. Then perhaps you should spend a few days somewhere else. Do you have a friend you could stay with? Your parents?'

Mel just snivels. She doesn't deserve this.

'Miss Langley, I have to go. I hope you understand that if the situation changes, we will of course require you to tell a court what you saw. But at this moment, your safety is paramount. I hope I won't need to be in touch again.'

She ends the call, then opens the car door and throws up all over the rutted concrete. She's barely eaten, so the vomit is just acid and water. She sticks her fingers down her throat and tries to bring up more.

Through tears, with the taste of acid and lies on her tongue, Tremberg looks across the car park. Between two vehicles, she can see Aector McAvoy talking to a short, hard-faced woman beside a little car. McAvoy is leading her into the station. He has an arm on her elbow, as if she is a refined old lady who needs a little help with the steps. Looking at him, the smell of vomit in her nostrils, she realises how much she wants to be like him. He doesn't manipulate. Doesn't strategise. He won't have thought to ingratiate himself with the woman by taking her arm. He won't be trying any psychological tricks. He'll have taken her arm because it's the right thing to do. It's what she needs, in this place, at this time. Helen wouldn't have thought to do that, and if she had, she'd have been too unsure of herself to see it through. She wants to be a good policewoman. She wants to catch villains. But nothing feels as clear as it used to. Her own investigation is currently stalled, Ray's suspension leaving her small team of detectives with little or no direction. Shaz Archer looks like a lost puppy without her mentor. She's spending most of her time on her mobile phone, talking to Colin and trying to find out what is going on.

As she heaves spittle onto her dowdy shoes and feels the hot emptiness in her belly, Helen is suddenly overcome with a need to prove her worth. She suddenly needs to remind herself that she is a good person who has simply been trapped into doing a terrible thing. She wipes her mouth and pops a piece of chewing gum onto her tongue, then checks her reflection in the rear-view mirror and manages to take some of the darkness from under her eyes with a stick of concealer. She sniffs, then steps over the vomit and crosses the now empty car park. She uses her electronic card to open the doors then heads for the major incident room.

Keep it together, keep it together, keep it together . . .

As she enters, Ben Nielsen is in the middle of an extravagant stretch. His shirt is riding up to reveal a belly with a Hollywood six-pack. He's a keen sportsman who hits the gym twice a day, though his stamina seems to be used for bedroom athletics rather than anything on a playing field. He's very good with the ladies. Helen looks at him and has to swallow down spittle and bile as she realises that such a man could easily be put to use by Downey's employers. She has begun to think of them as talent spotters. Businessmen adept at spotting rising stars. Without realising it, she has mentally christened them Headhunters.

'All right Hell's-Bells? You bored?'

Helen manages a smile. Nielsen looks a little wide-eyed, as if he's been staring too long at a computer screen.

'We're a rudderless ship, Ben,' she says, sarcastically. 'Without Colin's example and leadership, we're lost in a fog. I thought I'd see if I could be of any use to you.'

Nielsen raises a suggestive eyebrow, then laughs. Nothing will ever happen between him and Helen. They're friends, and she knows too many of the places that his penis has been to want to go near it herself.

Nielsen smiles, sitting forward in his chair. He leafs through the pile of papers on his desk then hands a list of names to Helen.

'The big man's asked me to look into those buggers. The family of the shrink who looked after Hoyer-Wood. You know where we're at with that, do you?'

'I'm in the dark, Ben.'

Nielsen quickly fills her in. She nods as he outlines McAvoy's theory.

'And the pathologist says that's feasible, yes? That her chest could have been caved in by repeated compressions? Like CPR? Fuck, that's awful.'

Nielsen nods. 'Aye, our killer's not squeamish. So, can I leave those names with you? It would be a big help.'

Helen nods, already jotting down important names, dates, times and places from the brief synopsis Nielsen has just given her. She needs this. Needs to work. Needs to atone. She crosses to her own workstation and starts bringing up databases. For the next forty minutes, the incident room is silent, save for the occasional groan or muttered phone call from Nielsen.

Soon, Helen is lost in work, her face lit by the glow of the computer monitor. She acquaints herself with Caneva's children. His daughter, Maria, is now twenty-eight years old and lives in West Yorkshire, alone. She has one police caution to her name, having been involved in a protest about the building of an incinerator in a Holderness village. A Google search shows that she has been active in several campaign groups for environmental issues and is a registered nurse. She has a Facebook page, but has not used it for several months and only has a dozen friends on it. Her profile picture is a photograph of a cat. Helen makes a note of her discoveries but fancies she has drawn a dead end. She turns her attention to Maria's younger brother, Angelo.

A moment later, Helen is nervously jigging her legs and tapping a pen on her teeth. She wonders if she has struck gold. Angelo Caneva was sentenced at sixteen years old to a stretch in a young offender institute in North Wales, half an hour from Chester, where his father now lives. He was sentenced for petrol-bombing a minibus, but had been getting into steadily worse trouble with the police over the previous eighteen months. The family lived in London at that point. His worsening behaviour coincided with his mother's suicide.

Helen pulls up a web browser and tries to find any reports on the inquest into his mother's death. She finds only a few *In Memoriams* that mention her name, and one paragraph in a London freesheet that said a verdict of suicide had been recorded.

Helen pulls a face. She wants more. The details of the court case are sketchy and she can't find any newspaper reports on it because Angelo's name would not have been mentioned in any press cuttings due to his status as a minor. She examines the date of the sentence. Notes that it was passed at a Crown Court rather than a Youth Court. She alters the boundaries of her web search. Finds the local paper for that region. Keys in a few choice words and waits for something to happen.

Helen lets herself smile for the first time in days. Angelo Caneva was jailed almost a decade ago for petrol-bombing a minibus carrying patients from a local private medical facility for physiotherapy at a nearby spa. It does not take Helen long to ascertain that Hoyer-Wood was a patient at that facility at that time. Nobody was hurt in the incident, which occurred more than a hundred miles from Angelo's London home, but the charge was arson with intent to endanger life. The boy's solicitor offered little mitigation. He said his client had refused to cooperate in the preparation of reports, and could only tell the court that Angelo had been slowly unravelling since the death of his mother. He told the court the boy had been a clever and diligent pupil at a high-class boarding school before his expulsion for continued misbehaviour, and that his father was struggling with business debts and the responsibility of raising two teenagers alone. The judge had given him six years.

Helen feels hungry, suddenly. She nips to the vending machine and comes back with two packets of crisps and a can of pop. She has almost forgotten the phone call to Mel. Has almost put Mark and Downey and the Headhunters from her mind. She suddenly feels like a detective.

Her mouth full of crisps, Helen punches a phone number into the landline on her desk and finds herself speaking to the hassled receptionist at the young offender institute near Wrexham where Angelo Caneva was an inmate. After introducing herself and stressing that she is part of a murder enquiry, she manages to get the governor on the line. He has a Liverpool accent and sounds less busy than his colleague. Helen tells him what she wants. Who she is. Asks him if he remembers Angelo Caneva.

'Posh lad? Yes, I remember Angelo. Didn't really fit in. We had problems.'

Helen tries to keep the excitement from her voice. 'Were you governor then?'

'No, senior warden. Angelo was nice enough, though he looked proper soft compared with some of the lads we get. He had the hard time you'd expect, really. He liked books and drawing and just being left alone. Took him a while to warm up but he got the hang of doing time. Served just over three years, I think. Never went to mainstream prison. Is he in bother again?'

Helen bites her lip, not knowing whether she should give too much away. 'We would love to speak to him in connection with the current enquiry. He's not a suspect, you understand. He just might be able to shed some light on a few things.'

The governor makes a noise that suggests he's thinking. 'I wish I had more to tell you. His file won't have that much more in it. He did a couple of courses while he was with us. Took his GCSEs, now I remember. Got good grades, considering. Earned his stripes with the lads in a couple of scraps. Was popular by the time he left. I thought he'd probably go into something useful. He did a City and Guilds course in something or other. Might have been plastering. I'll check and get back to you. I do remember he was always in a world of his own. Always had his mind somewhere else. I hope he's got himself sorted out, Constable. We always expect the worst but Angelo seemed to have more about him . . .'

Helen leaves her contact details and hangs up. She rubs her nose and it makes a squeaking sound. In her bag, she notices her phone is ringing, but decides to ignore it. She doesn't want to be distracted from this feeling. She clicks back to the Police National Computer and looks into the eyes of Angelo Caneva's mugshot. He's young. Small. Dark-haired and frightened. But there is something else in his eyes. Something that could be called determination.

Helen prints the image. She is about to cross to the printer when the phone on her desk begins to ring. Impatiently, she snatches up the receiver and barks her name.

'Constable Tremberg,' comes a familiar voice. 'Please don't ignore my calls. I could be in distress and require your assistance.'

The joy of the previous moment dissipates as the colour drains from Helen's face. She sinks into her chair.

'I did what you asked,' she hisses, spittle hitting the receiver.

'Indeed you did, and your services are hugely appreciated. I understand that Miss Langley is busy recanting her calumnies as we speak. No, I am seeking your assistance in one more matter. You may not be currently aware, but one of my well-informed young uniformed constables told us some days ago that when he was apprehended, Mr Downey was spitting and cursing with regard to having had his money taken by a girl of decidedly Romany appearance. I am not of the opinion that Miss Langley could be described in said terms. No, I require a little clarification from yourself regarding the identity of this unknown creature.'

Helen feels herself begin to shake. Jesus, no . . .

'I am not a great believer in happy accidents. I don't find the idea of serendipity to be reliable. But sometimes the universe does play along. I'm referring to McAvoy. Like yourself, Detective Constable, he will soon become a little more manageable. And it would seem Sergeant McAvoy has a wife who caused considerable embarrassment and distress to our Mr Downey.'

Helen leans forward. Rests her head on the cool corner of the desk. She can feel herself coming apart.

'Don't,' she says, softly. 'Whatever you're doing, whatever you're planning, don't go near her. You don't have any idea what you would be starting.'

From the other end of the line comes a faint laugh.

'So, you concur. The young Mrs McAvoy is indeed the person to whom we should be addressing our petition for recompense. Thank you, Detective Constable. Now, please do not trouble yourself any further. I can assure you that your contributions to our cause have been appreciated. The funds deposited in your bank account will remain there as a gesture of gratitude. Do not be foolish enough to warn your superior about the information we have in our possession. The fates have actually succeeded in saving Mrs McAvoy from our original plan. Mr Downey will not be pleased but Mrs McAvoy will be grateful her identity has become known to us. I am an adaptable man. But I guarantee you that our plans will become more severe in execution should you go running to her husband with your stories. I thank you for your time.'

Helen holds the phone to her ear long after the call is terminated. She feels part of herself leave her body and die in the hot, static-laden air. Then she wipes her face with the heel of her hand, and manages to stand up. She needs to find McAvoy. She needs to help him catch a killer. She just hopes that she can look him in the eye.

It's cold in the interview suite. Although it's a small, airless space, the walls have shielded the little room from the heat of the day. The walls are damp and the air cool. The hairs on Ashleigh Cromwell's arms rise as she crosses them on the chilly rubber surface of the desk.

McAvoy sits down opposite her and hands her the can of fizzy pop she had asked for, along with a see-through plastic cup. She takes it gratefully and pours herself a drink. She watches the bubbles bounce on the surface, then drains it. She closes her eyes, trying to compose herself. McAvoy lets her take her time. He sits back in the chair, content to wait.

Ashleigh Cromwell had been living with her husband and children for more than ten years when Sebastien Hoyer-Wood had taken a shine to her that winter day in Bridlington fourteen years ago. She was no holidaymaker. The house where he tried to rape her was the family home, on a quiet street near the seafront. She'd seen him looking at her a few hours before the attack. She and her husband, Johnny, were having a drink in one of the boozers off the promenade. He'd stared. Stared until her husband had asked him what he was looking at.

'He seemed out of place,' says Ashleigh. 'Everybody knew Johnny. He was a bit of a character. He was a tough man and everybody knew we were a couple. The way he was looking . . . it just wasn't . . . Johnny gave him a look to say clear off and he did. We just laughed about it. It didn't matter. He was just a bloke. It didn't seem to matter.'

It had mattered that night, though. Sebastien Hoyer-Wood had got into their house.

Ashleigh plays with the empty cup. She'd told him on the way in that she didn't like coppers, didn't like police stations or telling tales. She seems uncomfortable here, as though she is being interviewed under caution. McAvoy is trying to put her at her ease. She looks at him before she speaks again, as if to thank him for his patience. Then she takes a breath, and stumbles on.

'I reckon he sneaked in when Johnny was having a fag with the back door open. They found his clothes later on. He'd been naked when he came in. Must have hidden somewhere in the house till we went to bed. My kids were there. That's the bit that I can't get past. My kids . . .'

Shortly before midnight, Ashleigh and Johnny Cromwell were woken by Sebastien Hoyer-Wood pouring petrol over their sleeping bodies. The bedroom light was switched on and a naked man in a surgical mask told them to take a deep breath. To sniff the air. To look at what he had in his hand.

'We were half asleep and wide awake at the same time,' says Ashleigh. 'You know when a light goes on and you sort of can't see properly? But we smelled the petrol. And we saw the lighter. And you only had to look between his legs to know what he wanted.'

Hoyer-Wood had ordered Johnny back against the bedroom wall. He told him he was going to do him a good turn. He was going to let the children carry on sleeping.

'He pulled the covers back,' says Ashleigh, eyes closed. 'I had a nightie on, and he poured more petrol on me. It stung. Stung my eyes. Then he told Johnny that if he moved, we would both go up like fireworks. The house would burn down. His kids would die. He told him to stay still like a good boy, and enjoy the show.'

Johnny Cromwell had never been the type to apply logic to a situation. He was a straight-ahead kind of man who had taken his fair share of beatings but handed out plenty more. He had looked at the naked man lying on top of his wife, parting her thighs, and he had reacted instinctively. He'd moved. He'd hit Sebastien Hoyer-Wood so hard in the face that he broke his own hand. And then Hoyer-Wood had dropped the lighter.

'He got himself more than me,' says Ashleigh, her fingers brushing the scarring at her hairline. 'I went up, like. My nightie caught fire. There was a whoosh of flame. I don't know how I knew to do it but I flung myself on the floor and rolled, like they do on the movies. I put myself out. Then I looked up and the curtains were blowing and there was glass everywhere and he'd gone out of the fucking window . . .'

McAvoy looks across at Ashleigh Cromwell. She's probably in her early forties but looks ten years older. She looks wrung out. It is as if a pretty, vivacious woman has been dehydrated. All of the moisture has gone from her flesh. Her softness has been burned away.

There is silence in the room as Ashleigh wipes her fist across her nose. A low, insistent buzz has started to penetrate McAvoy's consciousness, and as he looks for the source, a wasp lands on the table between them. Instinctively, he takes Ashleigh's empty cup and drops it over the creature. It knocks, ineffectually, against the plastic.

'Johnny went after him. I ran to see the kids were okay. They were still sleeping. Then I went out onto the street. Johnny had caught up with him. He was smashing his head on the pavement. I don't know why I told him to stop. I guess I thought that with Johnny's record he would do time. I don't even know if I was thinking at all. I was sore and scared and there was this naked man all bloody and burned in the snow on Bridlington seafront and the next thing there are all these people and somebody is putting a coat around me and Johnny is being held back and the police are there . . .'

On the table, the wasp has begun to beat against the plastic. Its tiny tinfoil wings are breaking as it fights, pathetically, in the sticky syrup that pools on the table. McAvoy cannot stand it. He lifts the cup and watches, gratified, as it buzzes angrily away.

'I didn't save him,' says Ashleigh. 'Other people saved him. The people who died.'

She seems to get smaller. Takes her face in her hands.

McAvoy reaches across, his arms rubbing the drips of orange soda into the tabletop. He puts his hand on her bare forearm and she raises her eyes to his.

'You said you thought the killer wanted you, Mrs Cromwell. Could you tell me what you meant by that?'

Ashleigh sniffs, noisily, and raises her eyes to the ceiling. She rubs at her arms.

'Johnny and me broke up not long after it all happened,' she says. 'I don't know if it was because of that night or all the other stuff. Johnny was always hard work. He had other women, but I usually forgave him. I had a few other men, though they were usually too shit-scared of Johnny to be tempted. I was a bit more of a catch then, as well. Johnny got himself into more bother. He stopped coming home. We split up then he got sent down for glassing some bloke. I don't even know what it was about. The kids and me moved away. The oldest has her own place but my son and me are doing okay.'

'You live locally?' asks McAvoy.

'Scunthorpe,' she says. The steel town is half an hour away, over the bridge. Not too far from Barton, where Yvonne Dale died. McAvoy wonders if it is significant.

'I have a sister there,' explains Ashleigh. 'We wanted a fresh start. She runs a newsagent's and I work there with her. We're doing okay.'

McAvoy nods. He licks his lips, unsure how to ask. 'Hoyer-Wood,' he says, gently. 'He wasn't sent to prison. He could be said to have got away with it . . .'

Ashleigh looks as if she has just cracked an out-of-date egg onto her tongue. She looks like she wants to spit.

'Me and coppers have never got on,' she says. 'I never expect much of them but I thought he'd have done a stretch. The copper in charge, George Goss – he said the bastard had been doing it for years. He reckoned they'd put him away for nigh-on life. Then his posh mates got involved and next thing he was living it up in some plush mental asylum. I don't know how I felt, really. I know he was suffering, so that was something. I sometimes wondered if Johnny would have got sent down if he'd killed him. I sometimes wonder why I told him to stop. I wonder a lot of things, but I keep it all inside, most of the time. Then something brings it back. Like now.'

McAvoy waits. He rubs at the sticky patch on his skin and watches the wasp as it crawls up the pale green wall.

'How did you know to ask for me?' asks McAvoy.

'George Goss,' says Ashleigh, looking at the floor. 'When I heard about the murders I rang for him. They told me he was retired. They put me through to CID and some bloke said he could get a message to George if it was important. I said it was and George rang me. Told me that I should speak to you. Said you were okay.'

McAvoy nods, embarrassed. 'The murders,' he says. 'What do you know about the victims?'

Ashleigh gives him an angry look, and for an instant, McAvoy sees the animated features of the woman she once was. There is a light in her eyes and a flame appears to have been lit behind her pale skin.

'I didn't know the paramedic, but I remember the two women and it doesn't take a genius to work out that they're all connected.' She says this with an accusing tone. 'I work in a newsagent's. I read the *Scunthorpe Telegraph*. I don't watch the news. But you hear, don't you? Somebody told somebody else and then my sister told me to read one of the other papers. I can't believe you haven't told people they're linked. I thought you might not know, but George says you already know about Hoyer-Wood and what happened . . .'

McAvoy raises defensive hands. 'That decision was made at a senior level,' he says, neutrally. 'Myself and the senior investigating officer are trying to change the thinking on that. We're trying to get in touch with anybody who may be at risk. I'm sure an officer would have been in touch with yourself at some point . . .'

Even as he says it, he senses that his words will not give Ashleigh much new faith in the police.

'Too late for me, Mr McAvoy. He already bloody got to me. That's why I'm here.'

McAvoy looks at her, trying to make sense of her words. Behind her, the wasp appears to lose its grip on the wall. It tumbles and lands on the cold floor, where it twitches and spins until, finally, the soft buzzing comes to a halt.

'I don't understand,' he says, and wonders if he should have it etched on his gravestone.

Ashleigh takes the can of drink and raises it to her lips. It shakes in her hand. The can is empty, but she makes a show of swallowing.

'A year ago,' she says, quietly. 'Maybe a little more. It happened again. I woke up with a fucking man sitting in my bedroom.'

The room suddenly seems smaller. The chill of this desolate, enclosed space seems to wrap itself around McAvoy like a damp shroud. He has to fight not to openly shiver.

'I'm not some wimpy lass,' says Ashleigh, as if this is an important point. 'I can punch my weight. I don't cry all the bloody time like a baby. I've been through stuff, but I've done my best to put it behind me. But when I woke up and there was a man in my bedroom I thought my heart was going to stop. It was like it had never gone away.'

McAvoy closes his eyes. Tries to imagine what went through her mind and then stops himself when it becomes too painful to endure.

'Was he . . .?'

'Naked? No. Didn't have the light on either. He was just a shape at the end of the bed. A weight. I'm not tall and I sleep with my feet drawn up but I stretched out and felt this lump. I thought I might have left the laundry basket at the foot of the bed or something daft like that, but then the weight shifted. I opened my eyes and could tell there was somebody there. Looking back, I suppose I might have thought it was my son, but it didn't feel like that. He felt wrong, somehow. I knew. Knew it was happening again.'

McAvoy scratches his head, hard enough to hurt. 'What happened?'

'I'm not a screamer,' she says. 'I shout, if I do anything. But I didn't even do that. I just sat up and asked if there was somebody there, and then he spoke. Just sitting there, on the end of the bed. He spoke, like we were friends or family and he wanted a chat.'

McAvoy can find no better way to express his feelings than by swearing. 'Fucking hell.'

'He said it was my fault. People like me. We'd saved him. Hoyer-Wood could have died that night but people like me had saved his life. He said he wanted to punish me. People like me.'

'Did he have a weapon? Fuel? A flame?' asks McAvoy.

'I don't think so,' she says. 'It was dark and I was trying not to wet myself. But even though I was bloody terrified, I was angry at him for what he said.'

'What did you say to him?' McAvoy asks.

'I told him that I'd suffered at that bastard's hands more than anyone. That if he thought I had somehow saved his life out of fear or compassion, he was out of his mind. I told him that I wished him dead every fucking day and that if he had the chance, he should find the crippled bastard and kill him – not me. Not people who had suffered enough.'

McAvoy pictures it. Pictures Ashleigh, scared yet defiant, talking to a voice in the darkness.

'Did he hurt you?'

Ashleigh gives what could be called a laugh. 'He started to snivel,' she says, eyes wide. 'Started to fucking shake. Said he was lost. Said he wanted to put things right but didn't know what to do. He even started to say sorry . . .'

McAvoy rubs at his eyebrow. Licks his teeth and tastes elderberry cordial and chocolate on his tongue.

'What happened, Ashleigh?'

'I put the light on,' she says, eyes closed again. 'And he ran.'

'You saw him?' asks McAvoy, sitting forward. 'You saw his face?'

Ashleigh shrugs. 'Maybe. A shape. Half a face.'

'And you never called the police?'

She shakes her head. 'I never told anybody. Not until now. I thought whoever it was had changed their mind. They were confused. Upset. They could have killed me as I slept but they didn't. Then all this started. I knew you had to know. So I'm telling you.'

McAvoy is about to speak when a knock on the interview room door breaks the silence. A moment later, Helen Tremberg enters, holding a sheet of paper. To McAvoy, she looks ill. She's pale and there is darkness under her eyes. She looks like she has been vomiting and there are sweat patches under the arms of her white blouse.

'A word, Sarge?'

McAvoy gestures at Ashleigh. Tries to suggest with his gaze that now is not a good time. He looks across the table at the short, red-headed woman who has endured more than anybody should have to. She is not looking at him. She is looking at the piece of paper trailing loosely from Helen Tremberg's hand.

Suddenly, Ashleigh stands and darts towards the door. She grabs the paper from Helen's hand and seems to crumple. She reaches out to the table, and McAvoy grabs her before she can fall.

She looks at him, uncertainty and confusion in her eyes. She brandishes the piece of paper; the print-out of a ten-year-old mugshot.

'Him,' she says, stabbing a finger onto the page. 'It was fucking him!'

McAvoy looks at the page and then up at Helen, who is opening and closing her mouth, wordlessly.

He takes the page. Looks at the image of a teenage boy.

Locks eyes with Angelo Caneva.

16

7.48 p.m.

Sodium street lights, the neon of a kebab shop and the faint cigarette glow of an unfamiliar sun.

A taxi office, just off Hull's Hedon Road. Knackered cars parked on double-yellow lines and a drunk pissing against the graffiti and chipboard of the boarded-up convenience store next door.

Inside the office, Adam Downey is leaning forward to snort a line of high-quality cocaine off the glossy front cover of a porno magazine. He's laid out the line on the thigh of a black woman. He likes the effect. Better yet, he likes the sudden rush that is thumping up his nose and eyeballs and into his brain, filling him with a sudden fervour and fury and causing him to emit a strange, animal growl as he raises his head to the ceiling and feels the drugs fill his system.

Downey has never been the sort of drug pusher to sample too much of his own product. He likes to smoke a spliff while watching a movie, and one of the girls he sees regularly has pretty toes that look extra special when holding a nice fat joint out for him to take a puff upon. But he hasn't taken much cocaine. Truth be told, he's a little frightened of it. Despite making his living by selling the white powder in bulk, he's seen too many people come to depend upon it to want to start sticking too much of it up his nose. Besides, the product that passes through his hands is a little too pure. Once it's been through a few dealers and been cut with glucose and a little bicarbonate of soda, he might consider the occasional line to help him stay awake or better enjoy a night out. But the idea of waking up and reaching for a cellophane wrap of the stuff makes him feel uncomfortable.

Adam Downey has decided to make an exception tonight.

Half an hour ago, the telephone rang in the taxi office. It was the voice that Downey has come to fear. He'd told him the name of the woman who had taken his money. Told him she was a copper's wife. Told him what he had to do. Downey had agreed, even as his insides turned to water. He'd thought he was just dealing with some pikey bitch. He'd thought that his boys could have a fun time with her and that would be the end of it. He'd entertained visions of sticking a few extra quid in her knickers when they were done, so she knew there were no hard feelings save the one in his pants. Now the evening's entertainment has become overloaded with risk. He's heard about the copper she's married to. Heard the rumours.

Downey is worried, even though he has three good men to lend a hand. Two Turks and Big Bruno are going to watch his back. They are each formidable and reliable. Bruno, in particular, is an intimidating specimen. He's a black guy with a Hull accent. He has long dreadlocks and wears shorts all year round. He has muscles on top of muscles, rippling like storm clouds across his skin, and Downey knows that despite his deep laugh and playfulness with the other drivers, Bruno has a violent side. He's killed before. Downey saw it happen. Saw Bruno smash a fifteen-kilo dumb-bell over the head of an enforcer who made the mistake of inviting him into his home to discuss a peaceful resolution to their differences.

As he stares up at the ceiling and fully opens his jaws, Downey feels the drugs fill his system. He bounces his legs, feeling tightness in his toes. He stands and looks at himself in the mirror that covers one full wall of the tiny space. It faces a desk that carries an old computer and a stack of unread paperwork. He examines himself. He's dressed for the occasion, in a baggy white T-shirt with a designer tattoo pattern across the chest. He's wearing tight jeans that sag, fashionably, at the arse, with slip-on shoes and no socks. He's accessorised effectively, with diamond earring and expensive watch. He looks good, and the bruises add an air of menace to the pop-star image he tends to affect. He stares into his own eyes. Tells himself he can do this. He has men at his disposal. He just beat a serious charge.

You're beautiful, mate. You're the prince of the fucking city . . .

As the drugs course through his system, he begins to feel untouchable. Begins to question his orders. He's been told to give Roisin McAvoy a message, but not in the way he had wanted to. He is under instructions not to hurt her. The voice had told him that the organisation has other plans for McAvoy. He's not to hurt her. Not to make a scene.

Fuck them!

The cocaine emboldens him. He had been looking forward to making that bitch cry. He'd been dreaming about closing his hand around that tiny throat, crushing those full lips until they burst like ripe fruit. He turns and spits on the floor. He looks at his hands and sees that they are trembling. He closes them into fists. His nose is running so he rubs it with the back of his hand. His movements are frantic. He is surprised to find that his dick has gone hard. He wants to do this. Wants it to happen now. Wants her in front of him, begging . . .

Downey pushes open the door to the main office, where Bruno and the Turks are sitting in mismatched chairs. He grunts. Tells them it's time. They stand up without saying a word. The Turks had signed up for the job even before learning what it was. He'd just told them he needed back-up and there was cash in it for them. They're a curious pair. Memluk is the taller of the two at just over six feet. Tokcan is a quiet lad who has fallen in love with Fruit Pastilles since arriving in England and always seems to be chewing. Neither is over thirty. They're tanned and unshaven, dark-haired and fit. They both liked Hakan. They know that, somehow, the woman they are going to visit tonight was responsible for his disappearance, and are looking forward to taking out their frustrations. Downey realises he should tell them the plan has changed. They're not to hurt her. Not to make a fuss. But he finds himself unable to.

'Time to play,' says Downey, and is rewarded with a trio of smiles.

They head outside, into air that feels baking hot despite the hour. The sky reminds him of a white towel that has been mixed in with a dark wash.

Downey and his men climb, wordlessly, into a large American 4x4. Bruno had turned up in it tonight and nobody has questioned him about its origins. It's large, comfortable and stylish, and Downey feels very much at home as he slides, dizzily, into the leather passenger seat and hears the throaty hum of the engine turning over.

'We good, Boss?'

Bruno asks the question quietly. The two Turks are on their team, but there is an unspoken agreement that the men in the front of the car are in charge.

Downey nods. His head is spinning. His eyes are open but he's struggling to take in much about the scene before him. He shakes his head and slaps his cheeks. Focuses. Sees . . .

The car is cruising down Hedon Road, past the entrance to the docks; the cemetery; the prison. He watches the landscape change as they approach the flyover. To his left is Sammy's Point, where the glass-panelled city aquarium sits on a jutting spit of land. They cross the River Hull, its muddy banks curving down to chocolate-coloured water. They pass through a city that Downey thinks of as his own. He finds himself giggling as he waves a hello to the statue at the crossroads. It's a man on a golden horse. It might be a king. It's stood there for as long as he can remember. Downey once heard a rumour that the sculptor killed himself because he got the stirrups wrong. It's outside a pub that used to be run by a local rugby legend called Flash Flanagan, a good old bloke who wore Elvis glasses and became a fixture in the Old Town after he retired from the game. Played on a Lions tour, apparently. The story goes that he turned up for the flight without a passport and carrying his clothes in a carrier bag . . .

My city, my people, my city, my people . . .

Downey's mind feels alive.

Wired.

Memories are fizzing inside his skull. The lights on the dual carriageway seem to be blurring and forming shapes. He wants to talk to Bruno. Wants to tell him that he's on top of everything and that this is just another step down a road he's already mapped out. But his mouth feels dry and his heart is beating too hard, so he says nothing. Just closes his eyes and lets the car drift towards the Humber Bridge. Enjoys a fantasy or two and lets his brain become a pan of popping corn.

You're the man, Downey. The man!

He feels powerful. A fucking king! Feels tired, too. Feels his eyes closing even as his blood fizzes with excitement.

Minutes later, Bruno's hand is on his shoulder, shaking him awake. The vehicle is parked on a nondescript side street in the small town of Hessle. He vaguely remembers telling Bruno this was the plan.

'This way.'

He points and sets off up the road, looking in the windows of the large, three-storey townhouses. Nice place. Decent folk. Could kill them all with a point and a nod . . .

He crosses a main road then down a little back alley, leaves and branches sticking out from the slats in the old fence, dead leaves crinkling and turning to dust underfoot. They emerge on the foreshore. Downey looks up at the Humber Bridge. He's walked across it plenty of times. His mam did some sort of charity jog for breast cancer across it a few years back. It's a familiar, comforting thing.

The Turks are muttering between themselves. He gives them a nod and they smile back, all teeth and stubble.

'Oh, we're going to have such fun . . .'

Downey checks his phone. Double-checks the address. Walks on, softly, until he finds the house. Four cottages, side by side. White paint and a pale blue trim. Picket fence and dainty eaves. Welcoming lights and herbs in a window box, freshly labelled, the soil a rich brown.

Cautiously, urging the others to stay back, Downey walks to the front of the property. The small fence shields a front yard of no more than two metres by three, and he can see straight into the front room.

'Bingo.'

She's there. The gypsy bitch. She's unpacking some cardboard boxes and turning to talk to somebody on the sofa. He angles his head and is surprised to see the seamstress. She's wearing a hooded jumper and is hugging a cushion, feet drawn up. Cross-legged on the floor is a young lad with red hair. He's drawing in a colouring book, his tongue sticking out of the corner of his mouth in concentration.

It's a nice scene.

There's no sign of the copper.

Downey wonders if he should just knock on the door. The orders are clear enough. He's to hold a phone to McAvoy's ear and play him a message. That's it. Roisin is not to be harmed. Not now. Not yet. But the bitch had hurt *him*. She'd kicked him in the balls and took his money. She'd made him doubt himself and reminded him what a pathetic little weakling he really is. He wants to hurt her.

Downey chews his cheek with his back teeth. Rubs a hand across the scabs on his chest. He begins to consider the consequences. His employers have indulged him this far. He's proven his usefulness several times and they moved mountains to get the charges against him dropped. Would they lose patience if he were to slap the bitch around a little? After all, it's his crew. His patch. It's his city . . .

He feels Bruno approach him. Smells marijuana and clothes dried in a damp room. He turns and looks into the big man's face. Downey looks at him, questioningly, and Bruno gives a nod that could mean anything.

'Playtime, Boss?'

With coke coursing through his veins, Downey takes it as an affirmation. Takes it as agreement that they should kick the door in and drag the bitch to the ground by her hair.

'That's them,' he says, pointing. 'It's the right house. There's a kid, but . . .'

'A kid?' says Bruno. 'Fuck.'

'Take him in another room. There's no need for him to see.'

Bruno presses his lips tight together. He sniffs. Turns to the Turks and tells them they're to follow him inside. Then he turns back to Downey.

'You sure, Boss? I'm game, but you're going to have to stuff something in his mouth not to wake the neighbours.' Bruno leers. 'Try his mum's knickers.'

Downey considers the adjacent houses. None of them seem occupied. While there are people strolling past and enjoying the warm air down by the water's edge, the area is quiet enough for him and his team to do what they want.

'She needs to learn her lesson,' says Downey. 'They all need to see.'

He opens the garden gate.

One step.

Two.

Three.

Fuck, fuck, fuck . . .

Before he can talk himself out of it, Downey bangs on the painted wood of the front door. A moment passes in which a part of him begins to hope that nobody will answer. Then Roisin McAvoy opens the door, smiling wide, halfway through enquiring whether he has lost his key . . .

It all happens fast and loud.

Bruno pushes past Downey, causing him to stumble against the doorframe. He hears Roisin let out just the quickest of shrieks and then Bruno's hand is around her mouth. He's dragging her down the hall, knocking a photograph from the wall so that it smashes on the cord carpet.

'Keep her quiet, keep her quiet!'

The Turks run past him too. Downey finds himself staggering, one arm on the wall to keep himself upright. He hears a door bang, then there are cries and shouts.

Christ, what are we bloody doing?

He slides along the wall, his mind racing, heart thudding like two rams butting heads. Then he staggers into the living room.

One of the Turks has Roisin against the wall. Her feet are off the floor and her face is turning purple. The other is pressing Mel's face into the sofa, yanking down her jogging trousers as he does so. There's a tattoo at the base of her spine. He suddenly wants to cut the thing off. Wants to stick her with pins. Sew her bloody lips together.

'Little bastard bit me!'

Downey turns to see Bruno, sucking a wound on his hand, kicking a sideboard over in front of a small door beneath the staircase. The muffled cries and screams within suggest that the boy inside is fighting to get out.

'Close the fucking curtains,' says Downey, and Bruno does as he is commanded.

Downey crosses to where Memluk is throttling Roisin.

'You like that, sweetie?'

He looks into her eyes. Sees nothing but fear. Sees frothy spittle pop from between her lips and land on her chin. The sight reminds him of an earlier fantasy, and he lashes out with his right fist, hitting her hard in the mouth. The blow bursts her lips and smashes her head back against the wall.

'Aw, did that sting?'

Behind him, he can hear Mel kicking and biting, and then mumbled foreign curses.

'Drop her,' says Downey to Memluk, and Roisin tumbles to the floor. Rather than lying there as he had expected, she scrambles to her feet, looking around for her child.

She fixes her eyes on Downey.

'He'll kill you,' she says, and blood sprays out to spill on the exposed skin above her vest.

Downey laughs, hoping Bruno will join in. But nobody does. The only noises are of violence and fear and there is nothing fun about any of it. He loses his temper. Fixes his venom on Roisin then lashes out with a kick. She's tiny and tries to dodge but he still connects where he had intended. She falls forward, both hands between her legs, as Downey finds himself giggling and pointing, excited, like a child . . .

As Downey turns to seek Bruno's approval, a figure appears in the doorway. Bruno senses him too and turns, just as a fist the size of a boiled ham takes him in the jaw. Bruno's head snaps back as if he has been struck under the chin with a golf club and he falls like a tree.

The Turks both move towards the new threat and Downey watches, entranced and motionless, as the giant flame-haired figure in the doorway lunges forward and hits them like a train.

'Stop, stop . . .'

Before Downey can finish the sentence, he feels pain screaming through his left leg. He looks down and locks eyes with the gypsy girl as she sinks her teeth into his skin. He opens his mouth to scream but before he can do so, a giant, pale, freckled hand closes around his lower jaw and he is pushed back across the living room and slammed into the wall.

A face is in front of his.

Broad.

Handsome.

Scarred.

Furious beyond words.

'A message,' says Downey, desperately. 'I've got a message . . .'

He winces, waiting for the fist to slam into his jaw, but the big man suddenly drops him as one of the Turks hits him with a punch to the lower back.

Downey's mind clears for a second.

Her husband.

The copper.

He watches as McAvoy turns. Watches as the big man grabs Memluk by his shirt and throws him at the wall so hard that a crack appears from floor to ceiling, the fresh plaster splitting like dry wood. Tokcan grabs him by the knees and the two of them go down in a melee of arms and legs.

Downey gasps for air. He reaches down and feels the blood on his leg and the sensation clears his senses for a moment. He looks down and sees Tokcan on McAvoy's back, his arm around his throat. Sees McAvoy stand, the weight upon him unimportant.

Downey wants to run. He wants to push his way free and run

into the warm air. He wants to be somewhere else. Someone else . . .

Without knowing why, without even realising he is doing it, Downey pulls the phone from his pocket. He fumbles with the buttons. Finds the message on his answering service and turns the volume up as far it will go. Then he lurches forward and presses the phone to the big man's ear.

McAvoy can't see. There is too much rage and fury in his eyes. But he can hear.

And he can hear his own voice, dribbling out of the telephone that is being held to his ear by some pretty boy in jeans and a T-shirt.

He stops. Shrugs the foreign man off his back and hears him swear as he crashes to the floor.

McAvoy listens.

Hears the words he sobbed at Sabine just yesterday.

'They would have died. All three of them. Roisin thinks they did. She's never asked. Never checked. I beat them unconscious and left them for dead. I don't know how the fire started but it would have cooked them and any evidence. But I couldn't leave them. I put Roisin somewhere safe and went and dragged them out of there. Then I left. I've lived with that ever since. Lived with her thinking one thing, and me knowing another. I let her down. Even now, I know that if it happened again, I couldn't have killed them. I'm not that man. It's not in me. She's married to the wrong man . . .'

McAvoy falls back. Looks up at Adam Downey. Feels the strength go out of him. Feels the man below him scrambling free. Hears them dragging the unconscious men away and the front door banging against the wall.

He feels Roisin's arms around him and hears Mel's cries.

'Fin,' he says, suddenly. 'Lilah.'

He finds himself tangled in a collection of limbs. Feels small arms hugging his knees and kisses from a bloodied mouth upon his forehead.

Through it all, one thought, over and over.

She taped me. She fucking taped me.

And then he is wrapping himself in the people he loves, trying to insulate himself with their caresses. He wants to hurt somebody. He wants answers.

He wants to be a different man.

17

Gnarled fingers of cloud are slowly closing over a nearly full moon. It is the only light in this ebony sky and seems to sit vulnerably on an open palm; a communion wafer waiting to be crushed.

'Stupid,' says McAvoy, again, through thin lips. 'Stupid, stupid.'

He has one hand on the wheel. The other is striking his forehead, the heel of the hand rhythmically hitting his sweaty skin.

It's gone midnight and the road to Beverley is quiet. He could press the accelerator to the floor if he wanted to, but despite his anger he knows where the speed-cameras are and can't afford the bump to his insurance premiums if he got caught doing more than sixty.

'Mouth shut, mouth shut, mouth shut . . .'

He beats the words into his brain, furious with himself for daring to believe there was any benefit to sharing the secret agony that has sat in his chest for a decade.

'I'm so sorry, so sorry, so sorry . . .'

For the past few hours, Roisin has been apologising. Telling him everything.

He thinks about it now. Pictures the scene. Sees himself, growing pale, shaking his head and scratching blood from his arms as she told him why Adam Downey was in their home, and why he shouldn't report the incident to his colleagues.

McAvoy hadn't lost his temper. He'd refused to shout at her. He wanted to shout, of course. Wanted to tell her she had been bloody stupid and demand to know what the hell she had been thinking. But the words got nowhere near his mouth. Besides, his own betrayal far outstrips her moment of weakness. Instead of shaking her until her false nails fell off, he'd sat her on the toilet seat in the bathroom and used a warm flannel to remove the blood from her skin. He had stroked her face and pushed her hair behind her ears. He'd hugged the children, straightened up the living room, and made Mel a hot chocolate. Then he'd led Roisin to their bedroom and told her to explain again. Told her he needed to hear it again so he could fully understand.

She'd been there, she said. Been in Mel's shop when Downey came in demanding the coat that contained the drugs. Downey had offered Mel money but she had refused. So he'd got tough. And Roisin had stood up to him. She'd phoned the police in her pocket and she'd kicked him in the bollocks. Then she'd seen the wedge of cash. It had been instinct. She'd picked it up and run. It had come to just under £600. She'd felt bad straight away and had offered it to Mel, but Mel didn't want it. So she'd spent it. Bought him a watch and some furniture for the garden. She was sorry. She hadn't expected this. She hadn't wanted to cause trouble. It was just a mistake . . .

McAvoy had held her. He said he understood. Told her he would fix it. Told her that the bad men wouldn't come back and then softly kissed her bruised mouth. At that moment he had been so damn relieved that she hadn't heard the message on Downey's phone, he would have forgiven her anything. Relieved, too, that he had arrived home when he did. He thinks about what would have happened had Pharaoh not told him to go get some sleep. Feels pitifully grateful that he hadn't stopped in at a takeaway or a supermarket on the way home for some snacks and a bottle of wine. He makes a squeezing motion with his hand and feels the pain in his fingers where his knuckles had connected with Bruno's jaw. He wonders how badly he hurt the man. Whether his jaw broke. Whether he snapped a vertebra as his head went back. Whether there will be repercussions.

McAvoy follows the road into Beverley. Passes down quiet streets and through the deserted town centre. He doesn't blink. Just follows the road until he sees the sign.

The village of Molescroft doesn't stop before it runs into Beverley. It's a conurbation rather than a suburb, but most people who live here think of the shops in Beverley as being the centre of their community. It's a pretty place, with a good junior school and neatly tended semi-detached homes, spread out around a playing field and a small row of stores.

Sabine Keane lives here. The shrink. The counsellor who betrayed him.

McAvoy bares his teeth as he thinks of it. He sees her, now. Sitting in her chair with her handbag open. She must have left her phone on the entire time. Must have called her other employers at the start of each session and let them listen in as he bared his soul.

It has occurred to McAvoy that perhaps the room itself was

bugged. Perhaps Sabine is an innocent party who will be as appalled and disgusted as he to learn that his confessions had been taped. But he fancies not.

McAvoy turns the car to the right, onto a silent side road, then quickly right again onto Finch Park. Sabine's bungalow is the first house on the left, a small, neat property with a separate garage and unusually petite windows that make the building look as if it was designed by a child with crayons and graph paper.

He sees her even before he has parked the car. She's sitting on the front step, lit by the light that spills out from her open front door. She's holding a glass and wearing a dressing gown, and even in this light, McAvoy can see tears on her bruised cheeks.

McAvoy steps from the car. Sees her recognise him. Sees her drop her head.

'You taped me,' he says, softly, as he walks up the drive. 'You taped our sessions.'

Sabine raises her head. She looks exhausted, like she's been slapped. Her cheeks are red and there is a dark patch above one eye.

Sabine just nods. Takes a sip from the glass.

McAvoy stands over her.

'You know you're finished,' he says. 'You must know that.'

She shrugs. Implies that she truly couldn't give a damn. Sniffs, noisily, and raises the glass again with a hand that shakes.

'Was it money?'

Sabine says nothing. Then she mutters something that might be an apology.

'Sabine, please . . .'

'My husband,' she says, at last. She raises her head. Looks at him with eyes that swim in salt water. 'He knocked a cyclist off their bike last year. Got sent to prison.'

McAvoy looks confused. 'I don't understand . . .'

'He's a teacher,' she says. 'He's not strong. He's got another year to go. At least.'

McAvoy rubs a hand through his hair. He slides down to a seated position, his backside on the cold paving stones, his back against the wall. He takes the glass from Sabine and takes a sip. It's vodka. He hates the stuff, and hands it back.

'When did they get in touch?'

'Not long ago,' she says, her voice cracking. 'Not long after you were referred to me. They showed me pictures. Emailed me photos of Graham. That's my husband. Well, we're not really married. That's why I got cleared to provide services for the police. He didn't show up on the background checks.'

'They wanted you to tape me?'

'Not at first,' she says. 'They just wanted to know what made you tick. Then they told me I had to call a certain number at the start of our sessions. To ask you about your secrets. What you felt guilty about. What you loved.'

McAvoy scrapes his boot along the stone. Kicks a pebble and watches it disappear into a flower bed. He draws his knees up, hugging them to his chest. He shivers, despite the clammy warmth of the night.

'You did as you were told?'

'I didn't push,' she says. 'I sort of hoped you wouldn't speak. You'd kept quiet . . .'

'And then I just blurted it out,' he says, so softly he can barely hear his own voice. 'I gave them everything.'

Sabine nods. 'They called tonight. Told me I'd done my bit. Said Graham would be left alone. They said you were getting your message tonight.'

She sounds as if she is about to say more, but she closes her mouth and looks away.

'Do you still have the numbers?' he asks. 'The pictures they sent you?'

She shakes her head. 'They told me to destroy them, delete everything.'

'And the person you spoke to?'

She frowns. 'Well-spoken. Quite wordy, like a solicitor or a politician. Very calm. Not old but not young.'

McAvoy stares up at the sky. The moon has disappeared, throttled by the fist of cloud.

'We could get your phone records. See what numbers you called. We could keep Graham safe . . .'

Sabine shakes her head again.

'I just want this to stop,' she says. 'I thought they might have hurt you. I can't think straight. Couldn't sleep. Couldn't look at the kids . . .'

'They hurt my family,' says McAvoy. 'I can't allow that. How do I begin to allow that?'

Sabine looks sick. Looks like she wants to smash the glass and draw one of the shards across her wrist.

They sit in silence for a time. McAvoy's anger is now just a hot rock in his guts. He's trying to think clearly. He has no doubts that the people who did this are the same outfit that Colin Ray has been chasing. He knows they are well connected, powerful and dangerous. They think they have him in their pocket. They have dirt on Roisin, and dirt on him. With a phone call they could end his career. With a call to Roisin, they could end his marriage. She believes he killed her tormentors. Married him in that belief. Fears, above all, that such a truth would drive her from his arms.

But he doesn't know what they will use their leverage for. He's not actively investigating them. He's not on Colin Ray's team. He's hunting a killer and hasn't thought of organised crime in months. He fancies he has time on his side. He needs to keep Roisin out of harm's way until he can find Angelo Caneva. He needs to stop a killer before he can make sense of tonight's events.

McAvoy makes a decision. In the morning, he will tell Roisin and Mel to take the kids and return to the old house on Kingswood. It's not much of a hiding place but they still have a few days before they have to give the keys back and he'll feel happier knowing they are somewhere they will take a little more finding and where there are plenty of neighbours to shout for help. Caneva is priority. Pharaoh has taken over the reins of the investigation once more and declared him prime suspect. He was released from custody a few years back and is no longer under the supervision of the probation service. The last place he was registered as living was in a flat in Coventry, but that was some time ago and since then he has dropped off the grid. His father is refusing to answer his phone. Tomorrow, McAvoy hopes to visit Angelo's sister, Maria. Nielsen is trying to get a current address, and Pharaoh will alert the media to the fact they are trying to find him. Things are going the right way. McAvoy's intuition and detective work have provided the breakthrough and he should be feeling proud of himself. But all he can see is the blood on Roisin's face and the terror in his son's eyes as he hugged his daddy.

'Did they tell her?' asks Sabine. 'Your wife?'

McAvoy shakes his head. 'They just let me know they knew. I might have to tell her.' He corrects himself. 'I am going to tell her.'

'She sounds a strong woman. You didn't do anything wrong.'

'There are different types of wrong,' he says, the words hanging in the air.

Sabine manages a little smile. 'Do the police really believe that?'

McAvoy looks at her, and then inside himself. Sees what he is becoming.

'I don't know what I believe. I don't know what I am.'

It is just gone 2 a.m. Dr Olivia Pradesh can smell antiseptic and rubber on her long dark hair as the wind blows it across her pale, delicate features. The storm that will soon engulf Hull has already broken here and a fine rain drives at an angle across the car park on a sharp breeze.

She fumbles in her bag for car keys. The bag may be designer but she treats it like a canvas sack, dumping everything in the same central compartment. She rummages inside it as she winces into the rain, turning her head so her dark hair billows behind her. She closes her hand around her phone and takes a quick glance at the screen. A couple of missed calls and a text asking her if she fancies the trip to Prague that some of her old university friends are planning over the next Bank Holiday weekend. She remembers that she was supposed to call some detective constable from East Yorkshire but fancies he will have gone to bed by now. She'll do it in the morning. She'll reply about Prague, too. She needs to recharge her batteries. Needs a toasted sandwich and a glass of milk then a few hours on the sofa under a crocheted blanket.

Dr Pradesh is forty-four years old. She's fit and slim, and though her mother is of Indian descent, her colouring does not proclaim her heritage the way her name does. She's an attractive woman. Her hair has always been jet-black but these days she has to use a dye to mask the grey roots. She's wearing a tweed jacket over a purple blouse, with a short, fawn-coloured skirt and soft leather boots. A string of pearls bounces around in her cleavage as she crosses the car park. They feel cold on her skin and she reaches inside her blouse to pull them free. Her hands betray her profession. Her skin is scrubbed painfully clean, her nails short and neatly trimmed.

As the rain plasters her hair to her face she plunges her hand back into the bag and closes her fist around the keys. She moves around to the far side of her unassuming Audi and reaches out to open the passenger door.

As she closes her fingers around the handle, something slams into her back. She feels the wind go out of her at the same moment as her middle and index fingers dislocate and mangle upon impact with the cold, wet metal of the car.

Dr Pradesh manages to shout but something strikes her left cheek.

In a moment she is semi-conscious; her face in a puddle, one ear and eye submerged.

For a moment there is utter blackness. Dead air. She raises herself, unsteadily, on one arm. Suddenly she hears tyres, squealing across the concrete. Sees a dark vehicle slam to a halt in front of her. Then she is being dragged up by her coat collar.

She hears her string of pearls snap.

Sees them dance as hailstones on the ground.

The doors of the van are pulled open. She feels a clump of hair come loose as she is slammed against something hard and the impact wakes her instincts. She shouts. Lashes out. Tries to turn so she can see who is doing this to her. Then there is a fist in her gut and she is being pushed back onto a patch of dirty grey carpet that masks the hardboard floor of the vehicle. She kicks out again. Feels pain as the van doors slam against her ankle. She draws them up and starts to shout afresh.

For a moment, her screams ring out, loud despite the whistling wind and driving rain. Somebody must have heard! Somebody must see!

She looks around, frantic now. Tries to get a sense of her bearings. Then a scream is ripped from her throat. At her side is a corpse. The skin has taken on a greenish tinge, like moss on an alabaster statue. The eyes are sunken, the mouth locked in a grimace of pain. She throws herself backwards, desperate to get her face away from the body before the stench crawls into her nose, but she is too late.

She smells decay.

Corruption.

Dead flesh.

Sobbing now, she wriggles onto her side and kicks at the corpse, trying to push it as far away as she can. Her booted feet go through the dead creature's torso as if she is stamping on a cardboard box.

And then she is thrown forward. The van is moving, fast and reckless. She tumbles, hits the van doors and one swings open with the impact.

She glimpses fresh air.

The dark, rain-lashed night.

She takes a step, as if to throw herself through the door, but a sudden jolt pitches her back. Her head hits wood. She tastes blood in her mouth. And then her eyes see nothing but gold stars and spinning blackness.

The body beside her slides on the wooden floor as the van slews left. The vehicle hits a speed bump and the doors swing open afresh.

Slowly, unseen by the driver, watched only by the street lights and the stars, the corpse slithers towards the exit.

The vehicle's wheels hit a pothole, and the rotten body teeters over the lip of the van.

And as the driver accelerates, the dead thing finally slips free.

Organs and innards and compressed gases explode in a damp spray as the long-dead sack of rancid meat collides with the unyielding ground.

Angelo Caneva's dead, staring eyes watch the vehicle disappear into the distance.

Steam rises from his ruptured guts, disappearing into the air like a cartoon ghost.

Part Four

18

5.05 a.m. Great Horton Road in Bradford.

It's too early to knock on a stranger's door, so McAvoy sweats and shivers in his car outside a row of grubby shops, waiting for the sun to come up. He hopes that when it does, the windows of the vehicle will stop reflecting his features back at him. He doesn't like what he sees. He's wearing yesterday's clothes and Roisin's blood and feels as feverish and pestilent as the skies he left behind when he set off for West Yorkshire two hours ago. He's unshaven and his face looks puffy and sore. His right hand, limp in his lap, is bruised across the knuckles. He's lost a fingernail, grabbing one of the Turks, and his middle finger is throbbing beneath the Elastoplast.

Well-connected.

Powerful.

Ruthless . . .

He can't stop thinking about the outfit that turned Sabine. Can't stop wondering what the hell to do next. He should be concentrating on the investigation. Should be thinking about Hoyer-Wood and Angelo Caneva.

Here, now, he can barely remember their names.

He looks at the clock. Still too bloody early.

The cup of coffee he bought from a petrol station an hour ago has gone cold, but he sips at it anyway, for something to do. He watches a spider industriously building a web around the wing mirror of the car. It's working hard. It's doing its job. It seems to know what it's doing and what's expected of it. He finds himself envying the little bastard.

He flicks on the radio. Starts listening to an early-morning phone-in show on Radio 5 Live, and switches off when he finds himself agreeing with everybody.

McAvoy knows there is nothing to stop him knocking on Maria Caneva's door immediately. He's a policeman looking into three murders and her brother is prime suspect. She hasn't responded to any phone messages. But to McAvoy, waking the poor woman up at this hour just seems too damned obnoxious and uncivilised. He doesn't want to be that kind of man. And besides, he's not ready for it. Doesn't know what noise will come out when he opens his mouth to speak. He doesn't feel like a policeman. He feels like a thug and a coward who has been manipulated and outplayed. There is so much guilt clogging his guts he feels as though he has been stuffed full of mud and stones.

Roisin, I'm so sorry . . .

His wife will wake up this morning with black eyes and bruised lips. His son will have nightmares for days. Mel may take the matter out of his hands entirely and tell his colleagues what happened.

More than that, Adam Downey might come back.

He has no fucking clue what to do.

5.06.

5.07.

5.08 . . .

At just after 6 a.m., McAvoy rubs a hand through his hair and scratches at his crown. His fingernails come away dirty. His patience frays, then snaps, and he steps out of the car into the cool air of the morning. He drops his bag and spills papers and pens on the damp stone of the pavement. Feels sick rise in this throat as he bends forward to start picking things up. Winces as his phone falls from his pocket. He looks at the image on the cracked screen. At Roisin and his children. Two smiles and one wet, pink, baby face. He wants to press the picture to his face. Wants to breathe them all in and be made better by their nearness.

He makes fists. Closes the car door. Locks it. Pulls his bag over his shoulder and sorts himself out. Steps over a cracked paving slab and nearly loses his footing on a discarded kebab.

Maria Caneva lives down Bartle Lane. The electoral register indicates that she lives alone, though given that it's a student neighbourhood he can't rule out that she rents out a room or two to somebody studying at the nearby university.

He turns off the main road and walks softly towards the small, bare-brick property. McAvoy tries not to think anything too derogatory about Bradford. The areas he has seen are dirty, rubbish-strewn and ugly. Most of the shops carry signs written in a language he presumes to be Urdu, but he feels far too Caucasian and guilty when he starts thinking about the socio-economic reasons for the neighbourhood's current state and usually stops himself before he can think anything negative. It's a community of halal butchers and general stores, where watermelons in damaged crates pile up outside graffiti-covered general stores that carry posters for English newspapers long since defunct. He would think of it as a rough neighbourhood if not for the unexpected flashes of class. Halfway up the main road is a glitzy, brightly lit restaurant that would not look out of place in London's West End, and most of the cars parked outside the takeaway shops and budget electrical stores carry Mercedes badges. It's an area McAvoy struggles to understand and he's grateful he's not a policeman here.

McAvoy finds the right door. Composes himself. Licks his palm and smooths his hair down. Rubs his lips. Closes his eyes and concentrates on breathing.

He knocks, politely, on Maria Caneva's door, then begins to count to ten in his head.

After just a few seconds the door is opened by a plump young woman in her middle twenties. She's wearing a pink dressing gown and has a pair of glasses on top of her head. Brown hair is pulled back from a plain but not unattractive face, and though she looks surprised to be answering the door at this hour, her expression is not unwelcoming.

'I thought you were the milkman,' she says, by way of greeting.

McAvoy shows her his warrant card. Gives a courteous, closed-mouth smile, and introduces himself.

'Are you Maria Caneva?'

She nods.

'I would like to talk to you about your brother.'

Her face falls, but an expression that may be relief also flashes over her features.

'What's he done now, silly sod?'

'Could I come in?'

'Please.'

Maria invites him inside. The door opens straight into an

untidy living room. On the sofa that sits beneath the large front window there are pillows and a quilt. In front of it is a coffee table covered in haphazardly opened letters, food wrappers and empty coffee cups. The TV is an old-fashioned and boxy affair that sits on a dusty glass cabinet and the electric fire looks sad and unlit inside a slate-and-breezeblock fireplace. There are books and old newspapers piled in one corner of the room and DVD cases in the other. It's not a nice room, but Maria makes no apologies as she kicks the duvet behind the sofa and waves McAvoy to sit down.

'Did I wake you?' asks McAvoy, indicating the pillow and trying not to mention how much of her fleshy thighs he can see as she sits down and draws her legs up underneath her.

She looks puzzled, then realisation dawns. 'Oh, I sleep down here most nights. There've been burglaries. I haven't got much to take but I don't like sleeping up there. Every time I hear a noise I think there's somebody in the living room.'

McAvoy looks around him.

'Have you lived here long?'

'A few years. I've never really got round to doing it up the way I want. I just rent, so if I spent too much tarting it up it would just be money down the drain.'

'And you live alone?'

Maria makes a show of sticking out her lower lip. 'Young, free and single. Apart from the "young". Or the "free".'

McAvoy plays with his collar. He's suddenly very aware of how he looks. He gets out his notebook, putting his warrant card down on the sofa beside him as he does so. Maria looks at it again and her mouth opens wide.

'Oh, you're McAvoy? I'm sorry, I was half asleep. Didn't twig . . .'

McAvoy takes his card and looks at it himself, as if for confirmation. 'I'm sorry?'

'You got the transcripts okay, yes? I wasn't sure I'd spelled it right.'

McAvoy feels a little lost, but he suddenly understands how Hoyer-Wood's psychologist sessions ended up in his hands and why the envelope was postmarked West Yorkshire.

'You sent them?'

Maria nods, innocently. She seems to be waking up a bit now. She reaches down beside her and finds a can of pop. She sips at it and smiles.

'I spoke to Dad after you visited him,' she says. 'He called me. He doesn't very often, but I think talking to you had shaken him up a bit. He said what you wanted. What was happening.'

McAvoy looks at her. She seems utterly without guile. She's a bright, open person and McAvoy feels himself warming to her. As she comes alive, she seems to examine him more closely. He feels her looking at the bruises on his knuckles. The Elastoplast. The blood and bruises. 'I'm sorry, have you been trying to get me on the phone?' she asks, raising a hand to her mouth. Her hands are cleaner than the room, with short, clipped nails. 'I'm only on a pay-as-you-go phone and it's off most of the time. I'm a nurse, you know that, yes? My bosses play merry hell with me because I'm such a bugger to get hold of. Dad does too.'

She says it all brightly. McAvoy wants to push.

'You and your dad are close?'

Maria shrugs. She seems about to speak and then stops herself. She closes her eyes and then suddenly stands. 'I'm going to make a coffee. Do you want one?'

McAvoy doesn't know what to say. He just looks down at his

notebook and stays quiet as she rolls her large rear end off the sofa and plods into the kitchen. He hears cupboards opening and a kettle boiling. Hears a fridge opening and closing and then she is back in the room, carrying two glasses of steaming brown coffee.

'No cups,' she says, apologetically. 'Hold it by the top or you'll burn your fingers.'

She hands McAvoy the glass of hot liquid and he sips it, scalding his tongue. He puts it down as Maria plonks herself back on the sofa next to him. She spills coffee on her bare leg but doesn't seem to notice. Then she looks at him so hard that he wonders if she is trying to imprint a thought on the inside of his skull.

'Angelo,' she says, at last. 'He's in trouble again, yeah? I know what you're thinking. You're wrong.'

McAvoy licks his thumb and dabs at a spot of blood on the back of his hand. 'What am I thinking?'

'You're thinking Angelo has killed these people, aren't you?'

McAvoy spreads his hands. 'We're open-minded. But he has questions to answer. This is a murder investigation that is very closely linked to Sebastien Hoyer-Wood. I feel like I'm swimming through treacle, but the one thing I'm certain of is that somebody is punishing the people who saved Hoyer-Wood's life. Yesterday I spoke to a lady who was there the night Hoyer-Wood should have died and who tells me that Angelo broke into her house with plans to kill her. Angelo has spent time inside. He has a record. The picture we're getting is of a dangerous man . . .'

Maria pulls the band from her hair as McAvoy talks and places it over her wrist. She pushes her hair back from her face and rearranges it into the same style it was before. She doesn't look worried. Just distracted.

'He's not dangerous,' she says. 'Not really. He's just been through a lot.'

McAvoy sighs. 'Do you know where he is?'

Maria considers him. 'You've read what I sent you, yes?'

McAvoy nods. 'How did you get the transcripts, Miss Caneva? And why did you send them to me?'

For a time, the small, untidy room is quiet save for the sound of the city coming to life beyond the glass. Steel shutters are being drawn up. Car engines are beginning to purr. A letter box bangs noisily as a newspaper is pushed through it too hard.

Maria finishes her drink. She pulls her legs up afresh. She scratches at her face and makes all the little adjustments that seem to help her decide what to say.

'You know what happened, yeah? You've read them properly?'

'All of them. Every word.'

'You believe him? Sebastien?'

It's a strange question, but McAvoy answers it. 'They helped me put some of the pieces together.'

She nods. 'I've had those transcripts for years, Sergeant. That man had an effect on all our lives. When you're young you ask questions. You need explanations. There was all sorts on Dad's computer, growing up. Angelo and me could quote you most of those sessions word for word.'

McAvoy shakes his head. Decides to be honest. 'Maria, I'm lost . . .'

She gives him an indulgent smile. 'I do prattle, don't I? The funny thing is, I've often wondered what I'd do if I ever had to tell a policeman about this. I didn't imagine I'd be in my dressing gown in a place like this. It's funny. The whole thing's just funny.'

As McAvoy looks into Maria's cheerful, pleasant face, he realises he is talking to somebody damaged. She is too light-hearted. Too sparkly. She's suffered and endured. She's survived, but at a cost to some part of herself. He wonders what she allows herself to feel. He's suddenly too hot, and yet the hairs on his arms are rising and he feels himself about to shiver.

'Angelo went off the rails when Mum was poorly,' she says. 'Got into trouble more and more often. Our lives were different then. We had money, for a start. We were very London in our outlook. We weren't exactly happy, having spent so much time at that bloody place.'

'You mean your dad's hospital?'

She snorts. 'Hospital? It was a factory. A money-making machine. The government was throwing money at private healthcare in those days. Dad always did have an eye for a few quid.'

'Living there must have been hard . . .'

'We never really lived there,' she says, looking at the dirty sole of one foot. Her actions are childlike, and put McAvoy in mind of Fin's schoolfriends.

'No?'

'Weekends and holidays,' she says, licking her finger and rubbing the dirt from the knuckle of her big toe. 'It was pretty, but Mum was never mad keen on us going up there too often. There was plenty of security and there really shouldn't have been any risks, but Mum said it was no place for kids. Even so, Dad got his way. He usually did. It was okay, to be honest. Mum would take us shopping or down to Hull or over to York or wherever. We didn't mind too much.'

McAvoy wonders what she is trying not to blurt out. He decides to steer the conversation.

'Sebastien Hoyer-Wood,' he says, gently. 'Tell me.'

Maria gives a high, girlish laugh. It's a near-hysterical sound, but there are no tears. She just giggles, as if the name is funny.

'We knew that him and Dad were friends at university. We knew he'd got into trouble because he was ill. We knew Dad was helping him get better and we didn't have any reason to doubt it when Dad said there was nothing to be scared of about having him in the house from time to time.'

'How did your mum feel about your father having these sessions in the family home?'

Maria flashes her teeth then shrugs. 'She never said.'

McAvoy waits for more. When nothing comes, he moves closer to her. Tries to hold her gaze.

'Maria, what is it you want me to know? You sent me those transcripts . . .'

She turns around on the sofa, kneeling up, and pulls the curtains aside to look at the street. McAvoy can no longer see her expression, but he can hear her words.

'When we met Sebastien he was in a wheelchair. He couldn't talk very well. He was in a lot of pain. He was a cripple, though you couldn't use that word around Dad. I'm a couple of years older than Angelo, you know that, yes? We'd do impressions of him. It's cruel, isn't it? But Dad would have him in his study and they'd be talking and sometimes Angelo and me would go and listen at the door or go outside and look through the window. Sebastien saw us, once. He was in his wheelchair, looking out the window. Dad had his back to us. He couldn't see what we were doing. Angelo was pulling this face and being silly and I was laughing and we saw that Sebastien was watching. We were so embarrassed. We felt really bad. He didn't look sad, though.

Not Sebastien. He looked like he was smiling. Like he found it funny. It was creepy, but it stopped us watching the sessions any more . . .'

McAvoy wishes he could see her face, wishes he could better read this strange young woman.

'After it all happened, our family was never the same,' she says, quieter now. 'It affected us all. Mum got sick. Angelo closed down. I don't know what happened to me. Dad started to lose everything. I needed answers. So did Angelo. It wasn't hard to get Dad's transcripts off his computer. I think he knows I took them, but at least it spared him having to talk to us about any of what happened. When he told me you wanted to see them I think he was trying to wriggle out of breaking the rules. I think he knew I would send them to you. I'm pleased I did. You seem nice.'

McAvoy just stays silent.

'You know what Angelo got sent down for, don't you? He was in a dark place. He'd started getting high. Sniffing glue, if you can believe that. It was easier for him to get his hands on than the hard stuff. He always looked young. Nobody would sell to him. He was a bit of a softy, really. Didn't make friends very easily. And he was an angry sod in his teens. He blamed Sebastien for what was happening to us. The money. The way he felt. Mum. He must have found out which hospital Sebastien was in from some of Dad's paperwork. Either way, he disappeared from home for a few days and then Dad got a call to say he'd been arrested. He'd thrown a milk bottle full of petrol and rags at a hospital minibus. Petrol-bombed it. We knew straight away which patient he'd been aiming at. The first question I asked wasn't whether Angelo was okay. It was whether he'd got him.'

Maria turns back, smiling.

'In a way, he did get him. The stress of it brought on a massive stroke. Hoyer-Wood ended up worse than he had been before. Proper vegetable.'

She bursts out laughing and McAvoy finds himself smiling out of politeness. He wants to put a hand on hers and make her tell him the bit that matters most, but there is something so brittle about the mask she wears that he fancies any contact would break her.

'The last transcript,' he says, as kindly as he can. 'It was missing from the bundle you sent me.'

Maria nods. She looks serious for a moment. 'I couldn't send that. I wanted to. I wanted you to understand about Sebastien. I wanted to help you. But I couldn't just send that to a stranger. That was where our lives changed. It would be like posting somebody a broken heart . . .'

McAvoy stays silent. Just looks at her and hopes she'll choose to help him.

'He wasn't crippled by the end,' she says, quietly. 'Sebastien.'

'I'm sorry?' says McAvoy, as he feels his heart begin to race.

'When he was first arrested and they nearly killed him and those interfering bastards saved his life. He was hurt. He was crippled. But you have to remember, he was a medical man. A physiotherapist. He knew just what to do and how much to show the people who were looking after him. He was months ahead of where he should have been, but we didn't know that until he stood up and put a knife to Dad's throat.'

McAvoy closes his eyes.

'That last session,' says Maria, into the cloth of the sofa. 'The alarm went off over in the main hospital while Sebastien was still at our house in Dad's office. We don't know if Sebastien set it up or just took advantage of the situation. Either way, Angelo and Mum and me were in the living room watching TV when the door of Dad's office burst open and Sebastien came out with a knife to Dad's throat. We screamed. We didn't know what to do. He was *the cripple*. He couldn't walk. Couldn't talk in much other than grunts and dribble. And now he had a knife to Dad's throat and was standing in our living room.'

McAvoy rubs his hand across his forehead, pushing the sweat back into his hair.

'What happened?'

'You know what happened.'

There is no gentle way to ask the question, but McAvoy still manages to drop his voice to a whisper. 'He raped your mother, didn't he?'

Maria gives a little snort.

'He'd have liked to take his turn with all of us. The way he looked at us . . .'

She stops and looks away.

'He'd have fucked Dad if it wasn't that he seemed to get so much pleasure from ripping his heart out.'

There is silence in the room. McAvoy tries not to picture the scene she has placed in his head but the image is too vivid, the colours and shapes in his mind too intense. He sees it all too clearly.

'Jesus,' he breathes.

'He knew how to play us all,' says Maria, softly. 'Knew we wouldn't move. He made us sit there. Made his wife and children watch as he held a knife to Dad's throat. He just laughed in Dad's face. He'd have started doing star-jumps if he thought it would have helped him make his point. Dad just seemed to deflate. It was like we saw something leave his body. He just seemed to crumble, there in front of us, when he realised he had been played all along. We just sat there crying as he told Dad everything. The names. The places. All his victims. And Dad, open-mouthed and wet-eyed and pitiful, losing all faith in himself and knowing, in his soul, just what he had exposed his family to.'

McAvoy says nothing. Just listens to his own breathing.

'It was the fire that ended it,' says Maria, pulling at the flesh below her chin and staring up at the ceiling. 'We smelled smoke. Saw flames. We heard people banging on the door. Sebastien reacted first. Dropped to the floor like he'd fallen from his wheelchair. And then there were people in the room and we were being evacuated to safety and Dad was telling us not to talk.'

'Why didn't he say anything?'

Maria looks at him kindly. 'His reputation. The reputation of the hospital. He'd said Sebastien was ill. Said he could make him well. He would have been exposed as a fucking idiot.'

'But after all these years . . .' begins McAvoy, before a sudden flash of temper takes him. 'I went to see him. Your father. He stuck to his story. Told me Sebastien had been ill . . .'

Maria rubs her cheeks. 'He's taught himself to believe what he wants to. We don't talk about it. Nobody ever talked about it. Not even Mum, when she was dying. That's probably why Angelo and me had to do our own digging. We were so angry. Our whole lives seemed so broken and it was all Hoyer-Wood's fault. We dug up everything we could on him. Found Dad's files. When we learned that he should have died that night in Bridlington it was like our hearts had been ripped out. What happened to us shouldn't have happened. Sebastien should have died. He should never have entered our lives.'

'But the people who saved him . . .'

Maria waves McAvoy's protests away. 'I know, they were innocent. When I heard about their deaths I was sad. This was never supposed to happen. It was just a fantasy. A way to make ourselves feel better.'

'But Angelo made it real.'

Maria sucks the inside of her cheek, then slowly shakes her head. 'Angelo was sent to a young offender institute. It was rough for him. Really rough. He was a posh boy. He suffered. Suffered torments you wouldn't believe. We didn't exactly lose contact, but when I went to see him it was so hard for both of us that the visits got less and less. When he was released I didn't even know about it. Then he turned up on my doorstep. I barely recognised him. He was scarred and tattooed and looked like death. He had a baby with him, if you can believe that. He came in and we talked and he told me he was trying to sort his life out. Said the baby was his brother's, then giggled. I think he was high again. We talked some more and I gave him some money and my phone number and he went away. I know you think he killed these people, but I remember him as a kid and he just wouldn't have that in him. I sent you those transcripts so you'd know more about the man responsible for everything. Responsible for our lives . . .'

McAvoy is about to speak again when his mobile rings. He looks anguished, but pulls it from his pocket, and is pleased to see that it's a call from Pharaoh rather than any bad news from home.

'Guv? I'm with Maria Caneva—'

'I know you are, Hector,' she says, and she sounds snappy and tired. 'You can tell her that her brother has just abducted the surgeon who saved Sebastien Hoyer-Wood's life. You can tell her he's dropped off a rotting corpse at the fucking scene.'

McAvoy presses his teeth together until he can taste blood and he hears something pop in his ear.

Another one.

He listens for a few more moments then hangs up, telling her he'll be as quick as he can. Then he turns to Maria. She's heard it all.

'If you know where he is . . .'

She shakes her head.

'Who he might be with . . .'

She shrugs.

He feels like crying.

'Please . . .'

Impulsively, she reaches out her hand and takes his. She looks at the bruised knuckles. Up past his blood-speckled shirt to his red-rimmed eyes.

'It can't be Angelo,' she says, though her voice quavers. It seems as though some part of her is waking up for the first time in years.

'Please, Maria. Does he have friends? How did he leave when he left here? Was he in a car? And the baby? Whose was the baby?'

Maria stares at the bruises on McAvoy's skin. Then she stands and crosses to the fireplace. She pulls one of the slates from the ugly construction and pulls out a scrap of paper. She hands it to him.

'That's where he was staying a year ago. Some mate. I never rang it.'

McAvoy turns the paper over in his hands. It's a phone number with a Hull code.

He holds the paper up to the light.

Sees. Sees it all.

He's up and out the door before he can say thank you. Before he can express his gratitude to the strange, broken girl, who took comfort in fantasising about the deaths of those who saved a rapist's life.

The echo of the slamming door is still reverberating in the room when she reaches under the sofa and pulls out her phone. She punches a number.

'Hi. Chamomile House? I was wondering whether . . .'

19

The path is thick mud and dead leaves, a tangle of stinging nettles and brambles. Thorns whip at Helen Tremberg's bare legs as she slips and slithers over the uneven ground, red welts and white spots appearing on her exposed skin.

It's just gone 7 a.m. and she is a little over a mile from her home. She's changed the route of her morning run and is regretting it. The path is almost impassable. The mud thrown up by her running shoes is halfway up her back and her ankle is starting to throb. Changing the route was a bad decision. She took a wrong turn, somewhere. Made a mistake. It's becoming a habit.

Helen focuses on her breathing and the music. Tries to inhale in time with the beat. Holds the oxygen in her lungs for two bars, then releases it.

'. . . and it feels just like . . .'

In Helen's earphones, Annie Lennox is screeching about walking on broken glass. As Helen loses her footing once more, she considers offering the singer a straight swap. She'd happily take the broken glass over the weeds and horse shit of Caistor's Canada Lane.

Helen used to walk up this overgrown bridleway with her grandad when she was a kid. They would pick elderberries in late summer. Pluck sloes from the hedgerows in early autumn. It's an overgrown and boggy track where the treetops lean in to form a natural steeple at various points. The light is never the same two days in a row as the shifting branches and leaves flicker on the constant breeze. It leads up to the broad green pasture where Helen used to go sledging with her friends when the snows would fall and cut Caistor off from the rest of the world for a blissful few days each winter. It's a place of happy memories and where the rich, earthy scents of the countryside combine to form a deep perfume that feels almost healing as she gulps it down.

But Helen did not fall asleep feeling proud of herself. She doubts she ever will again.

Her thoughts keep returning to the man on the end of the phone.

To Roisin.

To McAvoy.

They were her first thoughts as she woke She keeps telling herself not to be so silly. Tells herself that nobody would be fool enough to attack a policeman's wife. Tells herself that Roisin knew what she was doing when she took that bloody money. Why the hell did she do it? She tries to harden her thoughts against her. But she cannot swallow her own lies. Cannot persuade herself there is anybody lower than herself.

As she runs, she finds her mind filling with pictures of McAvoy. She remembers their first meeting. Remembers that agonising walk from Queen's Gardens to Hull Crown Court. It had rained the night before and the damp pavements were patterned with the crushed shells of snails that had not got out of the way as the city's commuters began their walks to work. McAvoy had kept stopping every five or six steps to pick up any snail he thought was in harm's way. He filled his pockets with them then ran back to Queen's Gardens to put them safely on the grass. Then he had run back to her, red-faced and embarrassed, while she had just stared up at him, open-mouthed, and wondered whether she should write the incident down in her notebook to be used as evidence should he ever go off the rails and shoot up a school.

The path begins to dip and the ground becomes more solid underfoot. Helen focuses on where she is placing her feet. Hears the music. Hears her own blood, pumping in her ears . . .

Two terriers run out from the driveway of the only house that stands on this stretch of the bridleway. It's a large white property, with apple and pear trees standing invitingly in the centre of an overgrown garden. Helen stumbles as a Jack Russell jumps at her legs. The shaggy-looking Yorkshire terrier barks loud enough to drown out the music, and Helen feels a sudden stabbing pain in her chest as she swallows her own shout of surprise. She starts to cough, and kicks out at the nearest dog as they jump excitedly up at her.

'Sorry, sorry, they think the whole path belongs to them . . .'

Helen whips off her headphones. A sixty-something woman with a healthy complexion and two too many teeth in the top row is crunching over the gravel. She's smiling broadly, exposing so many incisors that her grin looks like it should be used by Druids as a place of worship. Helen recognises her from the pub. She tries to smile back, to say it's okay, but can't seem to remember how to do it. She just ends up waving both hands around her face as though warding off a wasp, and then she gets flustered and pushes herself off from the gatepost at a sprint.

The dogs bark louder but are called to heel.

Over Annie Lennox's voice, Helen fancies she can hear herself being referred to as a 'stroppy cow'.

Helen staggers down the sloping path. She feels her ankle turn again as she slips on the old bricks that have been used to patch up the many gaps in the rubble and earth. She wants to be at home, suddenly. Wants to shower the dirt and the shame from her skin. Wants to slip into her plain work clothes and hide herself away behind a computer monitor. Wants to pretend. Wants to be somebody else, or perhaps a different version of herself. She's no good at this. No use at introspection and analysis. No good at thinking about right and wrong . . .

The music in her ears switches unexpectedly. Her phone is ringing.

Helen slows and pulls the phone from the clip on her running shorts.

It's from a withheld number.

Helen feels her hands tremble, as if she needs sugar or sleep. She feels a sudden desire to throw the phone into the nearby field. To change her number. To just keep running.

'Helen Tremberg,' she says, breathless and shaky, as she takes the call.

'Good morning, Detective Constable. I trust you slept well?'

Helen closes her eyes. Leans both arms against the trunk of a tree and waits for her breathing to slow down.

'You said you wouldn't call . . .'

'Indeed, indeed. And for that, may I express my sorrow and regret. You have been of considerable service to our organisation and to further impose ourselves upon you is not something I undertake lightly. However, I do believe that the information I am about to impart to you is of considerable importance.'

Helen presses her finger and thumb to her eyes so hard that brightly coloured spots of light seem to explode behind her eyelids.

'Just tell me what you want,' she says, and her voice sounds childlike and weak.

'Last night,' comes the reply. 'The young gentleman whom you have had in custody. He made an error of judgement. He has caused great distress to your sergeant and his family. Distress we had not intended. For this reason, the young man in question is no longer under our protection. More than this, he is yours to do with as you will, should you find him before one of my associates does. However, I am advised that Mr Downey has not taken kindly to the indignities he suffered. More than that, he feels that the lady who took his money and embarrassed him is personally accountable for all of the inconveniences he has endured. I have every faith in my associates' ability to locate him and bring this situation to resolution, but you may be well advised to keep Mrs McAvoy somewhere safe. I do not think her husband would respond to this communication in the same manner as you. Having done so, I feel a lightening of my conscience. For this reason alone, I am grateful to you, and can guarantee that there will be no further communications from myself or my associates. I thank you for your time, and hope that you enjoy the rest of your morning jog. Goodbye.'

As Helen stares at the phone, it returns to playing her music.

Helen looks behind her, up the dirt track, through the tunnel of overhanging, interlocking branches. Her world seems to be narrowing. The scent in her nostrils is suddenly thick and overpowering. She can smell dead creatures in the hedgerows. Can hear the sound of spiders chewing on desiccated corpses in their webs. She can hear the screams of dragonflies and ladybirds and the crunch as sloes are squashed beneath careless feet.

Helen is no longer jogging.

She wants to run for her life.

The sky seems to be moving in a series of freeze-frames. As McAvoy looks up, the dragon he had previously spotted in the skies becomes a cliff face, then jerks, unsteadily, into a choir congregation.

He turns back to the road. Watches as the first spots of rain begin to kiss the glass.

Looks up again.

Now the heavens are a snapshot of a storm-lashed ocean. The clouds broil as waves, curling and crashing in upon themselves in an explosion of black and grey.

McAvoy looks at his phone. It may be due to the fall from his pocket or a consequence of the storm clouds that block out the light, but he is struggling to get a signal. He has managed to call Pharaoh and update her, but was halfway through a garbled conversation with Ben Nielsen when he lost his phone signal, and he cannot seem to get it back. Thankfully, he had already received most of the information he needed. Got the address. The name. The next piece of a puzzle that's turning his brain to paste.

The car comes to a lazy halt in a parking space on Rufforth Garth. He's on the edge of Hull's Bransholme estate. It used to be Europe's biggest council estate, though nobody ever took

the time to write that on the marketing materials or 'Welcome
to Bransholme' signs. The area has had a lot of money spent
on it in recent years, and while it has not exactly become an
address to boast about, living on Bransholme is no longer a tick
in the 'against' column when applying for a job. It's a sprawling
community of small, near-identical houses. Most are crammed
into cul-de-sacs that branch off from main roads sporting so
many speed-bumps they look corrugated.

McAvoy takes a deep breath, steps from the vehicle.

Wincing into the fine rain that has begun to blow in on a harsh
wind from the east, McAvoy looks around at the nearby vehicles
for one that matches the registration plate he has scrawled on his
notepad. He can't see it. Can't see the van that screeched away from
a hospital in Norfolk with Hoyer-Wood's surgeon in the back, and
then deposited a rotting corpse on the tarmac. It's all Volkswagen
Golfs and old BMWs – their suspensions lowered so they give off a
pretty shower of sparks as they scrape the speed bumps.

McAvoy rubs some colour into his cheeks then heads for the
address Ben had shouted down the phone at him over the sound
of static and rushing wind. He pushes open a metal garden gate
and walks down a well-tended front path. He finds himself in
front of an old-fashioned and single-glazed front door. The two
panes of frosted glass at its centre do not look particularly sturdy.
Were he to lean on it he fancies it might fall down. He decides
this could be useful, so files the information away without
allowing himself to think too hard about it.

Three raps on the glass: a policeman's Morse code for 'open
the fucking door'.

No answer.

Tries again, louder now.

He opens the letter box and feels cold air against his face as he looks into an untidy kitchen and down at dirty linoleum. He wonders what he expected to see. Feels an urge to giggle as he imagines seeing Angelo Caneva standing over Dr Pradesh with a scalpel and some surgical rib-spreaders. He wonders if he should have uniformed support. Whether he should wait for Pharaoh. Whether he has got the whole fucking thing completely wrong.

'You won't get him during the day, love.'

McAvoy turns. A woman in her late thirties is standing by the front gate. She has a small child on her hip. The woman has a wrinkled, puckered mouth and features; her hair is long, lank and bottle-black and she has a leather jacket on over a small vest top and tight black jeans. She's wearing a lot of make-up and has a vaguely Gothic look about her, though the effect is spoiled somewhat by the tiger-feet slippers.

'You're after Nick, yeah?'

McAvoy turns away from the closed door. Gives the woman his full attention.

'When did you last see him?'

She looks up, her eyes revolving unnaturally, as if she is scanning the inside of her skull.

'You a copper?'

McAvoy isn't sure how to answer. He wants her to talk to him. Wants her to like him.

'He's a bright-looking lad,' says McAvoy, at last, nodding at the child in her arms. 'What's his name?'

The woman smiles, showing smoker's teeth. 'Reebok,' she says, with a laugh.

McAvoy doesn't know what facial expression to pull. 'That's different.'

She shrugs. 'He's not mine, don't worry. I think it's bloody daft, but if she wants to name her kid after a running shoe, who am I to judge? There's a kid in my daughter's class called Pebbles. Could be worse.'

McAvoy walks towards her, ready to show her his warrant card. He is reaching into his pocket when the child fixes him with a piercing look, and then bursts out laughing. McAvoy and the woman look at the boy, who is pointing at McAvoy and giggling hard.

'Am I that funny?' asks McAvoy, trying to look offended.

'Brave, Brave,' says the child, and sets off in another fit of hysterics.

The woman shrugs, good-naturedly. 'He must think you look like someone from the film.'

'Which film?'

'Disney cartoon. Scottish princess, wants to be a warrior. Billy Connolly's the voice of the dad . . .'

She stops herself. Looks him up and down and appears to agree with the child. She sniggers a little, then uses her sleeve to wipe the rain from the child's face.

McAvoy gives in to a little laugh of his own and then closes his fingers around the warrant card. Holds it tight enough to hurt.

'You're a neighbour?'

'Next door,' says the woman, jerking her head. 'I'm Jen.'

McAvoy shakes her hand. It's cold and slim and the palm feels slightly clammy. He introduces himself.

'I was hoping to talk to Nick.'

'He works days. Some nights too. Busy man, but you've got to go where the work is, don't you?'

As they talk, the rain begins to come down harder. There

is a low rumble and the face in the clouds tears itself in two. The sky becomes an ocean, upended and draining onto the city below.

'Jesus, look at this,' says Jen, huddling into her coat. 'Do you want to come inside?'

McAvoy pulls up his jacket collar and follows her into the neighbouring property. In moments he is soaked to the bone, his hair stuck to his face, shirt clinging to the muscles in his chest, arms and back.

McAvoy shakes himself like a damp dog. Looks up. He finds himself in a square kitchen. A small patio table and chairs sit next to a plain white door. The table supports a basket of unwashed laundry, which contains an unfeasible amount of leopard-print underwear and jogging trousers. The heat in the room comes from the far side, beside the metal sink that overflows with pots and pans soaking in a sea of cold water and dissolving bubbles. The door of the oven is wide open and heat emanates like dragon's breath. Three small children and a Dalmatian are sitting in front of it, eating biscuits and playing with blocks.

'I'm a childminder,' says Jen, filling the kettle. 'That's Pauline, Luke, and the little one's Colin.'

McAvoy looks at the toddler, who is sucking on a plastic brick and trying to get his hand into his nappy.

'He looks a Colin,' he says, and then leans himself against the wall. He tries to order his thoughts.

The phone number that Maria Caneva supplied him with is registered at the house next door to this one, on Rufforth Garth. The electoral register shows the occupier to be a Nick Peace. Before he lost the phone signal, McAvoy had instructed Ben Nielsen to dig up anything and everything on Peace, and to cross-reference those checks with Angelo Caneva. Like shapes in the clouds, McAvoy is starting to see fuller pictures.

'Like I said, I was hoping to talk to your neighbour,' says McAvoy, as chattily as he can manage over the sound of the playing children and banging pots. 'Well, his friend, more accurately. Angelo?'

Jen stops what she is doing and turns to him, drying her hands on her trousers.

'You said you were Old Bill, yeah?'

McAvoy nods. 'I'm investigating several murders. It really is important.'

Jen seems to be weighing things up. This is an estate where talking to the police is only acceptable when the community officers are running a tombola at a family fun day, or providing safety checks on your children's bicycles. Jen seems about to clam up.

McAvoy decides to help her see sense.

'You heard about the murder off Anlaby Road, I'm sure . . .'

Jen nods, then drops her voice, as if it's wrong to say 'murder' in front of children.

'I heard he pulled her heart out, or something. Sick bastard.'

McAvoy looks at the children, then gives a gentle jerk of his head to tell her to come closer. She does so. Her head only comes up to his chest and from here he can see her grey roots and smell her perfume. He can breathe in the sunflower oil and fabric softener of her hair.

'He didn't pull her heart out,' says McAvoy, quietly. 'He caved it in. He performed CPR on her body until her ribcage cracked open and he turned her insides to mush. Then he sliced open the femoral artery of a nice mum over the water. Her kids found her.

Then he battered a bloke to death with a defibrillator machine in a rage because he couldn't electrocute the poor sod to death. Last night he abducted a surgeon and left an unidentified corpse at the scene. All that these people had done wrong was save the life of a man who was far worse than they were. It really is important I speak to Nick, or Angelo. Please, Jen, what can you tell me?'

There is silence in the room, save for the gleeful chatter of the children and the rain beating hard against the glass. The kitchen feels too dark, suddenly, and Jen switches on a light. It breaks the spell. McAvoy recoils from the light like a vampire. He feels too exposed. Too visible. He's aware of his scars and scrapes and creases and knows that Jen must see them too.

Jen looks him up and down.

'Sick bastard,' she says, again, and McAvoy hopes she is referring to the killer.

'Please, Jen . . .'

The woman gives a little shrug, and seems to make a decision. She doesn't seem overly horrified at what she has heard. Just grimly accepting of further proof that the world can be a horrible place.

'I've lived here two years,' says Jen. 'Nick's lived next door the whole time. He has a little girl. Well, I say he has . . .'

McAvoy leans closer, wondering if he should suggest they go into another room or put the kids somewhere else. He does neither. Instead he asks her about Angelo Caneva.

'His friend,' he says, softly. 'Angelo.'

Jen smiles. 'Little chap, yes? Slightly built. Big brown eyes. Very shy. Yeah, he lived there for a bit. Bit of a weird set-up, two grown men and a little girl, but you get all sorts on this estate . . .'

McAvoy wants to pull out his notepad but fears spoiling the moment. He concentrates on breathing and listening.

'What do you know about Nicholas?'

'Nice enough chap,' says Jen. 'Helped me out a couple of times. My boiler went off and he came and fixed the pilot light and I once got locked out and he jimmied the bathroom window. Brought me a bottle of something on New Year. Yeah, nice enough bloke if you could stop him talking about football.'

McAvoy pauses. Thinks hard. 'When did you last see Angelo?'

Jen looks up and to the left. 'Few weeks, maybe? Maybe more. I don't know.'

'And Nick?'

'Oh, just a couple of days back. He always says hello. He tries to stay cheerful but it can't be easy after that bitch waltzed in and took his daughter . . .'

McAvoy looks up at the ceiling. There is a damp patch spreading out from the corner above the sink. In it, if he squints and cocks his head, he fancies he can see the same leering, sunken-eyed face.

'His daughter?' asks McAvoy.

'Nick's ex-wife won custody of little Olivia,' she says, looking as if the information pains her. 'Broke his heart, I reckon. She's such a lovely little girl, too. Big eyes and the cutest smile. She'll get a nicer tan over there, of course, but it was Nick that brought her up . . .'

'Over where?'

'Benidorm, I think,' says Jen. 'Somewhere sunny, anyway.'

McAvoy looks down at the floor, hoping it will give him something more than the ceiling.

'How did Nicholas take that?'

'His world fell apart. He must have been hell to live with because I never saw Angelo much after that . . .'

McAvoy rubs at the bruise on the back of his hand.

'They worked together, yes? Nick and Angelo?'

'Well, it was Nick's business,' says Jen, back to full volume again. 'Builder. That sort of thing.'

Inside McAvoy's mind, images drift together. He sees the new railings outside Philippa Longman's house. The flat roof at Yvonne Dale's. Dimly recalls that Allan Godber's bank statements showed a hefty withdrawal recently that his wife said had gone on repointing the brickwork.

McAvoy purses his lips. Feels water trickle down the back of his shirt.

He suddenly sees it all. Can imagine Philippa bumping into her builder in the street and stopping for a chat in the glare of a lamp post, moments before he dragged her into the darkness and caved in her chest. He sees so many perfect opportunities for surveillance. For near-invisible proximity to victims.

McAvoy pulls out his phone. The screen is blank and, as he curses, Jen hands him her own. He manages a smile and a thank you, then dials Elaine Longman from memory.

'Elaine? Aector McAvoy. Fine. Yeah. Yes, possibly. Look, Elaine, your mum had had some new railings put in, hadn't she? You said somebody had bodged the job . . . Yes? Okay. No, thank you. Thank you.'

McAvoy hangs up. He imagines the tap on Philippa's door. The sudden appearance of a passing tradesman who had noticed the railings in a poor state. Willing to finish them off for a bit of cash in hand . . .

McAvoy apologises and makes another call.

When he hangs up, he looks at his own phone for a while. Tries to smooth out the crack on the display using his thumb. Tries to make the picture whole again.

'I don't suppose you have a photo of Nick or Angelo, do you?' he asks, quietly.

Jen shakes her head.

McAvoy stares some more. Smells baking bread and wonders if a pizza crust is burning at the back of the open oven. Hears the older child ask Jen who the big man is. Hears little Colin shit his pants and sit in it.

Eventually, Jen's phone bleeps. The forensic report he has requested flashes up in her Hotmail account. She had hastily spelled out her email address as he spoke to Ben, and McAvoy had turned crimson as he'd typed in *tygerpants69*.

He scrolls through the report. It's accompanied by a list of Angelo Caneva's associates from his time in the young offender institute. There are no names that sound familiar, but one was incarcerated for crimes committed within the Hull boundary.

McAvoy flicks his fingers across the screen. Finds the section he was looking for. The organic matter, found at the crime scenes. It has been identified as sap from lime trees: the sticky, corrosive substance that eats through the paintwork on expensive cars parked down shaded avenues.

McAvoy breathes in, hard, as if trying to fire more oxygen into his brain.

Where?

Think, you silly fucker, think!

He sees the name of the gamekeeper's cottage, written in bright letters across the shifting cloudscape of his thoughts.

Tilia Cottage. *Tilia*. Latin for *lime*.

He flicks back to the list of Caneva's associates. Returns to the name of the lad sent down in Hull. He has a sudden flash of recognition.

He turns to Jen. Gabbles something almost unintelligible and nearly steps on Colin as he begins to pace the small room.

'I'm sorry, just one more call . . .'

For the next ten minutes, McAvoy watches the rain run down the glass and listens to the thunder grow closer.

He waits for a call that could mean everything.

Finally, Ben connects him to a sleepy, angry woman in Benidorm.

'No, of course not,' she snaps, in answer to McAvoy's question. 'She's with her dad in Hull. Bastard won't let me see her. Why, what's . . .?'

As lightning tears through the sky, McAvoy throws the phone to Jen.

He blunders through the door and into a day turned to midnight by cloud that hangs as sackcloth over a city that fears the rain.

20

Roisin's face is sore and tender to the touch, but she still makes the effort with her lipstick. She flinches a little as the frosted pink gloss bites into the wound on her mouth, but she will feel better when she looks better, if her mother's wisdom is to be believed.

'He'll come back,' says Mel, gently, from the doorway. 'He adores you. He's just gone to work.'

Roisin slept with her face on a black bin-liner full of old clothes, with her children curled up in her arms. Aector was not here when she woke. His phone won't connect. Her stomach is climbing up her ribcage and all she wants to do is hold him and say sorry a thousand times.

He'd said he forgave her. He'd held her and kissed her sore places and wiped her tears with his bruised fists, and then he'd left her to a fitful sleep, peopled with dreams of loneliness and violence.

'I don't know why I took it, Mel. I'm so sorry.'

Roisin has apologised endlessly to her friend and Mel has told her it's okay. She is still a little shaky after what happened last night, but despite the violence she witnessed and endured, she seems to feel safer with Roisin than anywhere else and has shown no desire to return to her own home. She would rather be here, in an empty house on the Kingswood estate, with its crying children and echoing rooms.

'It was just there,' says Roisin, again. 'He'd offered it to you. He'd made you sad. It was your money. I just picked it up . . .'

'Ro, it's fine, I understand.'

Roisin falls silent. She finishes applying her make-up and checks her reflection in the small compact mirror she has plucked from her handbag. They are sitting on the floor in the living room of the empty house. Fin is playing a game of football in his head, passing an imaginary ball to himself and scoring goals at the far end of the room. Lilah is asleep in her carry cot.

'Why won't he answer his phone?' asks Roisin, despairingly.

Mel gestures at the living-room window. The rain is coming in off the Humber in waves and it's dark enough for the street lights to come on. 'He probably can't get a signal. And he's a murder policeman, Ro. He's up to his eyes. He'll be sorting it all out. You said that's what he does.'

Roisin touches her fingertips to her bruised face. She wants to know what was said to him. What the voice at the other end of the phone had whispered in his ear. She wants to know if McAvoy would have killed her attackers had the voice not stopped him first.

'He went through them like they were made of paper,' says Mel, blankly, as if examining a memory. 'He looked like he was from another time. Like an old king, or something. I don't know. I'm talking shit, aren't I?'

Roisin smiles, then shivers at the pain. She gives her friend a little hug.

'Will you come with me?' she asks. 'To the new house? I don't want him to see it in a state when he gets back. There'll be blood. Mess. I want to put this behind us. All of it.'

Mel looks uncertain. 'He said to stay here. To keep our heads down.'

Roisin points at the scene beyond the window. 'It's chucking it down. Nobody who's going to do anything will do it in weather like this. We'll only be an hour. We're fine. It's important, Mel.'

Mel sighs and smiles and together they begin getting the kids ready for the short journey across the city to the new house on Hessle Foreshore.

They fleetingly appear in the large, curtainless window at the front of the house.

A few feet away, an angry young man spits on the misted windscreen inside the stolen car.

Bitches!

Despite the rain and the darkness and the water that slashes diagonally across the windscreen, Adam Downey recognises the two women who have fucked it all up.

He lowers his head. Sniffs another line from the mountain of cocaine in his lap.

Feels himself filling with fire and rage and sunlight.

He looks at the hammer on the passenger seat. At the grenade that rolls in the coffee holder.

Downey watches the women load the children into the car and reverse out of the driveway in the driving rain.

He turns the key.

Drifts along behind them, his vision marbled and opaque, his quarry a blue blur beyond the cascading water on the glass.

This is his chance.

His last opportunity.

He's going to show them who he is and what he can do. He's going to make the gypsy bitch pay.

11.14 a.m. Courtland Road Police Station. An incident room buckling under the weight of paper, people, bustle and noise. A long, unwelcoming office, painted in puke and buttermilk, that stinks of sweat, fast food and fly spray.

Leaning her head against the cool glass, Trish Pharaoh watches the light die.

Sees the clouds swallow the pale halo of the sun. Sees rain fall like the blade of a guillotine. The dying light puts her in mind of an old halogen bulb, covered in dust and dead flies, that seems to be giving out precious little illumination up until the point it gives out none.

'Bloody hell . . .'

Wind tears in through the open windows. Wind and water and the dirt of the city, and in a moment the incident room is a storm of billowing paper. Officers hang up phone calls to lunge for errant forensics reports and witness statements. A carton of milk tips over on a civilian officer's desk and spills across keyboard, lap, chair and floor. Trish's hair tangles in her earrings, and as she runs to the window the rain plasters loose strands across her features and dampens her breastbone and neck.

'Ben! Ben, Christ, get that one. Fucking hurry up . . .'

A row of harsh lights flicker into life overhead and the last sash window slams down.

'Jesus, it's bloody biblical out there!'

The officers crowd around the glass, watching the tempest beat upon the city. The darkness beyond the window turns the glass into a mirror and each man and woman has to squint through themselves to make sense of the furious scene. Already gutters are being turned into streams and waterfalls by the deluge and the few cars that had been negotiating this quiet area of the Orchard Park estate have slowed and then stopped. It is as if the sea is trying to reclaim the land.

'Come on, come on, it's only rain,' she says, turning away and clapping her hands. 'Killer, yes? That's what we're here for. Nasty man, killing nice people. Remember him? Could we catch him, please? It would be such a help. Thanks.'

Muttering and apologising, the team disperse back to their individual desks. Somebody begins mopping up spilled milk with a tea towel and DC Andy Daniells has his head in his hands after trying to put the papers that have blown from his desk back into some semblance of order.

'Ben,' says Pharaoh, looking around. 'Helen? Word.'

Pharaoh's office is up the stairs, near the head of CID, but she is happier here, in the engine room. She remains by the window and is joined by Ben Nielsen and Helen Tremberg. Ben looks fit and wide awake, though he has likely spent the night engaged in one of his sexual marathons. He's wearing the same shirt as yesterday and hasn't shaved, but still looks stylish and presentable. Helen looks worn out. Her eyes are red, there are crumbs of chocolate on the lapel of her dowdy blazer and she seems to be limping as she walks.

'You okay, Helen?'

Pharaoh looks up into Helen's swollen eyes. This is how she leads. How she inspires. In this moment, the killer is forgotten. She cares, here and now, whether her constable is okay.

Tremberg nods. Seems about to speak and then clams up again.

'I wish you'd been on this from the start,' says Trish, softly. 'Nice that Everett noticed you, though, eh? You must have been doing something right. Bloody good to have you with us though. We wouldn't have got to this stage without you. You should feel proud of yourself.'

Pharaoh hopes for a smile or a thank you but gets neither. Helen just looks down at her feet. Pharaoh reaches out and strokes her arm. 'We'll talk later, yeah?'

Helen nods. Swallows, and closes her eyes.

Pharaoh turns her attention to Ben. 'Talk to me, Handsome.'

Nielsen gives his face a slap on both cheeks, then shakes his head back and forth. His lips wobble a little, then he slaps his face again. Trish has no idea why he does this. He seems to be awake enough already.

'Well,' says Ben, animatedly. 'Caneva may as well have a big sign around his neck with the word "killer" on it. We've got his description to all units within the force boundary and beyond. The vehicle seen leaving the hospital has fake plates but the description has still been sent out for all to see. We've contacted Dr Pradesh's relatives and apprised them of the situation and Andy is using every resource to warn everybody who was in the operating theatre with her when she operated on Hoyer-Wood. The operations she performed on him are bloody complicated, but let's just say that if Caneva is planning to carry them out on her, there won't be any happy ending.'

Pharaoh takes it all in.

'Caneva,' she says, then lets her thoughts drift to the information McAvoy had blurted down the phone before he lost his signal. 'Nick Peace,' she says, turning to Helen. 'You've been back onto the facility where Caneva was an inmate, yeah?'

Helen takes a breath and keeps her voice even.

'I've asked the governor if there were any other inmates that Caneva was especially close with. He didn't recognise the name Nicholas Peace but did mention that Caneva had a very hard time fitting in at first. He was a little bloke, not much about him, with this posh London accent. Read a lot of books. Did drawings. Wrote short stories. He's sending us the lot on the inmate you flagged up. The one who got sent down in Hull.'

'Crime?' asks Pharaoh.

'Attempted murder,' she says. 'Kicked some bloke half to death outside a bingo hall. Was the latest in a long line of escalating crimes. He was thirteen when he was sent down. Spent almost six years at the facility and became mates of sorts with Caneva. Governor remembers bits and bobs.'

Pharaoh licks her lips. Absent-mindedly, she reaches into the pocket of her biker jacket and pulls out her black cigarettes. She places one to her lips and though she doesn't light it, rolling it on her damp lips seems to help her concentrate.

'So we're thinking Caneva went to stay with him when he was released. Got a job working for him. Used the cover to take his revenge on the people who saved his family's tormentor. How am I doing?'

Helen nods her assent and the three fall silent. They turn to watch the storm.

'His phone's still off, yeah?' asks Pharaoh.

Ben grunts an answer.

'And have we any bloody idea who *tygerpants69* is?'

Ben starts to laugh.

Together, the three of them watch the rain make the city into a whorl of dribbled shapes and half-formed slabs. They look, for a moment, as though they are trapped inside an unfinished painting.

'Norfolk CID,' says Pharaoh, at last. 'They know what we know?'

Ben shrugs. 'They know our angle. They're still treating it as a local crime. Belt and braces. They've promised to call when they have an ID on the body.'

'And we're thinking that it's going to be his mate, aren't we? Nick Peace, or whatever he used to be called.'

'Makes sense,' says Helen. 'He must have found out what Caneva's been doing. Confronted him, maybe. If you watch the CCTV of the doctor's abduction, the body fell from the van. It wasn't dumped on purpose. It was a mistake.'

Helen seems about to say something more when a shout from halfway across the room interrupts them. There's a phone call for Ben.

'Is it McAvoy?' asks Pharaoh, and is greeted with a shake of the head from the civilian officer holding out Ben's phone.

Ben crosses the room. Pharaoh watches as he jots down some details and pulls a face. Then he sighs, looking angry and lost. He hangs up and comes back to where they stand.

'The ID is through on the body left at the hospital,' says Nielsen, and he seems to be struggling to keep the anger from creasing his features.

'And?'

'And if we're looking for Angelo Caneva we can fucking relax. He's on a slab. Been dead for weeks, rotting away in a warm, dry space.'

Pharaoh closes her eyes.

'The name,' she says, softly. 'The bloke who was arrested in Hull. Angelo's friend. The lad who might have become Nick Peace. What did he use to be called?'

Helen crosses back to her desk. She sifts through a pile of papers and finds a rain-spattered document. She brings it back to Pharaoh.

'Him,' she says, pointing.

Pharaoh looks at the name. Something in the back of her mind fizzes for an instant, like the last breath of light in the filament of a dying bulb.

And then she sees him. Sees his fillings as he laughs. Hears his voice. Hears him talking football and handing her and McAvoy a business card. Sees McAvoy on the phone in the great hall of an abandoned stately home.

She sees the contractor.

She sees Gaz.

21

Gary Reeves watches the lightning through the gaps in the red tiles. He is soaked to the bone. His blue overalls stick to his skin. His hair hangs lank, touching the back of his collar. His eyes are open, wide and staring; the very image of the dead man in whose name he has become a killer.

He stares.

Doesn't blink as the raindrops bounce off his face.

Watches the patterns in the sky.

The dark sky is a raven, the clouds its feathers. Each fork of brilliant white is a paper dart, thrown by some celestial hand. Reeves isn't sure he believes in God, but he sees the shapes above him quite clearly. Sees the bird's eye, beady and perfectly circular, fix itself upon him. It seems to approve. Seems to like the scene, far below.

He sees himself in its gaze.

Sees a fit young man, lying motionless on an old operating table.

Sees the woman at his side.

Naked.

Bound.

Sobbing and drooling into the stuffed toy wedged in her bleeding mouth.

Gary Reeves has answered to many names. He enjoyed being Nick Peace. It was the name he'd chosen when they let him out. He didn't bother changing it legally but he felt that it fitted him. The 'Nicholas' had honoured the flamboyant Arsenal striker whom one of his foster fathers had always admired. The 'Peace' was a nod to one of his psychologists. She'd told him to find the peace within himself. To find a calm, soothing place in his soul, and try and live within it.

Gary has never really managed to follow her advice. He has spent most of his life in trouble. Doesn't remember his mother or father. Has a birthday that was given to him by Social Services. He has had more foster homes than he can remember. He has spent time in children's homes and on the streets. The only stability he has ever experienced was when he was sent to the young offender institute at fourteen. He'd been living in Hull at that time, a fireball of rage and resentment. He wanted solitude and he wanted company. He wanted silence and chaos. He interpreted every action through a filter that hung behind his eyes like a side of rotting pork. Whatever was given to him was given with spite and the things he needed were absent because nobody loved him. His mind was a ball of wool, pulled apart by warring thoughts and desires. He spat when he talked. He twitched and swore and struggled to make himself understood. He would spend days making himself as filthy as he could before scrubbing his skin until he bled. He had headaches. He masturbated until he was sore. He stole then wept when nobody believed his denials. He took the possessions of those who were kind to him and then used them to violate himself. His education came at a variety of pupil referral units and schools for children unable to be taught in mainstream education. He spent time at a residential school for bad lads, where he found a way to get past the Internet security restrictions and spent a few months with access to every kind of pornography he could imagine. And he could imagine a lot.

Reeves's run-ins with the police led to cautions and community service orders. He didn't mind the community work. Liked getting his hands dirty. Painting old ladies' fences and sweeping streets. He'd go back later, of course. He'd go and graffiti the same fence he had spent the day painting white. He couldn't seem to help it. Nor could he help the calling of his blood. Couldn't help what it told him to do when he saw that perfect fucking family with their perfect house, having their perfect picnic and perfect game of badminton on their perfect front lawn.

Gary Reeves had been as much a witness to his early crimes as he had been a perpetrator. He had not really been in control of his body. He was a passenger in a vessel piloted by some other, unstoppable, force. He had been as surprised as anybody to see himself walk into the front garden of the house. Had simply watched, entranced, as Gary Reeves had kicked over the barbecue, grabbed a hot coal from the glowing pile and pressed it into the face of the portly accountant who'd been standing grilling sausages in his perfect fucking apron with its stupid fucking picture on the front. By then, Gary's blood was in control of his actions. He took lighter fluid and set fire to the smouldering coals. His hand hadn't hurt, despite the ugly flap of burned skin that hung from it. Then he'd begun to shovel the coals through the letter box of the perfect fucking house, where the rest of the perfect family cried and cowered while Dad writhed on the grass as a teenage boy kicked his ribs, rhythmically, purposefully, until they snapped.

Gary arrived in the young offender institute determined not to be bullied. He had three fights on his first day. He smashed a pool cue into the face of one of the prison officers, giving him a scar that he reckons is probably still there. For the first few months he spent most of his time on lockdown in his room. He was sixteen before he began to control himself. The counselling sessions helped. It was nice to talk to somebody who was paid to listen. He didn't think they cared, but the fact they were paid to be there meant they had no choice but to pay attention as he told them how it felt to be him. How his blood called to him. How he sometimes saw things that weren't there and often left his own body and watched it all from above, like an angel.

As he grew older and more physically capable, Gary began to take advantage of some of the courses offered at the centre. He learned metalwork and woodwork with a retired schoolteacher who didn't mind letting him use the more deadly-looking equipment. He made a spice rack for the old bloke's missus. Gave it to him with a grunt but was pleased to see it meant something to him. And then he met Angelo Caneva.

Angelo was a feeble little thing. He was scared and flighty and reminded Gary of a baby rabbit, shivering and ready to bolt. Gary hadn't thought much about him at all, other than the fact he didn't fit in. He had little to do with him. But he saw another side to Angelo when one of the older lads took the physicality too far.

The facility was short-staffed. There weren't enough wardens to cope with so many teenagers. So there was nobody around when Byron Alexander dragged Angelo to the reading room and started smashing his face in. Gary had gone along to watch. So had some of the other lads. The show they were expecting never took place. Instead Angelo turned into the devil. As soon as he realised what Byron was going to do he seemed to come alive. He unleashed a strength that nobody knew he possessed. He got on top of the bigger lad and punched Byron until he was unrecognisable. Instinct made Gary react. He wasn't saving Byron when he dragged Angelo away. He was saving the kid. Saving him from a murder charge. It was a profoundly moving moment for Gary Reeves. He found himself fascinated by the younger boy.

Nobody ever told the screws who had left Byron like that. Nor did anybody ever try it on with Angelo again. They left him alone. Left him to his books and his drawings. Gary wanted to know more about him. Wanted to talk to him. But he didn't know how to. He tried making him something in his woodwork lessons, but he smashed up the toy aeroplane he'd made for him out of balsa wood when he imagined himself giving it to the younger lad.

In the end, Angelo did the hard work for him. One day, out of nowhere, Angelo presented him with a book of short stories. Told Gary he might enjoy it. Said there was a yarn in there about a bloke in solitary confinement who tunnelled his way to freedom behind a big poster of some Hollywood pin-up. Said it was a classic and that the movie version was amazing. Gary was not a comfortable reader but had taken the book anyway. Gave it a go. Asked Angelo for more. Their friendship developed. They began to share stories. Secrets. Despite their different backgrounds and the age difference, they became more than friends. They told one another about what had led them to the facility. They unburdened themselves and each found somebody who understood.

Gary had felt sick when he heard what had happened to Angelo's father. When he'd heard about the rich prick with the double-barrelled name who'd fooled everybody into thinking he was a cripple. He'd laughed when Angelo told him about fire-bombing the bus and the posh wanker suffering a stroke that left him shitting in his pants and unable to move. He'd held Angelo whenever he cried and Angelo had done the same for him. Angelo had told him his fantasy. Told him his dreams. Told him what he and his sister were going to do some day. Told him the people he was going to kill. Told him about the cunts who'd saved the posh prick's life. Gary had liked the plan.

When he was older, Gary was sent to serve the remainder of his sentence in adult prison. He had never felt loneliness like it. His separation from Angelo was the most excruciating sensation he had ever endured. He tried to find a new friend. Ended up in fights. Grew frustrated and began to seek out fresh violence. Had time added to his sentence. Only the letters from Angelo kept him going. They spoke of what it would be like when they were both free. About getting a place for themselves. They would start a business, maybe. Gary would take him to the football. They'd drink beer and watch movies on a Saturday night. They'd get girlfriends but tell them they were for the chop if they ever came between them.

Gary was released first. He headed for Hull, purely because he knew the streets better than he did in any other city. Social Services had found him a flat and a job as a labourer. He stuck it out. Kept his head down. Saved his money. Even got himself a girlfriend. Mandy, she was called. Bit older than him and twice as streetwise. Gave him the eye in a McDonald's and opened her legs for him an hour later, sitting on a pile of wooden pallets and blowing the smoke from her cigarette over his shoulder as he emptied himself inside her. He hadn't expected her to get pregnant. She hadn't wanted the baby but he was delighted when she told him. He imagined being a dad. Imagined being a strong and noble influence on a child. Imagined Angelo and himself raising it together. He'd told her he would take care of her. Of the child. She'd given him a daughter, then fucked off to Spain with somebody else. Gary had written to Angelo. Told him they were parents. And Angelo had told him he was happy.

The day Angelo left the institute, Gary picked him up in his new blue van. It had been a couple of years since they had seen one another and Gary was struck at the change in Angelo. He had fresh scars. His skin clung to his small, birdlike frame. He was quiet and uncommunicative. It seemed in those two years the fight had left him. Bad things had happened to him. He had not always been able to fight people off. He was tired and his voice did not sound like his own. Gary soon discovered that Angelo had started using drugs while inside. He'd started sniffing glue again. Got one of the staff in the kitchens to start bringing in LSD and ecstasy. Gary wanted his friend to be happy so he scored him some drugs. Watched him became his old self again as the high took him in its embrace. Watched Angelo cuddling their daughter, and for a time he felt anything was possible. He moved them to the house on Rufforth Garth. Angelo had to stay in a flat Social Services had got him, but after a few months he was able to slip through the cracks in the system and come home to Gary. Sometimes he'd go and visit his father for money. Once, they went to see Angelo's sister, though the fat cow had changed and wanted nothing to do with the murderous fantasy they had both enjoyed in their teens and which had sustained Angelo through his incarceration. But Gary stuck to his word. He thought the plan was a good one. He thought revenge would help his friend. Angelo wanted it to happen, so he said he would help him. Even drove him to the house of the slag who'd been raped by Hoyer-Wood up in Bridlington the night he should have died. Had sat in the darkness with the engine running and watched Angelo break in.

When Angelo returned, it was clear something had changed. He just didn't have it in him. Didn't have the strength to kill. He saw the people on his list as innocents. They didn't know what they were doing. They'd made a mistake but didn't deserve to die. The fight went out of him. He began to take more drugs. He closed down. Stopped talking. Wouldn't play with their daughter. Wouldn't come out of his room.

A month ago, Angelo took his own life. He parked their blue van in a lock-up they had rented. Turned on the engine and opened the windows. Breathed in blue smoke until his lungs gave out and his eyes closed.

He couldn't have known, Gary told himself, when he found the bodies. *Couldn't have known their daughter was in the back. She just climbed in. Snuggled down in a place she felt comfortable. Angelo couldn't have seen her. The fumes would have reached her first as she lay with her toys in the back. She'd have slipped away as if to sleep. Angelo would never have known, as he sat and waited to die in the front seat, that their daughter was dead.*

Until then, Gary had been Nick Peace. He'd found that peaceful place, within him and without. He'd begun to imagine a future. He'd stopped listening to his blood. As he found the bodies of his friend and their child, he felt himself drifting out of himself in a way he had not done for years. And his blood told him what to do next.

Told him that Angelo was another victim of Hoyer-Wood.

Told him his daughter was too.

Told him they needed to be avenged.

He couldn't bring himself to get rid of the bodies. Drove around with them in the van, even when the stench made him feel sick.

It hadn't been difficult to find the do-gooders who had spoiled all of their lives. Philippa Longman. Yvonne Dale. Allan Godber. Hadn't been hard to get to know them. He was an odd-job man, after all, a contractor. He'd fixed Philippa's railings. Yvonne's roof. Done some pointing work at Allan's place. Got to know them. Became invisible. Peered into their lives as he planned their deaths.

Philippa had been the hardest. Despite what she cost him, she had seemed a nice lady. She'd given him a big smile that night as she spotted him on the street on her walk home from work. Chatted to him about the weather and her grandkids and told him he'd done a grand job on her railings. But Gary's blood wasn't listening, and Gary hadn't returned to himself until Philippa was dead on the ground with her chest caved in.

It had been the same the next time. Yvonne had died quietly but there had been more blood than he expected.

But he'd made a prat of himself with Allan's death. The defibrillator had been too fucking complicated. Had shown him up. Gary never left his skin that time. Stayed very much awake as he battered the former paramedic to death on the cold floor of the lock-up.

As he looks at Dr Pradesh, he wonders how much of today's work he will actually experience, and how much he will simply watch.

The surgeon is still blubbering. She's got one of Olivia's fluffy toys wedged in her gob and it's turning pink. She's bleeding from the mouth. He can't remember if he punched her in the stomach or not. He wonders if she might have internal bleeding, or has just bitten through her cheek.

He rolls off the table. Brushes himself down.

Looks around.

Gary likes this place. It's a ruin now. There are holes in the roof and the bare brick walls are surrounded by a chain-link fence topped with barbed wire. The remaining internal walls are smoke-blackened and the carpet has turned into something organic and squelchy beneath a covering of lime-tree sap and leaves. Still, it has character. It's quiet. And he likes knowing that Angelo had, for a time, been happy here. He can feel him nearby.

Gary shed a tear this morning when he realised he had lost his friend's body. He blames Dr Pradesh. Blames her for a lot of things. The woman on the table saved Hoyer-Wood's life. She opened him up and stopped the bleeding. Stitched his spleen back together. Repaired a laceration to his kidney. She's going to learn how that feels. And then she's going to bleed into her own exposed abdomen until she drowns and dies.

Gary pushes his hair back from his face. He's a little hungry. In one corner of the room are a few empty tins. He's been living on cold beans and spaghetti. Been kipping in his van some nights and lying here, looking through the holes in the roof, on the nights he knows the security guards won't be patrolling.

It had been more luck than design that he'd landed the job of looking after the mansion house. He'd driven up purely to see the place for himself, having heard Angelo's descriptions so many times without ever laying eyes on it. He'd been parking up on the gravel when a load of posh blokes in suits and accents had walked out, looking over blueprints and chattering excitedly about their big plans. They'd approached him and said something about serendipity and needing somebody to keep an eye on the place. They'd hired him on the spot to keep the place clean and tidy. Given him a business card, and told him to email his details across. Agreed to pay him cash in hand. It had felt like somebody was smiling on him.

Angelo had still been alive then. But he wasn't communicating much. Wasn't coming out of his room. Gary didn't even really trust him to be left alone with Olivia. He'd taken to bringing her with him everywhere. She'd sit and chatter and play with her toys in the back of the van. She liked it in there. It was warm and dry and smelled of Daddy.

He couldn't have known . . .

Gary looks down at Dr Pradesh. The light isn't very good and her face is only illuminated when the lightning flashes. She's quite pretty, and her body is in good shape. She even has a little heart-shaped tattoo where her pubes should be. He'd expected more from a surgeon.

Gary looks into Dr Pradesh's eyes. Sees himself reflected in them. Realises he's forgotten the mask. He stole one from a dental practice a few weeks ago, along with some latex gloves and a fistful of scalpels and scrapers. He wants to do this right. To get it as close to perfection as possible. He hopes the doctor doesn't think that he's stripped her for any perverted reasons. He would like to put her in a surgical gown, but he doesn't have one, and feels uncomfortable using this old pine table to operate on instead of a gleaming, cold slab of steel. But he has to make do.

Gary tears his gaze away and looks up at the sky. The rain

patters onto his face and he closes his eyes to enjoy the sensation. When he opens them again, the jackdaw in the sky is staring again. A black pupil is turned upon him. He realises he has an audience. That time is precious and Dr Pradesh has already been alive too long. At some point, he'll be caught. He's already been stupid enough to give a name to those two coppers who turned up last week. He was trying too hard. Trying to be too friendly. Plucked a name from the air that could be exposed as bullshit with a phone call. He'd wanted to seem helpful so they didn't sniff too hard and breathe in the rotting corpses in his van. He'd phoned security the second he'd got away from them, but they both seemed pretty bright and he knows that he has a limited amount of time left before they begin joining the dots. Before they catch him, he has more work to do. There are the nurses who tended to Hoyer-Wood after his operation. There are those who helped him with his rehabilitation. It struck him recently just how incomplete Angelo's list had been. So many more people could be justifiably killed. He intends to right that wrong . . .

Feet squelching on the carpet and the dirt, Angelo crosses to the back door of the derelict property. His mask is in the van, parked behind the screen of lime trees. The scalpel that will be used to open Dr Pradesh's belly is in his pocket. He hadn't been able to purchase the surgical rib-spreader he had wanted but he has a hydraulic foot-pump in the vehicle that should do a similar job in splitting her ribs and allowing him the freedom to poke around inside her with his blade.

He takes the door with both hands. The wood has expanded over the years and sticks on the uneven floor. He yanks it hard and steps out into the darkened day, rain turning the ground beneath him into a swamp of mud and standing water, its surface bouncing and rippling beneath the deluge.

Gary pushes aside the sagging fence and ducks under the dangling barbed wire. His work boots sink into the soft earth and he feels water up to his shins. Carefully, he pulls one foot free, then the other, and manages to slurp his way onto harder ground. The van is only a few feet away.

A sheet of lightning rolls across the blackness and for an instant the scene before him is illuminated.

A big, broad-shouldered man is climbing out of the back of his van.

He's holding the decaying body of Olivia in his arms.

Gary's blood takes over.

He takes the scalpel in his fist. He throws his head back.

Feels the jackdaw's eye upon him.

The flash of recognition is lost in his rage. Even as he realises that the man who holds his daughter is the policeman who spoke to him a few days ago, the knowledge is swept away on a tide of angry blood.

He runs forward.

And sticks the blade in the big man's back.

McAvoy doesn't hear Gary Reeves approach.

The thunder and the driving rain mask the sound of footsteps on sodden earth and it is only as pain rips down his spine that he realises he is in danger.

He pitches forward. His first thought is not for himself. He just doesn't want to drop the dead girl who he holds in his arms as if rocking her to sleep.

McAvoy places the little girl on the hard floor of the van. Only then does he turn.

Steel flashes past his face. He jerks his head back just as it whistles past his cheek, then does so again as the screeching, howling features of Gary Reeves are lit by another flash of lightning.

McAvoy feels the van at his back. Tries to find somewhere solid to put his feet and looks down for the briefest of instants. It is long enough for Reeves to lunge with the knife again and McAvoy sucks in a gasp of agony as the blade digs into his hip.

He pushes hard with both hands, sending Reeves back and onto his arse. McAvoy looks down, expecting the weapon to still be stuck in him, but there is nothing there save a spreading patch of warmth. He looks back up and sees Reeves pulling himself back to his feet. The blade is still in his hands. McAvoy scrabbles in his jacket pocket for his extendable baton but Reeves runs at him again. Savagely, the smaller man stabs and stabs again, opening wounds in McAvoy's arms as he throws his hands up to protect himself. There is suddenly warm wetness upon his face and his vision turns red as the scalpel slices down to the bone above his eye.

In desperation, McAvoy grabs Reeves around the middle, shouting out as the blade sticks in his left bicep and stays there. They go down together, splashing to the ground in a spray of mud and blood and dirty rain.

Reeves slithers free and kicks out, the steel toe of his boot catching McAvoy in the throat. McAvoy raises his hands to his windpipe, gasping for breath, and suddenly Reeves is on him, kicking his hands away and forcing his head down into the great puddle of rain and leaves.

His mouth and nose are suddenly full of mud and water. He

can't see. Can't speak. Can feel only cold pain in his lungs and the weight of Gary Reeves upon his neck, holding his head below the surface.

McAvoy tries to push himself back but the ground is too slippery and his hands give way, forcing him deeper under the water. The sound of the storm dissipates and he realises his ears are under water too. His lungs feel as though they are bursting. His face is agony.

Despite himself, his mouth opens and filthy rainwater fills him.

Lights dance in his vision. He feels himself growing weak. Feels his limbs shake.

Sees, for the briefest of moments, Roisin's face, picked out like a constellation in the dancing stars of the fading darkness.

McAvoy reaches under himself. Through the dirt and the leaves and the swirling water, his hand closes on the scalpel that sticks in his left arm.

In one movement, he pulls it free and stabs, weakly, desperately at the man on his back.

He feels the blade hit home. Feels a momentary loosening of pressure.

McAvoy throws himself backwards, gasping for air, eyes opening into the rain and the storm.

Gary Reeves is a few feet away, pulling the scalpel from his collarbone. His fingers are slick with the blood and his hair hangs forward across his features. It's black, like a jackdaw's wing over his eyes.

McAvoy puts his whole weight into the punch. Throws it while staggering forward in a half-run.

His right hand connects with Gary Reeves's jaw. McAvoy feels a knuckle break with the impact. Then his feet slip out from under him and he lands on top of the unconscious man, a wave of brown water rolling away from their entwined limbs to break against the chicken wire and brick of Tilia Cottage.

Drowsily, feebly, McAvoy gets back to his feet. He staggers a little and presses a hand to the wound at his hip. He feels the warmth of fresh blood, but keeps his footing long enough to cross the grass and stumble through the lime trees to his car. In the glovebox he finds the tie-wrap cuffs he should have had in his pocket. He takes them in his blood-soaked fist and slithers his way back to where Reeves lies. He's half submerged in a puddle, and his jaw hangs slack to one side. McAvoy tries to stop his hands from shaking and slips the cuffs around Reeves's wrists. He drags him clear of the rising puddle, then climbs back to his feet.

He almost falls: his progress across the grass is that of a man trying to stay on his feet on the deck of a boat in a force nine gale.

He ducks under the barbed wire. Pulls open the door.

Sees.

Dr Pradesh.

Naked.

Bleeding.

Alive.

He crosses to her quietly. Begins untying the blue ropes that lash her to the table.

Blood-soaked and mud-spattered, he knows he looks terrifying and fearsome. He talks to her as he would to a startled horse.

Locks eyes with her for a moment.

And then her arms are around him and she is sobbing into the soaked cloth of his jacket, her body heaving as she holds him tight.

He strokes her hair, leaving blood upon her crown. Looks around at the ruin of Lewis Caneva's old home. Imagines, for the briefest of moments, what Angelo witnessed here.

And then he is pulling out his broken phone.

'It's okay,' he whispers, disentangling himself from Dr Pradesh and putting his jacket around her shoulders.

And then he falls to the ground.

Before he loses consciousness, he repeats it.

'It's okay.'

And then, as blackness washes over him: 'I'm a policeman.'

22

Hessle Foreshore. 1.26 p.m.

Downey hadn't expected to see this place again. He wishes she had gone somewhere else. This was the scene of his humiliation. The place where his revenge turned sour. He'd nearly pissed himself when the husband came home.

He lowers his head and snorts up another line. Feels it blast through his system. Feels as if he has opened a window at 35,000 feet.

Bitch!

He watches her climb from the car, rain coming in sideways to patter against her attractive face. He watches her arse as she leans over and into the back seat of her friend's stupid little car. She emerges with her baby in her arms. It's crying, and she hushes it, cooing and singing, as the pouring rain turns her white top see-through, and her mate stands there gormlessly huddled inside a waterproofed coat.

He sees the lights of another car, further up the road. Sees them as the eyes of something powerful and monstrous moving towards him. Has to shake his head to turn the lights back into something safe and unthreatening.

The women run through the rain to the front door of the house. There is some complicated fumbling with keys and then they are pushing inside.

Downey has to time it just right. He wants the door to be closing as he puts his weight behind it. Wants to see her face as she realises who she has dared to cross.

He pulls himself free of the car and splashes through the fast-moving water that covers the road. He hears thunder above and looks up, past the Humber Bridge and into a pewter sky that rolls and twists as if pregnant with a belly full of snakes.

Stumbles.

Curses.

Charges hard.

He puts his shoulder to the door and hears the squeal of surprise.

'Bitch!'

Downey doesn't hesitate as Mel slams into the wall. Just jabs his right fist into the seamstress's face and watches her crumple, falling in a tangle of arms and legs in the doorway.

'Where are ya!'

He's bawling and screaming, his own voice alien to his ears.

The bitch appears from the living-room door. Her eyes widen in surprise as she sees him and then she turns her back on him, moving fast. The baby is over her shoulder, bobbing comically, and Downey almost giggles at the silliness of it all.

Roisin bangs at the back door, desperately rattling the handle, then looks around for a weapon. Her eyes are furious. If she had a blade she would stick it through his heart.

'I'll blow you fucking up!'

Downey hadn't rehearsed the line. Had planned to say something else entirely. But it erupts from his lips unbidden.

'He'll kill you,' she says, turning on him, hissing through bared teeth.

Downey pulls the grenade from his pocket. Looks at her and laughs.

'He wouldn't kill a fly for you, you bitch. Couldn't even kill those blokes who whipped you bloody you when you were a kid. Let them go with a big bunch of flowers and an apology. Move and I'll blow you and your baby into a million fucking bits.'

Roisin looks at the object in his hand. At the cocaine-fuelled hysteria in his eyes. Feels her world tilt as his words slide into her consciousness.

'Please, I'll get you more money. I'll give you everything—'

Downey giggles, high-pitched and effeminate.

'Too fucking late. You've spoiled it. I was supposed to be prince of the city, you know that? Supposed to get some fucking respect. And some pikey bitch just waltzes in and it's over? You have to pay. Have to!'

Downey steps forward. He doesn't know if he's going to throw the grenade or not. He just likes the look in her eyes. He wonders what she'll do if he pulls the pin out and holds it in front of her. It won't detonate unless he throws it. He could have fun. Could make her piss her fucking pants . . .

Downey pulls the pin from the grenade at the exact moment Helen Tremberg clatters into the room.

She has her phone in one hand, her baton in the other. She'd arrived outside just as Downey ran from his vehicle and smashed through the door. She hadn't hesitated. Knew the right thing to do. Knew she would rather be shot or stabbed or have her heart squeezed in a fist than stand back while somebody hurt McAvoy's wife.

Helen lashes out with the baton. It cracks across Downey's arm.

The grenade tumbles onto the floor.

Four pairs of eyes turn to watch the object rolling in a lazy semicircle on the carpet.

Then there is a flash.

The explosion can be heard even above the sound of the thunder.

There is silence for a moment.

And then nothing but the sizzle of rain falling on flame, and the rumble of falling stones.

EPILOGUE

2.06 a.m.

A small hatchback, quiet and dark on a cold country lane.

Chamomile House sits brooding and silent beneath light rain and a half-full moon.

Maria Caneva whistles something she can't quite place. The news is on the radio but she's not really listening. The evening bulletin had been full of reports from East Yorkshire. The doctor who operated on Hoyer-Wood has been found alive. A 25-year-old man was arrested at the scene on suspicion of three murders and abduction. The body of a child was also recovered from a vehicle at the remote former medical facility in Driffield. A police officer has been taken to hospital with life-threatening injuries . . .

Maria had tuned herself out. She reckons she knows who the policeman is. Reckons that the man arrested at the scene is either her brother, having given a false age, or some mate he met inside. She can't think about that. Can't open that door in her head. There are too many screaming ghosts inside.

No, all she can do is this.

She can do what somebody should have done years ago.

The boss of the care home had been friendly. Had told her they tended to use agency staff but would be delighted to take on somebody with her experience and obviously caring demeanour. Told her she could see her fitting right in and that they had one particular patient who would be delighted to hear about her fondness for the arts and interest in poetry. She'd apologised for the smell and told her the septic tank had just been emptied a couple of days ago. It would be years before it would need to be done again, she reckoned. Could she start straight away?

Maria steps out of her car. She's still dressed in her smart interview clothes. She locks the car and crosses the quiet country road. She throws one leg over the low stone wall and painfully climbs over and into a small copse of trees. Then she heads to the back of the building.

She pulls out the swipe card she has stolen from the receptionist and lets herself in, as quietly as she can. The facility is in half-darkness, with only a couple of bulbs in the corridor proving any illumination. She crosses to his door. Turns the handle and steps inside.

Sebastien Hoyer-Wood is on his back. His eyes are shut and he's sleeping soundly. Maria would like to look at him for a while. Would like to savour the physical humiliation and degradation he has endured since their last meeting. But it's not important.

He wakes as she pulls him from the bed. He isn't heavy. Weighs less than a child. He begins to thrash and a low, whinnying sound emerges from his slack mouth, but Maria clamps her hand on his lower jaw. It feels as if he is trying to bite her, so she sticks a thumb on his windpipe, then silently carries him from the room, down the corridor and into the night.

Maria's footsteps sound loud on the leaves and gravel, but nobody comes running. Through the trees she can see moonlight bouncing off standing water.

She follows her nose.

Lays Hoyer-Wood down on the cold ground.

She has no torch or phone, so has to find the lid of the septic tank by touch alone. She feels around amid rotting leaves and damp moss, sharp stones and mud. Feels two plastic handles. Puts her back into it, and pulls.

The smell hits her. The tank may have been emptied but it still stinks of accumulated gases and shit. She looks down into the darkness. Almost vomits at the stench. Sees a stagnant pool of brown, scummy liquid, about a foot above the bottom of the tank.

Without a word, Maria turns her head back to Hoyer-Wood.

He seems to understand. Tries to get away. Tries to stand. Tries to scream.

She doesn't give him the chance.

'Not today, Sebastien,' she says, quietly. 'But some day. I want you to keep the thought of this moment in your head tomorrow when I'm introduced to you. I'm your new nurse, Seb. I've got myself a contract and living accommodation and I'm going to be here at your beck and call for as long as I can stand it. And believe me, Sebastien, we are going to have some fun.'

Maria closes the cover over the fetid blackness and turns back to Sebastien. She picks leaves from his pyjama top and smiles into his terrified eyes. 'They said there was no way to punish you. They said that letting you live as you are is punishment enough. Let's see if they were right, eh?'

Maria scoops Sebastien up and carries him back towards his

room. As she lays him back in his bed she feels his body trembling like a frightened puppy's.

'See you tomorrow,' she says, and switches off the light.

As she slips out of the room and into the cool of the night, a shaft of moonlight spears through from the hazy clouds. She looks at her hands. They are covered in dirt and leaves and filth that makes her want to gag.

She has never felt as clean.

Acknowledgements

Thanks, as ever, to the Quercus team and Oli Munson – agent and friend.

Thanks too, to the crime writers who have influenced, inspired and welcomed me. Stav, Mari, Martyn, Steve, Peter, Tom, John, Mark and Val, you are owed more drinks than I can afford.

Special thanks to Dave and Babs Watson, who allowed me to use their computer to write this damn book when burglars took mine.

Love, gratitude and a look of perennial bewilderment go the way of George and Elora. I couldn't do any of this without you. And I'd have nobody to do it for.

Finally, thanks to the burglars. You really helped me imagine a whole new raft of gruesome deaths.